THE MISTAKE HAS A NAME

Inspired By A True Story

To Christi —
Blessings!
Anne Weihsmann

Anne Weihsmann

PRESS

ACKNOWLEDGEMENTS

To Kathy Firestone: Your definition of 'creative non-fiction' helped give me a framework for this book—a blending of real and imagined people and events into a narrative that is greater than the sum of its parts. When I understood that all of the real names, places, and many events could be changed without diminishing the power of the story, I was ready to swing for the fences.

To my loving husband Steve: Thank you for encouraging me to chase my dream.

To Therese Black: Your tough questions stretched my ability to find the best words for each circumstance.

To Virginia André: Your editing skills were invaluable—you are 'too' good!

To Carly, my oldest daughter: Your meticulous attention to grammar and details was priceless.

To my church family: You are the great 'cloud of witnesses' who encouraged, prayed, and cheered me on to the finish line.

The seven-year journey of writing would not have been possible without all of you.

PREFACE

The afternoon is a feast for the senses: every known
shade of red and orange is breaking into a kaleidoscope
of color, dancing through the trees in unpredictable rhythm.

The sweet smell of burning wood rises up boldly from
countless backyards and collides with the sound of waves
rearranging the sandy beach. All of this is a backdrop for the
crunching gravel under my feet and the deep azure of the
cloudless sky. Heaven's refracted light slides under earth's
door, and contentment finds a home in my soul.

The women's fall retreat weekend at Strand Lake Bible
Camp affords me relaxing times to meet women—some for
the first time, and others with whom I've shared church life
without benefit of time to connect on a deeper level, which
is something I treasure above everything else. This retreat
affords both motive and opportunity.

Julie is one of those acquaintances from church; until
now we've shared only first names and a love of books.
This weekend changes everything as I begin to push out
the edges of our friendship. By inquiring about her past, I
discover someone who is refreshingly forthcoming, delight-
fully honest, and an excellent storyteller. The long-dormant
desire to write a book awakens and pushes to the surface, as
I realize that Julie's astonishing life is a story demanding to

be told. It is an idea that is one part exciting and two parts terrifying.

◆

I am deeply humbled by Julie's willingness to open windows into her troubling past. Throughout the time she shares her story, I understand that shock value and revenge are not the desired goals of her life, nor are they to indulge a negative self-esteem and justify it by years of accumulated wrongs. Julie seems, instead, to be about *soul*-esteem as her life reveals the work of a loving and gracious Heavenly Father ... a Father who tears down walls of deceit and rebuilds a home of forgiveness ... a place where memories are a constant healing-in-progress, and where the goodness of God trumps the unfairness of life.

Your Shed Blood

Your shed blood of Grace is an ocean
Breaking over me in ceaseless waves.
My weary spirit returns only tears
Lovingly collected in your bottle.
Blood is the water of renewal.
Tears are the water of praise.
Tears fill a well of rejoicing,
Blood flows into a river of life.
My weary spirit offers tears
Collected in Your bottle of remembrance.
Your shed Blood of Grace is a sea
Sweeping over me in waves of forgiveness.

PROLOGUE

April 1, 2000

Julie awoke to overcast skies Easter Sunday morning.
Spring had crept into Michigan, coaxing tired clumps
of dirty snow into their melting fate. Thin sheets of waxed
paper ice covered ponds bubbling with life. Lengthening
days encouraged the sun to pry loose winter's pale-knuckled
grip.

Today was Julie's forty-fourth birthday. Dressed for
church in simple khakis and a blue button down shirt, she
stared into the full-length mirror in her spacious bedroom.
The beginnings of crow's feet crinkled the corners of her
intensely brown eyes, deep-set and compassionate, framed
under carefully arched eyebrows. A small chin sat squarely
in her oval-shaped face, highlighted by a radiant smile show-
casing teeth as white and straight as piano keys. Usually
fastidious about her short, stylish, auburn hair, she didn't
fuss with it today. In a little while, it would be drenched and
plastered to her head.

A newly washed, bright burgundy, '98 Olds Silhouette
minivan idled in the driveway like a duty-bound chariot
waiting to take Julie and her husband to First Evangelical
Free Church. The fifteen-minute ride was barely long enough
for Julie to think about all that had happened during the years

when her life had been fueled by a primal need to survive. She had often escaped into cruise control to protect herself from overwhelming hopelessness. When she had finally reached the end of herself, God had been there to reclaim her life and return it to her. She had found a fresh start in the words from Psalm 34, verse 18: "The Lord is near to the brokenhearted, and saves those who are crushed in spirit."

The parking lot was already overflowing a half-hour before the eleven o'clock service. Inside the sanctuary, Julie and her husband and extended family searched for seats in a small room made even more compact by the removal of the first two rows of padded chairs to accommodate the portable baptismal tank. The three-by-six-foot tank was covered in a dark wainscoting that made a dignified backdrop for the carefully placed Easter lilies.

I spent so many years wishing that the people who hurt me would get what they deserved ... and now I'm glad that God chose not *to give me what I deserve.* She smiled at the musicians playing contemporary worship music during the 'gathering time,' and hoped she could settle her nerves by the time Pastor Tim called her name as a candidate for baptism.

Part of this day seemed like another of Julie's many dreams—yet she knew that today was very real. Her dreams had often been full of hideous demons wearing masks; today the disguises were gone, and Julie saw the exposed ugliness of a past that no longer had power over her. As Julie and Pastor Tim faced the congregation, he recited a verse from First Corinthians as she whispered it in her heart: 'Blessed be the God and Father of our Lord Jesus Christ, the Father of mercies and God of all comfort, who comforts us in all our affliction so that we will be able to comfort those who are in any affliction with the comfort with which we ourselves are comforted by God.' *Maybe someday God will use me as a wounded healer for someone who's drowning in rage-filled anguish and despair.*

As Pastor Tim helped her climb into the blue fiberglass-lined tank and then lowered her under the water, Julie hoped it would wash off years of blame and shame …

CHAPTER ONE

NINETY-NINE BOTTLES OF BEER ON THE WALL

Julie Sandford wanted a doll to dress. Not just any doll, but the perfect one. The one in the Sears-Roebuck catalogue, where she'd torn out the picture and then taped it to the faded pink wall above her rollaway bed. Every night, alone in her room, Julie whispered goodnight to the doll and imagined it life-sized, with skinny arms and legs like hers. But the doll's long, jet-black hair wasn't *anything* like her not-quite-blonde-not-quite-brown hair. Julie liked to pretend she looked like one of those Breck models on TV with the beautiful, wavy, auburn hair. The game ended at the beginning of each month, when she was ordered to climb up on a rickety metal stool in their drab kitchen. While her mom chopped her hair into a pixie cut, she'd sit and stare silently at the walls of the kitchen, wondering how they could be the same color as her hair—a color that she couldn't find anywhere in her small box of broken crayons.

♦

The doll would *have* to have a dress. The Sears catalogue didn't have any, but in Julie's mind, the dress would be puffy, yellow seersucker and would make a swishing sound when she twirled her doll. She had another secret: that someday the two of them would have matching dresses.

The used-up dresses hanging from a rusty metal rod in a dark corner of her room were the has-beens. Over-wear and under-care had long since faded the bright colors to apologetic shades of something. *At least the dresses with no color will match my hair.*

♦

Second grade was starting in six days. Julie assumed the monthly position on the stool and patiently endured another haircut. When it was over, she picked up the cracked hand mirror, looked at her reflection, and laid it back on the green countertop.

"Please, oh please, Momma, can I have a new dress for school? Maybe a yellow seersucker one?" Julie wasn't sure what would happen if she begged for a dress, since she had never seen her mom in one. As far as she knew, her mom didn't even *own* one and maybe didn't want to. Still, she thought her mom looked like a movie star. With her slim waist and dark, wavy hair, she reminded Julie of Dorothy in "The Wizard of Oz," except that her clouded eyes made her look old and sad, like the sun had left the sky a long time ago.

Arlene Sandford ground her half-smoked cigarette into the bottom of the glass ashtray, pulled the towel from around Julie's neck, scrunched it, and dropped it on the floor.

"Okay, let's see what you've got for dresses."

Julie leaped off the stool and skipped to her bedroom, hands smacking the walls of the narrow hallway in anticipated victory. As she burst through the door she dove onto her bed, springs moaning in protest.

Arlene was right behind Julie. She stopped in the doorway, kicked off her high heels, leaned against the frame, and lifted one foot at a time, checking for runs in her nylons. "We won't be able to buy you any new dresses if you break your bed!" Arlene pushed against the frame, stood up, and straightened the belt around the waist of her long, green tunic top hanging loosely over her white pants.

Julie sat on the edge of her bed. She knew that if she got too close to the middle she would sink into the trough formed by who-knew-how many bodies had done who-knew-what in her bed before it was given to her. "Yes, Ma'am," she whispered, and breathed very quietly.

Arlene walked to the corner and began rifling through the dresses, each hanger scraping along the rod in noisy protest of the judgment. Her hand suddenly stopped as she stared up at a spot on the ceiling. Julie had seen her mom do this before in other rooms in the house. It was like she vanished into another world. *Maybe this time Momma is thinking back to when she was a little girl and owned pretty dresses.*

Dropping her gaze back to the rod, Arlene grabbed a hanger, turned around, and held up a mousy brown jumper with small ink stains dotting the front.

"This'll do," she declared. "This'll do fine. What do you need a new dress for anyway? School ain't no big deal."

Julie thought that all of those dresses were ugly. After her mom had re-hung the jumper, walked back to the doorway, stooped over to pick up her shoes, and disappeared down the hall, she fell back into the bed trough. With tears in her eyes she stared at the doll picture. Wiping her eyes on her sleeve, she exclaimed, "That's it! When I get that doll I'll name her 'Thistledew'—sounds kinda like 'This'll do.'" She giggled at her joke and her world righted itself on its axis again. Now she just needed to be rescued from the center of her bed.

17

Begging Dad to fight her dress battle never occurred to Julie. She didn't know whether he paid any attention to what she wore. It was different for her, because she noticed every-thing about her handsome father. He had bigger muscles than any man she had ever seen except the ones on the TV commercials for exercise stuff. One time she had overheard her parents arguing in their bedroom. "Hey, Mr. Bigshot," Mom had yelled, "If you could train for the 'Mr. Olympia' title, how about throwing your weight into a decent job?" The next thing she had heard was the slam of their bedroom door. She could smell her dad's Old Spice even before he walked in to the living room. While she lay on the brown carpeting in front of the TV, he came in, sat on the green plaid couch, put on his Wellington boots, placed his welder's cap care-fully over his wavy hair, checked the crease on his jeans, ran his hand over his well-trimmed beard, got up and walked out the front door without stopping to check his reflection in the hall mirror. *Did he know I was in the room?*

Julie felt like that mirror: neither one of them ever got a sideways glance. They were both invisible to Danny Sandford, and she wanted him to really *see* her. Sometimes, though, she had to admit that she was glad she was ignored, especially when he drank out of the brown bottles from the back of the fridge. Then he'd get angry and yell really loud, and it was scary, but also kind of funny, because he sounded like he had marbles rolling around in his mouth. But lots of times he'd spit out horrible words at her mom; she didn't know what the words meant, but her mom would spit them right back until it sounded like they were playing volleyball. That's when she made sure to stay away from them so that she didn't get caught in the net.

♦

In eight years Julie had already moved many times. She didn't remember any of their other houses, or any of the classmates she kept leaving behind. The cold, blue beauty of the distant mountains was like an older sister who wouldn't have much to do with her, but who Julie imagined coming home from dates, patting her on the head, and saying, "You're all right, kid," before heading off to bed. Julie had never had any close friends, because Momma and Daddy wouldn't allow her to invite any girls over to their house. *And even if they did, my friends would hear them fighting and wouldn't want to come back again.* She never got invited to other girls' houses, and thought maybe it was because those girls lived in houses that looked like the Cleaver house, and hers definitely didn't. The two missing front window screens made her house look creepy, and the inside smelled like old shoes, fried onions, and cigarettes. The odor clung to the torn sofa, the stained, beige drapes, and her clothes, and it seemed like she could never get away from it.

Julie's best friends were her library-discard books, her stuffed animals from Goodwill, and most of all, her active imagination. She wished that her six-year old brother Dan were one of her good friends, but he was mainly a pest. Someday she hoped to have Thistledew as her special friend, and then maybe her Mom would buy one of those Easy-Bake Ovens with the little pan big enough for a cake for two. She and Thistledew would share secrets about what each of them would be when they grew up.

♦

Grandma Leona Hagstrom, Danny's mom, was coming to live with the Sandfords. Julie skipped around the house, short hair lifting around her head like dandelion fluff, while the untied laces from her saddle shoes slapped against the black-checkered linoleum floor in the kitchen.

"Grandma's coming! Grandma's coming!" Julie's secret spilled out. "Maybe she'll buy me a doll, and an Easy-Bake Oven, and some little boxes of cake mix, and a little tea set." Wasn't having a Grandma living with you the best of all?

"What are you talking about?" Arlene was washing dishes with her back turned toward Julie.

Julie decided not to say any more. "Momma, why isn't Grandma's last name 'Sandford' like ours?" She had a hard time figuring out all of this family stuff.

"You ask too many questions." Arlene turned and stared at Julie, eyebrows creased in intense thought as her mind filtered through memories. "Because ... I think Grandma remarried after your grandpa died—"

"I don't get it—"

"And his name was Roy Hagstrom. He also died a few years ago. Maybe."

All Julie knew for sure was that she was going to have a real grandma right in her house. She never thought to ask why Grandma was coming to live with them. *Does she need money? I hope not, because Momma says we never have enough. Will she bring us money or food? I don't care—I just want her here!*

On a warm September night, Julie was sitting outside on the front steps, looking up at the sky and trying to remember what she had read about the Milky Way in one of her books. *There must be a million stars up there! I hope I see a shooting one.* Just then a Yellow Cab pulled up in front of her house, the back door opened, and an old-looking woman got out. The cab driver went around to the trunk, opened it and pulled out a tan, dented suitcase. He handed it to the woman, who was also carrying a bulging plastic bag. The woman said, "Why'd you bring me here anyway?" Then she turned around and headed towards Julie.

This must be Grandma Hagstrom! No one had told her when Grandma was going to come. When she had asked her mom about it, the only answer she got was, "When the spirit moves her." The woman walked up the steps and around her into their house without even knocking. Julie got up and followed her.

Arlene came out from the kitchen, wiped her hands on her apron, went over to Leona, said, "Hiya, Lee," and motioned for Julie to come closer. "This is your grandkid Julie. Julie, kiss your grandma." She stared. *Grandma's hair looks like the water in the kitchen sink after mom does all the dishes. It looks like* my *hair, all short and stick-straight.*

Julie closed the gap to her grandma, stood on her tiptoes and tried to reach her orange powdered cheek. She mostly kissed the air. Leona hadn't let go of her suitcase or bag, and stood as still as a statue. Finally she said, "Well, hi then." Julie didn't know how grandmas were supposed to act, but she didn't think Grandma Hagstrom seemed too excited to be in their house. She backed up and tried to hide her curiosity about her grandma's clothes. *She's wearing a dress, but it doesn't have any lace, or fancy buttons, and it's not even pretty.* Leona's lime green dress was too loose around her bosom, and too tight around her waist. The color was faded around the cuffs, and a button was missing near the bottom.

Suddenly dropping her suitcase and bag, Leona walked to the couch, rubbed her hand across a cushion, lay down on her stomach, and turned her head towards the back of the couch. Arlene grabbed Julie's elbow and pulled her out of the room, without saying a word.

♦

By the end of the first month with Grandma Hagstrom, Julie couldn't hide her disappointment. Her grandma didn't seem to know anything about dolls, or dresses, or little girls. When she had tried to get her to play paper dolls, her grandma had taken the scissors and cut them into shreds before Julie could find her mom and get her to take Grandma away. She wished her Grandma would wear the glasses that hung from a chain around her neck. At least they would hide eyes that were too blurry to tell what color they were.

Another time, Julie showed her Grandma how to play "Go Fish." She was starting to have a good time until Grandma asked her four times in a row if she had any 'eights'. She didn't know what else to do, so she gathered the cards together in a pile, told her grandma she was tired, and turned on the TV. Not long after, Grandma fell asleep sitting up, her head tipped to one side and still gripping her cards.

Grandma Hagstrom drank and smoked with Julie's momma and dad late at night around the kitchen table. Long after she was ordered to bed, she would sneak back down to the living room and hear the adults talking really loud. Pretty soon they were arguing. Then they used those words she had already heard from her mom and dad. She heard caps pop and knew they were drinking from the brown bottles. Finally all the noise stopped, and then she would gather the bottom of her nightgown into one hand and quickly run up the stairs, closing her door right before heavy footsteps followed her. From the other side of her door, it sounded like people were dragging-carrying someone, and she thought she knew who that was.

On the school bus Julie heard the word 'alcoholic' from some of the older kids; and once she found out what it meant, she thought maybe Grandma Hagstrom was one of those. She had never heard the word at home, but started using it when she talked about her Grandma at school. It didn't make Grandma Hagstrom sound very nice, but she didn't know what else to say about her.

◆

Connect-the-dots was one of Julie's favorite rainy-day games. She was lying on her bedroom floor with her bright pink pencil, and the dot picture was almost done. *It looks like a giraffe! I love them. I wish Daddy and Momma would take me to the Seattle Zoo sometime. My teacher says it's only thirteen miles from Bremerton, but that must be a long ways away, because whenever I ask Momma, she says, "We don't have time for that."*

When Julie had finished the last page of her book, she doodled on the inside back cover, drawing pictures of her mom, dad, brother, and grandma, and then a big dot under each person. *I can connect all these dots, but then what kind of a picture do I have? Dad doesn't know I'm here; Mom and Grandma do things I don't understand; everyone yells more than they talk; and if they really wanna be heard, they use bad words. When that doesn't work they slam doors.* She wanted her connect-the-dot family to be a picture of the Cleavers, but she knew that couldn't happen. *Besides, June Cleaver always vacuums in a dress.*

CHAPTER TWO

SCHOOL DAZE

The lilac bushes made the air smell like someone had sprayed perfume everywhere. Julie loved spring, especially after the long, cold, snowy winter. *I wish I still had my bike. I wonder what happened to it after we moved last year.* It was Saturday afternoon, and she was trying to decide what to do for the rest of the day. She was kneeling on the sofa with her arms propped up on the back, looking out the window at the pretty yellow and red and blue birds landing on the feeder in the neighbor's yard across the street. She had to keep swatting away the flies that buzzed in and around her head.

A noise from behind her made Julie turn around. Grandma was standing in the living room holding the same suitcase and stuffed plastic bag, and wearing the same lime green dress she had worn that night she had come to their house back in September. Arlene's voice carried from the kitchen. "Julie, kiss your grandma goodbye!" She hadn't grown any taller since the fall, and this time she really did want to kiss her grandma. She ran to the hall closet, got out the hair-cutting stool, brought it to the living room right next to Grandma, climbed up on it and kissed her on the cheek.

"Bye little girl." Leona walked to the door, set down her plastic bag, opened the door, walked out, and left her bag behind.

♦

Right before Grandma Hagstrom left, Julie had remembered overhearing her telling Momma and Daddy that this 'Grandma thing' wasn't for her, and that she was moving in with a friend of hers in Seattle. "Besides," Leona had declared, "You people keep taking my purse, my glasses, my toothbrush ... if I'd have known you needed stuff, I would have bought it for you." Julie hadn't been able to hear any more of the conversation. *Why didn't anyone tell me Grandma was leaving?*

Leona was gone, and the house had returned to something familiar to Julie. As she was sitting in front of the TV watching Saturday morning cartoons, her mom lugged an old, scratched, blue suitcase into the living room. "Pack all of your clothes, books, and other junk in this." She walked away before Julie could ask her where they were going.

♦

As far as Julie could tell, her family was moving across the country. She had heard that Kankakee was somewhere in a place called the 'Midwest,' but she didn't know where to find it on the map. She was glad about leaving her grandma behind, and excited about living somewhere new, and even going to a new school. One good thing about her parents never letting her have any girlfriends over, or letting her go to anyone's house, was that she didn't get too close to other kids, and didn't have part of her heart torn away when she had to move.

And maybe, now that Grandma Hagstrom was gone, her parents would drink less, and talk nicer to each other, too.

♦

It was the Tuesday after Labor Day and the start of third grade for Julie and four other girls from her new neighborhood. They all stood at the bus stop, along with Dan and another first-grader, at eight forty-five; Julie hoped her instant oatmeal would stay down, and that she would feel calm enough to eat her lunch when the time came. *I hope Momma made me my favorite peanut butter and grape jelly sandwich, and that she packed a box of Animal Crackers to go with it. I wonder what we'll have at snack time?* Her thoughts were interrupted by the yellow school bus, which had turned the corner and was headed down her street. She took off her pink cardigan sweater, tied it around the waist of her sleeveless, robin's-egg blue dress, picked up her school supplies, where she had laid them on the sidewalk, and climbed the steep steps onto the bus. The fifteen-minute ride to school was the longest in her life. *I can't wait to get there!*

Hubert Elementary was a red brick, two-story, no-frills building, surrounded by a gravel parking lot, a paved playground, a baseball field, and a row of stately maples along the street. It stood as a proud tribute to functionality and stability. Teachers started and ended their careers there; seniors from the neighboring high school returned to thank their former teachers for expecting more than they thought they could give; and parents went to conferences, affirmed the work of the same teachers, and hung out in the hallways sharing the easy camaraderie of people who have known each other since kindergarten.

Hubert had earned its membership in the Fraternal Order of American Grade Schools by the universal smell in the hallways—a combination of floor wax, stale milk, Elmer's glue, Lysol, and fish sticks—and it made Julie feel like she was back in Washington again. She knew she'd be okay here. Teachers' aides directed the kids to the appropriate classrooms as they poured out of the busses like escapees from an anthill. She followed the rest of the third graders, with the boys punching each other, girls straightening hair ribbons, and everyone's energy level on high alert.

Once in the right room, the kids each staked out a desk, marking their territory with pencil pouches and boxes of crayons. Some kids also had metal lunchboxes; a few of the better-dressed kids had the sixty-four boxes of Crayola crayons. Julie looked at her Woolworth's ten-crayon box, and hoped no one would make fun of her for it. She felt lucky to have that much, and that it was a new box.

When a woman marched into the room, the kids instantly folded their hands on their desks and looked straight ahead. Julie immediately noticed her powerful-looking arm muscles, and bet she could take on her dad! The boys started whispering about who she might 'whoop' while Julie wondered how her new teacher could ignore the dress code by wearing black pants and a plain, white, short-sleeved blouse. And, while Julie was used to her mom's dark, shoulder length hair, styled in soft waves, and her dad's neatly-combed, collar length hair, Miss whoever-she-was had short, reddish hair that stuck straight up. The light was shining right through it to a place on the chalkboard behind her. Her square-looking face looked pale; her eyes were squinted in little slits; her spread-legged stance looked like she was protecting her ground in 'King of the hill.'

"Class, I am Miss Meyer." She cleared her throat like a growling dog. "You will pay attention at all times. There is to be no talking when I'm standing up here unless I call on you. There will be no gum chewing. You will raise your hands at all times."

For the next ten minutes, Miss Meyer read the rules in her low voice, even deeper than Julie's dad's when he was mad. Julie's excitement was slowly turning into a kind of fear. When she climbed back on the bus, the school gossip was that Miss Meyer had been kicked out of the marines. She didn't know what that meant, but she was already scared of saying or doing something wrong in class. *I've become invisible to my father; hopefully Miss Meyer won't notice me, either.*

By the end of the next day, Julie saw that even the bravest-looking kids kept their hands folded in their laps or tightly gripping their number two pencils during teaching time. No hands were waving for attention. No one whispered or passed notes. Miss Meyer looked like she wouldn't just take prisoners out to the hallway and have them sit on the floor, like her last teacher had done with some of the naughty kids; she might do something else, and Julie didn't want to ever find out what that 'something else' was.

♦

"Class, where does oil come from?" demanded Miss Meyer one rainy morning during the third week of school. The students had already figured out that their teacher was full of 'trick' questions, and they didn't know whether or not this was one of them. "It's not necessary to raise your hands—just shout out answers." Miss Meyer had never changed her rule about hand raising. None of the kids knew what to do.

Silence.

"Come on, let's have fun! Show me what you know!"

Finally, one big boy yelled, "Rocks!" Everyone giggled. And from near the front, "The ocean!"

More silence. The kids looked around. Julie was starting to feel nervous and sweaty.

Miss Meyer walked over to her. "Sandford?" She barked.

Oh, no. "Oil wells?" she whispered.

Miss Meyer lunged at her like she was the enemy. Grabbing her by her dress collar, she pulled her up out of her seat and hauled her to the front of the room. More nervous giggles erupted from students mostly at the back, the ones with a clear escape route.

Miss Meyer was panting. "Class, I want you all to see what happens to stupid kids. Sandford here will write her name in my *Student Stupid Answer Book*." Miss Meyer turned her face until it was inches from Julie's. "And when you're finished, you'll drop and gimme ten." The class was pin-drop quiet.

"Ten what?" squeaked Julie.

"Man, you're even dumber than I thought. After you sign my book, you'd better spend some time in my *Student Stupid Answer Chair*."

I'm glad I didn't eat any breakfast, 'cuz it'd be all over the floor by now. Julie signed her name in the book of shame, sat in the stupid chair, ate lunch by herself, then returned to her desk for the rest of the afternoon, occasionally glancing at the other kids snickering and rolling their eyes and making weird faces at her, especially the boys. When she walked into her house that afternoon, she wondered whether she should tell her parents about what had happened to her. If they took her side and pitched a fit with her teacher, she would be called a 'tattle-tale' for the rest of the year. If they said, "Your teacher knows what she's doing," then she would feel even stupider than ever. She decided the best thing to do was to push the day way down inside of her, and then maybe she'd forget all about it. And she sure had to figure out a way to keep it from ever happening again.

Miss Meyer didn't run out of 'stupid' students who kept her attention away from Julie for the next several weeks.

As word began to circulate about Miss Meyer's classroom teaching methods, a group of parents made an appointment to observe her class in late October. Although these parents, along with many other teachers, were appalled at her thinly veiled abuse, the administration seemed as overpowered by her as her students were. Rather than taking any action to have Miss Meyer removed from the school, they instead assigned her responsibilities on the textbook committee and extra-curricular activities committee, praying that as she worked with the other teachers, some of their kindness and genuine concern for the kids would smooth her edges.

♦

I know I'm stupid in Miss Meyer's class, but it'd be so cool to get a part in the Christmas pageant. Then I'd be popular and everyone would forget about what happened to me. I'm gonna try out! Wearing her best dress—an only slightly worn, red polka dot one with a Dutch girl collar—and her hair held back by a red, plastic headband, Julie snuck into the gym after school one day in late November. Walking across the gym to the stage, her Ked's sneakers squeaked on the waxed floor, announcing her arrival long before her courage caught up. When she reached the stage she looked up at the adults sitting in folding chairs behind a long table, papers and cups spread out around them. *What is Miss Meyer doing up there?* Julie felt her throat close. A girl in her class, who had been running errands for the judges, jumped down from the stage, ran up to her, cupped her hand around Julie's ear, and whispered. "Miss Meyer knows you're here. I wonder if she brought her *Stupid* chair with her." When the girl pulled back, Julie saw a mean look on her face and turned around, hoping for a quick getaway.

"Sandford! What're you doing here? This play is for *smart* kids." Everyone in the gym froze, as Miss Meyer's words bounced around the walls. Julie turned and ran back across the gym, which suddenly felt as big as the whole school. She hoped she'd make it through the double doors before Miss Meyer heard her sobbing. *I'll never try out for anything!* As the door banged behind her, she collapsed on the hallway floor and buried her head in her arms.

♦

School was finally over. Julie had a wonderful, long summer ahead of her before she had to start worrying about the fall. *I hope Miss Meyer doesn't move up to fourth grade. If that happens, I don't know what I'll do!* And then came great news: her family was moving again. This wasn't going to be another cross-country move—just to Wisconsin. Julie didn't have any close girlfriends, so she was glad to leave Illinois and Miss Meyer forever.

"Mom, why're we moving?" Sitting on the sofa next to her mom, Julie knew she was allowed to ask questions during the commercials.

Arlene ran her hand down the sleeve of her taupe, silk blouse, smoothing out a little wrinkle. "Why, why, why? How do I know?" She kept her eyes focused on the screen, while Julie wrapped and unwrapped a yoyo string around her finger until "The Fugitive" was over. Arlene got up, walked over to the TV and turned it off. Then she swiveled and put her hands on her small hips.

"Your dad says he has buddies from Washington who live in Platteville now, and they're ready for us to exercise our visitation rights." Arlene laughed, turned, and headed toward the kitchen.

Maybe I should turn the TV back on and look for a rerun of "The Twilight Zone." That's gotta *make more sense than Mom.*

The Sandford belongings fit in a five-by-eight U-Haul, which Danny hooked to the back of their tan, Chevy Nomad wagon on the last day of June. The family was packed and ready to leave Kankakee by late morning.

Their car didn't have air conditioning, and Julie had overheard her dad saying that they had 'a hundred seventy miles and four hours of dad-blame driving.' Or something like that—the words were hard to hear with the air blasting into her ears through the window. She felt like one of her stuffed cats with its legs all stuck out and lying face down on the back dash. Her cut-off jean shorts and yellow tank top were plastered to her skin, and the inside of the car was hotter than anything she had ever felt before. She tried focusing on the fields racing backwards as their car sped forward—and for a while she was too hypnotized to notice the heat. But when the tall things growing in the fields started to look like upside-down, dancing brooms, she couldn't look out the window any more, either. She hoped her stomach would make it the rest of the way to Wisconsin.

♦

A man, a woman, and three boys with haircuts like Miss Meyer's were sitting on the porch when Julie's family pulled up to their house. By the time she had unstuck herself from her seat and got out of the car, the adults were already hugging and laughing. "Rich!" "Lorraine!" "Arlene!" "Danny!" Julie, Dan, and the strange boys stood around staring at each other. "The Andersons, as I live and breathe!" Arlene laughed.

"Everyone come in!" Lorraine put one arm around Julie and the other around her dad. *I hope it's not as hot in there as in our car, otherwise I'm coming back out and finding a shade tree.* As soon as they were all inside Lorraine made an announcement: "Go relax in the living room, and I'll call you when supper's ready," and then disappeared behind a swinging door.

The children followed their dads into a small room with a brown-plaid sofa, stuffed chairs, and a braided rug on the floor. One of the windows had the shade pulled down over it; the other one had a big contraption stuck in it that was pumping out cold air at full blast. No one paid any attention to Julie as she dropped down on the rug, spread out her arms and legs, and closed her eyes. The next thing she knew, Mrs. Anderson was standing over her whispering, "Dinner time." She got up slowly, not sure if she wanted to leave this cool room, even though her stomach was making noises. She'd been too sick to eat since they'd left Illinois.

There was a large table in the middle of the kitchen, with picnic benches on both sides. The table was covered with a white cloth, and on top of it were dishes filled with sliced ham, little potatoes swimming in something creamy-looking, biscuits, strawberry Jell-O, and a big pitcher of iced tea. On the counter next to the stove was a tall cake with coconut icing. The smells all hit Julie's nose at once, and she knew she was starving.

After supper everyone headed back outside. The adults settled in lounge chairs on the porch, which Julie noticed wrapped around three sides of the house; Dan and the three Anderson boys, Jimmy, John, and Joe, ages ten, eleven, and thirteen, ran around catching fireflies in the cool dusk, while Julie asked permission from Mrs. Anderson to explore the house.

Julie wandered around the inside looking at things she figured must be treasures. A framed picture of the family hung on a wall in the living room; a deer head with big antlers and wide-open, pretty and sad eyes hung on another wall; one of the bedrooms had a bookshelf with lots of books, a golden statue of someone holding a bowling ball, and tall, fat coffee mugs with wooden handles. Her favorites were the paintings and drawings that must've been done by the Anderson boys, taped to the refrigerator. *I've never been in a house like this.* The only things her mom ever hung were stained potholder gloves and a wooden key-shaped thingamajig with hooks to hang keys.

I hope we end up living near the Andersons. At least for tonight, we'll get to sleep in their guest rooms.

The next morning Julie awoke to the smell of frying bacon. The stars outside her window were still shining brighter than the top curve of the sun peeking over the horizon. She was ready for breakfast and a new day.

There must have been a rainbow arching over Platteville with the pot of gold sitting in the Anderson's yard. After breakfast Mr. Anderson announced to Julie's family that he and his wife had decided to let the Sandfords live in a trailer that his family wasn't using. It was eight-by-twenty-eight feet; it was only a year old; it was parked near the western edge of their farm; they wouldn't accept any rent for it; and that was that. Julie had never, ever heard anything so good before.

♦

Long, hot, humid summer days were full of adventure for Julie, Dan, Jimmy, John, and Joe. They started calling themselves the 'Fab Five;' and, for once, Julie was okay with her shoulder length, straight hair. *If we're going to pretend to be the Beatles, I can do my part and try to look like one of 'em.*

There was always something to do around the farm: during the day, the Fab Five watched Mr. Anderson butcher geese and chickens. Julie thought it was gross to see blood spurting everywhere, but also funny to see headless chickens running around for a while before they fell down. The best part was when Mrs. Anderson fried the chicken and invited her family over for supper. It was crispy and hot and tender and delicious.

As long as Julie stayed with all of the boys, her mom didn't seem to care what she did. The lawn around the Anderson farmhouse was always neatly mown; but beyond that there were swamps, meadows, and good climbing trees. Sometimes the Fab Five became Tarzan, Jane, Cheetah and assorted monkeys. Other times they went on an African safari. When they decided to be farmers, they drew straws to see who would be the first one to ride the five hundred pound pig named Benny, who was the family mascot.

When Julie walked in to her trailer for supper, her shirt and shorts were usually covered in hay, mud, or dirt, with parts of the farm clinging to her shoes. As soon as she was finished showering and eating, she'd be back outside with the boys. At sundown they'd catch fireflies, play midnight tag, and stalk skunks; by the time Julie dragged herself back inside for the night, her sneakers were wet from dew.

The oldest boy, Joe, told the others one night after a game of 'Red Light, Green Light' that he often saw all of their parents drinking together when he and his brothers would go into their house for bed. Joe also said that he would hear a lot of yelling and cussing, but that no one ever sounded really mad. Julie thought back to when Grandma Hagstrom had lived with her and figured that when grown-ups got together, they drank. If they had a good time and left the kids alone, then she wasn't going to worry about it. Besides, it helped her forget about Miss Meyer, which was probably the best thing of all.

◆

Julie was practicing a new word: she was at the 'threshold' of fourth grade at Christ Lutheran Church School. She didn't know what 'Lutheran' meant, nor did she care, as long as her new teacher didn't look like Miss Meyer.

Christ Lutheran was a stucco, rectangular building, with a stained-glass window on every side, a steeple, and a heavy, oak front door. It sat on a large, neat lot with flower boxes on the east side of the building and maple trees giving plenty of shade to picnic tables behind the church. The congregation was a close group of a hundred-and-fifty people; sometimes, family members spanning three generations shared the same pew on Sunday mornings.

Mrs. Anderson drove her boys and the Sandford children to school and back every day. On the first day of school, Jimmy, Julie and the other twelve fourth graders gathered in the hallway outside their classroom. Some kids were sharing their what-I-did-last-summer experiences with their friends; others, like Julie, were looking around for any other new kids, the ones Mrs. Anderson said had the 'deer-caught-in-the-headlights' look. After spending a summer living on the Anderson farm, Julie had seen a lot of deer when the sun went down. She and the boys would get a flashlight and shine it in the deer's eyes, and now she knew what that saying meant.

As soon as the bell rang the fourth graders walked quickly into their room. Julie wore a hand-me-down uniform—navy blue jumper and white blouse—with white socks and loafers, and had her hair pulled into a high ponytail. Her freckles were evidence of a summer spent living outdoors. *When Miss Meyer folded her arms she looked like Mr. Clean, except she had a little more hair. I wonder what my new teacher will look like?*

The students scattered to find desks that were either new, used, covered with drawings and initials, scratched, dented, squeaky-hinged, rusted, or plain and small. Julie walked around looking critically at each desk until she settled on one that was scratched. When she sat in the seat and lifted up the top, she saw a big dent on the inside. *It's perfect for me.*

The class held its collective breath as a woman with jet-black, shoulder-length, wavy hair glided into the room. Her light pink, knee-length dress looked as stiff as a board. *Definitely not the clothes of an ex-Marine.* Julie didn't understand why her stomach felt like someone had tied a knot in it.

"Good morning, students." *Her voice sounds like a bird's.* " I am Angela Ryczek. You may call me 'Mrs. R,' and I'll call you 'Miss,' or 'Mr.' Today I'll start by calling all of you 'special.'"

Mrs. Ryczek reminded Julie of the mom in "Ozzie and Harriet." By the end of the first day, her stomach had unknotted itself.

◆

Christ Lutheran required all of its students to attend church each Sunday, and Mrs. Ryczek put a check in her *Special Book* every time one of her students went to church. *I can finally get my name and a checkmark in a book for doing something good.* Julie really wanted to please Mrs. Ryczek, who was one of the kindest women she had ever met — but she couldn't tell her teacher that her parents spent every Saturday night drinking with the neighbors, and then fighting when they got back to their trailer. The next morning they'd sleep until noon, while Julie and Dan ate their bowls of Fruit Loops in front of the TV. The Anderson house was quiet, so Julie thought maybe they were all at church.

◆

It was the first week of December, and Julie was still trying to solve her church problem. She had thought about it during the ride to school that morning, and was even thinking about asking Mrs. Anderson if she and her family ever went to church. Julie took off her jacket, mittens and boots in the cloak room, put on her shoes, and entered the classroom ahead of some of the kids who had a longer ride to school. She straightened her jumper, sat at her desk, and opened her reading book. Mrs. Ryczek was at her desk with her reading glasses propped on her nose.

"Miss Sandford?" Julie looked up. *Her voice is always soft. And her eyes look like the color of Windex.* "Could you please stay in for a few minutes at noon recess? I need to talk to you." Mrs. Ryczek smiled and then returned to whatever-it-is-teachers-do-at-their-desks work.

What have I done? Oh, please, I hope she's not mad at me! The knot from the first day of school came back and stayed in Julie's stomach until the lunch bell rang. After everyone had finished eating, they quickly put on jackets, scarves, hats, mittens, and boots, and raced outside to see who would be first to climb the six-foot high snowdrifts piled alongside the fence. She walked slowly up to the wastebasket, threw her bread crusts and apple core away, and stood next to Mrs. Ryczek's desk.

"Sit down, dear." Julie sat in the desk-for-kids-who-need-extra-attention, and hoped she wouldn't start crying.

"I've noticed you don't have any checkmarks in my *Special Book.*"

She cleared her throat and looked down.

Mrs. Ryczek gently put her hand under Julie's chin, and lifted her head. "Do you go to church?"

"No," Julie whispered.

"Would you like to?"

"Sorta."

Mrs. Ryczek didn't waste any more of her twenty questions.

"Listen, Julie, you are a very smart young lady."

'Smart?' 'Lady?'

39

"I've seen how easily you memorize facts. And I think I know how we could get your name in my book."

Oh, I'm listening! Julie clasped her hands tightly together.

"If you memorized a Bible verse each week and recited it to me during Monday noon recess, I'd be happy to put a check next to your name. What do you think?"

"Could ... could I take home a Bible?"

"Absolutely."

"Oh, then I could do it!" Julie jumped up and threw her arms around her teacher. "Thank you, thank you!"

Mrs. Ryczek had smiled through the whole conversation. She waited for Julie to finish her hug and step back. "Julie, here're three index cards with a different verse on each one. You can pick whichever one you want to start with. They are John 3:16, Genesis 1:1, and First John 1:9. I'll be ready to hear you recite next week."

Julie would already have done *anything* for Mrs. Ryczek, and now she'd get her name in the *Special Book*. She couldn't imagine trying to get through the rest of the school day before she could go home and start reading and memorizing verses. That night sitting on her twin bed, Julie opened to the first page, expecting to find an index that would show her how to get to First John. Instead she saw the words 'This Bible is given to," and next to them was written 'Julie Sandford.' The next line down said 'On this date,' and someone had written 'Christmas 1966.' *My very own Bible! Mrs. R did this for me!* Julie held the book like it was a treasure, even better than the doll she had always wanted.

Before the end of school in June, Julie had memorized over twenty verses. And she did way more than that by finding whole stories to read, some that Mrs. Ryczek had already told to the class, and others that she found on her own. Some of the stories were exciting, like David and Goliath. Some were sad, like when Jesus was crucified. The ones she liked best, though, told about women like Mary Magdalene. Jesus had loved her even when people made fun of her, and she knew what that was like. *I know Jesus loves me and Mrs. Ryczek loves me. I wish I could stay in her class forever!*

CHAPTER THREE

CHILDHOOD, INTERRUPTED

Julie was moving again. As she packed her clothes, stuffed animals and books, she saved her Bible to put on top of the box so it wouldn't get squished. She felt sad at the thought of saying goodbye to the Andersons, who had treated her like she belonged to them; and especially of leaving Mrs. Ryczek, who had made her feel smart. This move was so much harder than when she had left Washington. *Mrs. Ryczek said that Spring Green is only 'a hop, skip and a jump' away from Platteville. I hope I can come back and visit her some day!*

Fifth grade *had* to be as good as fourth. And she had all summer to make new friends before school started.

♦

Home was another trailer; Julie was used to them by now, and didn't think she'd ever live in a real house again. But this trailer wasn't a clean, almost-new one parked in a clearing next to a big farmhouse; instead, it smelled like the Anderson barn when it needed mucking out. The linoleum floor had big cracks in it; the door hung crooked; and some of the windows didn't close all the way. The trailer was in a 'park' surrounded by lots of other old-looking trailers, all squished together with a little bit of brown crabgrass around them. Julie thought most of the trailers looked like the TV news that showed houses after they had been hit by tornadoes.

When the Sandfords unpacked their trailer on a sticky, muggy night in early July, there was no family waiting for them with a home-cooked meal and an air-conditioned room. Julie's mom welcomed them to their new trailer with a Spam casserole, which they ate outside sitting on the prickly grass, swatting mosquitoes.

Julie ate Spam almost every day that summer—usually for supper, but sometimes even for lunch. Her mom found lots of different ways to make it, but it never really tasted good, not like the ham Mrs. Anderson had made. Since she ate Spam so often, she added Julie plus Spam and got 'Jammy'.

♦

Julie had wanted a bike ever since they left Washington. There were two used ones for sale by a family one block over from them; Arlene gave her kids five dollars each for the bikes and warned them "not to wreck 'em, 'cuz I ain't buying you no more." The blue Schwinns were rusty and mud-splattered, and their chains fell off as soon as Julie and Dan hit a curb at break-neck speed on their first ride. They fixed the chains, wiped their greasy hands in the grass, and took off again. Stones shot out beneath the fat tires, sometimes hitting innocent bystanders like well-aimed BBs from Dan's gun. Deep potholes and crooked speed bumps made the ride seem like a big adventure. With hair whipping back and pedals pumping furiously, they attacked the roads and sidewalks like they were being chased. The previous day's cloudburst had created huge puddles, perfect for spraying a trail of glistening, oily water in a rainbow that arched behind the bikes.

Julie began to attract a lot of attention. Even though the trailer park was teeming with kids, her bike came at people like a heat-seeking missile. Some neighbors laughed, some cursed, and everyone got out of the path of destruction.

One man stood outside for hours, watching all of the kids ride their bikes. Julie seldom slowed down long enough to notice anybody, but every time she rode on the sidewalk in front of his trailer, her eyes were drawn to him because of his Wellington cap, which was like her dad's. She also noticed that he had dirty-looking, gray hair hanging limply below the rim of his cap, which wasn't anything like her dad's hair; and his flannel shirt looked the same as her dad's, but it had holes around the pocket and collar. The shirt hung loosely on his skinny body for dear life, but Julie's dad's shirt always stretched tightly across his chest muscles. She thought it was good that this man wore Wellington boots, but his right pants leg seemed glued to the top of the boot, and that looked really strange to her.

One day the man stood right in the middle of the sidewalk, not looking like he was going to move. Julie threw her feet back on the pedals; when the brakes caught, the back of the bike fishtailed, the tires screeched, and a squiggly path of burned rubber decorated the sidewalk. Other kids saw what happened from a distance, stopped their bikes, and looked terrified at what the strange man might do.

"Hey, I'm Mr. Thomas. What's your name?"

I'm in deep, dark, doodoo now! "Julie."

Mr. Thomas looked down the street at the group of frightened kids and laughed. "Whoever burns the longest and waviest path of rubber," he yelled, "will get a Tootsie-roll pop!" Their fear instantly turned into cheering and hollering as they lined up their bikes, while one of the older boys shouted, "Start your engines!"

Fierce competition eventually drew the trailer park kids into a close friendship. Julie never noticed any of the adults talking together outside their trailers, so she figured they were inside, like Mr. and Mrs. Anderson and her parents always were.

The almost-bald tires on the Schwinns signaled the end of the summer. While Julie was out for one last ride, she started thinking about the beginning of school. *Will I fit in? What is Spring Green like? Who will be my fifth grade teacher? Will she be like Miss Meyer, or like Mrs. Ryczek?* Her mind and her bike were turning simultaneous circles.

"Look out!" Julie heard, barely in time to avoid a chain-link fence. Somehow her circle had flattened into a line headed straight for disaster.

"Thanks, Mr. Thomas!" Julie shouted.

"That's okay—anytime. Hey, I can give you a Tootsie-roll pop even though you didn't burn any rubber today! Come on over and pick one out!" Mr. Thomas shouted back.

Julie headed out to the street to make one more circle, and then cruised over to Mr. Thomas' trailer. *I wonder if he's married? And where is his wife?*

"I actually left the Tootsie-roll pops in my trailer. You can come in and pick out whichever one you want." Julie hesitated because she hardly ever saw the grown-ups going in to each other's trailers, and the kids usually played outside. But Mr. Thomas was a nice man; all of the kids liked him, and he watched out for all of them. She would be in there only long enough to get her candy, and then back on her bike for the rest of the day.

Mr. Thomas opened the aluminum door ahead of Julie and leaned against the railing.

"Go ahead in, young lady."

Julie stepped in, and then turned around. Mr. Thomas swung the door closed and walked towards her. Before she could ask about her Tootsie-roll, he reached out with both hands, grabbed her tank top at the bottom, yanked it up to her neck, cupped both hands around her developing breasts and rubbed them.

"I've been waiting for a long time to do this," he breathed heavily. "And I know you want me to do this, or you wouldn't have come into my trailer."

Julie's lungs burned. She couldn't move. *Where's Dan? Where's my mom? Why is he doing this?* Out of instinct, Julie suddenly ducked under Mr. Thomas's right elbow and momentarily froze at the door, trying to remember how to open it. Then she jerked it open, ran down the steps, and caught her foot on the edge of the bottom one. She stumbled forward, regained her balance, pulled her top down and ran to her bike. For the first time ever, Julie forgot how to ride; she threw the kickstand back with her foot and walked her bike with her brain all fuzzy, hoping she could remember how to get home. *I hope Mr. Thomas isn't following me. What if he tells my parents I stole his candy or something?* Hurling the bike against her trailer, Julie collapsed on the dry grass, buried her face in her hands, and sobbed.

All the next day, Julie stayed in her bedroom as much as she could. The August sun beat on the metal roof of the trailer until the inside felt like the car the day she had moved to the Andersons'. But she *had* to stay in and be safe, so she closed her window, pulled down the brittle shade, and sat on the floor in front of a small fan. She tried to play with Mr. Potato Head, even though most of the parts were missing. Her puzzles also had missing parts; and it was no fun playing Sorry by herself. She was bored and hot, and wanted to open her window, but she wasn't going to take any chances on having Mr. Thomas peek in, especially when she was getting dressed. *I'd rather burn to death than see him again!*

Julie was glad her mom didn't ask her about why she was staying in, otherwise she might have had to tell about her awful shame. She was used to keeping things to herself, like when Grandma Hagstrom lived with them, and when Miss Meyer said things that hurt.

But this thing was worse, and harder to keep a secret. She felt like she was trying to hold a balloon down under the water; pretty soon it would pop up somewhere else. Mr. Thomas had turned her inside out and stomped on her, and she almost hadn't escaped from him. One time her brother had stepped on a bunny in the yard; Julie had watched it gasp for breath, stretch out its paws, and then it was still. *That's how I feel.* Only Julie wasn't still, and she couldn't stay in her hotter-than-a-furnace room any longer. It was time to talk to her parents, or maybe just to her dad. *He'll know what to do!*

Late that afternoon, Julie went outside, sat on the side-walk, and waited for her dad to come home from work. She knew that as soon as he got home was the best time to talk to him when he wouldn't be stumbling around or yelling, or plain mad at her about something.

Danny pulled up to the trailer, got out of his truck, slammed the door and walked toward her. He took off his cap and ran his fingers through his hair. "Man, it's hotter'n blazes! I need a cold one. What are you doing out here?" Julie was about to lose her chance.

"Dad, I need to talk to you." She stood up and tipped her head down.

"What's eating you?"

She stared at a crack in the sidewalk. "Well ... you're not gonna like this."

"Are you in some kind of trouble?"

"I don't know." She kept her head down, and stuttered her way through her story. When she was trying to figure out how to say the embarrassing part, her dad suddenly turned away from her and ran up the steps into their trailer. *What've I done now? Am I going to be sent to my room? Is he going to tell Mom?* Julie sat down, picked up a stick, and started poking ants racing out of the sidewalk crack.

Ten minutes later, Danny came back out of the trailer wearing ironed jeans and a red t-shirt that showed off his muscles. His hair was wet and neatly combed, and Julie was surprised to see him without his cap. *I wonder where he's going?*

As Danny walked down the sidewalk and turned the corner, she decided to follow him. When she realized where her dad was headed, she panicked. *He's going to Mr. Thomas' trailer!* She ran back to retrieve her bike and rode as far in the opposite direction from Mr. Thomas as she could. If she thought she could get away with it, she would have ridden for miles and miles.

Danny walked up the steps of Mr. Thomas' trailer and banged loudly on the door. "Hey, Ed! Get your sorry butt out here!"

Mr. Thomas ambled to the door and peered through the screen. "Yeah?"

"I know about lizards like you. There's a hole for you somewhere, but it ain't here." Danny was very loud, very sober, and very threatening. He made sure everyone around him heard about what this 'pervert' had done.

"Get off my property now, before I call the cops!" Mr. Thomas stayed behind the door.

"I'd love to see you do that. Maybe they'd like to hear what you did to my daughter." Neighbors were quietly leaving their trailers and standing on the sidewalks, pretending to be interested in each other's conversations.

"Everyone knows I love all these kids. Your kid's just mad 'cuz she didn't get the Tootsie-Roll she wanted." Drops of sweat appeared on Mr. Thomas' forehead.

Danny was menacingly cool. "Watch your back, Thomas." He turned around, ignored the gathering crowd, and walked back to his trailer.

♦

By the time Julie returned, the sun was casting long shadows across the park. When she abandoned her bike and went in to the trailer, she was hoping her dad would be there to tell her that everything was okay, and that he had 'cleaned Mr. Thomas's clock.' But he was gone, and she didn't know whether or not her mom had been told about Mr. Thomas. Arlene pointed to a bowl of macaroni and cheese sitting on the table without taking her eyes off of the TV. Julie choked down the cold, congealed blob of food, said goodnight, and headed for her bedroom. She pulled up her shade and her window, and collapsed onto her bed without changing out of her sweaty clothes.

Julie was done with bike riding. The next morning, she walked her prized bike to the back of the park where the dumpsters were, and left it there.

♦

One of Julie's few really strong memories from her earliest childhood was brushing her teeth by herself. She was four years old and had climbed up on a stool to reach the sink. Grabbing the tube of Crest, she'd unscrewed the top and aimed it at her toothbrush. When a gentle squeeze didn't work, she'd squeezed harder, and a huge thing like a piece of long Playdoh had shot out and landed on the sink. She'd been terrified of her mom finding out, but didn't know how to get the toothpaste back into the tube.

That's how Julie felt now: like she had been squeezed, something important in her had come out, and there was no way to get it back in again. Mr. Thomas had done it, and she felt ashamed for letting him.

♦

The start of fifth grade was a week away. *I remember when I used to care about who my teacher would be. Now all I want to do is hide from Mr. Thomas.*

The possibility of getting a man for a teacher was something Julie hadn't ever thought about. Mr. Davis was short, mostly bald, and wore the same white shirt every day, except with a different tie. He was nice, he spoke softly, and he never lost his temper. He told funny knock-knock jokes; and every day he told one of his students something special he liked about them. His classroom was covered with posters of animals in funny poses; one hung on the wall behind his desk with a picture of a big, furry calico cat. The balloon over its head read, "Never hold grudges ... they shed terribly!" The best part of Mr. Davis' room was all the books lined up on shelves under the windows. He encouraged the kids to borrow his books anytime, so Julie took home at least one a week. Her favorite books were the "Trixie Belden" mysteries and "Tom Sawyer."

If I like school so much, why does my head hurt when I'm here? And what about my stomach pains? At first, they came once or twice a week, then once or twice a day; by Christmas time, they were lasting all day. Julie was afraid to go to school, because she started aching as soon as she got there. But she was also afraid to stay home. She'd seen "Name That Tune" on TV, and this was like "Name That Fear," and she didn't like the game.

♦

On the last day of school in June, Julie and the other kids got off the bus at the trailer park. As soon as it pulled away, a pick-up truck towing a U-haul drove in. The kids broke into a run and followed the truck. Julie was the first one to stop when she saw where the truck was headed. *Is he moving? I wanna see everything ... maybe I can get closer and still be*

51

safe if I stay in the group. As strange men came out of Mr. Thomas' trailer carrying boxes, the boys begged to help, and were instantly recruited. The girls hung back; they looked at each other, quietly shook their heads, and returned to their own trailers. As Julie walked back home, she wondered, for the first time, if any of those other girls had ever followed Mr. Thomas into his trailer.

As soon as Julie got up the next morning, she quickly changed out of her nightgown into shorts, a t-shirt and flip-flops, ate a bowl of Frosted Flakes, and walked over to Mr. Thomas' trailer. The truck and U-haul were gone, and so were the lawn chairs, push mower and grill that used to sit on the grass outside. Julie felt like throwing a party—but all she could do was run to the chain-link fence and throw up her breakfast.

◆

Julie's headaches and stomachaches went away. She talked her mom into taking her to the Salvation Army to buy a bike—*I hope she doesn't ask what happened to my other one*—and they came back with a shiny blue Schwinn. It was missing a pedal, but it had a big bell on the handlebars. The kids in the park now rode in a posse, with everyone taking turns being Wyatt Earp. While they spent the summer making the streets safe, the adults gathered on the sidewalks a little more often than the previous year, and talked about President Johnson, school bussing, the weather, and Elvis.

◆

Sixth grade meant a change of schools, but only because Julie would be going to a brand new middle school. All of her friends from last year would be there, and she knew she didn't need to be afraid of who her teacher would be. The summer had been good, Julie hadn't been sick, and after all, this was *middle school*. She almost felt like a grown-up.

The ghost of Miss Meyer lived in Mr. O'Keefe, who told his homeroom class the first day that he used to be a Marine. *This can't be happening!* He didn't have a *Stupid Chair*, but he seemed to enjoy whacking the knuckles of students who didn't catch on to their work quickly enough for him.

Mr. O'Keefe was Julie's science and math teacher; and soon into the year, her headaches and stomachaches were back for an encore. To keep things from getting boring, Julie started to experience nausea as well. She had grown since third grade, which made her too tall to hope Mr. O'Keefe wouldn't notice her—but didn't know what to do about it.

◆

"Mrs. Sandford, please sit down. *Now.*" Arlene easily folded her five-foot-five frame into her daughter's desk chair in the middle of the classroom. It was four o'clock, and the last student doing detention had left. Jim O'Keefe paced in front of Arlene, then stopped, squared his shoulders, and squinted his eyes at her. "I'm not sure your daughter is going to make it through sixth grade. She can't seem to pay attention." Julie's mom simply stared. "And I've heard that her younger brother seems to get into a lot of trouble. Maybe it has something to do with your family living in a trailer court—"

"And that makes my family, what—'trailer trash?'"

Mr. O'Keefe folded his arms and let the words float around the room.

"I already live with a bully; you're going to have to do better than that if you expect to win this battle." Arlene narrowed her eyes into slits.

"I don't need to win anything."

"My husband is one part snake charmer and two parts bull fighter. You don't want to mess with him."

"Is that a threat?" Mr. O'Keefe's voice rose slightly.

"It is if you come in to my barn and start slinging manure."

"We're not getting anywhere here."

"That's good, because I'm not going anywhere with you. I already got a roller coaster at home, and that's enough of a ride for me."

Mr. O'Keefe and Arlene glared at each other, neither conceding any ground. The janitor walked in and started to sweep the floor. Arlene disengaged from the conference by getting up, walking slowly to the door and closing it behind her. There had been a slight opening of a pressure valve, apparently needed to release tension from both Arlene and Mr. O'Keefe—tension that probably had nothing to do with Julie's welfare, and certainly not with her knuckles, which stayed raw for the rest of the year.

CHAPTER FOUR

FRIENDS IN LOW PLACES

Christmas was a week away, and Julie expected her family to celebrate the season like they'd done every year for as far back as she could remember. Her dad would start drinking beer until he got drunk and fell asleep, usually on the floor. That would make her mom really mad, and then she'd use cuss words like a bat to beat up on her and her brother. When it seemed like she'd finally used up all her words, she'd clamp her lips shut and not talk to anyone. Julie would try her best to stay invisible until about the middle of January, when something mysterious would happen to make everything calmer again.

Julie jumped off the bus the last day of school before Christmas vacation and took her time climbing over all of the snow banks before she walked up the front steps of her trailer. She opened the door quietly, hoping to escape to her room before either of her parents saw her. *Maybe Dad'll be passed out somewhere, Mom'll be in the bathroom, and I can sneak by both of them.* What Julie never counted on was finding her mom standing next to a small evergreen tree propped in a metal stand in the living room. A big bowl of popcorn was on the coffee table, and a box of ornaments

Julie had never seen was on the floor. A tangled string of big lights was draped over the back of the couch.

Dropping her books and construction paper star, Julie said, "What're we doing?"

"What does it look like? It's about time we put up a tree around here. We need to do something special for Christmas."

♦

By the time the tree was decorated, it had been dark outside for a couple of hours. Julie's stomach was growling from hunger, but she hadn't wanted to stop until the lights were hanging on the tree. When her mom plugged in the cord and the tree was lit in red and green and blue, Julie was sure she'd never seen anything so beautiful. *I don't know where Dad is—but I hope he leaves the tree alone when he gets home.* There were even a few wrapped packages under the tree, which made everything look like the picture on the Ace Hardware calendar hanging on the wall in their kitchen.

For the next five days, Julie sat on the couch reading a book, waiting for it to get dark enough outside to plug in the tree lights. After that, she'd stare at the tree, barely noticing her mom and brother eating supper in front of the TV, until her mom chased her to bed.

On Christmas Eve, Julie found her Bible from Mrs. Ryczek and lay on her stomach on her bed, flipping through the first part of the New Testament to find the story of Jesus' birth. As she started reading in the book of Matthew, she noticed it was already getting dark enough outside to light their Christmas tree, even though it was only four in the afternoon. She turned her Bible over and heard a smashing sound coming from the living room. *Oh, no!* Julie got up and ran out of her room in time to see red and blue glass balls flying around, while her dad was cussing and her mom was crying. After the ornaments were reduced to a sea of glittering shards, Danny grabbed the pot of meatballs and sauce from the burner and threw it against the wall, laughing and yelling, "Mortared mush!" Then he walked over to the tree and kicked around the presents with his Wellington boots. Julie walked backwards to her bedroom, threw herself down on her bed and soaked the Bible with her tears. *God, why does Dad have to smash all of my dreams?*

♦

A February thaw in Wisconsin wasn't too rare—but a sixty-degree thaw definitely was. Julie left her home on a Saturday afternoon and saw young children wearing shorts and riding bikes through piles of snow. *All of these kids probably have nice parents who're looking for someone to baby sit. If they'd ask me, I could get out of my trailer.*

"Look out!" Julie was almost knocked over by two grade school-aged boys riding their bikes at mach speed, headed right for her. The memories of her bike riding—and of being hurt by Mr. Thomas—made her head start to pound. *Stop it, Julie. Not everyone's like him.* As she jumped to the edge of the sidewalk, a voice yelled, "Michael! Brian! You goofballs be careful! You almost ran that girl over!"

"We're sorry, Mom!" came the stereo reply. The boys jammed on their brakes, bikes fishtailing. They turned towards Julie in unison. "Hey, girl, we're sorry."

"That's okay. I used to ride my bike the same way."

"Boys, invite that girl over here, so I can give her something to drink, and maybe you can practice acting like gentlemen for a change."

Wow! Are there really moms who talk to their boys like that, and who expect them to show respect? Julie tried to slow her heartbeat, not wanting to look over-anxious to have friends. She walked over to the boys' trailer as normally as she could.

"Hi. I'm Mary Nelson. You can call me Mary. And you've already met the knuckleheads."

Now that Michael and Brian were so close to Julie, they seemed overcome with shyness. Ducking their heads in tandem, they parked their bikes next to the porch and scampered up into the house.

"So, what's your name and what's your game?" A pleasant smile played around the corners of Mary's mouth.

"My name's Julie ... and I'm not really sure what a game is ..." Julie tried to cover her confusion by looking down. No one had ever asked her anything that didn't already have an assumed answer—a math fact, or a "Yes, Ma'am, I'll never do it again."

"Well, what do you like to do? Are you in any sports? Do you read? What are your dreams? What would you like to be when you grow up?" These rapid-fire questions made Julie uncomfortable, but also curious about this woman. After that first encounter, she started inventing a different excuse to walk over to the Nelson trailer every day after school. Sometimes, it was to borrow a cup of sugar, even though Arlene never baked anything; another time, it was to ask Mary to sew a missing button on her favorite red blouse; and lots of times, it was for help with homework. After a couple of weeks of this, Mary asked Julie to stay at the kitchen table after she had closed her math book.

"Would you like something to drink?"

"Yes, ma'am."

Mary got up, pulled a bottle of Coke out of the refrigerator, flipped off the top and set it down in front of Julie.

"We need to talk." Mary's pleasant smile never left her face.

Uh oh. I've really been a pain over here. If she tells my mom, I'm going to catch it.

"About what?" Julie gulped down her fear.

Mary reached out for her hand. "I don't want you to keep making up excuses for coming over here. I really enjoy your company. If you'd like, I could teach you to cook and sew— if that's okay with your mom—and maybe even take you grocery shopping."

Tears pooled in Julie's eyes. "Mary, no one's ever done any of that for me. I don't know what to say."

"Don't say anything. Give me a hug, and we'll see about sending you home with some fresh chocolate-chip cookies in about an hour-and-a-half. Will that be all right?"

Julie didn't know life could be like this. Mary was a mom, grandma, aunt, teacher, and friend, all rolled into one of the nicest adults she had ever known. And, by the end of March, her headaches and stomachaches had almost disappeared.

Mary took Julie grocery shopping with her the following Saturday morning, and for every Saturday after that. They'd each put a hand on the cart as they pushed it through the produce section, snitching grapes, laughing at the strange-looking fruits, and looking forward to the first ripe strawberries of the season. When they got back from the store, Julie would help Mary put the groceries away. *I don't see a can of Spam in any of these bags.* Pretty soon Mary was showing Julie what different pots and pans were used for, how to make pasta al dente, and then lasagna. The best thing of all was when Julie was invited to stay for the supper she had helped cook.

By April Julie had her special place at the table, between Mary and Lee, and across from Michael and Brian. Each person shared something special about his or her day; everyone listened, analyzed, laughed, and encouraged each other. Julie was sure "The Twilight Zone" theme song was playing in the background somewhere. *This must be another world. I never knew people really talked and acted like this— and I get to be a part of it.*

♦

On a Saturday night in May, Julie was sitting at her usual place at the Nelson table. Mary had taught her how to make baked curry chicken, mashed potatoes with chives and fresh green beans. While the family raved over her good cooking, she found the courage to share her fear of Mr. O'Keefe. When she was done, and everyone had shown more sympathy than Julie had ever known before, it was Michael's and Brian's turns to talk about school; then Lee talked about his job; and finally, Mary talked about wanting to start selling Tupperware.

Mary got up from the table and asked Julie to help her clear the dishes. As they were standing at the sink working in perfect washing-and-drying harmony, she suddenly said, "So Julie, what's it like at your house at dinnertime?"

Maybe I could pretend I cut myself drying a sharp knife, and Mary would forget about her question. If I tell her what my family is like, she'll never want me here again.

"Well, Mary," Julie decided to take a detour. "My mom makes stuff like sausage and sauerkraut, and the trailer stinks so bad I have to run away!"

Mary didn't follow the rabbit trail. "But I mean, what's it like around your table? Does everyone talk at once, like Lee's family, or do people take turns talking, like here? I'm really interested in how different families do things."

You're right about that. My family is about as different as you could possibly get.

Before Julie could think of anything to say, Mary dried her hands and walked over to the phone. "I know! I'll call your mom, tell her what you said about her sausage and sauerkraut—and after we laugh about it, I'll get a chance to ask her some of these questions without sounding too nosy."

The gig's up.

"Hello, Mrs. Sandford? This is Mary Nelson. My family and I live in the trailer court, and Julie's been spending a lot of time over here the past few months. I've really enjoyed getting to know her. You have a delightful daughter."

I wonder what my mom's saying?

"Well, anyways, I was calling to share a funny story with you ..."

Julie threw down her towel and ran to the bathroom, slamming the door behind her. *My heart might as well break in here—the pieces will be easier to clean up.* Julie sat on the plush rug, trying not to think about what Mrs. Nelson might be hearing from her mom. After about ten minutes, she knew it was crazy to sit in the bathroom any longer ... there was no help for her anywhere. She got up, quietly opened the door, and tiptoed back down the hallway towards the kitchen.

"Julie, please come here." Julie had never heard Mary use a stern voice until now. "I talked to your mom, and she said she has never, ever made sausage and sauerkraut. Why did you lie to me?"

"I ... I don't know ..." *Please, Mary, don't make me leave you!*

Mary walked towards Julie. "Well, everyone deserves a second chance. But don't ever lie to me again," was her gentle rebuke.

After that, Mary seemed to forget about pursuing a conversation with Julie's mom. It seemed to Julie that Mrs. Nelson was good at figuring things out. Maybe something in her mom's voice had spoken louder than her words; or maybe Mary had 'heard' between the lines and knew something wasn't right. Julie felt like a beggar who was hoping for stale crumbs, and instead got a whole, fresh, hot loaf of bread. Whatever the reason, she didn't care: she was back on Mary's good side, and that was all that mattered. She could keep shopping with her, eating with her family, and being with people who didn't seem to realize that they were shining a flashlight of kindness into a shadowed heart.

At the beginning of the summer, Mr. Nelson announced that he had transferred jobs, and his family would be moving to Colorado. Julie ate one last dinner with them, after which Mary hugged her and said she promised to write to her. Michael and Brian gallantly volunteered to 'escort' her back to her trailer. A couple of weeks later, Julie looked out her bedroom window and saw a moving truck drive by—and her heart felt emptier than it ever had before.

CHAPTER FIVE

"STICKS AND STONES MAY BREAK MY BONES"

The Sandford trailer was a compact firing range. Julie sought refuge in her bedroom, but soon discovered that paper-thin walls made good verbal-assault conductors.

"Tell that damn kid—tell her right now!" she'd hear her dad scream. *Tell me what? Why is he calling me names?*

"I'll do it when I'm good and ready! I'm hardly ever good, and I sure ain't ready!" Arlene would then slam their bedroom door, and the next thing Julie would hear was the sound of the TV turned up to full blast. Her head would feel as though it was going to split open like the melons she and Mrs. Nelson often cut and arranged on a platter for a fancy dinner. *Oh, Mary, I miss you!*

About fifteen minutes later, Julie would hear her parents' door open and bang shut again, followed by the slamming of the trailer door and then the gunning of her dad's truck. The last thing she'd remember was crying herself to sleep.

When Julie would wake up the next morning with puffy eyes and an aching head, she'd hear the squealing test pattern on the TV as she walked into the living room; and once she got there, her stomach would turn cartwheels from the smell of cigarette butts still smoldering in an overflowing ashtray on the coffee table. She would always pick it up carefully, trying to balance it with the empty beer cans. On her way to the kitchen to dump everything, she'd usually stumble over crumpled bags of Fritos or Cheetos, and then the clean-up job would be bigger and stinkier than ever.

The pitch and rhythm of the song never changed. After a while, Julie started thinking of herself by the name her dad had called her, and was becoming numb to its sting. She found out that she could turn on her little transistor radio that was sitting on the table next to her bed, and fall asleep listening to her favorite songs, or even to people arguing about war and baseball.

♦

Julie's family had never gone anywhere special for the Fourth of July—not like her friends, who always got excited about going on picnics with their families at a lake or a park, and afterwards watching fireworks when the sun went down. The summer her family had lived on the Anderson farm, all of them had had a picnic together, and then the kids had found a tall ladder and climbed up on a flat part of the house roof to watch fireworks, while their parents stayed in the kitchen. That was Julie's best memory of the Fourth of July.

All the other years, her dad was always gone somewhere, and her mom would stay inside and watch the New York City fireworks on TV. She would use the excuse that she didn't want to "become a mosquito feast," but Julie and Dan would spray themselves with Off and try to find a high place to at least *see* the fireworks, even if they were too far away to *hear* them. It was the Fourth of July again, and the flight pattern was about to change.

♦

Arlene turned off Julie's radio and shook her shoulder. "Julie! Get up! Here's your shorts and shirt. You can throw them over your nightie. Come on, we gotta go find your dad." She then left to go to Dan's room and do the same thing. When the three of them were semi-dressed and semi-awake, they climbed into their automobile wannabe, rolled down the windows, and headed out of the trailer park.

The smell and haze of burnt fireworks and firecrackers hung over the city. It was a balmy night, but Julie felt chilled and scared. *We're patrolling a beat without a siren, and where are we going to find Dad? Besides, why are we looking for him?*

Julie saw her dad's truck parked in front of the U-Com-In bar and wondered why so many people were standing outside. She didn't want to get out and walk through all of those loud people, but it was even scarier to think about staying alone in the car. Besides, she knew her mom wouldn't let her do that. The three of them got out of the car, and Arlene led the charge through the crowd, which somehow parted to let them through.

Inside the bar, the air was as hazy as outside, but Julie knew that this thick air was from cigarette smoke. She saw people laughing and bumping elbows; some were asleep hunched over little round tables scattered all over the room; others were sitting at a long, skinny counter in front of a waiter wearing a white apron, who was pouring stuff from tall bottles into tiny glasses.

"Here. Take this and go buy yourselves a 7-Up." Arlene shoved a dollar bill into Julie's hand, turned her kids around and pushed them towards the bar, while she wove her way through the crowd.

Julie and Dan found stools, hoisted themselves up on them and bought their sodas. No longer chilled, Julie was now hot, sweaty, and even more frightened. She took a few sips of her soda, laid her head down and cried quietly until she fell asleep. When she awoke for the second time that night, her mom was shaking her shoulder again. "It's time to get home." While her mom half-dragged her to the car, Julie suddenly felt as helpless as her Grandma Hagstrom must've felt.

♦

Julie never thought she would have to go into a bar again after the Fourth. One month and many bars later, she stopped paying attention to the smoke and the people. There was one good thing about the nightly trips: no one was at their trailer to fill ashtrays or leave a mess on the floor. When she got up in the mornings now, she went to the kitchen right away and ate her cereal. If it was early enough, she had time to watch TV and enjoy the quiet house before her mom woke her dad up to go to work at his construction job. Julie made sure she was done eating and back in her room before her dad stumbled around the trailer, yelling and cussing.

I know the Anderson family and the Nelson family were different than ours. Why do Mom and Dad keep doing this every day? How come they can't love each other?

CHAPTER SIX

THE O.K. FARM

ℰℓ

While crickets, spring peepers and owls fought for supremacy in the night choir, Arlene quietly swung her legs out of bed. Tiptoeing down the hall and into Julie's walk-in closet-size bedroom, Arlene leaned over her bed, lightly tapped her on the shoulder, and held a manicured finger across her tightened lips. Julie shook herself awake. *Why are we going out again? We already made the nightly bar run.* She looked at her mom and tried to figure out why she was supposed to be quiet. *Wherever we're going, my brother has to come with us. Who cares how much noise we make?* Something in her mom's face demanded unquestioning obedience, so Julie suppressed her urge to yawn out loud. While she was stretching, Arlene reached under the bed, grabbed the handle of a suitcase with a broken latch, pulled it out and set it quietly on the end of the bed. Julie was wide-awake now. She scrambled out of bed and stood, not even sure if she was supposed to get dressed. Arlene pointed to Julie, and then to the dresser. Julie figured out the clue: She took hold of one knob, while her mother grabbed the other one. They gently pulled the drawer out together, so that it wouldn't squeak on the metal slide. Arlene grabbed a handful of clothes and tossed them into the suitcase, while

Julie picked up the remaining clothes and did the same. *What about my socks and underwear and stuff in the other drawers?* "This is all we have time for," Arlene whispered as she walked over to the suitcase and tried to close it. The hinge kept popping out, almost like it was refusing to cooperate with this different-kind-of-adventure. Arlene looked up at the bungee cord attached to the curtain rod at one end and a hook in the ceiling at the other.

"Tiptoe to the hall closet and bring the stool here." Julie did so, and then her mom told her to climb up on it and remove the end of the cord from the ceiling hook.

"But mom—"

"Do it!" Arlene hissed.

As soon as Julie unhooked the end, the curtain rod came crashing down. For an eternity of seconds, mother and daughter held their breath, staring at the open door with horror-filled eyes. The only sound coming from the adjoining bedroom was raucous snoring, and Julie couldn't remember a time when her nerves had actually been *calmed* by that noise.

Arlene hastily wrapped the cord around the bulging suitcase, attaching the curved wire ends together. She grabbed the handle and motioned for Julie to follow her. Dan was standing in the hallway, still in his pajamas and holding another beat up suitcase wrapped with a piece of twine. Danny's family walked quickly to the front door, threw on jackets and shoes, and sailed through like victims fleeing their captor.

With one hurdle jumped, there was still a large one looming before the escapees. A faded black '54 Buick—their most recent purchase—profaned the gravel driveway like an immovable object, challenging passersby to a smack down.

"Kids! Even though the engine's blown, we can still drive this heap if we stop to pour oil into it every fifty miles."

I've got a dad who can't seem to do anything without a drink—and now we've got a car that's the same way.

"Where are we going?" Julie whispered.

"To see your grandparents in Pineville."

"Where's Pineville? What grandparents?" Julie's words were lost as Arlene cursed the jammed driver's side door. She ran around to the passenger door, yanked it open, and motioned for Julie and Dan to follow her.

After piling their suitcases on the back seat, they climbed in, stepping on crumpled papers and petrified food remnants. Arlene pushed the seat back and slid across to the driver's side as all three settled into the car, enfolded by a reckless sense of anticipation. Arlene spotted a large, unopened bag of sunflower seeds on the dashboard and announced, "Look, guys, we've even got food!"

She started the car and turned on the headlights. As she was throwing the gearshift into reverse, a shadow appeared in the low beam of light. She let out a curse, while Julie sat paralyzed. *Please don't let that be Dad.*

A man wearing a sleeveless t-shirt and work pants walked up to the driver's side and motioned for Arlene to roll down her window. Arlene turned the crank a few times.

"Hi, neighbor. I've seen a lot of what's gone on around your house with your kids and husband. It wouldn't have been right for me to interfere – but it looks like maybe you're trying to run away."

"Please don't call the cops on us," pleaded Arlene.

"Lady, if I was going to call the cops on anyone, it'd be on that no good excuse for a husband of yours. I came out here to help you."

The man disappeared behind an old shed and then reappeared a few minutes later, dragging a decrepit trailer to the Buick and hitching it to the back. Arlene and her kids scrambled back out of the car, scurried into the house and grabbed armfuls of belongings to load into both the trailer and the

car. Fifteen minutes later, with Danny's snoring still reso-
nating throughout the house, Arlene bounced the car down
the muddy ruts and merged onto the main highway.

The radio and the odometer were both broken. Arlene
and her kids rolled down the windows and sang "Row, Row,
Row Your Boat," "Camp Town Races," and "You Are My
Sunshine," until their music overpowered the songs of the
night creatures. When Julie started to feel like someone had
lifted barbells off her shoulders, she knew they'd driven
enough miles to escape her dad's tantrums.

◆

Julie wondered if being with these grandparents would be
like her time with Grandma Hagstrom … and what Pineville
was like. By the time the sun was starting to heat up their
car, they drove into a town past a sign that read 'Pineville,
Michigan: population 318.' *Make that '321' now.* The town
looked like a postcard, with one-story houses on both sides
of Main Street, guarded by the fire department at one end and
First Lutheran Church at the other. The countryside spread
out beyond the town like it was keeping a polite distance,
and the farms all looked neat, although Julie noticed a few
tractor graveyards. The swamp of cattails made a dividing
line between the town and the country, and she knew that in
the fall the swamps would look like big, frothy heads of root
beer.

◆

Tired, dirty and hungry people pulled into Arlene's
parents' driveway right before noon. Richard and Rosalynn
Cerbé walked out to the car and wrapped their daughter and
grandchildren in enormous hugs. Gulping deep breaths of
safe, fatherless air, Julie wondered how long this unknown

peace would last. *When will Dad find us and drag us back to the trailer again?*

Julie was too tired to worry about anything except stretching out on a soft bed. Maybe, after she'd had some sleep, food, and a little more sleep, she'd be able to concentrate on getting to know her grandparents.

"Here, darling. And call me 'Grandma Rosie.' You can sleep in the room your mom grew up in." Even though Julie was dog-tired, she couldn't help noticing that her grandma looked like an older version of her mom—same height, same petite build, only her hair was grayer, and she was wearing a straight, pink-checked, below-the-knee dress with a matching belt tied around her waist. Julie walked into the room, collapsed on the bed, and the last thing she remembered, before she fell asleep, was being kissed on the cheek.

◆

When Julie awoke, the moon was shining brightly through a window, and the air felt a little chilly. It took a while for her to remember where she was, which was immediately followed by the realization that she needed a bathroom. She got up, walked out into the hallway and down a flight of stairs.

Voices from another room reached Julie's ears. "Arlene, you can't stay here. You and them kids need a place of your own. Why don't you see if Orville Koski has anything for you?"

"Ma, I don't want to beg from O.K.!"

"Like I care—"

As soon as Julie reached the kitchen, her grandma stopped in mid-sentence. "Hey, we thought you were going to sleep 'til next week! Are you hungry?"

"Yeah, and I need a bathroom."

"It's around the corner. Go wash up, and I'll fix you something to eat." Julie walked out, glad to find the bathroom, but wishing she'd had the chance to finish hearing whatever it was her grandma had been saying to her mom. *Are we going to live in another trailer? And who is 'O.K.?'*

At the end of the week, Arlene and her kids moved in to a farmhouse owned by Orville Koski—who, Julie gathered, was a childhood friend of her mom's. The farmhouse was surrounded by more land than she had ever seen, even at the Anderson's. At the entrance to the farm was an arched, peeling wooden sign with "The O.K. Farm" painted in barn red.

The farmhouse was old and deserted-looking, not clean and inviting like the Andersons' had been; but still, it was big, and had a climbing tree right outside the window of the room Julie chose for her bedroom. She could climb out her window onto a thick branch, take a book with her and not be found by anyone.

Julie overheard her mom telling Grandma that the rent was "only twenty-five bucks a month." *Maybe there will be enough money for me to get some new clothes before seventh grade. It would be too embarrassing to wear those torn things we brought from Spring Green.*

♦

The Pineville School had kindergarten through twelfth grade in one building. Julie started school wearing Salvation Army castoffs, but couldn't help noticing that not long after Arlene got a job as a school bus driver, she started bringing home shopping bags with polyester pants, print blouses and high-heeled shoes. *I guess there's no money left to buy anything for me, otherwise Grandpa Richard and Grandma Rosie wouldn't have to bring ground beef and chicken and fresh vegetables to us all the time. Maybe we would have more if Dad was here ... but then again, things are peaceful now ... and I don't know what I'd do with new clothes anyway.*

♦

The seventh graders had finished reading "A Christmas Carol" when Danny appeared in Pineville early in December.

"Please, Arlene," Julie heard her father beg her mom in the kitchen. "I've stopped drinking. I promise I won't take another drop." *He sounds like he's seen the ghost of Christmas future.* Julie began to see a new, sober, busy dad. Danny fixed the holes in their walls, fiddled with wires until the outlets worked, painted all the bedrooms, and reattached the door hinges.

"And thanks to you," Julie had heard her mom say to her dad one morning, "we don't have to pay the twenty-five buck rent anymore." *I'm really glad he did all this stuff—the house looks nicer. But will it stay as calm as it was before he came? I wonder what Grandpa and Grandma think about having him around.*

♦

The kitchen was comfortable and inviting, even though there wasn't a picnic table in the middle of it. A big, black stove—one that Julie had heard her grandpa call 'older than Patton'—stood guard in a corner, making everything warm and cozy, even when the rest of the house was freezing, and all of the windows were fogged over. *I thought Wisconsin was cold!*

Julie knew the familiar drill by now: her dad would start drinking and stay drunk until sometime after Christmas, while her mom would swear for whatever reason, do her search-and-destroy missions on easy-to-reach self-esteems, and then hide in her room for only-she-knew-how-long.

◆

On Christmas morning there was no coal for the stove, and the house was drafty, with the wind whipping through every crack. Ice built up inside the kitchen windows, diffusing the sunlight shining on the orange and pineapple wallpaper.

Arlene entered the kitchen dressed nicely and wearing make-up. "Julie, you and your brother get your sleeping bags and bring them in here!" She raised her arms and swept them theatrically across to the gas cooking stove, turned on the burners and lit the oven. "Your Granny Rosie sent homemade cinnamon rolls that only need to be baked! Now get!"

Julie ran out of the kitchen and up the stairs, passing her dad coming down with an armload full of wrapped presents. *What's going on here? Presents? He looks happy! And I'm freezing!*

◆

"Who's ready to go out and make a big bonfire?" Danny jumped up from Julie's spread-out sleeping bag, licked the frosting off his fingers, ran out of the kitchen, and came back a minute later wearing his Carhartt overalls. His family scattered to find their coats, hats, gloves and boots.

"Last one out's a rotten egg!" screeched Julie, running outside and heading for the nearest snow bank.

"Come on, you guys, we gotta find small sticks for kindling for the fire. I'll go back to the shed and drag some big logs over to the pit." Danny stepped into his own footprints from earlier that morning to make his way back to the shed.

The four adventurers piled kindling on top of Danny's elaborate log design, and when it looked right, Dan yelled "Ready! Aim! Fire!" Danny touched his Bic to the tinder, and within a few minutes the blaze was shooting perfectly vertical orange arrows into the cloudless sky. Julie never wanted to be awakened from this dream, which was so unlike anything she had ever imagined with her family. *Maybe Dad has stopped drinking for good, and we can do things like this every night.*

When the blaze had settled into glowing coals, Danny disappeared behind the shed, reappearing with four large, sharpened sticks pointed into the air like conquering spears.

"Ta-da!" Danny triumphantly walked around the bonfire, carefully handing a stick to his wife and children with a kiss on the cheek for each of them. From inside his left pocket, he then pulled out a slightly squished bag of marshmallows; the right pocket had Hershey's chocolate bars. While he handed everything to Arlene, he began singing "Let Me Call You Sweetheart" in a quiet tenor voice. *I've never heard him sing before. Wow—this night is full of surprises. I hope it never ends.*

◆

Richard and Rosalynn called a friend of theirs who owned a coal delivery business and was willing to take a load to the Sandford farmhouse on Christmas night. After Danny scooped snow onto the pile of smoldering ashes, he followed his family into the house and shoveled coal into the stove. Pretty soon, the house was as toasty as the bonfire had been. Julie couldn't remember when she'd had a more perfect day. And there were still presents to open under the tree.

◆

One frigid evening in early January, Julie was up in her room using the colored pencils and sketchpad she'd gotten for Christmas.

"Julie! Come down here! Your dad and I are watching an 8-millimeter. We want you to watch with us. Come here!"

Julie dropped her orange pencil on her desk, jumped up from her chair and headed downstairs. Entering the darkened living room and waiting for her eyes to adjust, she saw her parents sitting next to each other on the sofa. *What's the movie? No one's ever taken home movies in our family, like the Andersons had. And we've never had a family vacation, so it can't be that, either.*

Danny undraped his arm from around Arlene's shoulder, moved over and patted the cushion. "Come on in, girl. The water's warm." Julie walked over and plopped down between her parents, with the movie projector humming behind them, directing its beam onto the white sheet draped across the curtain in front of the window. The images were grainy, and the sound was garbled, but Julie could pick out three dogs and a man. They were all climbing on top of each other, and the man was pulling his pants down … *stop!* Her hands shot up to her face, tightly covering her eyes.

"Mom, I want to leave," whispered Julie. *Why did they want me to see this?* While Julie's parents were cackling, she got up and fled from the room.

Julie threw herself on her bed and sobbed. *I wish I could wash my brain out. If I'm going to sit next to my dad on the couch, I want him to tell me that he loves me. That I'm pretty. And smart. I don't ever want to remember that awful stuff!*

♦

It was January and the end of the first semester. Seventh grade hadn't been too hard; the teachers were mostly nice; and Julie had a surprise for her dad. She bounded into the house with her report card tightly clasped in her mittened hand. Without stopping to take off any of her winter clothes, she ran through the house, tracking snow on all of the old, dark-gray, braided rugs.

"Dad! Dad! Look what I got!"

Julie followed her voice up the stairs, with her boots leaving imprints on each step. At the top, she heard her dad humming softly as she burst into the bathroom doorway, panting and giggling. Danny put down his screwdriver, unbuckled his tool belt, and sat down on the curling linoleum floor. After handing him the report card, Julie began pulling off her mittens, boots, and wet socks. Even though her dad sat with an unreadable expression on his wind-burned face, she *knew* he'd be happy with her.

Danny talked into the card. "What did you get this B for?"

"But Dad," Julie's eyes brimmed with tears. "I got five A's—in English, Spelling, Science, Social Studies—"

"But you got a B in Math. That'll never do."

Oh, but that'll *do. And* this'll *do. It's Thistledew all over again. Where is she when I need her?*

Danny handed the report card back to Julie, who turned and walked out of the bathroom, leaving her boots and jacket drowning their sorrows in a puddle of melting snow. She shuffled to her bedroom and threw the report card down. If she hadn't had to get her mom's signature on it and return it to school the next day, she would've torn it into a million pieces.

♦

If that's the way my dad's going to be, I'll have to look for a father somewhere else. It was the middle of March, and Julie had given up trying to get her dad's attention. She was glad to have a nice, newly painted, clean-smelling house to live in—but she would have gladly traded it all to hear her dad say, 'You're the best daughter ever.'

Julie couldn't help noticing Orville Koski, with his sparkly eyes and silver hair that reminded her of Santa Claus. He seemed to spend more and more time around the farm, which made sense to her, since he was the owner of their house and all the land. One day he announced to Julie, Dan, and the other neighborhood kids, "You can all ride my horses for free in exchange for doing some chores around here." It was the perfect thing to chase away Julie's depression; by early May, she had learned to help mend fences, feed the horses and clean their stalls. All of the kids fought over who would get the honor of doing the best chores, which was anything that had to do with the horses.

Spring eventually gained the victory over winter by the end of the month. Patches of dirty snow were still hiding in the shadows of oaks and maples; the brighter, longer-lasting sun was encouraging the grass into the promise of deep summer green. The earth smelled like worms and damp rocks; new life was approaching the starting gate.

It was a bright, warm Saturday morning, and Orville had invited the kids—*like another posse*—for a long ride. "The horses are all Quarters, and stand fifteen hands high," Mr. Koski explained that morning, "and there are Bays, Chestnuts, Sorrels, Arabians, and Paints."

Julie couldn't decide between a gray, black, spotted, or white one. All six kids scrambled to get to the ones they liked best. *Mine's 'Lightning.'* Julie climbed up and waited for instructions.

The morning was spent trotting, cantering, and galloping. Mr. Koski led them on a big adventure, riding on acre after acre of his land, stopping when the horses needed a drink from one of the many ponds. When they were walking the horses, Mr. Koski pointed out Queen Anne's lace, Indian paintbrush, Mullen, Goldenrod and Burdick. And when the kids tipped their faces up to soak in the warm sun, they learned about Chickadees, Goldfinches, Brown-headed Cowbirds, Evening Grosbeaks, and Starlings—also known as Grackles, Mr. Koski had explained to them.

It was early afternoon before he told them it was time to return. When the sweaty kids rode even sweatier horses back to the barn, arguments broke out over who would work the hardest at taking off bridles and saddles, rubbing down the horses, brushing them, and feeding them. *I could stay here all day.*

Julie was the last child in the barn, inhaling mingled scents of horse and hay. Things in the barn were always right: Even the pungent manure was used for fertilizer around the farm. Nothing was wasted, and everything made sense.

Glancing around the barn, Julie noticed Orville sitting on his usual hay bale, watching her with pleasantness playing around the corners of the warmest eyes she had ever seen. With impetuous glee, she ran over to Mr. Koski and plopped down on his knee, not in any hurry to return home to a father who had no interest in knowing anything about her life. Mr. Koski reached into his pocket and dropped several sugar cubes into her hand—treasures for her to share with her horse on their next riding adventure. Her excited tears pooled in her eyes as Mr. Koski softly crooned words of love and comfort, wrapping his arms around her and gently rocking her with the tenderness of a father drawing his child into sweet sleep.

With the same gentle motion, a hand slowly worked its way inside Julie's jeans ... down ... down ... while the other hand reached up inside her denim shirt. Caressing hands mocked caressing words, as Julie's world exploded. Powered by the fuel of betrayal, she jumped up from Mr. Koski's lap, tearing her shirt in the process. Orville reached out and grabbed her by the wrist, wrenching and twisting it as he pulled her back.

"Don't you tell your mother what happened today, or you won't be living on my land anymore." Orville hissed vehemently as he flung Julie away. She threw the sugar cubes on the ground and raced out of the barn, tripping over a tractor rut outside the door and tumbling into the dirt. At least now she could give her mom an excuse for why her shirt was torn.

Beams of silence supported the roof over Julie's house. Silence about this incident would keep her parents in the farmhouse for free. *And besides, who would believe what Mr. Koski did to me? All the kids love him. All the parents love him, probably because he keeps us busy for hours at a time.* Julie wondered if any of the other girls, last in the barn like she had been, had had the same thing done to them. She would probably never know, but she would make sure she was never alone with him again. She'd help her brother Dan with the horses—do chores with him, or with one of the others. She would have to get even better at her hide-and-survive game plan.

CHAPTER SEVEN

SWIMMING UPSTREAM

"Get up, Julie. Your dad's moving us to Black Bear, Wisconsin. He's got some fool idea he can find work there." Arlene expelled the words in one breath before Julie had opened her eyes. *Thank You, God.*

"Did Dad—"

"Don't ask any of your usual fool questions, because I don't know anything." Arlene turned around and walked out.

Did he find out what Mr. Koski did to me, and decide to move us away? I really don't care, as long as we put distance between him and us.

♦

Danny had never had any problems finding work when he was sober. A big construction firm in Black Bear hired him within days of their move into a clean, modern, three-bedroom apartment. Julie was proud of her bedroom with the pale lavender walls, love beads in her doorway, and posters of David Cassidy, the Monkees, and the Beatles hanging everywhere. It was the nicest room she had ever had, which gave her extra confidence to start a new school.

As soon as Julie walked in to Kennedy Middle School for eighth grade, she was overwhelmed with the smell of chlorine. *I almost forgot that I used to dream about being an Olympic swimmer.* Since the whole school was buzzing about fall sports, it wasn't hard for her to find out where to sign up for tryouts for the swim team. *If I don't do anything else this year,* she whispered into her locker, *I will make the team!*

By the next week, Julie was the newest member of the swim team, and trying to catch up with all of the other girls who had started their training in mid-August. It was grueling training for an hour-and-a-half every day after school. While the other girls complained about how hard it was, Julie reveled in it. Every stroke was a pulling away from her life at home; and in her fourth meet, she set the school record for the 100-meter breaststroke, finishing at 1:11:27.

Julie's world became swimming, swimming, and more swimming. It felt so good to be a part of a team and to be recognized for something besides being the "new kid." Her plan was to go to the University of Wisconsin-Madison, where she heard they had an Olympic-sized swimming pool! Fellow teammates Abbey and Suzanne talked of sharing an apartment with Julie during college.

◆

Their season ended mid-November. Thanksgiving and Christmas—except for the previous year—had never been celebrated in the Sandford household without including a recipe for disaster: one part alcohol and three parts anger. *Will it be different this time?* Julie hoped her dad would stay sober until the following spring, when she'd try to talk her mom into letting her join the local YMCA swim program. She needed to maintain her stamina and speed until the team began training again in August.

♦

"Julie, we're moving back to Michigan to be near Grandpa Richard and Grandma Rose. They'll help us out when we need it. At least they'd be good for something, because right now they're good for nothing." Danny finished his speech and grabbed a beer from the fridge, strangling it by the neck as he yanked off the cap. Julie figured she was watching the end of his sobriety. *Time of death: 6:19pm.*

Arlene, strangely mute, listened to her husband mocking her parents. *Does she agree with him? Does she want to be close to her parents? Does she get along with them? Shouldn't we have stayed near them before, instead of moving away? But what about Mr. Koski? Dear God, I hope someone ratted him out by now – or better yet, maybe he got thrown from one of his horses and is paralyzed. How will I keep from running into him again?*

But a new job and another move? That wasn't in Julie's plans. No one told her that her dad's job wasn't working out, and Julie didn't even understand what that meant. *You put your head under water—pull, glide, breathe—and you make it work.* A job was no different, was it? There was *no way* she was going to move; her family could do what they wanted, but she had to stay here. Maybe she could live with Suzanne or Abbey. The team needed her next year, and she definitely needed the team. How could Julie leave the only place that had meant anything to her? *I'll talk to Mom when she's in a good mood, whenever that is.*

♦

Saturdays at the Sandford house were quiet until Danny and Arlene began stumbling into the kitchen late in the after- noon. Hell could stay tightly wound, or break loose, but it was usually in evidence somehow. This particular Saturday

83

afternoon, Julie was in luck. Her dad was nowhere to be seen. Now she could have a reasonable conversation with her mom. Julie crept quietly into the kitchen only to find Arlene slouched in a metal chair, using one long thumbnail to dig dirt out of the grooves in the red Formica table. The other hand cradled a cigarette hanging limply out of her mouth while she squinted her eyes against the smoke curling in front of her.

"Please, Mom." Julie swung for the fences. "Can't I live with Suzanne or Abbey during swim season next year? You wouldn't have to feed me or drive me home from practice or—"

"Absolutely not. What would the neighbors think if I wasn't taking care of my own kid?"

Julie heard footsteps behind her. *Oh no. And here comes Dad. I thought he was still sleeping.*

"Arlene, don't you think it's a good time to tell her the truth, for crap's sake?"

What truth? This is the second time I've heard this. What are they talking about?

"No it's not, and you shut up about it! I'll tell her if and when I'm good and ready!" Arlene's venom spewed into the air, dangling over the three of them.

"Suit yourself. You always do. All I need is some good, mud-black coffee, and I'm gone."

Julie learned an important lesson that day: her welfare wasn't as important as what the neighbors thought. Her mom had to maintain a reputation at all costs. *How can a family that has never been a real family care about staying together?*

♦

The angry blizzard held the town hostage. Swirling, blinding snow, fueled by sixty-mile-an-hour wind gusts, made the snowstorm look like a sandstorm. Barely-identifiable humans, with eyes the only things unbundled against the hostile snow, were in a battle of brute strength with the regal drifts, some already eight-feet high. Snow blowers shot plumes of spray in an arc of white blindness—plumes which formed white flags of surrender. The club of determined conquerors conceded defeat, storing their snow blowers back inside garages. Busses, taxis, tow trucks and snow-plows were pulled off the streets and highways, waiting for this powerful force to have the last word.

◆

"Maybe winters in Michigan will be easier," Julie heard her dad mumble, and then he laughed like he'd told a clever joke. A few weeks after the 'blizzard to end all blizzards,' snowdrifts were still piled high enough to obliterate street signs. Without waiting for spring and dry roads, Danny ordered his family to put everything they wanted into the back of the Ford pick-up. Julie helped her mom stuff clothes into orange crates and heap them into the truck bed, along with their old bikes, a black-and-white TV that only got reception on one channel, an old Hi-Fi that played 78's, a hot pot, and cardboard boxes of unmatched dishes and pans. *The Salvation Army would reject the stuff we're leaving behind.*

Julie wasn't sure how all four of them were supposed to squeeze into the cab ... nor was she sure whether or not the truck would make it as far as Michigan ... but some questions were better left unasked. Besides, what did it matter? She was leaving her friends, the swim team, and the nicest house her family had ever had.

◆

Starting school in the middle of the year was something Julie should have been used to by now, but somehow it never got any easier to be the new kid, even if it *was* in a familiar, one-size-fits-all school with twenty-five kids in each grade. The school didn't have a pool. But since her family moved so often, and this was only February, she was hopeful she'd be starting high school with a swim team somewhere else. She could train extra hard and regain the strength she needed for the backstroke. For now, she'd focus on getting good grades, so a coach would definitely want her on his team.

Every time Julie moved, the kids wanted to know where she'd come from. Her standard response was always, "My parents moved around a lot when I was young, and I always managed to find them!" She dodged the question and let the kids think her dad was in the military. *That's partly true: Our house is definitely in a war zone. And the battles never seem to end.*

♦

Julie's first period class was math with Mr. Carl Eriksson. On her first day, she made sure she was at school early enough to slip into class before anyone else arrived. As Mr. Eriksson marched in and dropped the tools of his trade onto his desk, Julie almost screamed out loud: *My God, he looks like Mr. Thomas! Does that awful man have a twin brother?* She couldn't explain the chilling coincidence.

By the end of the week, Julie's paranoia had morphed into terror, and she started to have serious nosebleeds every day in math class. She was pretty sure that if she told her mom what was happening, she'd be accused of making up stories to gain sympathy, or to hurt her dad's chances of getting a good job. *He seems to have done that just fine on his own.* She didn't know any of the other girls—even her 'old' friends—well enough to unload her secret. The school nurse acted increasingly concerned, and eventually explored all the possibilities of illnesses or allergies to find the source of the nosebleeds. When she finally called Julie's mom, Arlene's response was, "Take care of it and don't bother me again."

When the nosebleeds started, Mr. Eriksson was solicitous toward Julie, giving her opportunity to turn in late work without any penalty. His patience deteriorated into harassments, the harassments became ultimatums, and then came humiliation. As he trolled the room, he'd stop behind Julie, lean over, put a hand on her shoulder and use his best stage-whisper voice. "You want to go to college? You need to get this right." Sometimes it was, "What are you doing in here? The dummy class is down the hall." Other times he'd bring her the wastebasket for her bloodied tissues, and then look in it and announce, "I hope there's no brain matter in there." Julie learned to wear a cocky attitude.

CHAPTER EIGHT

ARLENE'S CAFÉ

Julie put her dream out of its misery by scrunching up her swimsuit and throwing it in the back of her closet. She was starting her freshman year in Pineville.

"Hi, Julie. It's good to have you back," said Jamie Anders.

"I guess."

"Are you in band or choir this year?"

"Nope."

"Would you like to be?"

Julie was momentarily quiet. "What's band like?"

"I love it!"

"What do you play?"

"Flute."

"Didn't you start playing back in sixth grade?"

"Uh-huh. But we're always looking for new people. Why don't you stop in and meet our band teacher? You'll really like him."

"I've always thought it would be cool to play the baritone."

"Perfect! Our bari player is moving to Chicago before Christmas."

"Thanks for telling me, Jamie. I'll see you in band."

"Watch out for Joey Green. You will be sitting in front of him, and he's ... well ... sort of strange and stuck-up."

"Will do."

♦

The town still reminded her of a postcard, but this time some of it looked a bit stained and worn around the edges. One building at the outskirts straddled two worlds, too poor to associate with the houses and too small to be useful to the farms. It had the haphazard, remodeled look of someone who had ignored the original design.

Arlene bought the building and announced to her family that she wanted to own and run a café. *Why is she doing this? Her definition of the four major food groups is frozen, boxed, canned, and instant.* Julie watched in mute amazement as Arlene purchased the most run-down, one-foot-out-of-the-grave building in town and nailed an 'Arlene's Café' sign to the front wall above the porch. Rough-sawn cedar siding clung to the building in waves of nausea. The garish front porch, wrapped around three sides of the café, was stained in faded burnt sienna. Wooden support posts, painted dark brown, were trapped between a sagging roof and porch. The three steps leading up to the porch challenged all customers to a match of wits and agility. A corrugated tin roof afforded diners suffocating heat in summer and finger-numbing cold in winter. Latticework, usually used to enclose porches, was nailed to either side of the first-story windows in a crude attempt at decorative shutters. A faded Pepsi thermometer graced a porch beam; a lighted Grain Belt beer sign hung from a curved pipe attached to the roof. The whole building looked like a little girl playing dress-up, with the colors and styles colliding in the ultimate clothing faux pas.

How can we afford this? My mother dresses up our tacky houses to look like mansions, but she's not fooling anybody.

*Then she dresses her body with flair, while I'm lucky to get
hand-me-downs. What gives?*

The Sandford family lived in a house right behind
Arlene's Café, bordered by a picket fence overgrown with
brambles and chokecherries in the fall. The convenience
of living next to the café was a trade-off for the size of the
house: the bathroom was slightly smaller than an airplane
lavatory and the two bedrooms rivaled walk-in closets. The
house had a yard inside the picket fence where a previous
owner had abandoned a camper, home to field mice, birds,
and squirrels.

♦

Arlene had another friend from childhood—Leon
Bittner—who owned a depression-era housing project in
Pineville. Every morning when he walked into the café in
pursuit of his usual breakfast of fried eggs, toast, bacon,
pancakes and coffee, he told Arlene that he could give her a
great deal on rent for one of his houses. After the umpteenth
time of listening to this annoying conversation, Arlene
decided to go home that night and tell her family they were
moving. It was either that, or she'd have to dump Leon's
breakfast in his lap and close the café for good.

The Jacob Bittner homes, named after Leon's deceased
brother, were plain, boxy, two-story structures spread over a
five-block area. After they had weathered decades of paint,
Leon had attempted to protect his investment with the addi-
tion of low-grade aluminum siding. Some houses were
completely sided; others were only half finished before he
had run out of money and interest. Arlene rented one of
the incompletely-sided houses that a previous tenant had
tried to jazz up by painting the top half in equal sections of
green, pink and brown. Julie thought it looked like a box of
Neapolitan ice cream.

Inside Julie's 'new' house were a kitchen, pantry, living room and bathroom downstairs, and two bedrooms with a small bathroom, converted from a shared closet, upstairs. Every wall and ceiling was painted the same battleship gray.

The night the Sandford family moved in, Mr. Bittner stopped by to check on them. When Arlene introduced Julie to him, she had to bite down to keep from laughing. *He looks camouflaged. His skin is almost the color of the walls! Good thing he's bald, or his hair might look like them, too.*

♦

It was the end of October, and the rent was due.

"Julie, take this envelope over to Leon's house, three blocks down, number 205. And make sure you're nice to him! He's letting us live here for cheap."

"I got homework. Can't I go later?" Julie didn't really have any homework; she simply didn't want to go to Mr. Bittner's house. She didn't like the way he looked at her when he saw her in the café, like a fish in a tank that swims up to the side and bugs out its eyes at everybody.

"Don't sass me." Arlene was hanging curtains on the kitchen window with her back to Julie, who stuck out her tongue, picked up the envelope from the table, said, "Yes, Ma'am," and headed out the door.

Bittnerville: that's what Julie had decided to name the neighborhood after her favorite movie, "It's a Wonderful Life." She didn't think Mr. Bittner was mean like the old guy in the movie, but he owned all the houses, and for all she knew, maybe even half the town. She liked their house okay. *At least it's bigger than our last one, it's not a trailer, and it doesn't smell too bad.*

Julie knocked on the front door. *Why doesn't Mr. Bittner live in a mansion somewhere? He must be really rich, since he owns all of these houses. If it were me, I would!*

Leon Bittner answered the door wearing tan trousers, a V-neck, white t-shirt, and slippers. "Hi, Julie-girl. Welcome." As he stepped aside to let her pass, Julie felt butterflies in her stomach. *The* last *time this happened, I was in Mr. Thomas' trailer.* She walked in, took a deep breath, and turned around.

"Mr. Bittner where's your wife?"

"She had to go grocery shopping, but she'll be back in a little while. I'm sure she'd like to meet you. You want a snack? We got cookies."

"What kind?"

"Oatmeal raisin or chocolate chip."

"Both. Please."

"Done." Leon walked to the kitchen, took cookies out of a canister, stuck them on a napkin, and put them on the table. "Come and get 'em!" Julie walked in, dug the envelope out of her pocket, handed it to Leon, and sat down.

"So. What are you doing at school?"

"Well, Mr. Bittner—"

"Hey, I'm almost like an uncle to you. Call me 'Leon,' or 'Uncle Lee.'"

For the next fifteen minutes, Julie told Leon about her teachers, her classes, and even some of the places her family used to live. As she talked, Leon got up to get her a glass of milk, listened intently, chuckled lightly, and paid more attention to her than her dad did. He seemed interested in everything she said, and even expressed pride in her for getting good grades.

"Leon—Uncle Lee—I'd better get home. My mom might wonder where I've been." Julie got up and took her glass to the sink, and then Leon was standing behind her. *Phew! His breath smells like garlic!* Suddenly she felt his arms reach around her, unzip her jeans and work his cold hands down inside her underwear, then back up underneath her shirt, rubbing his palms over her bare breasts.

"Don't worry, I'm tickling you," he whispered. "I do this to all the girls I like."

Julie tingled and burned in fear. *Oh, God, please help me! I'm trapped!*

A big, white car pulled into the driveway right outside the kitchen window. "That's enough fun for today." Leon removed his hands, turned and walked to the door.

Julie zipped her pants and ran out the front door before Mrs. Bittner could see her.

♦

Another month passed. "You must have made a big impression on Leon, because every time he comes in to the café, he talks about how much he liked being with you last month." Arlene was holding out an envelope for Julie to take.

"Mom, please, can't you go this time?" Julie was almost in tears.

"Don't be an idiot! If that jerk Leon likes you, maybe our rent will stay down. Besides, what're you crying about?"

Julie wiped her sleeve across her face, and said, "Would you go with me?"

"Heck no! I'll never get away from him and that sappy wife of his."

"But, mom—"

"Forget it. Go." Arlene dropped the envelope on the sofa and returned to the kitchen.

Mom will never believe me if I tell her what her old friend did to me. But I can't go over there again! What am I going to do? Julie ran up to her room, tucked her blouse into her jeans, put on an old sweatshirt and zipped it up. She went back down, put on her winter jacket and walked out the door headed for the Bittner's. *Please, God, let Mrs. Bittner be home.* At their house, Julie waited on the porch, afraid to knock.

The door opened; Julie was shocked to see Leon wearing a black suit and bright, red tie. "I clean up good, don't I? I just got back from a meeting with a bunch of bigwigs, and I seen you standing outside our house. Come in and relax while we wait for Mrs. Bittner to get back from shopping."

Doesn't she ever stay home? Julie walked in and stood in the narrow, dark hallway.

"You need to come with me to the living room. Mrs. Bittner and I went on a vacation out west, and I want to show you some of our pictures." Leon loosened his tie, took off his coat, hung it on a hanger in the closet, and draped his arm around Julie. Julie's feet were frozen to the floor. "Let me take your jacket."

"That's okay."

"No it's not! My wife keeps it way too hot in here!" Leon unzipped Julie's jacket, eased it off of her and hung it carefully in the hall closet.

There weren't enough layers to shield Julie from this repulsive man, who smiled almost politely as he unzipped her sweatshirt, pushed her gently against the wall, slowly unzipped her pants and pulled them down, ran his hands around the inside of her underwear, and then up her shirt. Julie couldn't even scream. This time no car pulled into the driveway, and there was nothing to interrupt Leon's 'tickling.'

When Leon removed one of his hands, Julie thought he was done, until he clumsily unzipped his pants and started panting. *I don't know what's happening, but I want this to be over! I think I'm going to throw up!* Leon sighed, muttered a "thank you," zipped his pants and said, "We're all done tickling for today. Where's the envelope?" Julie pulled her pants up, zipped them, dug the envelope out of her pocket, threw it on the floor, picked up her sweatshirt, and flew out the door. *What if Mom asks me what happened to my winter jacket?*

By the end of December, Julie knew there was *no way* she would ever walk into Leon's house again. *Somehow I have to tell Mom what happened to me. Dear God, I hope something will change. Mrs. R used to talk about how You are our protector. Can You do anything for me now?* When Julie finally opened the can, worms spilled out everywhere. Arlene accused her of telling lies to get out of doing "the only stinking job I ask of you around here, to pay our stinking rent." Julie's mom left her no choice.

♦

It was the end of January, and Arlene was sitting at the table with her checkbook. Julie wandered into the kitchen for something to eat. "Get my purse, look in my wallet for a stamp, and bring it here." Arlene kept her eyes on the phone bill.

That's it! When Julie's mom handed her the rent check the next day, Julie snuck into her mom's purse, got a stamp out of her wallet, found an envelope in her desk drawer, wrote out the Bittner's address, slid the check inside, sealed the envelope, licked the stamp, smacked it on the corner, and walked to the closest mailbox. *I hope she doesn't keep a stamp inventory.* She stayed out long enough to make her mom think she had actually gone to Leon's house. *I don't care if mom finds out about what I did and we have to leave. I'm never, ever going over there again!*

A week later Leon walked into the café for breakfast and caught Arlene's elbow. "Hey, I never see my Julie anymore." Arlene noticed Leon's eyes were bugged out even more than usual.

"Whatever." Arlene smiled. Back in the kitchen later that morning flipping pancakes over a hot griddle, she muttered, "That man's cake is only half-baked."

♦

Along with owning and managing the café, Arlene took another job as a school bus driver. It was the one-year anniversary of the move to Michigan, and Julie had watched one swim season pass without her. Unbelievably, it looked like they would be living in Pineville longer than she had ever thought possible. Her nosebleeds had finally stopped when school was done the previous June and she no longer had to see Mr. Eriksson every day. She had grown so hardened by constant teasing that, along with her blood, her emotions had also clotted.

This particular day in February was not one of those glorious winter days that made Julie dream of skiing, making snowmen, and burying her low self-worth in the nearest snow bank. The day was cloudy; the unforgiving winter wind was powerful enough to blow the snow sideways across the road in front of the school. The window screens were covered with blotches of heavy snow that looked like they had been attacked by an angry snow cone machine. The plows fought and conceded the battle, while Julie's thoughts were piling into their own drifts. *The maintenance crew must feel like they're trying to bail the Titanic with a teaspoon. I hope we get out of school early; otherwise we might get stuck here overnight. Where would I want to be stranded? Washington? Illinois? Wisconsin? Michigan?* A crackly voice came over the intercom, paging Julie to the office. Did her mom want to drive her home before the start of an early dismissal? Was she in some kind of trouble? She trudged down to the school office, wearing defiance like a shield.

Mrs. Evelyn Johnson, the school secretary, was accustomed to students like Julie, the ones who used prickly attitudes to protect empty hearts. "Julie, your mom was taken by ambulance to the ER at St. Michael's a little while ago."

Evelyn paused, waiting for Julie to put on her best 'I don't care' look.

"Your mom couldn't back the bus out of the garage until she hoisted up the door herself. It seems that the automatic door opener was broken. Anyways, dear, she slipped on a patch of ice; as she was going down, she let go of the garage door, which came crashing down on her."

The facemask cracked and Julie knew instantly that she needed help. Mrs. Johnson came around the counter, opened her arms, and stood quietly. Julie momentarily hesitated, then walked into those arms and realized how much she needed someone to sustain her fragile reality. After a long hug, Mrs. Johnson made a phone call to a neighborhood school volunteer who showed up with a four-wheel drive truck to drive Julie to the hospital.

Arlene had broken her back, which was gradually followed by a break in the wall of resentment and hostility that had been building in Julie ever since she'd had to give up being on the swim team. While Arlene was in the hospital, Julie was surprised to discover love for her mom growing in her heart. She waited anxiously for her mom to become less groggy, so that Julie could show her sympathy.

"Mom! You're awake! What can I do for you?" Julie was standing near the bed.

"You can get out of here and go back to the café. It isn't going to run itself. And you can forget about being in volleyball anymore. Your dad isn't going to pick you up after school every day at five. You kids don't know how much I do for you."

I don't care about the stupid café. I want to hear you say you love me and you're glad I'm here. "Yeah, whatever." Julie picked the chip back up and set it securely on her shoulder.

◆

It was Friday night and Julie was on an adrenalin rush after spiking the ball for the winning point on her volleyball team. Her dad had stunned her—after she had returned home from her disappointing visit with her mom—with the announcement that he'd be glad to pick her up after volleyball practice during the week in exchange for her working more hours at the café on the weekends.

Julie opened the door to Arlene's at nine-thirty to help the last of the customers and then do her closing jobs. Since no one looked like they were waiting for anything, she busied her hands wiping down counters and refilling salt- and pepper shakers, ketchup and mustard bottles, napkin dispensers, and the all-important toothpick holders. She could hear her dad humming behind the swinging kitchen door and assumed he was cleaning the griddle. *He's been in a good mood lately, and I hope it stays that way. But hey! If that changes, he can take out his anger on something greasy back there.*

At ten-thirty, Julie closed and locked the door as Danny sauntered into the room wearing a food-stained apron tied loosely around his waist, and with his hands hidden behind his back. "Ta-da!" He proudly produced a bottle of Bali Hi and shouted, "Julie-girl, let's you and me go to the back room and play a game of pool. A dollar a game sound good?"

When was the last time he asked me to do something fun? Julie raced ahead of her dad to the poolroom, flicked on the fluorescent light hanging precariously over the old table, grabbed the triangle off the nail on the wall, and readied the pool balls—all in one unbroken motion. She was ready to beat her dad at something! By the fourth game, Danny was joking, laughing, and enjoying his daughter without the jokes being at her expense. *I don't know what's happened to him, but I like this new and improved version.*

After three games, Danny's hand-eye coordination had gone AWOL, closely followed by his reasoning skills. "How about Pinball?"

Julie laughed at her dad's inability to keep his hands from slipping off the wooden handles. "Say 'Uncle!'" she laughed as she pushed him aside and positioned herself to take over.

"C'mon, it's no fun drinkin' alone." Danny bumped Julie's elbow with his and some of the wine sloshed onto the Plexiglas, slanted top of the machine.

"Oh, ick!" Julie used her sleeve to wipe up the liquid. *I can't stand the smell of that stuff, and now it's on my clothes.* "All right, I'll try it." She kept playing as Danny disappeared into the kitchen, returned with a small juice glass and poured as much wine on his arm as what he managed to get into the glass.

"Here—bottom's up!"

I guess I should be happy he's treating me like an adult. Julie turned away from the lights and bells, tipped the glass and drank the contents all at once. Her dad laughed as she gagged and barely kept from coughing it back up.

"Thatta girl! Try another glass. It'll help keep the first one down." Before Julie could object, Danny had refilled her glass and brought it up to her mouth. This time she drank it a little more slowly, and noticed after the last swallow that she started feeling warm and tingly. *When did he start sounding so funny?*

Suddenly Danny left the room, Julie heard a bell ring, and then her dad walked back in with his arm sticking straight out and his hand clenched in a fist. "Lookee what the reg'ster drunk and coughed up." Danny opened his hand and a shower of quarters fell to the floor, with some landing on their edges and rolling in all directions. Julie giggled, crouched down to pick one up and fell over. Danny pulled her up and walked her over to the jukebox, where she aimed and dropped her quarter into the slot. The song titles and numbers were spinning, but she leaned her elbows on the glass, concentrated and pushed the buttons under E, 3 and 2.

"Ray's the man!" Julie turned, threw her arms around her dad's neck and started to sing. "I can't stop loving you, I've made up my mind ..." They danced their way to the pool table, where Danny grabbed the bottle of wine sitting precariously on the edge and took a big gulp. Julie grabbed it out of his hands and finished the rest, and then both of them dropped to the floor. "So I'll just live my life in dreams of yesterday."

◆

When Julie awoke in a pitch-black room, she was lying on the floor with an excruciating pain in her back. Her mouth felt like it was stuffed with cotton while a crushing weight was pressing down on her, and someone was pinning her arms back at a crooked angle as pain shot through her shoulders. *What're you doing on top of me? Why're you tearing my clothes?* Words fought their way through Julie's pasty lips. "Don't do this! Don't!" Danny continued to maul his daughter until she blacked out.

◆

The next time she awoke, Julie was completely naked, covered only in vomit and shame. She tried to focus her eyes on a Schlitz wall clock. *Five thirty? Is it day or night?* She gingerly sat up, checking all of her arms and legs for movement. Although she had never had a hangover before, she knew this was it. Someone must have removed her head, beaten it to within an inch of its life, and then cruelly set it back on her neck. Her back was still screaming in pain, and her shoulders felt like they had been ripped out of their sockets.

Julie found a dirty, white apron on the floor and cleaned some of the mess off of her with it. *I wonder who was wearing this?* Then she collected her twisted clothes and tried to put herself back together, although it was easier to slip her blouse on backwards. Crawling over to the pay phone, she used the hanging metal cord to pull herself up while waves of dizziness rolled over her. As she focused on a quarter sitting on the ledge next to the phone, she had a fuzzy memory of having used one for something last night. With one arm wrapped around the cord for support, she reached out with the other, picked up the coin between shaky fingers, carefully aimed it at the slot, and dropped it in. She picked up the receiver, brought it slowly to her ear and almost collapsed at the deafening sound of the dial tone. Uncoiling her arm from the cord and using her elbow for balance, she set the receiver on the ledge and threw all of her focus into pushing each button of her grandma Rosie's number. She picked the receiver back up again and prayed for someone to answer the phone.

She hardly ever hears from me; and when she does, I'm usually mad about something. I wonder if she'll even want to talk to me.

"Grandma? It's Julie. Please come … and get me … here." As Julie dropped the receiver, she heard "Has your father done something to you? Why did Arlene marry that no-account drunk? I'd love to get my hands on him for sure and for good." She sank to the floor. *I forgot to tell her where I am! And I can't get up again!*

Julie never figured out how her grandma knew where to go, but by the time she had crawled to the front door, both she and Grandpa had used their key to unlock it. Once inside, Grandma flipped around the 'Open' sign. *Oh yeah, I guess I forgot to do that last night.*

Richard Cerbé picked Julie up while Rosalynn found her jacket and wrapped it around her. As the three walked outside, Rose sputtered and fumed like the getaway car Arlene had driven when she and her kids had escaped to Michigan. Back at their house, she helped her granddaughter get undressed and into the shower, adjusting the water for her before she left her alone. Julie could never have imagined her grandma seeing her like this ... but then, embarrassment could only come with dignity, and Julie's had been robbed. When her grandma closed the shower door, she sat down on the tiled floor, tipped her face back into the steamy spray, and wondered if there was enough water in the world to wash away the dirt from her soul. *Was he protecting me from Mr. Thomas so that he could save the merchandise for himself? What kind of father does that to his daughter? He was so drunk ... does he even know what he did? Am I even sure I know what he did?* When the water started to get cold, she stood up carefully, turned off both faucets, opened the door and wrapped herself in a terrycloth robe hanging on a wall hook. Julie walked in to her mom's old room, sank into the four-poster bed and cried salty tears that stung her cheeks. After a fitful sleep, she awoke to shadows falling across the room. *The darkness is a one-size-fits-all for my life ... a life where everyone's dreams become my nightmares.*

♦

Rosalynn never asked Julie what had happened to her that night, and Julie certainly never told anyone, especially not her mom. *If Grandma or Mom found out, would they do anything about it? In case they* wouldn't *or* couldn't, *I'd better keep it to myself.*

CHAPTER NINE

SPAM-EATIN', WHITE-DOG TRAILER TRASH

When Arlene was released from the hospital after a month, she returned to bus driving part time. She also spent a few hours each day at the café, but still demanded that Danny and the kids cover all the shifts. Julie avoided her dad when she could; when she had to be in the same room with him, she made sure customers were always nearby. She refused to help her dad clean up and close the café at night, and it seemed that her mom was blind to her morosely defiant attitude that dared her dad to push the issue. *Maybe he feels sorry for what he did. If so, why doesn't he say something to me? If not, why is he backing down?*

Julie had never wanted the café from the beginning, even when she was sure the money was needed for their basic needs. Now she realized that they were never going to see more food in their cupboards or refrigerator, only more clothes and shoes and jewelry adorning Arlene. If the restaurant was some kind of dream recycler, then Julie desperately wanted the building to be dynamited. *And then we could toast marshmallows over the ashes.*

♦

It was April Fool's Day; Julie walked into the house after school expecting to hear the radio in the kitchen and TV in the living room, both of which were usually left on all day since Arlene claimed the noise would "scare off the idiots." *It's way too quiet and spooky ... I wonder what's going on.* "Oh, well." She talked to the dark TV screen. "I think I'll raid the fridge for that Mounds bar I hid in the veggie drawer last night." Plopping her books on the horsehair sofa, she went into the kitchen and yanked on the handle of the old GE refrigerator painted gray to match the walls. Julie couldn't comprehend the fact that *anyone* could assault an appliance with such a hideous color. "They used ugly wall paint *and* left thick globs hanging on the sides for dear life! Sheesh!" Jerking open the door, she didn't realize at first what was wrong. *Okay, there's no light in here, which probably means no electricity anywhere in the house, and that explains why everything is so quiet.*

Lounging in the living room with her lanky legs hanging over the arm of the unreclinable recliner, Julie was reading a book and enjoying 'quiet hours' in the house when Arlene noisily entered and slammed the kitchen door behind her, rattling the pots on the wall hooks.

"So what, you couldn't start dinner?" shouted Arlene from the kitchen. Peering around the corner into the living room, she modulated her voice a bit. "What are you doing reading without a lamp on?" Julie twisted her body, swung her legs to the floor, closed her book, got up and headed towards her room, hoping to send a signal to her mom that she was weary of the constant arguments. "Did those idiots at the electric company turn off our power again?"

Julie turned towards her mom's voice. *How about paying the bill?* "I don't know, Mom. Why would they have done that?"

Arlene threw her purse on the table as the contents spilled out like they were running for cover. She grabbed her checkbook and four pens, trying each of them and tossing all but one into the garbage. After hastily writing a check, she tore it out of the book and held it up. "Here, take this down to the power company." Julie stared at her mom without moving. "Those good-for-nothings can wait for the rest of their money until we get more." Julie knew that her dad worked construction jobs at least six months at a stretch, and thought he made more than enough to support them year-round if they saved during the 'down' times.

"So what does that make me? The elected officer-of-deceit?" The darkness emboldened Julie in a way she would never have considered otherwise.

"Watch your mouth!"

"Okay. I'm sorry." *Why do we have to spend half the year living on food stamps and Spam?* Julie took the check from her mom and headed out the door, convinced that her life was an in-house arrest—and when she finally escaped, it would be into a state of humiliation.

♦

The long line at the power company was filled with people who had dim pilot lights, shuffled forward like they had pebbles in their shoes, and avoided any eye contact. Julie felt out of place, but knew she wasn't leaving anytime soon.

It took thirty minutes to reach the Delinquent Accounts counter where Julie overheard a clerk say 'Spam-eatin,' white-dog, trailer-trash.' *We don't live in a trailer anymore; is she talking about me?* Julie felt as naked as the night she was in the café with her dad, only *this* disgrace came from someone who was *sober.* She threw the check across the counter, turned and ran through the line of semi-comatose people and out the door.

♦

It was one-thirty in the morning when Julie awoke to arguing, cussing, and the sound of the phone being ripped out of its wall socket. She ran downstairs, peeked into the living room, and wondered if there would be a stay-of-execution for the furniture. "Julie!" Arlene screamed. "Go to the neighbor's and call the cops!" *Which neighbors? They're all going to play by the rules of non-engagement. We've lived here for over a year and no one's done anything about the screaming they've heard. Where am I supposed to go?* Julie threw a sweatshirt over her pajamas and ran out the back door.

The house on the corner, four doors down from the Sandfords, still had a front porch light on. *If the cops come after me, at least I can take them to my house.* Julie lifted her fist to knock when the door suddenly opened to a woman about her mom's age, wearing a terrycloth robe loosely tied around her trim waist and short hair mashed on one side of her head. The lingering aroma of gingerbread made Julie's stomach growl.

"Come in, dear." The woman smiled. "There's hot chocolate on the stove, and you can sleep on our couch if you want."

Julie was shivering from cold and fear, too tired to be suspicious. Everything she wanted was here: hot chocolate, a couch, and a warm blanket, all offered by a woman who obviously had an abundance of sympathy. "Thank you, Ma'am," Julie whispered as she sailed through the door, collapsed on the couch and cried silent tears. The woman disappeared into the kitchen and reappeared almost immediately with a steaming mug. Julie sat up and reluctantly drank as quickly as she could, knowing that she was expected to dial 911 and get back home.

◆

Officer Seaver banged on the front door. "Come on out, Mr. Sandford." Julie had made her third emergency run that week and was dealing with guilt over how good it felt to leave the arguing of her house and find shelter with the kind Mrs. Moore. *I wish I could stay there all night.*

"Danny, open the door."

No response.

A little louder, "What's the problem this time? Go back to bed and sleep this off. We got more important things to worry about—bigger fish to fry." The monologue was always delivered to a closed door. Since there was a momentary lull in the hurling of words and objects, Officer Seaver and his partner had no choice but to turn around and walk back to their cruiser, hoping this song-and-dance would end someday. Officer Seaver always mumbled, "God helps those who help themselves," and then his partner would say, "That's unbiblical hogwash. Danny has to admit that he's powerless to help himself and turn his heart to the One whose help will change his life." The men would open their doors in tandem to the radio squawking a report of a crime, usually a home burglary somewhere nearby. The robbing of material objects was definitely not more important than the robbing of souls; the officers at least agreed on that. It was simply easier to prosecute.

◆

A few hours of respite were sandwiched between the police calls and the arrival of dawn, when Danny would pass out on the couch, lying on top of a bent table lamp or torn cushion. Arlene and her children would collapse into troubled sleep, a kind of rough idling until the sunlight overpowered the darkness and shifted the parents into overdrive again. The trophy for midnight fighting always went to Danny, while the morning one went to Arlene, whose job was to harass and manipulate her husband into another day of work—the only way she knew to avoid the stigma of poverty.

CHAPTER TEN

MAMA "T" AND TEDDY-BOY

It was the beginning of May, and Norwegians spilled out of their homes looking like they had spent the winter swimming in Elmer's glue. Julie came home from school, dropped her books on the kitchen table, and headed back outside. Roller-skating would have been fun, but most of the neighborhood sidewalks were a maze of broken chunks of concrete. She decided to walk in the opposite direction from her usual route, and certainly not anywhere near the Bittner house. The red, yellow and purple tulips and bright daffodils bloomed in miniature gardens in almost every yard Julie passed. *Mrs. Ryczek always had a vase of fresh flowers on her desk in the spring. Maybe if I walk backwards I can find her again ... or Mrs. Anderson, or Mary.* Julie's black and white world wasn't enough for her Technicolor dreams; she hadn't realized until now how lonely she was for a grandma-kind of friend.

Step on a crack, break—no wait, that already happened! I wish Mom and I were close ... but there will never be enough evidence to convict her of 'intent to do good' to her daughter.

Several blocks from home Julie saw a little, brown gingerbread house, with gabled windows and blue trim. A

111

sixtyish-looking woman was sitting on the front porch in an enormous wicker rocker, knitting and singing. She wore a red-checked dress with a matching scarf tied around her head. When she looked up and smiled at Julie, her bright lipstick and arched eyebrows complimented a full, perfectly symmetrical face. *If she had dark skin, she would be a dead ringer for Aunt Jemima!* The woman put down her knitting needles, waved, and said, "Come up here und talk to me" as she motioned for Julie to sit in the other rocker. Julie slowly walked up the front steps.

"I'm Mrs. Tannenbaum, but everyone calls me 'Mama T.' Und who bist you?"

◆

Julie felt like the only guest on Mama T's daytime talk show. For the next hour she shared every big and little thing in her life. She wondered why she hadn't done this with Mrs. Moore, but then realized that the Moore house was only for physical safety. Julie had never volunteered any personal stuff, nor had Mrs. Moore ever asked for any. That seemed a good way to protect everyone.

But with Mama T it was already so different. She listened and listened to Julie, and her attention fed Julie's starved heart. When Julie reluctantly got up to leave, Mama T exclaimed, "I vill pray for you! I haf calluses on my knees from praying for so many years, but I down can't get no more, so now I pray sitting on my backside. Der Lord Gott hears from me every day!"

◆

Summer vacation was starting, and Julie headed over to Mama T's as often as she could. The hot weather chased Mama T inside, so Julie quickly learned to ignore the formality of knocking on the door. She'd burst into the house and find Mama, who had a no-big-deal way of turning everything into a party for two.

"Come, my liebchen, is time to haf a cuppa." The coffee pot was always on, and Julie figured it was time for her to learn to like the nasty stuff. "Ven you come tomorrow, ve make dark rye brodt." Mama T turned on the window fan in the kitchen, poured mugs of coffee, and motioned for Julie to sit down across from her.

"So. I hear you go to school vit my boy."

Julie almost choked on her first sip of the bitter liquid. "Ted? Teddy Tannenbaum? I thought he was your *grandson!*"

Mama laughed, and Julie noticed that her smile lines connected with other lines crossing her face.

"Ach, an easy mistake! I vas forty-two ven I Teddy had."

"Wow!"

"Ja, he vas big surprise to his fater and me. I alvays say I had da caboose to give birt to da caboose der Gott gave me!"

Julie was shocked, and then burst out laughing. "Mama T!"

"Ah, Gott has humor. He gifs us all tings to enjoy!"

Julie didn't know what to say to that. She had never thought of anyone being close enough to God to share a joke with Him. Mama got up and brought an apple pie back to the table. "Next you vill learn to make fruit pies. Ve haf lots to do!"

While other teenagers headed to beaches, pools, and movie theaters that summer, Julie found a different kind of refreshment with Mama T. When it got too hot to bake in the kitchen, the women went out shopping. Mama showed Julie how to find nice clothes at second-hand stores, and alter them or freshen them up with different buttons or rickrack so that they ended up looking new. Mama would say, "Oh, ja, ve can take da collar off here und move in da side seam dere." Julie's mending eventually became sewing clothes from scratch. *I hope Mom doesn't care that I'm wearing clothes someone else helped me sew.*

◆

Julie was surprised that she never saw Teddy during all of her visits at Mama T's. She figured he had a job bagging groceries at the IGA or pumping gas at Bob's Standard, but he never came home for supper the nights she was there. Mama T's husband had apparently died not long after Teddy was born, and Julie didn't know where the rest of the kids were. They were probably married and living far away, but Julie couldn't imagine *anyone* staying away from a wonderful mom like this unless they didn't have a choice.

The dog days of August were barking at the door, and Julie and Mama T were sitting in the living room in front of a window fan, alternating between drinking iced tea and holding the cold glasses up to their hot foreheads.

"Mama, you once called Teddy your 'caboose,' so you must have other children."

Mama set down her glass of tea and picked up her knitting needles and a ball of soft blue yarn. Julie knew she was making a baby blanket for a neighbor's new grandson, and marveled that anyone's heart could be as big as hers.

"Ja, I haf Barb, who ist probably about twenty years older dan you. She's married to Bob Fechner, und dey live in Omaha."

"That's funny—my mom has a cousin named Bob Fechner, and I'm pretty sure he lives in Omaha." Julie and Mama T looked at each other and burst out laughing. "So I'm kind of a part of your family after all! Wait until I tell my mom! She always says it's a small world, and when things get strange, it gets even smaller." *I don't know about the size of the world, but I feel like I'm the only moon in Mama T's orbit.*

◆

Pineville was a small school, and Julie ran into Teddy Tannenbaum at the beginning of their sophomore year. *I was wrong about his summer job: He must have been doing heavy work outside!* Teddy was lean, muscular, and deeply tanned, and his long, blonde hair was bleached almost white. For the rest of the day Julie was barely able to concentrate on the meet-the-new-teachers-while-they're-still-nice orientation. She did have Teddy in one of her electives—fifth period art class, where some of the most talented students had work from previous years displayed around the room. Teddy had an acrylic of a fire-eating dragon coming out of the top of a Cyclops' head; a charcoal of a robot tying a noose around its neck; and a colored-pencil drawing of an eagle in flight carrying a snake in its talons. The only thing Julie knew about art was still life. There was definitely nothing tranquil about those drawings.

◆

"Hey Sandford! I hear you've been hanging around my ma." Julie was carrying her hot lunch tray, turned around and almost dropped it as she looked up at this guy who obviously wasn't in the dark about how cute he was.

"I have been. She's been really good to me." *Okay, that sounds dumb.*

"Yeah," a girl standing next to Teddy put her oar in the water. "He does anything he wants, and his mom thinks he's got it all together. He parties and does drugs and tells her whatever she wants to hear." The girl reached for Teddy's hand.

A guy smacked Teddy's shoulder. "Parents can be so stupid!"

Julie was suddenly uncomfortable. *Maybe I'm more of an artist than I realize. I'm already painting a picture of Teddy-boy. I need to stay away from this guy.* Julie took her tray to an empty table and ate her fish sticks. She was so lost in thought that she even ate her dull-yellow wax beans.

◆

Teddy was an edgy guy in a charming package. A couple of weeks and several stolen glances after that first encounter, Julie was hoping for the chance to hitch a ride on his star. She didn't have to wait long.

Julie was walking down the middle of the hallway at the end of school one Monday in early October, when suddenly Teddy was standing in front of her. "Hey Jules, you're looking mighty hot today." Teddy flashed his butter-melting smile, and she blushed as much from the other kids forming a circle around them as from Teddy's comment. "So, you got a date for Homecoming?"

Julie looked down. *If he's going to humiliate me, he's got the perfect audience.* "No, not yet." *Not ever.*

"How would you like to go with me?" Loud applause echoed off the walls, which saved Julie from finding her fickle voice.

Mama T was easily persuaded into sewing Julie a new, ankle-length blue dress with long, sheer sleeves. She wasn't told that the dress was for a date with her son, and she couldn't have explained why it was important to her to keep this part of her life separate from Mama. Maybe she had seen enough of the underbelly of life to know what people might do if they had leverage against her. She loved everything about Mama and had opened up some deep places in her heart, yet still held back a portion of trust.

Teddy had officially become Julie's first boyfriend; she wore his I.D. bracelet, and they became a recognized 'couple' at school. Julie went from having a few friends to suddenly being in the popular crowd, one of the many perks of being with a guy who both chose the play *and* starred in the leading role.

Most of the high schoolers waited for a chance to go out with Teddy and Julie. Teddy's black Firebird convertible led the pack to Friday-night movies, or to McDonald's, or just to drag race down the main street in town. Everyone assumed Teddy would pick the time and place for the hang-outs, and that made Julie feel special. *Her* boyfriend was good-looking, strong and decisive.

◆

The tide of Danny's drinking was in the ebb stage, which meant less frequent 911 calls at the Moore house. Julie was glad her dad drank less, but found him almost scarier when he was menacingly sober and tried to control even the obvious and inevitable parts of his family's lives. *Okay, so what's the diff between him and Teddy? Teddy's strength is starting to look more like stubbornness, and his decisiveness is very controlling. Maybe he's a younger version of my father.*

But Teddy is so cute and fun! And since I've learned to put up with Dad's drinking, this really isn't a big deal. Besides, I know Teddy really loves me, and he would never hurt me.

◆

"I'll come by after I get off work and take you for a spin on the Honda. We have to get in a few more rides before it

117

gets too cold. Wear the leather jacket I got you, and your red bandanna. I'll wear mine too. Okay, babe?"

"I can't wait!" Julie hung up the phone and sighed deeply. No guy had ever treated her like this before, and it put a knot in her stomach—*for the* right *reason this time.*

When the Honda wailed into the McDonald's parking lot, Julie and Teddy saw some guys from their class throwing punches in front of a Mustang with a dented back fender. One of the guys was Teddy's best friend. A crowd of guys and girls was standing around cheering. Teddy stopped the bike and barely waited for Julie to swing her leg over the seat and jump off before he pushed down the kickstand and sailed into the middle of the fight. *I've seen him do this before; most of the guys will probably cut a wide path around his temper.* Julie ran inside the restaurant without waiting to see the outcome. *Who am I kidding? I can't do this anymore. Teddy has so many girls lined up to date him, that I'm sure it won't bother him to lose me, especially if I make it seem like* he's *dumping* me.

By the time Julie walked back outside, there was no longer any evidence of a fight. Teddy was alone in the parking lot, leaning up against his bike and smoking a cigarette. "What do you say we get out and do something fun, babe?" Teddy flicked the cigarette into the weeds and motioned for Julie to climb on the bike.

"Great! Yeah!" Julie secured her feet on the pedals and waited for Teddy to climb on, then wrapped her arms tightly around his waist. *I should probably do this now before I chicken out.*

Within five minutes the Honda was cruising down interstate thirty-five going seventy. "Teddy!" Julie shouted into the wind. "Let's turn off at that exit!" Teddy gave the thumbs-up and flipped his right turn signal. Julie was hoping for a slower, quieter ride, but as soon as he could, Teddy found a dirt road and pushed the speedometer back up to sixty.

Julie loosened her arms. "Teddy, I don't think we should go out anymore," she yelled. After several seconds Julie was ready to repeat herself, until Teddy suddenly spun the bike in a three-sixty. Rocks flew out from under the tires, and Julie never knew what kept them from laying the bike down.

"Stop!" Julie screamed. "Let me off and I'll walk home!"

Julie quickly climbed off and caught the bottom of her jeans on the tailpipe, yelping as a small hole burned through the jeans to her ankle.

"Maybe you should go back to my mommy and see if she can fix your leg." Teddy sounded frighteningly sarcastic.

"That's okay," gasped Julie, who was sitting in the middle of the road holding her ankle. *I won't let him see me cry ... that'll make him angrier.* "Take me home and I'll be fine. And I'm sorry I said anything ... of course you're the guy for me." Julie had learned how to survive.

Back at school the next day, Teddy acted like nothing had happened between him and Julie. He sat next to her at lunch and told everyone that they were going to a movie that night, and that this date was "for the two of us. The rest of you losers can make your own entertainment."

"Oooooh! Aaaaaaah!" Everyone laughed and pointed at Julie, who blushed without really knowing why.

♦

The cramped back seat of a Firebird was not where Julie had ever thought about losing her virginity. She had the image of strolling across a bridge spanning a clear, peaceful river ... until the wind picked up and the water began churning angry images of Mr. Thomas, Mr. Koski and Mr. Bittner. By the time the roaring water had swallowed the bridge, Julie knew that there would never be any return to innocence. *And besides, 'losing my virginity' is a silly and wrong phrase. It can be stolen or given, but never lost.* Hers had been partially stolen by evil men, and now she had given the remainder away freely. The only way she could live with that was to find something in it for her: She was now assured of holding on to Teddy, as well as the far greater privilege of staying in Mama T's life. *Everyone needs a safety net. Maybe I've found mine.*

♦

It didn't take long for the net to tear and Julie didn't feel especially safe anymore. Her dates with Teddy usually ended in verbal attacks, the result of too much drinking and too little care. The gap between life with her Dad and life with Teddy was narrowing, and Julie desperately needed some control over at least a small part of her world. *It's time to get out of this. Teddy is great looking and talented, and he can have any girl he wants, especially the unsuspecting ones.* Teddy was coming to pick her up for a date at the movies; tonight was the night.

"Teddy," began Julie on the way to the theater.

"Yeah?" He popped open a can of Schlitz and drank most of the can in one gulp. "What is it, babe?"

Please don't call me that anymore. I know it should make me feel loved, but it makes me feel controlled.

"I really don't think we should be together anymore ..." Julie ran out of steam.

Teddy hit the accelerator; Julie glanced over and saw the needle at seventy. *Not this again!* Without warning, Teddy reached across her lap, gripped the door handle, yanked it up, and hurled his weight against Julie's shoulder. The door jammed.

"Please, Teddy! Stop and let me out!"

As Teddy hit the brakes, Julie's right side smashed against her door. She didn't want Teddy to see her crying—being a 'weak chick,' he called it—but she couldn't help it. She was tired of this relationship.

"Go on and get out. I've had enough of you anyway. You're about used up—it's time for me to find a new chick who'll appreciate me." Teddy dropped his head back on the seat, closed his eyes, and shut Julie out. She got out of the car and headed back to the main highway, hoping to hitch a ride home.

♦

Julie was equal parts devastated at the prospect of losing Mama T and relieved at the expectation of losing Teddy. She continued spending time with Mama, but it never felt the same after the break-up with her spoiled son. Julie had nothing to feel guilty about, and was sure that if Mama knew everything, she wouldn't defend her son—but who knew? Maybe it was time to move on. *I hope Mama T keeps praying for me. I need anything that will tip the scale in my favor.*

CHAPTER ELEVEN

THE WRONG ROOM

~

Julie longed for a girlfriend—a *close* girlfriend, not like the bottom feeders who had sucked the life out of her when she had been with Teddy. As soon as the 'break-up' was advertised, she had become road kill anyway. *Oh well, I guess I deserved it.*

The stormy January weather kept everyone indoors as much as possible; Julie hadn't walked down to Mama T's since before Christmas. Even her own mom would have been some shield against the loneliness, but Arlene was in the hospital recovering from another back injury, which meant that Danny suddenly had less of an excuse to perfect his rant-and-rave routine. She hadn't been to the Moores in almost a month.

The sun broke through the clouds for the first time in— *what did the weather guy say? Three weeks? No wonder I've felt icky!* Julie bundled up and went outside—even freezing to death was better than dying of loneliness.

A house on the next block had three gallon-cans of bright yellow indoor paint sitting on a metal table next to the garage with a "free" sign taped to one of the cans. Julie faced a long Saturday ahead of her. *What could it hurt to take the paint?* She made two round trips to her house and lined up the cans in a corner of her bedroom. Paintbrushes and drop clothes were in the bathroom closet. She was armed and dangerous, ready to attack her bedroom walls. *'Attack' is the right word. The battleship gray on these walls looks like they've been at war for years.*

How am I going to move my dresser away from the wall to paint? It's as heavy as a boat anchor! None of the kids at school would risk loyalty to Teddy by venturing into enemy territory. Julie's mind scanned the rows of desks in her homeroom class until she stopped at Chris Anderson. She grabbed the phonebook off of her desk and started looking for Chris' number. *With the last name of 'Anderson,' I'm amazed I found it!*

While Julie was dialing, she felt stupid about thinking that moving furniture and painting would be the ticket for a fun afternoon. However, Chris also sounded bored, reassured her that she thought Teddy was a creep, and said she'd be over in an hour. By the end of the day, the girls had painted, laughed, and sung slightly off-key to albums. They discovered shared likes and dislikes of jokes and teachers and music. *This is like being with Suzanne and Abbey again. We could use a fourth for our apartment!*

Chris and Julie remained acquaintances at school; they had decided to enjoy their friendship away from the shallowness of the other girls. As soon as they each got home from school they'd talk on the phone for at least an hour. Before long, Chris had invited Julie to spend the weekend with her family at their house in nearby Oak Creek.

This Anderson family was like the other one in Platteville: Julie felt both seen *and* heard. She began to think of Chris as her biological sister. Someone at school started a rumor that they were cousins, and that they must have had some reason for trying to hide it. Both girls were a slender five-eight and shared fair-skinned, German-Norwegian facial features as well as shoulder length auburn hair. As the rumor took on its own life, it stood uncorrected by girls who had each found a friend and decided not to be secretive about it anymore.

♦

Arlene's release from the hospital was a green light for Danny to resume his midnight terrors. At the appointed hour Julie threw on her jacket and ran down to the Moores. Officer Seaver showed up at the familiar house and delivered his monologue to the same closed door. Julie walked back home and made her own speech in the frosty air: "I'm tired of doing this—it's getting embarrassing. Let Mom start doing it—I'm done. Nothing ever changes anyway."

The human heart is defined anatomically as a muscle, but philosophically it can act like a ligament: tough, sinewy, and able to stretch and connect. Julie's heart connected with Chris' and made a bypass around her dad; she was no longer emotionally involved in his tossing-and-throwing of innocent furniture, as long as he left her alone.

♦

"Saturday night's all right for fighting/Get a little action in ..." Julie cranked up the volume on her stereo and laughed at Chris, who had pulled an enormous pair of sunglasses out of her duffle bag, slapped them on her face and started playing 'air piano.'

"Elton John you ain't!"

"Thank God!" yelled Chris.

Julie had been with Chris' family every weekend since they'd met, and really wanted Chris to be at her house for a change. Danny seemed to be in a long stretch of catching his breath before the next round of toss-and-fling, so Julie took advantage of the break in the action to have Chris over. *A friend is finally at* my *house.*

It was after midnight before Julie and Chris finished looking through yearbooks, snacking, and listening to a stack of albums. Both girls fell asleep in mid-conversation on Julie's double bed while the stereo needle was stuck in a groove on "Send In the Clowns." Julie awoke, grabbed the needle arm but carefully picked it up so that it wouldn't scratch her album. She pushed the arm down into its cradle and drifted back to sleep.

♦

As the bright moon shone through the window, Julie fought to pull herself out of a troubling dream. *Why is my hand wet, and why is it moving? What's the matter? I need to wake up!* Julie forced her eyes open and brought them into focus on her dad, who was standing above her naked, one hand holding a Styrofoam cup, the other gripping Julie's hand to pleasure himself.

Julie withdrew her hand in horror.

"Get out of here!" she shrieked.

Danny dropped his cup on the Judy Collins album cover lying on the floor as the smell of whiskey filled the room. Julie sat up and saw the liquid forming on Judy's face. *Now both of us will be stained, probably permanently.*

Danny staggered out of the room, tripping over Chris' shoes as he headed for the door. He caught himself on the doorjamb with his shoulder, let out a curse, and disappeared through the door.

Julie's heart ached. *God, aren't there any 'do-overs'?* When word of this horror spun through the school gossip, her life would be over, and Chris would never speak to her again. She ran to the bathroom, yanked off her sweatpants and sweatshirt, and climbed into the shower. Turning on the water, she stood sobbing and shaking until her tears and the hot water were used up. She'd been gone at least a half-hour, but when she got back to her room Chris was sitting up in bed.

"Look, Julie." Chris pulled up her knees and wrapped her arms around her shins. "I will *never* tell anyone about this." Chris let out a long sigh. "You know what else we share? My grandpa is like your dad. He makes me feel like hazardous waste."

"Chris, you know you can't ever sleep here again. I don't know what my dad would do to you." Chris' head nodded slightly as she quietly got up and dressed, organized her suitcase, and waited for Julie to take her home.

◆

Julie was coming unglued. She managed to drive Chris home while her mind drifted over a mental wasteland. *Don't think ... don't think. Drive.* She had no idea where she was. Not even the railroad tracks in the distance looked familiar.

I'd better be careful when I cross those tracks. Every time the gas pedal in this stupid car is jammed to the floor, it sticks and then the car dies, and it takes a crap load full of cranks to get it started again. I don't want to get stuck on the tracks ... stuck on the tracks ... stuck on the tracks ... I wonder if I'd die instantly ... if I'd feel any pain ... Julie looked around and didn't see any other cars at this rural crossing. She eased halfway across the tracks, stomped on the pedal, listened to the engine sputter and die, and sat back to wait. *The stars are beautiful tonight. There's the Big Dipper. It's getting cold in here. I'm waiting ... anticipating ... I wonder if Carly Simon will get over her stage fright and do a concert anytime soon? I could have been on stage if Miss Meyer hadn't called me a loser. I'll probably lose weight if I keep skipping meals. I didn't even eat supper. But Chris and I had popcorn and M & M's tonight. That was a long time ago.* Julie's thoughts bounced around the inside of the car for another thirty minutes until the sound of a train whistle jolted her back into the horrifying present tense.

Oh God, this isn't what I want after all! Julie started the car, stomped on the gas pedal and finished crossing the tracks as the train—whistle shrieking—barreled down on the space she had vacated. Panting in rhythm with the train engine, Julie lowered her head on the steering wheel and sobbed. *What happened, God? Are you trying to tell me something? Is Mama T still praying for me?*

When the sun spread oranges and pinks across the eastern sky, Julie woke up, lifted her head and winced at the crick in her neck. Even though there was so much wrong with her life, apparently she still wanted to hang on, at least for a little longer. For now she was in a hurry to get to a bathroom. She turned the key, threw the shifter in drive, stomped on the gas pedal, and the car died.

♦

When Julie was finally able to sneak through her front door and run up to the bathroom, she was thankful that everyone was doing their usual sleeping in on Sunday morning. *These steps are so creaky ... how come they betrayed me when they should have warned me last night?* Returning to her room, she tore all the sheets off her bed, threw them in her hamper and dug an old sleeping bag out of the closet. The floor, though not as comfortable as her bed, seemed somehow safer.

♦

Early in the afternoon Julie slogged into the kitchen in a bleary-eyed daze, grabbed a mug out of the drain board and a coffeepot sitting on the burner, and poured a mud-like substance into her cup. She then poured the contents of both down the drain and plopped onto a chair at the table across from her mom. *How can she drink that poison?* Arlene was staring at the newspaper folded crookedly on the table; a cigarette was perched on the edge of an ashtray next to the paper. *I think I made that ashtray in third grade. Was my life any simpler then? Well, there was Miss Meyer. I hope she quit teaching. The Marines can have her.*

Julie drew her brain back and heard loud snoring coming from the living room.

"Mom." Julie swallowed, wishing she had kept her mug of bitterness. "I need to tell you something."

Arlene looked up, pointed her pencil and glared at her daughter, who had violated the rule of don't-interrupt-Mom-while-she's-doing-something. "Can this wait? I'm trying to think of a four-letter word for 'hodgepodge'.

You mean like my life? How about 'crap'?

"Please stay with me." Julie wasn't used to begging.

"Oh, all right." Arlene pushed the paper aside and tossed her pencil over to the counter. "Spill."

Even though Julie had been the victim, it was embarrassing and humiliating to look at her mom, so she stared at a glob of grape jam on the floor. *That's about how I feel right now.*

"Last night Dad came into my room—"

"So?"

Julie rubbed her eyes and looked up. "And he was naked and drunk and grabbed my hand and did stuff to himself and then I woke up." Julie started crying and hoped she would find a point of entry into her mom's heart, or at least a crack in the thick wall around it. She wasn't prepared for a twisted loophole.

"Oh," Arlene pointed a thumb towards the living room, "your dad was just in the wrong room." Arlene picked up the newspaper and got up to retrieve her pencil.

Julie wiped her nose with a balled-up napkin sitting on the table. Her face turned red as she looked at her mom's back. "Doesn't he know the difference between your room and mine?" Her voice was hoarse from anger.

"Shut up!" Arlene turned around. "You've caused enough trouble already!" She glided to the table, took one more drag from her cigarette, ground it into the bottom of the ashtray, and walked out of the room.

♦

Danny took the same detour several more nights on the way to his room. Julie thought she could stay awake and somehow avoid him, but emotional fatigue always won the battle and left her with the casualties of war: disgust, horror, and helplessness. *I still have one way of escape: my mind. I'll relive my time on the swim team. I wonder how long I could hold my breath under water? Are Suzanne and Abbey still on the team? With one more girl, we could have had an awesome relay.* Sometimes her dad wasn't satisfied until he actually thrust himself inside of Julie, which took longer. *I'm pretty sure I'm drowning. Is there anyone out there who can rescue me?*

♦

The dried leaves crunched under Julie's Converse All-Stars as she ran around her neighborhood. If she was up early enough—and she never slept much after her dad's 'visits'—she could run before school. *Even though I'm already a junior, maybe it's not too late to go out for track next spring. If I can't swim, I can at least tear the cover off the track.*

Julie got back home with enough time to grab breakfast and a shower before school. She poured milk over a bowl of Cheerios, stared out the window and sighed. *If I kept stubbing my toes over sidewalk cracks, I'd be an idiot not to start running a different way. I've stubbed my whole self over his*

abuse long enough. There's got to be a different way to run.
Julie knew her mom wouldn't go to the mat for her, and she
was tired of feeling out of control. She looked down and saw
that she'd forgotten to get a spoon.

Pulling open the silverware drawer, Julie stared at the
knives and saw her 'different way.' Grabbing some in both
hands, she ran up and into her bedroom, dropped the knives
and slammed the door shut. She then picked up one knife at
a time and jammed it into the gap around the door until the
knives looked like the stuck out quills of an angry porcupine.
*The next time he opens the door the knives will come crashing
to the floor, and I know I won't sleep through that! Danny-
the-drunk will meet his match in Julie-the-determined.*

That night in her room Julie listened to albums, snacked,
and did her homework. She put her new security measure in
place, lay down between fresh sheets, pulled her bedspread
over her and fell asleep.

Long after midnight Danny climbed the stairs; whiskey
sloshed out of his regulation Styrofoam cup and ran down
his arm. Julie awoke to the sound of her door handle jiggling,
with the knives trembling in protest but holding firm in their
resolve. While Julie held her breath, Danny gargled vulgari-
ties around in his mouth, rattled the doorknob a little while
longer and then stumbled back downstairs. Julie's racing
heart kept her awake the rest of the night.

The next night Danny repeated his attempt at breaking
and entering, and for several more nights after that. Julie's
security system held. Arlene ranted endlessly about their
'god-awful garbage disposal,' but never found her knives.

CHAPTER TWELVE

"THERE'S NO PLACE LIKE HOME"

⌀

The utensil locking system created a daytime refuge for Julie and Chris—kindred spirits who pretended they were normal teenagers by teasing each other about zits and fat, even though both had clear complexions, weighed one hundred eighteen pounds, and were the envy of half the girls at school. Julie saw Chris shrug off the jealous, petty comments of those girls—but she was becoming more and more convinced that *she* was fat. *I'm already running every day ... maybe I should also start exercising at home.* She had once seen a picture of her mom as a slim twenty-something, and knew she had inherited a 'skinny' gene. She had also watched her mom fatten, and determined never to let that happen to her. She looked in the huge, oval mirror hanging on the wall above her dresser and announced to Chris on the phone one afternoon, "I'm going to get skinny again!"

"But Julie, you're already a bean pole!"

"Uh-uh, I can still pinch a little around my stomach."

"Girl, you're nuts!"

That night Julie started her new exercise routine of ten push-ups, twenty sit-ups and twenty-five crunches. Three

Dog Night would be the workout album-of-choice. "Jeremiah was a bull frog ..." She hummed along as she rose, fell, rose, fell, in perfect sit-up cadence. When the song ended she got up and stretched before the next set of exercises. Glancing in the mirror to check her progress, she squinted her eyes to get a better look. *Is there light coming through the mirror?* Oblivious to the next song blaring from her speakers, Julie approached the mirror like a detective on a crime scene investigation. She carefully unhooked it from the wall and turned it around. Every cuss word she had ever learned flew out of her mouth. Someone had drilled a small peephole through the wall and the mirror. Since her parents' room was right next-door, it was easy to figure out who had done it. *He's horrible! He finds new and different ways to violate me. What did I ever do to deserve this?* She put her mouth right up to the hole. "How can you do this to me? What have I ever done to you?" She had learned to live with the loss of her childhood, her innocence, her dignity, and her virginity ... and now she had lost her sanctuary. She put the mirror on her bed, opened the door and slammed it behind her. The needle skipped on the album as her feet pulverized the stairs. *With any luck they'll break.*

Arlene was lounging on the burnt orange couch in front of the TV surrounded by a stack of old newspapers, a half-eaten cheeseburger, and a Coke can balancing on the news-papers. Julie burst into the room with her eyes burning.

"This time Dad was *not* looking for the wrong room. He was in your room, and he drilled a peephole through your wall into the back of my mirror. He's probably watched me exercise and undress ..." There weren't adequate words to finish the sentence.

Arlene's eyes never left "The Tonight Show." "Well, cover it up the best you can. You're nothing if not resourceful. I never worry about you."

WHAT? Is that it? She's not going to protect me from my alcoholic, perverted father? Is she really that pathetic? Or does she stay with him because she gets the money to buy what she wants? In the meantime, he gets her and me for his pleasure, and I get pain.

Julie dragged herself back upstairs. Where was the hole you were looking to drop into when the world was too much?

◆

Duct tape, it turned out, had many uses. Julie drove to Ace Hardware early the next morning and bought a jumbo roll of gray. Back in her bedroom, she pulled and ripped, pulled and ripped, until she had an inch thick layer of duct tape strips covering the hole behind her mirror. And just to be safe—*what an interesting phrase*—Julie slapped a coat of black paint on top of the duct tape. The nightly exercise routine now had an added step: Check the painted duct tape and proceed with caution.

◆

After gym class, when the junior girls were in the locker room changing out of their gym suits back into street clothes, Julie felt a tap on her shoulder.

"Hey Julie."

"Hey yourself."

"I heard you're trying to lose weight."

"Who told you that?"

"Who cares? I think it's great. When you're skinny, you're in control of everything."

I'd settle for being in control of anything. "Yeah?"

"Yeah. So follow me into the bathroom after lunch, and I'll show you what to do."

"Whatever." *Colleen's always given me the creeps, and she looks way too skinny. Wonder what she's doing?*

The girls' bathroom was always crowded and smoky right after lunch, so Julie and Colleen hung around until they were the last ones in there, with less than five minutes left before they had to get to class. Julie watched in horror while Colleen leaned over the toilet, shoved her finger down her throat and made herself lose her lunch. Then she calmly flushed, walked to the sink, rinsed her mouth out with a little bottle of Listerine she pulled out of her purse, and wiped her mouth on a paper towel. "See? Do this every day and you'll never gain any weight!" Colleen looked in the mirror, fixed her hair, and left the bathroom.

Julie was pretty sure she had absolutely nothing to lose by trying this—whatever it was. At first it was hard and gross, but after a few days she got used to it. Colleen encouraged her every day, and it felt good to have another friend besides Chris, even if the common bond was strange.

A week later, Chris walked into the bathroom as Julie was finishing her after-lunch tossing. "Colleen, is Julie in here?"

"Yeah, she's almost done." Colleen slipped something into her purse, walked around Chris and out the door. Chris heard a sickening noise.

"Julie, are you okay? Should I get the nurse?"

"No. I'll be out." Julie walked into the sink area looking slightly green, and headed for the sink.

"You don't look good! Are you sure you're not sick?"

"NO! I'm—"

"What? Pregnant? Because maybe I'll report your father—"

"No, I'm not. It's—"

"What?" Chris put her hand on Julie's arm, and suddenly there was no shut-off valve for Julie's tears.

"Jewel, what's wrong?"

"Oh, Chris, I wanted to get skinnier ... and Colleen said I'd have control—"

"You're doing this on *purpose?*"

"But my throat hurts, and I'm getting these really, really bad headaches every day like I used to get years ago—"

"Why did you listen to that idiot Colleen?"

Julie walked three steps over to the sink, leaned over, turned on the cold water and tried to wash her face. "I can't do this anymore."

"For sure not. It's got to be dangerous."

Julie dried her face with the bottom of her sweatshirt. "I'm pretty sure I can exercise harder."

"You're my best friend, but you're a knucklehead." Chris put her arm around Julie's shoulder and walked her out the door. "Please promise me that after my family and I move to New York, you won't start hanging around with her."

"I'll do better than that—I'll quit before you move."

"Excellent."

◆

Up, down, up, down. *I can't believe I'll be finishing my junior year in high school.* Up, down, up, down. *I'm really glad Chris is still my friend. I can't imagine my life without her.* Up, down, up, down.

Up. Catch a breath. Wait for the song to end. Stand and stretch; get ready for the next set of exercises. Julie always checked herself in the mirror between sets. And there it was: a steady beam of light shining through her mirror. *Can this be happening again?* Julie yanked the mirror off the wall: the duct tape had been torn off and the hole re-drilled. Rage gave Julie the strength to shove her heavy dresser across the room and up against an outside wall. *I'll re-hang the mirror tomorrow. I'm not putting* anything *against that wall again!* The leftover roll of duct tape hung on a nail in Julie's closet, waiting to be pressed into duty. Julie pulled and ripped strips of tape until the covering over the hole looked like a cancerous growth—*not unlike whatever's in Dad's brain.* Julie jumped on her bed, took down the framed picture of her and Chris at a football game, and hung it where the mirror had been.

The room had become another place of betrayal in Julie's life. *I'll never exercise or change clothes in here again.*

♦

Arlene walked upstairs and into Julie's room a few days later, and handed her a laundry basket full of her clean, wrinkled clothes. "Something's different in here. Did you move your furniture?"

"Mom, you haven't listened to anything I've told you. Dad molested me when Chris spent the night last year. He drilled a hole through your bedroom wall and made a peephole into my room. I covered up the hole months ago, and I found out he did it again!"

Arlene dropped the basket, put her hands over her eyes, and made a pitiful sobbing noise. "How can you do this to me?"

Picking up the basket, Julie clenched her teeth. "How can I do this to *you*? I've been telling you this over and over! I showed you the peephole in the wall! I can't do this anymore. Get rid of him!"

♦

Julie thought that a snake curled up on a rock was always preferable to finding it in her boot, as long as she knew where the rock was. The night after her confrontation with her mom, Danny didn't come home, nor did he show up the next morning. *Did Mom finally kick him out? Did Dad get sick of Mom and decide to leave? If he left, how far away is he?*

A shaky peace settled over the house until Danny showed up a week later, sober, mean, and threatening to kill Arlene. It struck Julie that her dad was way more dangerous sober than he was drunk, when he had the advantage of hand-eye coordination and the motive of revenge. After wreaking his special brand of destruction, he vanished only to reappear a week later and threaten to "kill you worthless scum and burn the house down." He settled for beating the furniture senseless, grabbing plates of spaghetti and meatballs from the table and throwing them against the wall. *I wish I could remember what kind of pasta Oscar hurled against the wall. Boy, was Felix mad at him!*

Arlene finally drew a line in the sand and got a restraining order against Danny. When he showed up a week later, Julie grabbed her running shoes and realized that she was looking forward to seeing Mrs. Moore again. Suddenly her mom tipped the scale, calmly picked up the phone and dialed 911. *Why didn't dad yank the phone off the wall?* Officer Seaver appeared almost immediately; Julie thought he did a poor job of covering his shock at actually entering the house. After he was handcuffed and hauled away, Arlene mumbled "Good riddance to a bad egg," and disappeared into her room.

Danny sat in jail for five days.

◆

Maybe Mom will figure out that she can have more than this merry-go-round she's been on forever. I'm not sure she really knows how to love me, but she's been so beaten down herself. If she left him in jail for a while, we could leave and start over somewhere. Since she lost the café, she could get a new job that would be good for her. That time before Dad found us was good. Mom seemed relaxed and almost nice sometimes.

Arlene bailed Danny out, and he thanked her by violating the Order of Protection so often that Julie thought the county jail should have commissioned a special cell in his honor.

CHAPTER THIRTEEN

STAND OFF

"We're blowing this joint. Time to haul." Arlene issued a take-no-prisoners edict.

"But Mom, I'm ready to start my *senior* year! We can't move now."

"Yes we can, and I don't want any more of your lip. You don't know how tough my life's been, and you haven't helped. Besides, we're only moving to Coldspring. You can still see your friends."

What kind of bug-infested place will we live in next? I wish I could live on my own. Before Julie and her mom and brother had packed their stuff into Grandpa and Grandma's station wagon, Julie had applied for a job at the Lakehaven Nursing Home. A buck-fifty an hour would be the start of her mutiny against poverty. She'd work evenings and every other weekend in the kitchen with bonus pay deposited in her self-esteem bank.

When Julie's mom announced, during their first-of-many macaroni and cheese dinners in their new apartment, "I got a part-time job as a caregiver for some old people in a nursing home," Julie almost choked. *I wonder what it would take for my mom to be a caregiver for me? At least the café is history.*

♦

Rent and groceries were at either end of an income rope that never tied in the middle of Arlene's salary. So, Julie did the only 'resourceful' thing she knew to do: called out the grandparent-cavalry. Richard and Rose made the thirty-mile round trip from Pineville to Coldspring every week in a big station wagon loaded with baskets of garden tomatoes, corn and green beans, quarts of freshly-picked cherries and raspberries, butcher-paper wrapped packages of venison from the previous season's deer hunt, some kind of hot casserole in a covered Pyrex dish, and a pan of lemon bars or brownies. Julie feared more visits to the power company in her future unless her mom got another part-time job or Julie dropped out of school—two scenarios high up in the category of 'least likely.' On a steamy August night, Julie woke up only mildly surprised that her mom was shaking her shoulder and saying, "We're out of here. A guy at work told me there's cheap, furnished apartments in Fairview." By the time the birds started singing at three forty-five, Julie was packing stuff into their car. *I'm always glad when we can move during warm weather and don't have far to go.*

A tenant unencumbered with cleanliness issues and good taste had probably vacated the apartment hours ahead of the arrival of Arlene and her kids. The gold- and green- and orange-striped kitchen wallpaper was splattered with grease and tomato sauce; the avocado-colored stove and refrigerator looked to be the losers in a food fight; and the rectangular, red, Formica-topped metal table was cowering under stacks of yellowed newspapers and overflowing ashtrays. The black linoleum floor was a sticky labyrinth of hardened food and crushed bugs. The rest of the scale-model-size apartment looked like it had given its all in hand-to-hand combat.

The late-morning sun raised the internal temperature of the apartment to life-threatening status. Arlene sought

relief lying on a flowered sofa in front of a window fan;
Julie attacked the kitchen with buckets of Spic-n-Span and
ammonia, in preparation for the making of the traditional
first-meal Spam casserole.

◆

It had been a tiring but satisfying Saturday evening shift
at Lakehaven; Julie parked her mom's car in front of their
apartment, unlocked the front door, slipped quietly into the
kitchen, and almost walked into the back of her mom's chair.
She hung her purse on a wall hook and stood behind her
mom.

"So what do you have there?" All of the usual tools—
coffee, cigarette and newspaper—were missing. Arlene
picked up the single sheet of paper from the table and handed
it to Julie.

"What's this?"

"Divorce paper." Arlene sighed. "Am I doing the right
thing?"

Julie dropped the paper and covered her shock by opening
the cupboard door and twirling the handles of several mugs,
making a show of trying to choose the right one, and finally
settling on an enormous dark navy one with "I don't suffer
from insanity—I enjoy every minute of it" stamped around
it. She pulled the pot out of the Mr. Coffee and poured a
thick substance into her mug. *One of these days I'm going to
show her how to make drinkable coffee.*

"How will we make it without your dad?"

Julie took a sip, grimaced and sat down. "Mom, I've been
waiting for years for you to do this. You're smart and you
know how to get along. One thing you learned from living
with Dad was how to survive. You've got lots of time to
figure out what you want to do with your life without having
a price on your head."

Arlene put her hand over Julie's and awkwardly patted it. Pushing her chair back she said, "Well, I'll think about it. Those are some good words." Arlene's slippers slapped against the linoleum as she left the room.

Julie was shocked: her mom had *almost* thanked her for her encouragement. *I have no idea what my mom did before she met my dad ... maybe I'll ask her about it someday.* Julie stared at a cobweb near the ceiling and got up to find the broken broom.

♦

Staff meetings at Lakehaven were an Olympic event. Words were lobbed back and forth across the room between aides, nurses, and support people in an in-your-face free-for-all. *I spent years training for this sport in my family, and no one's going to intimidate me!* But the outcome was different than anything Julie had expected. People were agreeable in their disagreements, encouraging of each other, respectful of opinions, and energized about their responsibilities. *I guess I've got some things to learn. This was really fun and everyone is leaving with egos unscathed.*

♦

A short, plump girl with straight, dark-blonde hair approached Julie after the next staff meeting at the nursing home.

"Hi. 'Julie,' isn't it? I'm Gloria Gustafson."

She's not the most popular girl at school. "Hey, Gloria. I think we might be in first hour together. You have Mr. Johnson, right?"

"Yeah, I do. I like him, but math will never be cool!" Gloria giggled.

"Too true. I just want to graduate."

144

The girls reached for the instant hot chocolate packets.

"Hey, Julie, how would you like to go to a YFC meeting with me next Friday night, if you're not doing anything?" Gloria was so confident, so pleasant, and so unlike any assumptions Julie had made about her.

"What's YFC?" Julie searched around for the pot of hot water, hoping not to embarrass herself by pouring coffee over her powdered hot chocolate mix.

"It's Youth For Christ, an organization for teens. We meet in the town hall to sing, pray, and listen to a speaker talk about stuff we're all interested in—like dating, drugs, stuff like that—and what the Bible has to say about those things. It's really fun, and a big encouragement for us."

"Does anyone else go from our school?" Julie was being reeled in.

"Yeah, there's a guy from our math class, and a bunch of others from our school, plus some from other schools. I could swing by your house on Friday; we could go together, and then some of us go out afterwards."

"Okay, I'm in."

◆

That Friday night, Julie and Gloria walked into the town hall at ten to seven.

"Hey, Glo! We saved some seats for you. Who's your friend?"

"Hey Just, this is Julie."

"Hi Julie, I'm Justine. But everyone calls me 'Just.' Like 'just too cute,' 'just too perky' ... I've heard it all. But I don't mind." Justine's almost-black eyes looked like marbles. "Come and sit with me—we're going to start pretty soon." Julie and Glo joined Just on an orange-striped, upholstered sofa. The many-colored armchairs and love seats and bean-bags scattered around the room in a clashing of shapes and styles were as offensive as anything Julie had ever had in her cumulative houses and trailers and apartments—yet they looked inviting and comfortable. Another girl came up to them and interrupted Julie's thoughts. "Hey, Just-fine." She looked at Julie. "I'm Jamie Anders. Aren't you in World Lit with me?"

"Guilty as charged. I'm Julie." Just popped up, said "Bye!" and ran off.

"There goes 'Just-in-time!'"

Julie laughed.

"Didn't you used to date Teddy Tannenbaum?"

"Guiltier than ever."

"I was always afraid to talk to you back then."

"Why?"

"You seemed so together—"

"I was pretty messed up." Julie sighed.

"What happened?"

Julie looked thoughtful. "I think he was kicking the tires to check out the car, and then decided against it—against *me*."

Jamie was quiet.

"I'm sure you didn't come here to listen to this."

"Oh, but I'm glad you shared. Have you been keeping this inside?"

"Pretty much. No one wants to hear my pity party. My best friend Chris moved to New York last year, and I haven't really found anyone to talk to since then."

"Well, I'm not going anywhere. I know I'm not Chris, but I'd be glad to listen to you anytime." Jamie smiled and touched Julie's shoulder.

"Thanks. Thanks a lot. I'll catch you at school."

The room quieted down when a few guys near the front started strumming guitars. Song after song washed over everyone in ripples of melody and harmony. Julie heard a song about a spark and getting a fire going and was back with her dad building a bonfire on Christmas day. *I don't want to remember anything good about him.* When the last chord hung in the air, whispered notes faded into intense silence.

A twenty-something guy carrying a duct-taped book strolled to the front of the room and hopped up on a wooden bar stool. He was wearing Nike running shoes, patched jeans, and a Grateful Dead t-shirt. When he turned his head to shout something to a guy on the far side of the room, Julie noticed a wavy ponytail hanging down under his John Deere cap.

"Hi. There's still couch space and plenty of floor space for those of you who are looking for a spot. I'm Bret."

Whistles and greetings filled the room.

"Great singing. And let's thank the guitar players."

Everyone clapped, some kids whistled again, and Bret waited patiently for the room to regain its equilibrium.

"So here we are again. I usually talk about dating and sex and peer pressure. *Is* there anything else?"

Julie joined the easy laughter.

"Tonight we're going to talk about God as our heavenly Father. I know that some of you come from divorced homes and your dads live far away. You hardly ever see them and you really miss them. Or maybe you're okay with them being gone because they drink too much, too often, and it makes you uncomfortable … or sad … or mad … or all three.

"I *know* some of you have really good and kind fathers. I met some of them when they helped carry in this cast-off furniture! They're the dads who order your homes—and sometimes you resent that, but mostly you feel safe. Your friends give you a hard time because your dads are too strict, and then they look for your dads when things start falling apart in their houses. They *want* someone to care about them, so they borrow your dads for a while."

Bret looked around the room and made eye contact with some of the kids. "Before the night is over, you will be asked to enter into the 'dad' world of someone else whose experience might be very different than your own—maybe much better, maybe much worse."

Bret paused again to let the students sift through his words. Some whispered to their friends; others crossed their arms and wore looks of challenge or disdain.

"Okay, so what haven't we covered yet? This is probably the toughest thing for me to talk about, and the hardest for some of you to hear ... the ones whose parents are still married, but whose dad beats you or your mom or your brothers or sisters ... or does stuff to your siblings that you wouldn't dare talk about."

Julie felt her face getting hot. *Did Glo tell this guy I'd be here tonight? Or is this a coincidence?*

Some of the students squirmed, stared down at their shoes, reached for a friend's hand, or clasped their own hands tightly together. The only sound in the room was the rhythmic humming of the Coke machine at the back.

Bret continued. "How many of you are waiting for the 'Jaws of Life' to snatch you out of your homes?"

Hands shot up and burst the tension bubble.

"Your Father with a capital 'F' knows who you are."

Hands lowered. Bret's voice was at the same time authoritative and soothing.

"The Bible uses lots of words for God: Protector ... Provider ... Creator ... Lover ... Grace-Giver ... Satisfier ... Healer ... Nourisher ... Restorer ... Jesus even called him 'Abba,' which means 'Daddy.'"

When Bret flipped open his book, Julie knew then that it was a Bible. "Psalm sixty-eight, verse five, says God will be a 'father to the fatherless.' Whether you have a loving father or an abusive father—or anyone in-between—you can leave here tonight knowing that your Heavenly Father, your Daddy, loves you with a forever-love ... a love that doesn't depend on your grades, your looks, or your accomplishments. He loved you enough to send His son to die for you, and He loves you enough to be your 'enough' every day."

John three sixteen: 'For God so loved the world, that He gave His only begotten Son, that whosoever believeth in Him should not perish, but have eternal life.' I got my very first check for memorizing that verse.

A tapping foot echoed loudly, while a girl's voice rose timidly from the back of the room. "Bret? Isn't one of the Ten Commandments to honor your father and mother? How do I honor a father who's a ... creep?" A slow burn crept up into her face.

Bret climbed carefully off the stool. *He looks like he's stepping into a minefield.* He put his Bible down on the stool, took off his cap and twirled it around on his fingertip before tossing it on the floor. Everyone watched and listened intently.

"I could easily concede defeat right now. I attended YFC meetings in high school, and then moved on to Concordia Bible College and Trinity Seminary. I've studied the Bible and spent a lot of time wrestling with God over things that make no sense to me. Up 'til now I thought the hardest battles were behind me.

Bret pointed to his cap. "Let me try to explain what I think God has shown me. We all want connections to our dads, and that cap's mine. Bret Johnson *senior* is a regional distributor of John Deere equipment. When I wear his only high school graduation gift to me, I am reminded that God expects me to honor him. And someday I really hope he'll see what I do as important and valuable.

"When I take off my cap at the end of the day, I remember that God is the Father who matters most. Even if my dad never says he loves me or is proud of me, I know that God loves me more than I deserve."

Bret noticed some of the guys removing their baseball caps and tossing them on the floor.

"The question was about the commandment to 'honor your parents.' I believe that when you do that, you're actually obeying God and giving honor to Him. Honoring your parents doesn't have anything to do with whether or not they've earned it. It's showing what I call 'U.R.': Undeserved Respect. You should actually give it to your dads *and* moms, your teachers, and even your bosses.

"And yeah, you might feel like that makes you a doormat. U.R. makes it easy for people to stomp on you and wipe stuff on you. But ... as Christian young people, you can choose a different picture. You can be a bridge ... still walked on, but really walked *across* by people who need to find God on the other side.

"I've done this with my father many times. He calls me every Sunday afternoon and asks me when I'm going to get a real job. 'When I was your age,' he says, 'I was already married, had three kids, and was working two jobs. I had a lot of responsibility—something you seem to know nothing about.' If I try to explain myself to him, it becomes a game of Battleship: Hit and a miss, hit and a miss, and eventually, hit and sunk. Even if I make a convincing argument—like how I think I'm making a difference in some of your lives—he disengages and moves on to some other game. I don't want to win an argument or a game. I want to win his encouragement. I want him to believe in me.

"After he hangs up I stomp around my apartment, yelling my anger and hurt out to God. And then I ask Him to help me exchange the picture in my mind from me being a doormat to a bridge—a bridge that will take my dad to God. He needs God's love and forgiveness like we all do every day."

Bret paused, picked up his cap and started twirling it again.

"Lately I've begun to realize that there's a hidden blessing in my relationship with my dad. It has shown me the same thing I'm telling you: that God loves me, believes in me, and is always in my corner. If I had the kind of father I've always wanted, maybe I would never have found a Heavenly Father." Bret put his cap back on.

One of the guitar players cleared his throat.

"Bret, what about someone who never knew their dad? My mom and dad were both sixteen when my mom found out she was pregnant and her boyfriend left her without a forwarding address. How do I honor him?"

"I'm really sorry that happened to you. But you can still show undeserved respect to your father by honoring him in your mind and in the words you use to tell your story to someone else. He may have fled the scene of the crime because he was scared; maybe he didn't think much about it ... but wherever he is today, he needs the bridge of Jesus to lead him to our heavenly Father. And remember: Even if our earthly fathers abandon us, God never does. Never will.

"We're going to try something now for about fifteen minutes. I want you to find a partner—guys, find a good buddy; gals, find another girl; when you've found your partner, get together in a quiet place. No pressure here—if you're comfortable, share with each other about your experience with your dad. It doesn't have to be much, just enough for you to be able to pray for each other. And I'd like you to promise to pray for your partner every day this coming week. Let's hold everything here in confidence. I'll let you know when the time is almost up. If you're one of those people blessed with an amazing dad, freely and happily share that. This time will be different for each of you. God knows who your partner needs to be, and so we'll trust Him to put the right people together."

Oh God! What would my life have been like with a different father? I can't ever forgive him, and You can't ask me to! He probably doesn't think he did anything wrong. And if You're my real Father, why didn't You protect me from my dad? Does that make You any better of a Father than he is? I want to believe Bret when he says You care about me.

As Julie leaned forward with blurred eyes, Glo and Jamie sat down on either side of her and each put a hand on her back. Julie wept as Jamie whispered, "I'm sorry he abandoned you," in her ear. *Is she talking about Teddy? All I can think about is my dad … I wish I could tell them what he did to me.* The new friends cried with Julie, and then she thought maybe God was also sad about her father. Maybe He really did love her like Bret said He did.

◆

Bret's shrill whistle quieted the room. "You're welcome to stay as long as you like after we're finished. I want everyone to grab the hand of the person closest to you, and let's form a big circle … or ellipse … or oval … or something." Everyone laughed and grabbed a hand while someone near the front started singing acapella. It was the most beautiful three-part round Julie had ever heard, and she found she was able to catch on to the melody and words quickly. She closed her eyes and joined the rest: "Father, I adore You. Lay my life before You. How I love You."

When the singing stopped Bret spoke quietly. "Abba, Daddy, some of us can't think about our dads without feeling blame or shame. I used to blame You for the father I thought you had cursed me with … but I'm trying to see the blessing in him, because that's how I found you—the best Father— the one who has never, ever left me. Please be the Father every one of these kids needs. In Jesus' Name, Amen."

It was ten-to-eleven before Julie, Glo, Just, and Jamie piled into Glo's car. Julie felt refreshed and unburdened as they headed to Pizza Hut. *God, I know I didn't deserve any of this tonight, but thank You for it all.* Julie got home at one-thirty and pulled out a box from her closet. On the bottom was her Bible from Mrs. Ryczek. *Did she suspect something wasn't right in my family? Thank you for putting her in my life when You did. Bless her!* Julie got comfortable on her bed and paged through her Bible, looking at all of the verses underlined in red pencil. Sunlight was beginning to dim the light from the stars before she fell asleep.

♦

The ink was still wet on the divorce papers when Danny appeared at the new apartment, sober and ready to defend his title. His boots trampled the defenseless ground as he exploded through the front door. If there had been a 'fasten seat belt' sign it would have lit up and given fair warning of expected turbulence.

Julie was in her room listening to Jesus Christ Superstar. As she turned up the volume it occurred to her that the soundtrack of her dad's life was really one song he had been playing forever—a predictable, methodical melody about an angry man toying with lunacy.

Julie's violence radar had learned to detect specific forms of destruction even from her bedroom. Lamps were being overturned, furniture was being tipped, and breaking glass was the exclamation point for every cuss word bouncing around the living room. The contents of the kitchen cupboards were the next targets. When Julie's curiosity eventually drew her out of her room, she found a totaled apartment. A pile of plastic plates had formed a fraternity of the safe-for-now in a corner of the kitchen. Every other flat surface was buried under the shattered remains of broken dreams.

Arlene was sitting on the brown-carpeted floor in a corner of the living room. *If you're hoping for invisibility, forget it. It never worked for me.* Julie's brother ran to the hall closet, snatched his denim jacket, went to the front door and grabbed the brass doorknob so hard it came off in his hand. He turned around and hurled it at his dad, catching him in the abdomen. Dan swore, stuck his fingers into the doorknob hole and managed to yank the door open. He was out the door while Danny was still doubled over in pain. Julie slipped into auto pilot mode, raced to the kitchen and pulled a serrated bread knife out of the kitchen drawer. She ran five steps back into the living room in time to see her father stagger over to her mother and cock his arm back. Julie reached out, caught his arm and planted herself between her parents. Trapped in a strange moment of time, she faced her dad. *I'm about to become either a murderer or a victim.*

"If you touch her, I'll kill you!"

Danny's eyes had the wild look of a trapped animal. His clenched fist, still in Julie's grip, began to burn from the drip of her salty sweat. "I could break your neck," he choked.

"Take your best shot." Julie hardly breathed.

Father and daughter looked at each other, and Julie wasn't even thinking about her mom whimpering. Danny looked down at his wife, shoved Julie aside and walked to the front door. Turning around, he leaned against the doorframe and pointed to Arlene. "You might want to tell her someday soon." He dropped his arm, turned around and walked out, leaving the door open behind him.

Julie slumped to the floor, overcome with relief but still angry. *I* didn't *honor my father; I* couldn't *kill him; and I* can't *stop hoping that someday he'll love me as his daughter. And for crying out loud,* what *is my mom supposed to tell me?*

CHAPTER FOURTEEN

REVELATION

Julie balanced the worlds of home and school like a lumber-jack on a log roll. The fear of losing her footing often competed with her desire to plunge head first into water that would swallow her, pain and all. It was a wobbly dance of survival and despair.

After Miss Meyer, Mr. O'Keefe, the nosebleeds and headaches, school had settled into an uncomplicated routine. Julie's teachers were practical people who actually seemed interested in her academic progress. A few were heavy-handed and self-absorbed, but they were lightweights, and no match for some of the tyrants who had buried Julie's innocence long before her childhood had ended.

Mr. Schroeder, the band teacher, was Julie's north star. Called 'Sir' by students and teachers alike during his twenty-plus years of teaching—although no one could remember where the nickname came from—he was a bright light in everyone's sky. Sir joked with his band students with a side-ways brand of humor, but also demanded hard work and expected great music. There hadn't been many honest and respectful men in Julie's life, and none as genuine as Sir. The best part was having band seventh period; it usually put her in a good and confident mood for the rest of the night.

The only thorn in band was Joey Green. Julie kept hoping that he and his family would move away, or at least that he would stop using his drum sticks to beat on her head. When he gave a play-by-play account of all his previous nights' female conquests, Julie dealt with him by ignoring him, and was greatly consoled by the evident and unusual disdain Sir seemed to have for him.

On a glorious Friday afternoon the band flexed its muscles, practicing for the halftime show at the home football game later that night. The windows in the room were open; brasses and reeds blasted their notes to an audience of squirrels, passing cars, and early-dismissal seniors heading out to jobs.

As Sir was giving last-minute instructions about the order of songs, Joey leaned over his snare and tapped Julie's ear with a drumstick.

"Hey Sandford, I got a scoop."

Julie turned and glared. "You idiot, I don't want to hear about your stupid date last night. Any girl who'd go out with you must have 'Loser' tattooed on her forehead.

Joey did a rim shot. "If you're the last one to hear about this, there will be no joy in Mudville."

Julie knew there was no way to get rid of Joey until she relented. "Okay, but make it quick. I really need to hear what Sir's saying."

"Are you sure you're ready for this?"

"Joey!" Julie turned back around and looked straight ahead.

"I'll tell you about it right after the bell rings."

Oh, great—now someone I don't even care about is dismissing me. Is there no end to these guys in my life?

The bell signaled the end of Sir's pep talk, the end of the school day, the end of the week, and hopefully the end of Joey's attempts to get Julie's attention.

As Julie leaned over and opened her baritone case, Joey plopped down into the vacated seat next to her, rested his drumsticks on a music stand, and tickled her back with his fingers.

Julie straightened, turned and glared. "This isn't a social call. State your business and leave me alone." Julie secretly wished she didn't take every opportunity to carp at Joey, but theirs was an oil-and-water relationship, and she still didn't have tools for dealing with guys who specialized in humiliation. "I mean okay, what did you want to tell me?" *I could at least give this guy another chance to act human.*

Joey pressed his advantage. "Sandford, maybe I should wait 'til Monday to tell you."

First my dad, now Joey. I wish someone would tell me what I'm supposed to know!

"Suit yourself." Julie bent back down to finish packing her baritone.

Joey gently touched Julie's shoulder and pulled her upright. The hard, cynical lines around his mouth softened; his eyes pierced a place deep in Julie. She felt strangely drawn to him.

"Julie, I was in our kitchen last night, really late. I'm sure my parents thought I had gone to bed much earlier. I was up in my room studyin' for our AP English test, and I came down to get some ice cream. It was Rocky Road. That stuff is unbelievable! Anyway, I overheard my parents talking in the living room. I figured they were saying mushy parent stuff, until I heard my mom say, 'I wonder if he knows that Julie Sandford is related to him? Her mother, Arlene, married my cousin Eugene. That makes Joey and Julie some sort of first cousins once-removed, or something like that. I never quite understand how the family tree works.' And then my dad said, 'We should probably tell him tomorrow.' Well, that's today, and my dad left for work before I got up, so I'll guess they'll tell me tonight."

Joey picked up the drumsticks and did another rim shot on the music stand.

"I really thought you were trying to be a nice guy, but I guess everything's a big joke to you. Why do I bother to listen to you?" Julie jumped up, almost knocking over her music stand, completely ignoring her open instrument case at her feet. She had a sudden urge to flee from this ridiculous, far-fetched, but strangely disturbing conversation.

Joey flipped his drumsticks and laid them back down on the music stand. "Julie, we've done lots of fighting. It doesn't take much for me to set you off. I could do that without making up something like this. I don't like it any more than you do, so why would I tell you if it wasn't true?" By the end of his last sentence, Joey was talking to Julie's retreating back.

"See you then." Joey picked up his drumsticks, set them back near his drum, and walked quietly out of the room.

♦

Julie couldn't concentrate on her normal after-school routine. Her backpack was forgotten in her locker; she didn't know how she got home, only that she was walking towards her back door. *God, if you're out there, please help me.*

Julie paced around the parking lot in front of her apartment building waiting for her mom to come home from work. She had no idea what she would say to her mom. *"Hey, Mom, I heard something crazy in school today. Is there something you want to tell me? And who the heck is Eugene?"*

The late-afternoon breeze cooled Julie's forehead and played a soothing melody through the trees. Julie was finally ready to go inside.

Grabbing a Coke from the refrigerator, Julie wandered into the living room and turned on the TV. Phil Donahue was interviewing some guy who had had a sex change operation. *Forget that!* Julie flipped the channel to an after-school special, something about a mom learning to love her son who was gay. *Isn't there anything 'normal' on TV? But why should there be—there's not much 'normal' in my life.*

By the time Arlene came through the door, muttering about her tired feet, her lousy job, and her empty checkbook, Julie was lightly dozing on the couch.

"So, are we having T-bone steak for dinner? With all the fixin's?" This was Arlene's standard after-work line.

Julie roused and rubbed her stiff neck. When the fog cleared from her brain and she remembered her conversation in the band room, she suddenly felt cold.

"Mom, can I tell you something I heard today?" Julie sounded far more tentative than she felt.

"Don't tell me coloreds are moving in next door to us!" Arlene looked dismayed.

Julie sighed. "Mom, can we please not beat that dead horse? They're called 'blacks,' and no, there aren't any moving next to us that I know of."

"Thank God!" Arlene dropped onto the couch and propped her feet up on the coffee table.

Julie made her approach on a different runway. "Do you remember when Dad used to beg you to tell me something?"

Arlene rubbed her eyes. "Your dad used to say lots of fool things. I never listened to most of it, and you shouldn't have either."

"The last time Dad left us, he looked at you, and said, 'Don't you think you should tell her soon?' So ... what was he talking about?"

Arlene got up slowly, peeled down her nylons, pulled them off, tossed them behind the couch, and crossed a leg under her as she sat back down. "I need a cigarette."

Julie jumped up, rifled through her mom's purse, handed her a flip-top box of unfiltered Lucky Strikes and an orange disposable lighter, and sat cross-legged on the floor.

Arlene lit her cigarette, took a deep drag, tilted her head back, and released a trail of pungent smoke. "Well," Arlene said, "Well."

I'm not letting her off the hook. I'll sit here all night if that's what it takes, until she tells me whatever it is I should have heard a long time ago.

"I guess you're old enough to hear this. Mind I'm not ashamed of any of it. I've done my best by you and your brother. You have no idea what I've been through."

"Okay." Julie waited.

"You know I went to high school in Coldspring. Well, Eugene and I were high school sweethearts. We started dating our freshman year all the way through high school, and kept dating for four more years. We were the 'Eugene-and-Arlene' team. It sounded so ridiculous and hokey, everyone figured we would get married and go on 'The Dating Game' on TV together!" Arlene stared at the gathering shadows on the far wall. "I just wanted to live with him for a while after we graduated, but that would have been very unacceptable, especially for this hick town. I actually did love him, but I still felt trapped."

Arlene glanced at Julie. "Anyway, we set our wedding date. The only thing I remember clearly from that day was standing next to my father in the lobby right before we walked in to the sanctuary. The 'Wedding March' was playing; I took my father's arm, leaned over, and whispered, 'I don't know, Dad. This doesn't seem right.' 'Don't do it,' my father said. 'We can stop this right here.'

"But, I did it anyway." Arlene clamped her lips tight.

"And?"

"And I figured since I done the right thing and married Eugene, instead of just living with him—which is what I wanted to do—that somehow God would reward us and we would have the perfect life together. Eugene promised me a big house, a white picket fence—the whole enchilada. The only catch was we would have to move to Washington to chase that dream.

"For the fifties I was a very independent woman. I owned my own car right out of high school. I had a full time job. I knew what I wanted out of life. If Eugene wanted to move me out to Washington, fine by me, as long as he could make good on his promises. Besides, I wasn't about to be embarrassed by returning all of our shower gifts and wedding gifts, and admitting that maybe I had made a mistake. This marriage was definitely going to work."

Arlene ground out her cigarette in a metal, beanbag ashtray. "I guess I wasn't completely honest with Eugene, but he wasn't honest with me, either. When we got out to Bremerton, I found out that there wasn't a house, no job for Eugene ... I have no idea why he even wanted to move out there. Maybe it was for adventure; we had both been feeling trapped in Coldspring. I was too mad and disappointed to ever ask him why.

"Anyways, when you were born there was finally some good that came out of living there. I hadn't really thought about being a mother, but that was another one of those expected things for the fifties."

Gee Mom, you really know how to turn a girl's head.

Arlene made a lane change without signaling. "But Eugene left me and you when you were three months old, and took up with a fourteen-year-old chick named Barbie; a while later I heard they got married. I guess he got what he wanted, and so did I. Well, I'm going to change into some comfortable clothes. Start some supper, will you?" Arlene picked up her nylons on the way to her room, dragging them on the floor behind her.

Julie stayed on the floor, eyes unfocused, thoughts whirling in a blender. *Why didn't I hear this a long time ago? I have a dad somewhere out there named 'Eugene.' So Danny Sandford isn't my real dad! At least the man who did that horrible stuff to me doesn't belong to me. I'm never going to forgive him for what he did. Maybe someday I'll find my real dad, and tell him what my life was like, and he can find Danny and ... and ... and ...*

Julie let her mind wander so far that it never came back the rest of that night. She still had to go to the football field and play in the pep band, pretending that her Friday was as normal as everyone else's; that her biggest decision that night was whether or not to go to the dance after the game. She had so much to think about. Julie remembered the YFC meeting, and Bret's teaching about earthly fathers and heavenly fathers. *Thank You, God, that Danny isn't really my earthly father after all! Maybe you have something good planned for me!* Julie slept more peacefully than she would have thought possible.

CHAPTER FIFTEEN

ERIK

The inscription under Erik Martin's high school yearbook picture read: "There was never a saint with red hair." Green eyed, freckled, cocky Erik played varsity football and attacked life with the same full-tilt, reckless abandon. He was six-two, muscular and handsome—and if that wasn't enough to seal his popularity, he swore, smoked, drank, and flirted with the boundaries of legal behavior.

Erik had graduated from Coldspring four years earlier. He lived in Detroit, worked construction, and came home in the fall for high school football games.

"Hey, Erik!" His sister Lori, slightly overweight and pleasantly quirky, motioned Erik to her seat on the top row of the home team bleachers. "I want you to meet my friend, Julie."

Erik walked through a gauntlet of high-fives and arm pumps, his legendary football prowess making him a Friday-night attraction.

"Hey yourself, little sis. Who's your pal?" Erik's mouth was well hidden under a bushy moustache.

"This is Julie—my friend, and hopefully, partner in crime."

Julie didn't miss the once-over glance from Erik or the hunger in his eyes. She was already in over her head.

"Hi, Erik." It would have been foolish for Julie to act like she didn't know who Erik was, or what he was. Her sixth sense from years of living with her parents told her that Erik lived on the wild side. *Here is a guy who picks his kicks and probably has no idea what the kickbacks are.*

"Maybe I should join you. It looks like you're coming apart." Erik had a keen grasp on old jokes, which was oddly endearing to Julie. Squeezing between his sister and her friend, Erik's letter jacket hung on him like the mantle of a conquering hero. For the rest of the game, Julie barely paid attention to touchdowns and extra points, aware instead of Erik's shoulder brushing up against hers, tingling sensations doing a tap-dance up and down her arm. When Erik leaned in close to explain the finer points of football to Julie, his breath smelling of beer and Fritos, Julie figured she was in trouble. *This guy is a definite bad boy. If I were smart, I'd get out of here while I still can.* But here was a guy—strong, older, probably a hard worker—paying attention to Julie, acting like it mattered to him that Julie understood a game that had represented all that was good for him. She was being invited into a guy's life for all the right reasons.

When the football game was over, Erik gave Julie a chivalrous kiss on the cheek, planted another tender kiss on the top of Lori's head, and wove through the bleachers, cradling an imaginary football, pretending to duck his opponents, and doing the 'touchdown dance' as he hopped down the final step to the grass. Erik waved a benediction over the crowd. "Smoke 'em if you got 'em!" he yelled.

"Come back and visit! Don't be a stranger—you're already strange enough as it is!" This was Lori's signature send-off to Erik. "And tell George to get off work next Friday night, so he can come back up with you!" Erik turned around and started running backwards as he waved and shouted,

"Later, Laurence!" Julie knew she was already swimming in deep water. *Hopefully it's not shark-infested.*

♦

Lori's boyfriend George, Erik, and two other guys all shared an apartment in Detroit. Erik, the oldest of the four, decided it was past time to christen their new apartment with the party-to-end-all-parties. The three guys' girlfriends all lived in Coldspring; Erik hoped Julie would be willing to drive down with them, and get to know him better. As soon as Erik returned from his trip to Coldspring, he had told George about Lori's friend Julie. He didn't even try to hide the fact that he was already smitten with her.

"Georgie-Boy, Julie Sandford is so different than any chick I've met here! The ones my age are too into their careers to get involved with a lowly construction worker. The younger ones are mostly airheads, even though it's nice to have them adore me for a while." Erik slouched back on the sofa, rearranging the cushions to cover the broken hide-a-bed mattress springs.

"Julie is sweet, and seems like the kind of girl who's a good thinker. She's got deep brown eyes ... I could lose myself in those eyes. Her hair is thick; she's got these bright, red lips ... it was all I could do to keep from kissing her and running my fingers through that amazing hair."

Erik and George raised their legs and plopped them onto the water-stained coffee table in a perfect harmony of protesting wood.

"Then it's settled." George used an economy of words. "When's the party?"

"How about next weekend? You're off work, and maybe we can get one of the girls' parents to let them all drive down here together. Do you think you could call Lori?"

"It's a done deal," said George.

♦

"Do I look stupid to you?"

Mom is famous for these unanswerable questions.
"Umm—"

"Why in the world would I let you drive down to Detroit to see a guy you just met? What do you know about him? What's his family like? Are you going to spend the whole weekend in his apartment? Does he have an extra bedroom for you and the other girls?" Julie heard the rapid-fire questions as thinly veiled accusations that she was too dumb to figure anything out on her own. *Well, I guess I haven't thought about some of this stuff; but she isn't exactly a poster child for wise advice.*

But wait: was that only three weeks ago when Bret talked about honoring our parents? Julie pushed aside the thought for now. *God, I promise to think about it again later if You'll let me do this one thing!*

Julie had already seen some of Erik's rough edges: She knew he drank, and his reputation for being a wild driver in high school was still talked about in driver's ed classes. But oh, he was tall! And muscular! And he had a good construction job. If he had a steady income, and intended to provide for her ... maybe someday ... well, who was she to pick nits? *After all, look what my father's like. If there's one thing he's done for me, it's lower the bar on my standard for men. It's not hard for any guy to jump over that. And Erik leaps over it!*

"Mom, I really, really want to do this with my friends. I promise I'll find out all the details before we go. I'll get you a phone number, and I'll make sure the four of us sleep in our own room together. I'm a senior; you have to start learning to trust me sometime."

Julie knew that Arlene had very little energy to drag herself to her part time job, and then home to veg out on the sofa for the evening. With no excess energy to do battle with her daughter, and nothing to gain from it, Julie figured her mom would eventually cave. Julie wrote little notes pleading her case, which she taped on her mom's bedroom mirror, the bathroom mirror, and the refrigerator. The notes disappeared without any explanation a few days later.

Arlene walked into Julie's room and stood in the doorway until Julie looked up from her English homework. Arlene crossed her arms. "Okay, I really don't care if you go, as long as you bring back the car with a full tank of gas. And, if you have a baby nine months from now, don't come crying to me, because I am not raising a bratty grandkid!"

Arlene stalked back to the living room. Julie raised her fist, pumped her arm, and said, "Yes, yes, yes!"

◆

Julie had had few adventures aside from moves, and none with three girlfriends. It was nearly impossible for her to concentrate in class for the remaining time until her trip. She actually couldn't believe her mom had given in to her – but after all, she would be graduating from high school in eight months, and then she'd be out on her own anyway. She also couldn't believe she'd gotten the whole weekend off from work, although she would have to take an extra shift of Glo's when she got back.

Tuesday night at Lakeview, Glo listened to Julie talk about Erik, about his roommates, about his construction job, and about how strong and capable Julie thought he was. "Have you prayed about Erik and this trip?" Glo's sincere eyes held Julie to her seat in the cafeteria. "No, but I know Erik's a good guy, and I can help him with the things that aren't so good. Once he falls for me, he's going to want to change those things." Julie spoke with more confidence than she felt at that moment. *Glo, if you only knew what kind of life I've lived with my family, you would realize how different Erik is from all of that. He definitely cares about me, which is more than I can say about my father.*

Glo got up from the table, pushed her chair in, said, "Julie, friend, I'll pray for you this weekend," and went back to work. Julie sat another five minutes staring at her pop can, hoping she was making the right choice.

♦

Michigan people love to joke with 'outsiders' about their four seasons: winter's coming, winter's here, Fourth of July, and road construction. Julie awoke Friday morning to a spectacular fall day, the kind that is a carefully guarded secret to keep out all of the 'undesirables,' she supposed. The humidity masqueraded as Phoenix—an insignificant topic of conversation. Late-summer tulips and phlox proudly bloomed in vibrant colors. The air was pungent with the smell of wood smoke. The sky was a deep blue, spread like a vast ocean undulating in gentle waves. Pencil thin clouds knifed through the sky, barely distinguishable from a jet trail arching over the horizon.

Julie felt like a racehorse at the starting block, ready to burst through the gate and explode down the track. She didn't know how she'd tolerate seven periods of classes before she and her friends began their adventure.

At three-thirty, Julie, Lori, Melissa and Jacqueline threw their backpacks into their lockers, slammed the clangy metal doors shut, and raced out to the parking lot. The cars and trucks were a mix of gleaming chariots—gifts from upper-middle-class parents—and rusted knights-of-old, held together with baling wire and prayer. Some, like Arlene's blue Chevy Nova, were on loan, pressed into humble service by semi-grateful kids.

The Nova's front and back bumpers were plastered with faded stickers which said things like "Kiss Me—I'm Desperate," "A closed mouth gathers no feet," and "Mr. Potato Head For President." As Julie and Lori climbed into the front seat, Mel and Jack stood next to the back doors, waving to friends, fixing their hair, and tipping their faces up to the sun, reveling in the magnificence of the day.

"Hey, you guys, let's boogie. This car's heading south!" Julie started the engine and rolled down her window. She and Lori looked at each other. Julie whispered, "One, two, three." On her cue she and Lori sang, in perfect timing, "Get your motor runnin' –"

"Head out on the highway." Mel and Jack joined in as they opened their doors, slid in, slammed the doors, and rolled down their windows. "Lookin' for adventure, and whatever comes our way. Born to be wild!"

The Nova hit cruising speed on interstate seventy-five heading to Detroit. The fall colors faded to summer green as they drove further south. With the gradual decrease in daylight and the increase in traffic, Julie concentrated on her navigation; the odometer crept up from sixty-five to almost seventy-five. *I hope the four of us have enough money between us to pay a speeding ticket.* With Mel and Jack giggling in the back seat and singing to the songs on the radio, Julie and Lori were more subdued in the front, watching the traffic, looking out for cops, and keeping an eye on the gas gauge.

At seven-fifteen the four happy travelers eased into a parking spot at their boyfriends' apartment on the south side of the city. As they spilled out of the car, Julie went around to the back and opened the trunk. The girls pulled out their duffle bags and heard "Incoming!" from across the parking lot. Erik, George, J.J. and Zeke were running toward them. George was the first to reach the quartet; pitching aside Lori's duffle bag, he wrapped her in a bear hug and swung her around until she screamed, "Enough already—I'm going to hurl!" J.J. and Zeke did the same with Mel and Jack. Julie and Erik stood facing each other, although not at all awkwardly. Erik put out his hand, Julie gingerly took it, and they walked slowly back to the apartment. It was natural and easy. *Where has this guy been all my life?*

Ten minutes later all eight of them were in the living room sitting on an 'L'-shaped sectional sofa, arms and legs wrapped around each other like tendrils. Erik disentangled himself and shot up, almost knocking Julie to the floor. "Let's get this party started!" As soon as he disappeared into the kitchen, more people appeared at the front door. By nine o'clock the party of eight had tripled.

Julie tried to stay in the background, feeling slightly out of place among Erik's roommates and friends. Julie assumed she and her girlfriends were the only high schoolers there. Everyone else looked much older: the guys sported bushy mustaches and beards; the girls had that 'been there, done that' look. Adding to Julie's nervousness was an empty stomach. The last thing she'd eaten was a bagel for breakfast. The living room was beginning to fill with the sweet-and-sour smell of marijuana and the yeasty smell of beer. It was suddenly too much for Julie.

Oh God—I think I made a big mistake. I shouldn't be here. I'm not sure why Erik invited me ... but I'd rather wait to see him again after he comes back up for a visit.

Their big adventure felt more frightening than daring. Julie had spent enough years living in the wake of the raging torrent of alcohol to know first-hand what kind of destruction it left. She had determined never to drink or do drugs, especially after that barroom episode with her dad. Now she found herself back in the water.

♦

J.J. sauntered into the living room with his unbuttoned denim shirt hanging over a pair of khaki shorts. "Presto!" He held up a pan of brownies like the spoils of victory. "Who's hungry?" he slurred. Julie caught the pan as J.J. tipped it forward.

"You're a lifesaver!" Julie had found the Holy Grail. She parted a group of guys standing in front of the kitchen door, went in and set the pan carefully on the red tiled counter. She yanked opened a drawer and found sharp knives and spatulas. Julie cut the brownies and took two before the others dove into the pan.

Plopping down on the only vacant space on the sofa, Julie quickly jumped up again when her backside made contact with broken springs. Hunger overcame good manners: Julie stood in the middle of the living room and consumed both brownies in four bites each. *I know there's an abundance of beer here—no good after brownies. I need cold milk.* Julie headed back to the kitchen, once again parting the sea of guys blocking her way.

Foraging through the cupboards, she found a plastic McDonald's cup. In the mostly-bare fridge was a lonely-looking carton of milk. Julie emptied the carton into her cup, tossed it in the sink, took her cup to the table and sat down on a duct-taped, vinyl kitchen chair. She gulped the milk, dropped the cup on the floor, folded her arms on the table, lowered her head and closed her eyes.

Bells were clanging in Julie's head. *That milk must have been bad. My head feels like it wants to leave my body, and my stomach doesn't feel too good, either.*

J.J. walked into the kitchen and used the knife to dig out a brownie. "Hey Julie, what do you think of the brownies?"

Julie muttered something incoherent, face still buried in her arms.

"Have you ever had hash brownies before? They're the best trip I know!"

Julie slowly raised her head. "What?"

"Yeah girl, you're going to be stoned good for the rest of the night!" J.J. seemed proud of his new convert.

Julie knew she would need the bathroom very, very quickly. She stumbled out of the kitchen, ran down the hall and found the bathroom vacant. After her stomach emptied, she opened the door and wandered farther down the hall to a room that looked like a bedroom. Piles of clothes, shoes, tennis racquets, record albums, and fast food containers littered every square inch of the floor. Julie didn't care what she stepped on, as long as she made it to the bed. Pushing aside a football and a cap, she sprawled on the bed. A cold wind blew through a wide-open window. *I wish someone would come in and cover me with a blanket.* That was Julie's last thought before she passed out.

♦

Erik hadn't seen Julie for a while. "Hey Tin Man, where's my woman?" J.J. was sitting at the kitchen table, using his finger to dig the remainder of the brownies out of the corner of the pan. "I don't know, man; she was here, she wasn't looking too good, and then she was gone." Erik wandered down the hall, looked in his roommates' bedrooms, and then checked his own, where he discovered Julie lying spread eagle on his bed, head turned to one side, a thin line of drool hanging out of her mouth. Erik crept inside, quietly closed the door behind him and turned the lock.

♦

Julie stirred while her hand instinctively reached up and gingerly pressed down on her forehead. With her eyes in slits she made out a blurry outline. It looked like Erik, but who knew what tricks her drugged brain might be playing on her?

And was this guy straddling her? She felt hands groping for her buttons, while a rush of cold air hit her exposed chest. Julie tried to push her numbed brain out of its fog.

"Don't … do … this …" Julie's voice was hoarse. "Please … wait … no …"

Erik finished, got up, pulled his shorts back on and left the room. *Have I been dreaming? Was Erik here?* Julie fell asleep again.

The next time Julie awoke, her eyes seemed to be in better focus. She sat up, swung her legs over the side of the bed, buttoned her blouse, retrieved the rest of her clothes and put herself back together. *I wonder how much time has passed since I stumbled, mostly dead, into this room? Maybe that was an hour ago. Maybe three. I'm freezing. I need to get out of here. Where are my flip-flops?* Julie wanted to gather her posse and leave. Even her mom's 'I-told-you-so' would be better than staying here any longer.

As Julie grabbed the doorknob, the door pushed towards her. Erik's surprised look turned to delight. "Hi, hon." He stepped inside, turned, closed and locked the door, grabbed Julie's elbow and pulled her back toward the bed. Too weak to resist, Julie sat down.

"I thought we could, you know, fool around a little bit. I locked the door so we won't be interrupted." Erik put his arm around Julie.

"Are you kidding me? Didn't you get enough last time?" Julie shoved Erik back and rose slowly to her feet. "Get over there and unlock that door or I'll think of a lot of words I can scream." Julie was shaking from fear, anger, and cold.

Erik erupted in an eerie laugh. "Who do you think you're kidding? No one will hear you from in here." The music was amped to the max in the living room.

Julie turned and glared. "There's nothing you can do to me that my own father hasn't already done. But you're no match for him. I had a showdown with him, and I'm not afraid to do the same with you."

Erik rose slowly, clapped his hands in mock applause, and strutted over to the door. He turned the lock, opened the door, bowed, and swept his arm across the air. "M'lady," he said in a British accent. Julie ran past him, resolve melting into despair. *Why do I always end up in these sink holes?* She hurried around the apartment in spite of the feeling that someone had attached a ball and chain to her ankles. Passed out bodies were scattered on the floors of every room like the aftermath of a train wreck. Lori, Mel and Jack were the lone survivors, huddled in a corner of the living room watching reruns of "I Love Lucy". When Julie spied them, she practically launched herself into them.

"Julie! What's the matter with you?" Mel had genuine concern etched on her face.

"Can we leave? I don't even know what time it is, and I can't talk about it right now, but I want to go home. If we take turns driving, we should make it home okay." Julie melted into tears.

"Sure girl, we're about through with this stupid party anyway." Mel unfolded her legs and got up from the floor, rubbing out her stiff muscles.

"Did my brother do something to you?" Lori's voice was equally concerned.

"I'll be fine." Julie couldn't believe how stupid that sounded. The girls quickly gathered their purses and duffle bags, left the apartment and walked to the car, huddling together for warmth. After wiping the condensation off the windows, Julie handed Mel the keys and climbed into the backseat.

Looking out her window at the sky spread with a million stars drew Julie back to the night in Washington when Grandma Hagstrom had stepped out of the cab; to the summer she, her mom and brother had patrolled the streets of Platteville looking for her dad's truck in front of whichever was his bar-of-the-night; and then again to the time they had made their escape. The common denominator in her life seemed to be booze: even though someone else bought it, she always paid the biggest price in innocence and dreams. That gun had already been fired and there was no reloading it.

No one talked or sang. Mel flipped through radio stations until she found one with a man's blaring voice lamenting the poor treatment of returning Vietnam vets. *At least the war's over for them. Battles keep finding me.* Julie turned her head from the window and wept silent tears the rest of the way home.

♦

The girls were climbing into their own beds by the time the sun rose on another day in Coldspring. The sun was low in the sky when Julie awoke again, her head not yet clear enough to discern dawn from dusk, or even what day it was. *I wonder why Mom didn't come in here to ask me anything. I should know better by now: As long as nothing rocks her boat, she'll let me struggle in the water by myself. An occasional lifeline would be nice.*

A shrill ring broke into Julie's thoughts. Moments later Arlene appeared at her bedroom door as though it was the most natural thing in the world for Julie to be home early and sleeping at ... whatever time it was.

"Your friend Erik's on the phone." Arlene twirled the receiver connected to the phone in the living room by a twenty-five-foot cord.

"No! I don't care what you tell him, I am *not* going to talk to him! Ever!" Julie's head began to throb again.

"Suit yourself—I don't care one way or the other." Arlene turned and walked back down the hall, the coiled cord trailing her in perfect submission.

Julie didn't figure Erik would take rejection casually, but that was her plan. He was only coming up for one more football game, and she could find an excuse to be somewhere else. *The avoidance infrastructure is secure. I wonder where my heart fits in.*

The next day, Sunday, Erik called repeatedly. Arlene quit answering the phone after the third call. Julie's nerves were on the ragged edge: Anything was better than the unrelenting ringing.

"Julie? Hi. It's Erik. Hey, I'm really sorry about the misunderstanding when you were down here."

"I understood perfectly." Julie gave no ground.

"Babe, let's start over again. The hash in those brownies, the beer ... everything made me looney. I'd never hurt you. We won't have sex until you're ready. I really want to see you again, and this time we'll go out to a movie or something. And hey, what did you mean by 'I had a show-down with my father?' Did something happen before you came down?"

"Not really." Julie hated that her heart was thawing.

"Would it help if I talked to your dad?"

If only. "No! I mean no, it wouldn't. My dad's a ... a ... pervert."

"So is mine, especially when he ogles the babes in the swimsuit issue of 'Sports Illustrated—"

"No! He really is! He's done stuff to me. When you did what you did last night, it was like him all over again."

"I'm sorry."

"I'm not looking for sympathy. I simply want you to know why I was so mad."

"Could we start over?"

"Really?"

"Really."

♦

Erik called Julie every night at eleven-thirty to make sure he'd catch her at home after her shift ended at Lakehaven. They talked about work and movies and books and high school and football—and each was reluctant to hang up on the other. Julie didn't think it was possible to have a guy for a best friend until Erik came along.

Erik didn't invite Julie down to his apartment again. When he traveled home to Coldspring over Thanksgiving, he invited her to share dinner with his family.

After a long and balmy fall, winter arrived early, carrying a grudge. An arctic wind roared down from Canada, plunging northern Michigan into temperatures hovering at zero, well below normal for that time of year. After a filling Thanksgiving dinner and a delightful time with Erik's parents, Lori, and his two younger sisters, Erik pulled Julie into the vacant den.

"Babe, let's you and me go for a drive. My Firebird has a good heater and we'll have a toasty ride up the shore. How about it?" Erik touched Julie's face. For a fleeting moment, her mind raced back to her times in the car with Teddy Boy. *I haven't driven with Erik before. Do I have any reason not to trust him? Okay, Julie, get a grip.*

"Sure, that sounds great." Julie and Erik hugged the Martin family members, bundled up and ran shivering and laughing out to Erik's car. Julie sat on her gloved hands, waiting for them to warm up.

"Hon, let's sit here for a few minutes. There's something I've been wanting to give you all night." Erik took off his polar fleece glove, reached into his parka and pulled out a small, black, velvet box. "This is for you."

Julie held her breath, pulled her hands out from under her, stripped both gloves off, and reached for the box. She opened it to a simple ring, with a diamond chip in the center.

Releasing her breath in a puff of cold air, Julie said, "Erik, does this mean what I think it means?"

Erik smiled. "What do you want it to mean?"

"It … it looks like a 'promise ring.'"

"That's exactly what it is. I want us to get married someday." Erik removed the ring and slipped it onto Julie's left hand. "When I can make some more money and move us into a nice apartment, I'll get down on one knee and do this the right way."

"Oh Erik, do we have to take a drive? I want to run back in the house and share this with your family!"

Erik shut off the engine. He took both of Julie's hands in his, one still hidden in a warm glove, and said, "Julie, you've made me a very happy guy. I'll do *anything* for you!"

For the rest of the evening they played Monopoly, Risk and Rook with Erik's family. By ten o'clock, hungry people were rummaging around in the kitchen for leftover turkey, stuffing, and pumpkin pie. It was the perfect end to a storybook day for Julie, whose life had been miserably void of happy families and the love of a good guy like Erik, her husband some day.

♦

Julie's days were filled with school, her job at Lakehaven, girlfriends, and Erik—everything she had always wanted. She spent a large portion of her paycheck on long-distance phone bills, counting the days until Erik would be coming back home. The only real sadness in her life was avoiding Gloria, who was pleasant, always solicitous, and continually inviting Julie to return to more YFC meetings with Bret. *If I go back to those meetings, I'll have to face the possibility that Erik shouldn't be in my life, and I just can't do that.*

With the approach of the Christmas season Julie's white knight was falling off his horse more frequently than ever. His visits home began with a pleasant evening with Julie and his family: board games were laid out, the popcorn air popper was brought out of retirement, and a game of silly-story one-upmanship was played into sudden-death over-time. But the increasingly predictable ending was Erik and Julie having a free-for-all argument either in the den or out in the driveway in his car. Julie would beg Erik to stop drinking; Erik would promise that this would be his last time. Each time was another dejá vu. At some point Erik had passed the social drinking mile-marker with his temper heading toward a dangerous curve. Julie longed for his family to step on the brake, but Erik's charm always won the day. He sent money to his parents every time his dad was laid off from work; and if they weren't completely blind to their son's drinking, they certainly squinted their eyes and saw a 'good ole boy' having a 'good ole time.' *What if my life with him becomes a bad copy of life at home?*

The next time Erik drove back for a visit, the family gathered in the den for a lively game of Life. At the end of the game Julie had three kids, a mortgage, and the prospect of bankruptcy. *My life really is full of irony.* "Erik, can we go for a drive?" As soon as they got into Erik's car parked in front of his house she determined to speak her mind *before* becoming trapped in a speeding bullet with an angry Superman.

"I need to tell you something." Julie reached for Erik's hand and wished her teeth would stop chattering. "These past months have been really great. I know you care about me, and I care about you." Erik stared straight ahead.

"You also know what life with my dad was like. Maybe another girl wouldn't have a problem dealing with how you get when you drink, but for me it pushes 'rewind' buttons that play too many bad memories. I can keep your ring—you know part of me will always love you. But I'm sorry, I can't marry you."

Julie waited for some sign of rage, but was instead shocked when Erik dropped his head on the steering wheel and started to sob uncontrollably. Julie had never seen a man cry, and it almost undid her resolve. She opened the car door, ran back into the house and found Lori coming out of the bathroom.

"Lori, please, please take me home and don't ask any questions. I'll tell you what happened when we get back to school Monday. Say goodbye to your family for me." Julie ran through the kitchen to the attached garage and waited in the Martin car for Lori.

Lori didn't say anything during the ride. Julie had used the blunt weapon of her emotion to chip at the impenetrable wall of silence that surrounds alcoholic families, but it was nevertheless seen as a threat, and she was locked out. By the time they were back at school Monday, Julie was no longer in the orbit of Lori's friendship.

CHAPTER SIXTEEN

THE REVOLVING DOOR

It was still too early to assess all of the damage done by hurricanes Teddy and Erik. The point of impact for both storms was Julie's self-worth, which had been tossed and blown and strewn around the fragile landscape of her heart. She intended to bury the leftover bits and pieces without any plan of rebuilding even a temporary relationship shelter.

♦

Christmas had come and gone without Danny's presence. Arlene's 'new' apartment was pitiable and bleak, but at least it was intact. Julie's plan was to focus on graduation, which was a little over five months away. Then she could pick a path for her life that would not be bordered by emotional and financial poverty. *If I* ever *get married, it's going to have to be to a guy who will work hard, drink easy and love me totally. In the meantime, I've got work and school to keep me busy.*

♦

A worn-down teacher in a threadbare sweater seemed way beyond caring whether or not his students understood the world financial markets during fourth period economics. Almost everyone in class was staring out the window at the enormous snowflakes swirling around the flagpole while 'Oblivious Mr. Silvius' was sitting in front of an overhead projector, using a pointer to illustrate a sequence of vastly tedious economic ideologies.

When Julie pulled her attention back to the room, she noticed a guy looking her way. *I shouldn't be thinking about anyone else! I'm not even over Erik yet!*

"Tom—Tom Dietrich. Do you have a minute?" Mr. Silvius usually did something to try to wake up his class about midway through the period. His most creative effort seemed to be reminding the students of their names, first and last.

So his name is Tom. *I wonder what he's like?* At the bell Julie gathered her books and headed out the door toward the cafeteria. Tom was already leaning against the vending machine near the lunch lady, watching Julie as she walked closer.

"Hi. I'm Tom. I noticed you back in November and I've wanted to meet you. Word on the street was that you were dating 'Gin Martini.'" Tom's easy smile reached eyes partially hidden behind glasses. He stood a few inches taller than Julie, and had a crease around his forehead, probably from the rim of a cap. Julie definitely noticed that his black t-shirt was stretched tightly across his chest and upper arms, barely containing well-defined muscles. The beginnings of a wiry mustache gave Tom a rugged look, and Julie knew instantly that she liked the whole wrapping.

"Would you like to go out some time? Maybe tomorrow after I get off work at six."

"Yeah—I'd like that." Julie felt her face flush.

"Okay, let's meet at McDonald's out on the highway. I'll be there around six-thirty."

"Where do you work?" Julie wanted Tom to stay a little longer.

"Knutson Sod. I load and carry big rolls. I'm really into grass!"

That's obviously a well-rehearsed line. What a goof!

Julie smiled, said "Bye then," and got in the hot lunch line. *I'm trolling through some unknown water here, and I don't know how deep it is. Maybe I should go slowly.*

♦

That first date with Tom set the relationship-wheels in motion. Julie loved the fact that Tom was a good listener, interested in her opinions. They had a lot of fun together going to movies, hanging out with Tom's friends, and driving around Pleasant Lake.

On a frigid Friday night in mid-February, Julie and Tom and four of their friends were driving in Tom's car, laughing and singing to the 8-tracks, checking out the movie theater, bowling alley, and pool hall looking for cheap entertainment, but not really wanting to leave the warm cocoon of their car for the icy blast of winter waiting in ambush for them. When his gas gauge and energy level eventually dropped to empty, Tom deposited their friends at Jim's house and shouted, "Close that door and move your dupas!" He laughed, cranked up the heater to full throttle, and blew out his breath in puffs of warm, moist air that immediately frosted the windows. He turned to Julie.

"Hey girl, wouldn't this be a good time?"

"A good time for what?" Julie's heart sank.

"You know. We've been dating for a while. Guys at school are starting to tease me about not getting to home base with you yet." Tom turned his head and began caressing the steering wheel with his left hand.

"So? What do I care about what your friends think? A bunch of jocks aren't going to decide anything about my life." Suddenly the car didn't feel so cold anymore. Julie's anger was a good furnace.

"Look Julie, I have a right to expect this. I care a lot about you, and I know you care about me. So what's the deal?" Tom was facing Julie again, eyes boring holes in her courage.

"Tom, I'm not ready for this. There's stuff you don't know … I need some more time." Julie was in the middle of a maze and couldn't find her way out.

"I don't need any more time! If you're not ready, then you're probably not the chick for me anyway. I'll take you home." Tom gunned the engine, cranked up the radio, and drove the next ten minutes in stony silence. When they pulled up to Julie's apartment, she turned to Tom, who seemed intensely interested in the streetlight. When she opened her door and turned to say goodbye, he kept his body stiff, eyes unblinking. Julie was being dismissed for the umpteenth time in her life. She slammed the door and ran to her house, tears freezing on her cheeks.

♦

Julie walked in on her mom lounging on the sofa in a housedress and fuzzy slippers, working a crossword puzzle. If there were any roads of sympathy that led to this house, they yielded the right-of-way whenever Arlene's welfare was in jeopardy. Julie's full-throttle, head-on collisions with both Teddy and Erik hadn't seemed to attract any attention from her mom. Julie shrugged out of her parka, hung it on a hook in the closet, and walked toward the kitchen.

"Julie, is that you?" Arlene didn't look up from her cross-word puzzle.

Yeah, Mom, it's really me. I walked right through your intersection. "What do you want—I'm kind of tired." She spoke into the refrigerator, desperately wishing for a comforting friend instead of day-old Spamloaf.

"Come in here, I need to tell you something."

Julie slid open the meat drawer, grabbed a slice of wrapped American cheese, slowly closed the drawer and then the fridge, and wandered back out to the living room. Unwrapping the cheese, she watched the clear wrapper flutter to the coffee table. "Yeah?" She folded the cheese into quarters and popped it in her mouth.

"We have to move again. This place gives me the creeps anyway. There's a guy down the hall who's always standing there watching me when I get the paper in the morning, no matter what time it is. I heard of a good apartment not far from here. You can take me to work and then drive your-self to school. I know you want to finish out your senior year there." Arlene's attempt at sympathy sharpened Julie's suspicion radar.

"Are we being evicted again?"

"What are you talking about?" Arlene seemed only mildly offended.

"It's taken me years to connect the dots, but I finally understand that we didn't move all those times because of a creepy neighbor, or a better job opportunity for Dad—for *Danny*—or to be closer to Grandma and Grandpa, or anything else. We moved because we couldn't pay our rent." Julie walked back into the kitchen in search of something to drink.

"That's not a very respectful way to talk to your mother!" Arlene crumpled up the newspaper and threw it at a defense-less spider plant, half dead, hanging in a plastic pot from a hook in the ceiling. A carpet of dried brown leaves was spread on the floor underneath it.

Julie popped the cap from a bottle of Coke, pitched it on the counter, and took a big gulp of the fizzy, throat-burning liquid as she walked back to the living room.

"I didn't mean to be disrespectful. I'm really tired ... and I'm trying to figure out life."

"It isn't rocket science. Some people say 'God works in mysterious ways,' but it's no mystery. When you're down he squashes you, so you gotta make sure you stay out from under His thumb." Arlene shifted gears. "So you think that Teddy-Boy friend of yours could bring over his truck and help us move?"

Julie froze. *Mom, try to keep up! For cryin' out loud, he was three boyfriends ago!*

"Why can't Dan help us?" Julie was perfecting the sport of deflection.

"When he got fired his truck was repoed. His fool boss didn't believe him when he said he got to work late last week because he had trouble with his truck."

Dan has to be Danny's biological son. Blame and excuses are both in their DNA, and there's obviously no lifeguard in that gene pool.

Julie had an inexplicable surge of sympathy for her mom; and after the earlier events of this long night she had no desire to fight her anymore. "Okay, I'll call Mama T and see if she knows where Teddy is." The last Julie heard, Teddy had dropped out of high school—*probably with Mama T's blessing*—to try to get into some over-the-road trucking school.

Julie climbed into bed aching for a friend like Glo, whom she was still avoiding. Erik's family had filled in the gap for a while, but that ship had sailed. All of Tom's friends would jump the fence when they found out he had dumped her.

Julie pounded and folded her pillow. *I wonder where Eugene is, and if he ever thinks about the infant girl he left behind?*

♦

After work the next day Julie dialed Mama T's number. On the third ring a voice answered. "Ja? Wo ist dis?"

"Hi, Mama T? It's me."

"Julie! Es ist so *gut* to hear from you!" Before she could even ask for Teddy, Julie had been invited over for dinner that weekend.

♦

Mama T's hugs were magic, as though she were 'unfreezing' kids playing a game of tag. Something in Teddy had changed; he didn't show any awkwardness about helping Julie's family move the week after her phone call. Julie had decided not to tell Teddy that their new apartment was up a long flight of stairs, and Teddy surprised Julie by counting the steps and good-naturedly laughing about it.

"Twenty-three steps! Good thing you packed everything in small boxes. And thank God for furnished apartments!" Teddy laughed and headed back down the stairs.

"Thanks for helping!" Julie shouted, thinking he was finished and heading home.

"I'll be back—got three boxes left." Teddy reappeared five minutes later. "Maybe 'twenty-three' is our magic number," he exclaimed to Julie after the last box had been stacked against a wall of the living room. Putting his arm around her, he whispered, "We could get married on March twenty-third; we could have twenty-three guests at our wedding; I could lay twenty-three rose petals on your pillow on our honeymoon night." For the moment, the surge of romance in Julie's heart was stronger than the warning bells going off in her head.

♦

In spite of the fact that Mama T had a wedding dress sewn for Julie within a month of her rekindled relationship with Teddy, and that Teddy had insisted on getting to know his future mother-in-law, his behavior returned to the rhythm of anger and apology, rage and remorse. *This is recycled Teddy. Or Erik revisited. I can't even keep the players straight anymore.* Julie felt like the ante in a high stakes poker game, tossed in to the middle of something she was increasingly desperate to flee.

Teddy was eating another Sunday brunch at Julie's and conducting a fact-finding tour of her mom's personality. *Good luck with that.* As Teddy kept up a lively monologue, Julie knew it was time for a talk with him alone. As soon as they finished eating, Julie took Teddy's hand and led him to the worn, brown, Naugahyde sofa in the living room. *Whatever happens in this conversation, I'm for sure not going to be doing sixty-five in a car or on a motorcycle.* And even though Julie hadn't seen her mom as any kind of a protector, she doubted Teddy would explode with Arlene nearby.

When Julie recognized the fact that she didn't trust more than a small corner of her heart to Teddy, she simply told him that she wasn't ready for any kind of serious relationship after all. Teddy got up and spewed a torrent of cuss words, then walked to the front door, turned around and erupted in a fountain of tears. As Julie sat staring at him, he opened the door, wiped his eyes on his sleeve, walked out and slammed the door behind him.

"Wait!" Julie leaped to the door, pulled it open and walked out in time to see Teddy pounding down each step, counting backwards from twenty-three as though erasing Julie from his life. As he shouted "thirteen!" he looked up in time to avoid plowing into Erik. Teddy blew past Erik, ran down and threw his weight into the front door, pushing it open so hard he practically fell out. Erik turned as a blast of lingering winter air snuck in before the door banged shut. Turning back around again he looked up at Julie and said, "Who was that?" as he took the remaining steps two at a time.

"Never mind. What are *you* doing here?"

"Babe, I haven't seen you in over three months." Erik put his hands on Julie's waist. "I've been here for the weekend and I found out where you and your family moved to. I had to come over and see you. Let's go in and sit down."

Julie was pulled into the apartment by a force from her past that left her feeling colder than the wintry air. Erik guided her to the sofa and sat down on the floor in front of her. "Julie, my family confronted me about my drinking the night you left. I promised them I'd quit, and I haven't had a drink since. I sold my car and bought a little Plymouth Duster. I'm going to change and I want you to marry me."

This can't be happening. If it were a 'Movie-of-the-Week,' people would yell 'Psych!' and flip the channel.

"Before you say anything," Erik continued, "I bought you a real engagement ring this time." He started to reach into the inside pocket of his camouflage hunting jacket.

"No! Stop!" Julie jumped up. "This is nuts! I can't marry you. I wouldn't marry Teddy—he's the guy who almost mowed you down on the stairs. Please, please, leave me alone!" Julie started to sob.

Erik slowly rose, wrapped his arms around Julie and pulled her head into his shoulder. Her arms hung loosely at her sides.

"Julie, I know this is what you want." Erik waited.

Measure twice, cut once. Julie pulled back her head, breaking his hold without touching him. "No, Erik, it's over. Please go."

Erik reached into his pocket, took out the velvet ring box, threw it through the still-open front door, and walked out. Julie ran into her bedroom and flung herself onto her bed. *How many girls are lucky enough to have one guy propose to them, much less two, and on the same night? I don't know what I want anymore.*

♦

Teenage romance was nothing newsworthy at Coldspring High School; a pre-graduation wedding was grist for the rumor mill. Sharon Dietrich, Tom's sister, had been told by a supposedly reliable source that Julie Sandford was going to marry Teddy Tannenbaum. Sharon liked Julie, had seen how happy her brother had been when he was dating her, and wanted to at least give her brother a chance to throw his hat in the ring.

Sharon was waiting for Tom when he got home from work. As soon as she told him about Julie, Tom quickly showered and drove over to her apartment, tires sliding over ice-covered roads.

Tom opened the front door of Julie's apartment and raced up the stairs. His attention was drawn to something hitting the wall and a guy headed down towards him.

"Erik Martin?" Tom stopped and grabbed the handrail.

"Yeah?" Erik glared, face and hair the same angry shade of red.

♦

Someone was shaking Julie's shoulder. "I don't know what's going on outside our apartment, but you better get out there!" Arlene disappeared like a ghost.

Julie sat up, rubbed her stiff neck, ran her fingers through her hair, and emerged from her room into the gathering darkness of the living room.

"Get out of my way!" A familiar voice was yelling outside her apartment.

Julie reached the front door and looked out as Tom and Erik were squaring off on ... *the thirteenth step?*

"Stop!" Julie's face was ashen.

Erik dropped his clenched fist, turned and glared at her. "It's him or me!"

"I'm sorry, Erik. Nothing's changed." Pity, fear, and anger all mixed together to make a sour taste in her mouth.

Erik shoved Tom into the wall, tore down the steps and out the popular door.

Tom looked at her. "This isn't exactly what I had planned."

Julie crossed her arms. "Oh? And what exactly *were* your plans?"

Tom ascended the remaining stairs and put his hands on her shoulders. "I don't know. I was wrong before. I shouldn't have pressured you, and I was dumb to let you go. I really want to marry you. I'll be good to you. I'll work hard. You know I will."

Tom knew when to fold his cards, at least for the moment. He let go of Julie, turned around, and slowly descended the stairs.

Three blind mice: see how they run.

CHAPTER SEVENTEEN

SMOKE AND MIRRORS

May is a fickle month in northern Michigan. Sometimes spring is reluctant to shake itself awake after winter hibernation; at other times, the afternoon sun bakes the world in its unforgiving kiln.

Julie stood in the narthex of Redeemer Lutheran Church adjusting the bobby pins that held her wedding veil in place. Ceiling fans circulated air-conditioned relief from the relentless heat outside the stucco building. Beside her was Grandpa Cerbé, looking both nervous and glad that she had asked him to share this special day with her.

Danny lurked outside in the shadow of a maple tree, dressed in his regulation blue jeans, Wellington boots, and cap. Julie saw him through the tall, narrow window next to the heavy oak door, and simply turned away from him. This was not a day for her to dwell on what he had taken from her. She was ready to begin a new life with Tom.

As the organist launched into the notes of the "Wedding March," Julie crooked her arm in her Grandpa's, and turned to him. *I wonder what it would be like if I was holding the arm of my* real *dad right now. Would he be dressed in a white tux, or a plain, black, slightly out-of-date suit, like Grandpa? What advice would he give me? If he thought he made a mistake in marrying my mom, would he tell me to stop the madness here and now?*

"Grandpa, I'm scared. I don't think this is the right thing to do."

Grandpa squeezed Julie's hand and whispered, "Don't make the same mistake your mother did. You can walk away right now. Or, you can run!"

Tears threatened to make rivers of mascara down Julie's cheeks. "I can't, I just can't." *I think this is a mistake—except that Tom works hard, and he'll give me financial stability. Besides, we have shower gifts, and wedding gifts, and we couldn't return all of those. I'm through the turnstile now—it's too late to back out.*

After the simple ceremony, a small group of friends and family gathered around Tom and Julie, balancing cups of punch and plates of cake and trying to stay cool in the basement fellowship hall. As the newlyweds prepared to leave the church, Arlene found her daughter in the restroom changing from her rented wedding dress into white dress pants, blue tank top and white blazer.

"Here, Mom. Could you return my dress for me?" Julie handed her mom the dress on a hanger. *I never* did *get a new dress, did I?*

"I hope you know what you're doing. We all make mistakes—"

Julie turned and looked at her mom's reflection in the wall-to-wall mirror over the double sinks. "It's a little late for this talk now, isn't it? I made the right decision. Tom will take good care of me." She picked up her white shoes, shoved them into a plastic Payless bag, and turned back toward her mom. "Could you take these too?"

Arlene shrugged, draped the dress over her arm, took the bag and said, "Well then, enjoy your honeymoon. Could you get the door for me?"

Julie opened the door, patted her mom's shoulder, and watched the door close behind her. Glancing once more at the mirror, she said, "Mirror, mirror, on the wall, I'm *not* my mother after all."

◆

The Coldspring Hotel was a perfect place for a romantic honeymoon, the kind Julie had always dreamt about before she had given in to Tom's sexual desires. Their wedding night wasn't memorable for Julie, who emerged from the bathroom in a new negligee and found Tom sleeping soundly. She hadn't known why they'd been given a room with two double beds, but decided that since Tom was already snoring in one bed, she would get a good night's sleep in the other one. *I'm not going to let this bother me—we can start over tomorrow.* Julie was surprised, both at how tired she was, and how content she felt to have her own bed.

At five-thirty the next morning, Julie pulled aside the heavy curtains and looked out at a spectacular view of Pleasant Lake, marveling at how the color of the water changed from light blue near the shore to deeper blue, then blue-green, and finally to a blue too intense to describe. *The lake is an eternity of mystery and promise.* She turned from the window as Tom sat up, ran his fingers through his hair and said, "I'm starving."

Okay, so he's not *the most romantic guy on the planet.* "Where do you want to eat?" Julie walked towards Tom, hoping he'd compliment her figure showing through her nightie, pull her into bed and start their honeymoon over.

Instead, Tom got up and headed for the bathroom. "I figured we'd grab a quick bite at that family restaurant back in town. We've got to get home. I've got work to do. We're burning daylight here."

Julie sank on to the bed. *Ohmigosh. What have I done?* Within an hour the newlyweds were showered, dressed, packed and out the door. *Remember, Julie, this guy is a hard worker, and that's what you wanted. Maybe romance is highly overrated.*

Three days after their wedding, Julie and Tom officially graduated. Julie returned to school to pick up her diploma cover, say goodbye to her friends, brag about how Tom had wanted her to have his last name on her diploma, and close the door forever on the Sandford years.

◆

I'm about to move in to another trailer. There's *a surprise.* But this time Julie really was surprised, since the trailer was both clean and nicely furnished. Days before the wedding, Tom had told her about a ten-by-fifty-five foot trailer he had seen for sale for three thousand. The seller was an older man who had nursed his wife of forty-five years through a hideous battle with brain cancer, and after she died he hadn't wanted any memories of those months. When Julie heard the story she hoped she and Tom would never have to live through anything like that.

What will I do if Tom tells me he wants to park our new trailer in a trailer park somewhere? Speaking of memories, I sure don't want that *one popping back up. I'm not ready to tell Tom anything about Mr. Thomas. He was depraved and I was deprived—sounds like a bad country western song.*

Bill Kenney was mayor of Coldspring and a good older friend of Tom's. When Tom introduced Bill to Julie at their wedding reception, he said, "Julie, meet my friend Bill, giver of great wedding gifts!" Bill's gift was bigger than Julie had ever known in her life: an acre of land outside of the Coldspring city limits on scenic highway twenty-three.

◆

Julie moved her few belongings into the trailer and rummaged through a small box of keepsakes, looking for something to hang on the bare walls. She found a picture of a doll with masking tape still stuck to the back, a framed picture of her and Chris, a certificate from Mrs. Ryczek for memorizing Bible verses, and a poster of zoo animals. *Is this all I have from my childhood?*

After work, Tom walked into the trailer, found Julie, took her hand and led her out and up a short path. As they tried to outrun the mosquitoes, Tom said, "Whenever I tell my grandma that the mosquito is the Michigan state bird, she tells me that it's God's way of reminding us there really *is* a hell!"

The path opened into a clearing surrounding a large farmhouse. A stout-looking, sixtyish woman was sitting in an aluminum lawn chair on a porch that wrapped around at least one side of the house. *Reminds me of how I met Mama T!*

"Julie, this is Grandma Emma." Tom smiled at his grandmother.

The woman hoisted herself up and laughed as she disengaged herself from the chair suspended in the air by her wide hips. Ambling over to Julie, Grandma Emma wrapped her in a hug that almost suffocated her. Pulling back, she then grabbed both of Julie's hands in a bone-crushing grip. "You feel dese hands? I haf milked tvelf cows mit dese hands for almost fifty years. My husband, he drank da beer too much, und could nefer do da work he vas s'posed to do. Dese hands raised kinder und grandkinder. I by myself am now, und I don't mind it at all!" Grandma Emma released Julie's hands and caught Tom in an adoring hug. "I haf my boy back home!" *And she even sounds like Mama T!* "Any ting I haf is yours. Now come in und haf some dinner mit me."

197

♦

After a simple, filling meal with Grandma Emma, Tom and Julie walked back to their trailer in the cool dusk of early June. "Julie, I know I never told you much, because this is kind of painful, and I've tried to forget about it all. But maybe you should know." Tom stared at the familiar ruts on the ground.

I thought I was the only one dragging overloaded luggage into this marriage. They had come to a fire pit, and Tom motioned for Julie to sit on a stump, while he eased down onto an overturned pallet.

"My dad was killed when I was thirteen." Julie sucked in her breath. *Every time I asked you why your dad couldn't come to our wedding, you shrugged it off and said he was 'busy.' I should have pushed you harder for the truth.* Julie remained quiet. "About six months after he died, Mom married a bozo named Archie, a real loser who couldn't stand me and my sister."

We have more in common than you think. This is almost bizarre. Julie got up and started collecting sticks to throw in the pit. When she thought she was out of earshot, she talked to the crickets. "How much should I tell Tom? Am I being fair to him? What should I do?" Julie wandered back, tossed her sticks and sat on the stump.

Tom got up and arranged the sticks on top of a few large half-burned logs. "Mr. 'Arch-enemy' was robbing me and my sister blind! We never saw one penny of our monthly social security checks! I don't know why my mom didn't stop him. But by the time I reached sixteen, I couldn't stand it anymore. If I wasn't going to get my money, and I hated that jerk besides, I figured I'd blow. I threw all my stuff into a big army duffle, got in my car, and drove over to Grandma Emma's. About six months later, Sharon came too. And that's where we were living when I met you." Tom pulled a lighter out of his pocket, lit the kindling wood, waited for a good blaze, and walked to the trailer. Julie stayed outside until the fire was reduced to embers.

♦

"Grandma Emma, can I fill these jugs with water?" Julie was doing her daily water run. She and Tom had been in their trailer for six weeks without running water. *Maybe I should be thankful that at least we have electricity.* Tom had run a very long, heavy-duty extension cord from the trailer to her house. Their temporary light source was a small K-Mart desk lamp, which Julie carried around the trailer, plugging it in wherever she needed it. *Thank You, God, that our stove is gas.*

♦

Since Tom had promised to take care of Julie, he picked up construction jobs with his buddies when his hours at Knutson Sod dropped below full time. Julie knew a good man was taking care of her, and she felt like she was finally on the right road and driving in the rhythm and flow of traffic. She was sad, though, to have to give up her job at Lakehaven, since it was twenty miles from their trailer, and they only owned Tom's truck. *I should be thinking about what I'm going to do when I 'grow up.'* Glo had graduated and been accepted at Michigan State. College was way too expensive for Julie for now, but she hoped to go when she and Tom were settled somewhere, maybe after they moved into their own home.

The Hot'n Cold General Store was a place for Julie to get a job, meet people, relieve some of her boredom, and contribute her buck-sixty-five an hour to the family treasure chest. Since she would have to depend on new friends to drive her back and forth to work, she hoped to be welcomed into the community as a full-fledged adult.

♦

"Tom, who needs an alarm clock when we have your Grandma?" It was only six o'clock and the sun was already hot enough to blister the siding off the trailer. Tom was getting ready to leave for work and Julie was rolling out of bed, when there was a familiar knock at the door.

Julie brushed past Tom. "You should have married your Grandma Emma, so you would have someone to take care of you. I am definitely not her," Julie sneered, as she opened the door and greeted Emma with a genuine smile. She was still puzzling over this relationship between Tom and Emma; it was unlike anything she had experienced with any of her grandparents.

"I yust wanted to know if you haf enuf to eat dis morgen." It seemed to Julie that Emma was annoyingly spunky for this early.

"Yes, Grandma Emma, we're fine. Tom is getting ready to go to work."

"Okay, den, I come back tomorrow."

Sometimes Julie's job kept her past four, when Tom got home from work. By the time Julie returned, Tom was at Emma's eating dinner. *I'm Tom's wife, and he should be eating* my *cooking in* our *trailer.*

By the end of July, the unrelenting heat was frying Julie's nerves.

"What are you doing here, Tom?" Julie had arrived home from work at five-thirty, and walked into an empty trailer, oppressive heat clinging to the walls. Without stopping to change out of her work clothes, she had angrily marched up to Emma's house and banged through the door without knocking first.

Tom swallowed a forkful of meatloaf. "Well, you weren't home, and Grandma had dinner for me."

Julie seethed, "Your house is over there! I am your wife; I cook your meals."

Grandma sheepishly responded, "Vell, Julie, you're velcome to eat mit us here."

"No, Grandma, I'm not hungry and Tom's house isn't here anymore."

"I am truly sorry, Julie. I did not mean to offend you. Of course Tom shoult be at his house mit you."

"Oh, Grandma, it's okay, I guess." Julie sat down at the table, rested her folded arms and lowered her head. A large window fan blew cool air across her back.

Emma opened her freezer, took out a frosted mug, dumped a handful of ice into it, then opened the refrigerator, pulled out the lemonade, and poured it over the ice. The crackling sound of ice-versus-liquid caught Julie's attention. She lifted her head as Emma placed the glass in her hand. "Here, Julie, I haf some ting to make you feel better."

After taking a large gulp, Julie held the glass to her forehead. *Am I nuts? Here is a kind, capable, loving woman, who's glad to cook for Tom. And if I come home hot and tired, she'll cook for me, too! Julie, get a grip!*

That night in bed while she was listening to Tom snore, Julie lay perfectly still, hoping to catch a breeze through their window. If there was one thing she learned that day, it was not to turn away from purposeful acts of kindness, especially when they came from someone as wonderful as the-woman-in-the-farmhouse. *Seems like people in farmhouses have been good to me.* Julie turned her head to see stars littering the sky outside her window. *Lord, thank You for Grandma.*

◆

Grandma Emma became a rock in Julie's life, strong and stable and dependable. If Tom picked up extra work on the weekends, Julie eventually wandered over to Emma's, where there was always a surplus of food and drink, wisdom and sympathy.

On an oppressively hot Saturday at the end of June, Emma's floral housedress clung to her back, as curly tendrils of gray hair lay plastered on her neck. While Julie sat at the table, Emma plodded into the dining room from the kitchen, humming and carrying thick slabs of German chocolate cake on chipped china plates with a faded floral pattern. She set a plate down in front of each of them.

"Ven I vas your age, Julie-girl, my husband Herman und I had a baby. A month later I vas carrying vater in jugs across my shoulders from da vell to da haus. It was one-quarter mile trip, und I vas balancing our baby boy on my hip vile I valked. It vas very tough life, but I saved all da money I could." Emma thoughtfully chewed and swallowed a bite of cake.

"Herman died of da cancer, und I know I shouldn't mean be, but he vas no gut! Venever he could, he vould take da money, go into town, und treat his friends to da drink. He vas a bugger, und dat's da troot!" Emma laughed, finished her last bite of cake, and scraped all of her crumbs onto her fork.

I don't own the real estate on broken families, that's for sure. Emma has a claim on her turf of hardship and grief. But she's not a miserable person seeking miserable company. This woman is full of joy. Her tough calluses only cover her hands. Her heart is soft. Julie was grateful that she had found the good sense not to push Emma out of her life.

CHAPTER EIGHTEEN

FIRST COMES LOVE, THEN COMES MARRIAGE

With the approach of Thanksgiving, winter made a dry run, coating grass, trees, abandoned trucks, and piles of tires with a layer of wet, heavy snow. Julie bundled into her fleece-lined jacket, pulled on her warm boots, and trudged over to Emma's, dragging her feet like someone had attached a ball and chain to them.

Emma always seemed to know when Julie was coming, and greeted her at the door with a steaming mug of hot chocolate. "Come in, come in, und da door close. Es ist *nicht* wunderbar!"

Julie collapsed on a kitchen chair, pushed back her hood, and wrapped her hands around the mug. "Grandma Emma, I have something to tell you." Her eyes pooled in enormous tears.

"Let me guess: You are wit da child already, ja?"

"How did you know? Oh, Emma, Tom and I have only been married six months. I'm not ready for this." Julie sighed deeply.

"Honey, du bist never, ever ready to be pregnant, no matter ven it happens. Da gut Lord sees fit to gif you every ting you need to get troo dis. And ven da baby comes, the tree of you will feel like a real family." Emma smiled warmly.

"But … I'm only nineteen! I don't know what I want to do with my life."

"Vell, it looks like some of it has been decided for you already, ja? Ven your baby comes, you'll be vay too busy to vorry about your future. Da best ting you can do now is sleep ven you can, eat vell, und stay healty."

Julie looked at this amazing woman, and then around the kitchen where things always seemed right. *Emma will be here for me. She's mom, grandma, aunt, and even best friend.* "I love you, Grandma Emma."

"I luf you too, liebchen."

♦

"Sleep when you can, eat well, stay healthy." Those had been Grandma Emma's simple words, given in broken English with a whole heart. Julie was confident in her ability to do those three things.

On Christmas night, a virulent intestinal bug knocked Julie down and out. Five days later, she was certain the vultures were circling when she awoke from a fitful sleep with her heart racing, her body sweating buckets, and her hands and arms numb. And then panic took over when she got up and felt something sticky running down her legs. She hobbled to the bathroom in a terror more intense than anything she'd ever felt before. Sinking to the cold linoleum floor, she focused on realigning her gray matter. *If I can crawl to the living room and reach the phone, Emma will know what to do.*

Emma had never driven anything but tractors and the occasional rusty pick-up truck around her land. Tom's '66 Ford was still in her barn for emergency transportation. Within ten minutes of Julie's call, Emma had thrown a coat over her robe, pulled on her boots and climbed into the truck—and amazingly, it had started on the first crank. She drove to Julie's, threw the gearshift in park, leaned over and opened the passenger door, and left the truck running as she opened her door. Inside the trailer, Emma lifted Julie, carried her to the truck, tucked some old wool blankets around her and ignored both the speed limit and winter driving precautions on the way to the hospital emergency room. "Dear Gott, spare Julie's life and the life of dis precious baby," she uttered over and over.

Anxiety filled all the spaces in Julie's heart. *Where's Tom? Did he come home after I fell asleep and then leave again early this morning? He never works on Saturdays. God, please get me to the hospital on time!*

◆

As soon as Julie was resting comfortably in the maternity ward, Emma found a phone in the family waiting area and began calling all of Tom's friends, most of whom had been in his life since childhood. No one knew where he was; a few joked that he had gone AWOL from the marriage army. Emma ignored the puzzled looks from the people in the waiting room staring at her pink robe and men's winter boots. Tucking some of the runaway gray hairs back into her bun, Emma headed back to Julie's room, whispering prayers for the courage to tell her what she surely didn't want to hear—that no one knew where Tom was.

Emma found Julie sleeping quietly, and settled herself into a leather recliner. The room was soon filled with soft humming; Emma had a head-full of hymns and was ready to pass the rest of the day singing peace into this room. Her friend Amy had once said that the word 'Peace' stood for 'Pray Early And Cheat the Enemy,' and that's what Emma intended to do. Julie may have been sleep-deprived, but she was not going to be peace-deprived if Emma had anything to say and pray about it.

The late-afternoon sun flashed its high beams across Julie's bed, flooding the room with optimism. She awoke groggy and thirsty, and saw Emma sitting in a chair with legs up and head tipped sideways, snoring lightly and smiling even in her sleep. Julie looked at the needle taped to her hand and at the tube attached to the IV bag. *Why did I ever doubt that I wanted this baby?*

A cheerful nurse came in bearing Epiphany treasures: toothbrush, toothpaste, and comb. Emma opened her eyes, looked down at her robe and chuckled. "Maybe I need fixing more dan you!" She got up, rubbed her back and watched the nurse raise the bed and help Julie comb her hair. When Julie suddenly grabbed her stomach and moaned, the nurse reassured her that she was fine and that these new pains were probably from hunger. Julie's stomach rumbled and Emma laughed as the nurse handed the comb to Julie and left the room to answer another call.

"Emma, could you —"

Julie's arm stopped in mid-air. "Vat is vrong?" Emma's eyes filled with alarm.

"Those footsteps ... in the hallway. They sound like Tom's. Oh, I hope they are. But, where has he been?" Julie felt like someone had pulled a string in her emotions and she was unraveling. She dropped the comb on her blanket, lowered herself onto the pillow and flung her arm over her eyes.

Heavy footsteps clumped down the hospital corridor. Someone was banging into metal carts and swearing. Julie didn't move.

Tom appeared in the doorway with his jacket hanging open, work boots untied, and a look of disdain on his reddened face. Bleary eyes glanced first at Julie, then at Emma, then at the floor. Julie's feeling of relief was overpowered by anger and sadness. *Where has Tom been all day? Does he care about my baby and me?* Our *baby? Is he glad we're okay? Will he ever tell me I'm beautiful?*

Julie pondered over whether there was really any difference between her husband and her *adoptive* father. And what about Eugene? Was he different? What if he knew he was going to be a grandpa? But then again, he had abandoned her when she was a baby, which left three men in her life who seemed to have more important things to do than care about her.

Tom walked unsteadily into the room, stood for a few minutes at the foot of Julie's bed, then walked over and put his hand on her forehead. "Julie, I'm sorry. I'll try—"

"Don't...say...anything. Just leave me alone. I'll be fine here with Emma." Julie's voice was muffled under her arm. *Go home.*

♦

Winter gradually threw off its heavy coat and flaunted a spring wardrobe. Buds burst into leaves and accessorized everything from dignified oak trees to flamboyant forsythia bushes. Emma made the short walk to Julie's almost every evening, cradling a thermos of hot tea and a Cribbage board. She entered the trailer like a fairy godmother in galoshes, and Julie felt her isolation and discouragement magically transform into belonging and contentment. Sometimes the women simply sat in companionable silence, drinking their tea and watching Julie's stomach ripple with the movement of unseen body parts. "I don't know if this baby will have good hand-eye coordination, but I'm sure he'll have good elbow-knee coordination!" The laughter helped them observe the code of silence where Tom was concerned. Most of the time he was gone when Emma visited; she never asked where he was and Julie didn't volunteer the information, usually because she didn't know herself. She knew that her mom was busy slaying her own dragons, making Emma the core of all things good and kind in her life.

◆

The pregnancy was in the home stretch. July heat and humidity had turned the trailer into a sauna, and Julie lugged around her extra thirty pounds in slow motion. Her doctor had off-handedly mentioned, during her final check-up, that she would probably be scheduled for a c-section, since the baby was positioned feet-first and unlikely to turn itself before labor began. Julie didn't understand any of it, but figured if she followed doctor's orders she'd easily reach the point where someone else could haul this baby around for a change.

Tom's friends occasionally dropped by to check up on Julie; after a while she found out that when Tom wasn't at work, he was drinking with Bill and Bernice at one of the Coldspring bars. Julie assumed 'Bill' was Bill Kenney, the terminal bachelor. The only time Julie ever saw Emma closed and evasive was when she asked her about who Bernice was. "She vas my sister-in-law. Dat's all." *And apparently as much of a 'bugger' as Emma's husband was.*

◆

With less than a month until her due date, any kind of rest was increasingly elusive. No sooner would she drift off, long after midnight, than Tom would pull up to the trailer, open and slam his truck door and stumble up the steps in a tragic-comical attempt at quiet. Julie would stir awake in time to see Tom standing over her with a silly grin on his face, holding out a can of Mountain Dew and a Snickers bar like the proverbial peace offering. Julie often wondered how

Tom drove home safely every night. *Exactly how many lives does he have, and which one is he on?*

◆

"Mom, this baby is coming soon. Could I stay with you until I deliver? You live so much closer to the hospital than we do."

"I suppose, if you have to."

On a muggy night, when air conditioners were losing ground in their battle with the unyielding humidity, Julie was lying on a bed in the emergency room at St. Michael's, shivering, crying, desperate to hear the familiar footsteps of her doctor. *I hope he gets here soon!*

The on-call doctor ran in and out of cubicles in a blur of frenzied activity, pulling privacy curtains back and forth like a magician on stage and reassuring Julie that he was monitoring her closely, even though her baby was still several hours away from entering the world.

Suddenly Julie wondered whether or not this doctor knew about her baby's breech position. Arlene paced around the cubicle muttering about going back out to find a cheaper parking spot on the street so that she wouldn't have to pay the crooks in the parking garage. Every fifteen minutes she vanished to the waiting room for a cigarette, then returned to Julie's cubicle, slightly more stressed after each trip.

Oh, I wish I knew what was happening here. Where is Tom? I hope they find my regular doctor soon. As her pain intensified, Julie felt like she was free falling through a haze of terror. *Why aren't they prepping me for a c-section? What's happening? Could I die from pain?* The baby's first step into the world was literally with one foot out and the other hung up in the birth canal. Julie was cut horizontally and vertically; she tore; she bled; she screamed; and Christina Rose Dietrich was born. Julie's last thought before she drifted off in a drug-induced euphoria was that she finally had a doll to dress.

◆

Five days later Tom appeared and drove Julie and Christina home from the hospital. As soon as he had them settled, he announced that his responsibilities toward his wife and newborn daughter were to get up in the morning, go to work, and bring home a paycheck every other week. It was Friday, so Tom kissed his wife and daughter goodbye and drove off to work, leaving Julie with all of the 'left-over' responsibilities.

None of her life experiences had prepared Julie for the punishing triathlon of diapering, breast-feeding and round-the-clock pacing with a colicky baby. A healthy body would have made everything easier, but Julie dealt with excruciating pain for six weeks, without the time or ability to lie down. Her bed became the most neglected piece of furniture in their trailer as Julie approached a meltdown. The energizing, late-summer sun mocked her weariness.

Julie was confined with a baby whose daily activities were nursing, gulping, burping, and projectile vomiting. Grandma Emma was the benevolent guard, making her rounds every morning at seven, delivering homemade cinnamon rolls with a hug, a smile, and the reassurance that "Dis, too, shall pass, liebchen." For the rest of the day Julie and Christina were alone. Julie never considered leaving the trailer: even if her body had been strong enough, her pride left her unwilling to take a colicky baby into a world of ideal mothers with perfect babies. There was too great a chance of encountering friendly fire.

Thanks to Bill's 'baby gift'—paying to have a well dug for Tom and Julie's trailer—their new Whirlpool washer became Julie's most cherished friend, while the old Plymouth

Duster—a recent better-than-soda-and-candy peace offering from Tom—sat forlornly in the weeds outside of the trailer.

♦

By the middle of October, Julie felt her energy returning. "Maybe if I get the wash done this morning," Julie whispered to Christina, "you and I could go for a drive. I'll put you in that cute, yellow, hand-smocked dress with the matching bloomers." The air was crisp and the sky a deep topaz. This had always been one of Julie's favorite times of year: the temperature was close to sixty; the bright sun was invigorating; wood smoke hung languidly in the air; and best of all, the mosquitoes were gone. It would be good for her to go out, maybe even show off her new baby to a few of her former coworkers at the store. Those friends would love her in the Midwestern-nice kind of way, and fuss over her baby, which was something she really craved. *Maybe I can do this 'mother thing,' after all. If I've survived these first months, I can do anything.*

Julie placed Christina in an infant seat on the linoleum floor, poured a cup of powdered laundry detergent into the machine, pulled out and twisted the knob to start the water, and gathered up an armful of clothes. That's when she noticed red spots on the back of the green shirt she had worn the previous night during Christina's last feeding. The spots looked like dried blood and could only have come from Christina's post-nursing vomiting. Julie dropped the clothes on the floor, slammed the palm of her hand into the knob to shut off the machine, picked up Christina's seat, tucked it under her arm, grabbed her purse hanging from the kitchen chair, pushed open the trailer door and raced out to the car. After belting in Christina's seat, Julie shoved the key into the ignition. *Jack be nimble, Jack be quick ...* The car started right away.

God forgive me—but maybe they'll ask me to take Christina to St. Michael's for an overnight stay, and I can pass out. I'd stretch out on a cot in Christina's room, be right there if she needed me, and let the nurses take care of her.

Julie shook herself out of her daydream as she pulled into the clinic parking lot ten minutes later and headed inside with Christina. After checking in, she took Christina to a waiting room filled with big plastic blocks, cardboard books, a variety of climbing equipment for toddlers, and four deep, leather armchairs. Julie set Christina's infant seat on the floor, lifted her out of it, and wrapped her arms around her baby as they both sank into one of the chairs.

When the nurse entered the waiting area fifteen minutes later, mother and daughter were zoned. She gently woke Julie and led her back to an exam room. The pediatrician walked briskly down the hall and entered the door right behind them.

Dr. Johnson patiently listened to Julie's concerns while he thoroughly examined Christina. "Mrs. Dietrich." The older doctor sat in his swivel chair, removed his glasses and looked kindly at Julie. "Your baby is fine. The blood in her vomit is from irritation in the lining of her throat. You need to settle down, maybe have a glass of beer. It will be easier for Christina to nurse that way, and easier on you." Dr. Johnson made a few notes on his clipboard and stood up.

I know I just woke up, but am I hearing you right? Do you know what damage alcohol has done in my life? "Doctor, I'm glad Christina's okay. Hopefully we won't see each other again unless it's at a party!"

"Deal." Dr. Johnson patted Julie's shoulder, rubbed Christina's head, and walked out the door. Julie was overcome with equal parts embarrassment and relief. This wasn't how she had pictured her first mother-daughter outing, but at least she found out she was up to the challenge. And for today that was enough. She drove home and laid Christina

down for a nap. Mother and daughter slept for five hours—
the longest stretch of uninterrupted sleep either had had since
Christina was born.

◆

The hoped-for outing to the Hot'n Cold General Store
never happened. Over the next several weeks, Julie and
Christina saw Dr. Johnson at least once a week. Julie was
usually convinced that Christina was dying from a variety of
childhood ailments. Her car—the 'green machine'—got used
to navigating itself to the clinic while Julie agonized through
all of the possible scenarios of Christina's impending death.
Christina never suffered from anything more than colds, flu,
congestion, or ear infections, while Julie suffered from an
acute case of affirmation starvation. In her high-alert level
of stress, she had only the minimum daily requirement of
energy to make it through twenty-four hours. Emma still
appeared at Julie's doorstep every morning at seven armed
with cinnamon rolls and ready to start the coffee pot, but
Julie turned her away more and more often. She was simply
too tired to be loved.

◆

Eventually, Christina's colic disappeared and Julie
was able to get six hours of sleep at night. On a Monday
morning a week before Christmas, Julie—full of remorse for
closing her door on Emma every day—surprised that gentle
soul by inviting her to stay for seven o'clock coffee. Emma
graciously accepted Julie's invitation, acting as if it was a
normal occurrence rather than one that had been interrupted
by months of distress in Julie's life.

◆

Tom no longer appeared at Emma's table for dinner. Julie learned to cook basic casseroles, set the table, wait, watch game show reruns while the food stayed warm in the oven, nurse Christina, put her down for the night, and finally give in to her own hunger pangs. She would then wash her plate, leave the other one on the table, and go to bed, all the while wondering when Tom would come home.

Julie didn't want to walk away from her marriage, and knew that that wasn't an option for her, anyway. She had no skills, no job, and no way to support herself. She was determined not to end up like her mom—who, Julie thought, could have left that horrible excuse for a husband if she had worked hard, saved her money, and carved out her own place in the world. For Julie, there were no do-overs. She couldn't go to her mom for any financial or babysitting help. Arlene lived thirty miles away and had already made it clear that she had raised her kids and wasn't about to be tied down with grandkids.

The noose was tightening: It was merely a question of who—or what—would finish the knot.

CHAPTER NINETEEN

SLEEPLESS IN MICHIGAN

J ulie was in a tug-of-war between her increasing joy over Christina and her sense of helplessness in her marriage. Looking out her bedroom window as she rocked Christina, Julie's thoughts were reflected in the changeable early April weather. Some days, the promise of spring hovered in the air as temperatures neared fifty degrees, beckoning people to page through catalogues advertising Burpee seeds, barbecue grills, and patio furniture. On other days, winter regained its place by freezing recently melted snow into hazardous patches of ice. Low-hanging clouds waited to dump wet snow on people who had packed away their warm clothes prematurely.

It had been several weeks since Julie's last visit to the clinic. She was finally convinced that Christina's bouts of cold and flu were the stuff of normal babyhood—and she was even learning how to adequately care for her baby. Her body had healed from the breech birth; she fit into her pre-baby clothes, and didn't have to worry anymore about wearing tops for breast-feeding.

When her nausea hit, Julie actually relaxed, figuring she was bound to get the same occasional flu bugs that hit

Christina. Tom never seemed to get sick—he wasn't home long enough to catch anything from them.

The nausea continued for over a week, and Julie began to notice her clothes hanging more loosely on her than they had when she had last worn them. This time she had no reason to take Christina to see Dr. Johnson; she wondered if he might be willing to check *her* out. *After all, my baby's pediatrician is a doctor, and I feel comfortable with him.*

♦

Julie held tightly to Christina's infant seat as she pulled open the door against the wind-whipped snow. The antiseptic smell inside the clinic intensified her nausea. Although she had wanted to come here to be comforted, she now had an increased sense of fear and dread. *What if something really terrible is wrong with me? People get cancer and other life-threatening illnesses, even mothers of babies.*

The familiar waiting room felt like home to Julie, and was deliberately decorated for the safety and enjoyment of toddlers. Three of the walls were covered with brightly painted murals of animal babies and human babies frolicking together. The fourth wall proudly displayed a magazine rack mounted high enough to be out of reach of tiny hands, and boasted magazines like *Parenting*. Mothers whose children were well behaved handed out *Highlights* like candy. Some overworked mothers—maybe all of them—were glad for a chance to share moments of uninterrupted adult conversation.

Julie thought for the hundredth time that this room would do far better at meeting her needs if there were a coffee pot and *Newsweek* or *Time* or *Reader's Digest*. She peeled off her coat, ski hat and gloves, and proceeded to unwrap the layers of bundling around her precious baby. The room was inviting and pleasant, and if Julie's nausea would settle down, she'd gladly sit in this comfortable warmth as long as it took for her name to be called.

After a routine check-up and a pleasant chat with Dr. Johnson, Julie was left alone in a room with pictures of animals painted on the walls. While Christina cooed and stared at the bright overhead light, Julie's head drooped forward onto her chest. Soon she was dreaming that she heard a knocking sound. Drowsily pulling her head back into wakefulness, she saw the door open cautiously and a nurse tiptoe into the room.

"Mrs. Dietrich, I have some wonderful news for you. You're not sick at all, just pregnant!" The nurse's face broke into a smile reaching to the tops of both ears, clearly enjoying this part of her job.

Julie covered her face and burst into tears. *Ohmigod, what have I done?* The startled nurse reassured her that everything would be all right. *No. Everything will not be all right. I don't even know what 'all right' is. But whatever it is, it is not my life.* Julie scooped up Christina and the diaper bag and walked back into the waiting room, avoiding eye contact with the other mothers. She threw on her jacket and forgot to zip it, quickly dressed Christina and sprinted out of the doctor's office. The snow turned to sleet that pelted against her face like sharpened needles, mixing with Julie's tears and freezing her face and spirit into numbness.

◆

When Christina was sixteen months old, Emma Lynn Dietrich was born during a January snowfall. She quickly showed herself to be the kind of easy baby paraded as 'normal' in all of the child development books. Julie whispered a word of thankfulness to God and crossed her fingers behind her back, intending to cover all of the bases in the games of faith and luck.

♦

Casting a wide net to pull in sufficient resources for her baby girls became Julie's daily ambition. Tom gave her five dollars a week to cover groceries, clothes, and all other needs. *I hope he enjoys the planet he's living on, because five bucks on earth buys a cup of coffee, a tube of toothpaste, and Spam.* Julie got some help from Mayor Kenney, who owned the Hot'n Cold and would extend credit to the Dietrichs during the winter months when Tom had fewer hours at work. If the grocery credit was paid up at the end of the month, Tom and Julie went out to the bar for a beer and a soda.

With the coming of spring, Emma taught Julie how to plant a garden and promised to teach her how to can the vegetables later that summer. Julie also learned to bake bread and sew her own clothes—things she had started to learn with Mama T. With some creativity and determination Julie knew she could provide for her family on a shoestring. She hoped someday she would own the whole shoe.

♦

Fairview State Hospital, built in 1937, was a well-ordered, sprawling compound of red brick cottages and two-, three- and four-story brick buildings all connected by walkways and tunnels. The largest and most imposing of the structures was the central building—the only one that boasted concrete steps leading up to a wide portico flanked by four enormous granite columns. The hospital complex was set back quite a distance from the highway; even from afar those columns drew admiring eyes up the gradually narrowing edifice to the copper-topped cupola towering over the grounds in a proclamation of good will.

Driving across Coldspring River, Julie had often stared at the beautiful, majestic hospital and meticulously manicured grounds, and wondered what went on in those buildings. When she finally decided to test the waters by asking Tom what he thought about her trying to get work there, he told her she was too stupid to pass a job placement test anywhere. *Okay, Miss Meyer, someday I'll show you I can do it.*

The January blahs that had hung over Julie since her teen years were still a part of her emotional landscape as an adult; this time she decided to fight the depression, bundle up her daughters, drop them off at Emma's and check out job openings at the hospital. An older woman at Hot'n Cold used to tell Julie about her years of working in maintenance at the state hospital—and how the basement was a labyrinth of tunnels opening in to storage rooms with antique furniture, outdated, fiendish-looking medical equipment, and even coffins in the old morgue. It had all sounded far more intriguing to Julie than her view of the cans of Campbell's soup on the back shelves of the store.

New snow covered the shrubs around the hospital in a layer of whipped cream, chasing away the apprehension that had threatened Julie's resolve. By the time she walked across the wide parking lot, she was determined to make some kind of change in her life.

Julie reasoned that the best place to start was in the central building. As soon as she walked up the steps and through the door, she craned her neck back to admire the twenty-foot ceiling and the massive white pillars spaced throughout the sun-drenched lobby. Feeling like she was somehow defacing the marble floor with her snowy boots, Julie stopped at the information desk and stomped her feet on a rubber rug, then asked all of the necessary questions to obtain an application. *There's no reason to tell 'Miss Meyer' what I did today. I probably won't be called back for an interview anyway.* Julie finished the application, gave it to a pleasant woman at the desk, and drove back home feeling like she'd left some of her blahs at the hospital.

A week and a half later, Julie received a phone call from someone in personnel at the hospital, asking to set up an interview with her. By the time Julie started her new job as a Human Services Technician, she'd already heard about a woman named Miriam Evans who ran a daycare a mile from her trailer—and who was willing to charge just a dollar twenty-five an hour for both of her daughters! Things were definitely heading in the right direction.

CHAPTER TWENTY

THE HOUSE THAT
TOM BUILT

Julie's job as Human Services Technician demanded at least forty hours a week; motherhood took a minimum of sixty; cooking, cleaning, tending a vegetable garden and splitting wood consumed another forty, which left a balance of four hours a night for sleep. The lines that separated hours from days, days from weeks, and weeks from months crisscrossed into a web poised to entangle Julie and swallow her few remaining functional parts, while Tom seemed caught in his own tug-of-war between his drinking buddies and home.

Grandma Emma unknowingly pulled on Tom's rope.

"Tomboy." Emma wrapped her hands around a cup of black coffee, sitting across the table from Tom as Julie sprang up to close the windows of the trailer against the late-fall air, chilly and damp, pursued by the almost-winter wind racing in from the north. As the storm windows rattled, Julie wondered again how much longer the four of them would last in this sardine can without becoming airborne.

Julie poured coffee for her and Tom and sat down next to him across from Emma. Emma tucked a loose strand of coarse gray hair back under her 'babushka,' as she called her headscarf.

"I haf a gift for you. There has a farm been in my family since mine fater owned it, und his fater before him."

Julie would never tire of the charm in Emma's convoluted English.

"It's a forty-acre farm in Kale, down road from vere you are now, und I vould like you to haf it. You can build a nice haus on it for your family."

Maybe now Tom will be home more than ever before. We can be a real family, and I can live in a real house that I actually own. Julie dropped her head on the table and cried, releasing tears of fatigue and relief.

◆

Through the winter months, Tom cut trees to clear an area for the house and hauled the trees to a sawmill. During the following spring and summer, while the boards were air-drying, Tom designed the house, had a well dug, removed rocks, and poured the concrete foundation. The boards were planed during a warm, dry autumn, and Tom used every spare minute to build before the snow flew.

On a cold, crisp Saturday in early November, Julie took a drive through Kale—a modest-looking town of seventy-one people living on neat farms with flower beds and miniature lighthouses along the road, and railroad tracks bordering the back of their land. Pick-up trucks parked in the front yards were stocked with hay bales and gun racks. *I'll bet they raise some Cain here along with the cattle.* Tucked in a knoll at one end of town were two churches whose front doors faced off across a dirt road. St. Andrew's had peeling wood siding, new oak doors painted forest green, and a third-story bell tower. St. Luke's had new white siding, cross insets in the door windows, and a fieldstone lamppost guarding the front steps. Spruce trees showing no denominational preference grew freely on both sides of the road and in the churchyards.

Julie slowed down as she passed the churches, and assumed that one of them was Lutheran, and the other Catholic. *This is Michigan—it's a good guess.* The towering spruces looked like they were protecting the churches, and Julie wondered if her new house would protect her from—*what?*

◆

I can't believe it's been seven months since I did the Kale tour, and that I've been married five years today. Sometimes I forget that I'm even waiting for anything special to happen in my life.

Julie shook off her pensive mood and laughed at her daughters playing in the inflatable wading pool like puppies tumbling over each other. The trailer was way too small and hot to stay in for long. Being outside in the scorching heat without a shade tree wasn't much different, except that the open space kept Julie from wanting to gnaw off her leg and escape to a place that was officially designated unbearable. Tom had promised they would be able to move into their new house by early July—and Julie was convinced that having more room would fix a lot of the problems in their marriage. *Okay: Click my heels together, say 'There's no place like home,' and open my eyes in my dream house.*

That night Tom and Julie took their girls and celebrated their anniversary with dinner at McDonald's and a drive out to their split-level house. Tom stayed outside and played with his daughters on the swing set while Julie wandered through the rooms imagining all of the decorating she would do. The kitchen counters would be reddish-orange and the walls would be paneled in dark tongue-and-groove walnut. Scandinavian teapots and plates and trivets would be displayed on shelves and special hangers. The dining room would have cream and tan wallpaper with a fern design. The three bedrooms would be decorated to match the personalities of the occupants. Everything in the house would be the best and classiest in country-living-on-a-budget.

Even the christening meal was planned way ahead of time: fried chicken, home-made biscuits with freezer strawberry jam, real mashed potatoes with sour cream, and iced tea.

♦

As soon as Tom's buddies unloaded the last of the boxes at the new house, he jumped in one of the trucks and didn't return until after bar closing time. The deliverymen had set up their new bed three days earlier; and with her bedroom door closed against the happy screeches of her daughters and a blanket thrown across the window to keep the room dark, Julie stayed in bed nursing a migraine while Emma came over and took care of everyone. Julie had hoped that the violent headaches and migraines, which had reappeared early in her marriage, would be deserted at the trailer, but they had obviously found her in the new house. When Emma suggested that her friends at the First Evangelical Free Church could help relieve Julie's stress and "achy head problem," Julie was willing to try anything and agreed to go to church with Emma.

♦

The church was a few miles outside Kale; by the time Julie, Christina and Emma had attended for three months, Julie had earned the nickname 'Shake-n-bake.' Her chicken casseroles, yeast rolls, cracked wheat bread and cinnamon buns were in demand for every wedding and funeral and potluck. Now when Tom cycled through his drinking binges, Julie was up late waiting for bread dough to rise instead of feeling her blood boil.

CHAPTER TWENTY-ONE

DANCING TOO CLOSE TO THE FLAME

Julie had expected her stress to magically disappear when they moved into their new house; she quickly discovered that little girls and household chores were still messy and unpredictable, and left no margin of error. Whatever else happened, control had to outrun chaos, which meant working five days a week, making meals from scratch, planting and weeding and harvesting her garden, canning the vegetables, splitting wood for heat, baking bread and rolls, and collapsing into a delirium-filled sleep for three or four hours before the cycle started again.

Patients who bit, spit and hit without warning constantly challenged the control Julie sought in her hospital job; order came from organizing and filing reports, ridding the floor of feces, and cleaning windows.

The persistent headaches made the edge of Julie's sanity dangerously thin. Home chores were seen as non-negotiable, but she thought maybe a job change would give her some relief. *If I don't find something else to do pretty soon, I'll be sharing a bed with one of the patients.*

♦

Tom's sister Sharon had recently been accepted into beauty school and Julie thought this might be the thing she was looking for. She remembered all of those times when her mom had sat her up on a stool and whacked her hair off in an offense against good taste. With beautician's training she could style her daughters' hair to look like dolls, they would all save money on haircuts, *her* hair would always look right, and she would work well with the customers — because *everyone* who came to her shop would want their hair cut precisely and styled a particular way.

"Tom." Julie scurried around the kitchen cleaning up the supper dishes while the girls were playing in the living room. *Tom is home, sober, and maybe even agreeable.*

"Hmm?" Tom was lost in the Dukes of Hazard.

"Sharon is going to beauty school." Julie scraped plates of half-eaten spaghetti into plastic storage containers.

"Yeah, so?" Tom got up, walked over to the TV, cranked up the volume and sat back down on the end of the couch.

"So I was thinking I might like to do that too." She sealed the lids on the containers and popped them into the fridge.

"Yeah."

"The tuition is less than a thousand." Julie was standing over a sink of hot, sudsy water, while beads of sweat dripped down her face.

Tom got back up, turned the TV off and watched the screen fade to black. He turned to Julie.

Here it comes.

"What have you been drinking? We don't have that kind of money. I need a tractor and other stuff to get this farm up and running." Tom fell back into the couch and picked up a magazine from the local farm-and-fleet store to emphasize his point.

226

Julie had him in the crosshairs. "Everything is always about *you*, isn't it? This house is *your* dream; you never, ever asked me to help you plan it. You don't even know what I want!" Julie dropped the dishrag in the water and stormed out of the room, shaking her hands over her head as she left.

The pastor had preached many sermons on the husband being the authority of the home; whatever he did was supposed to be supported by the wife. What Julie heard was, "You need to do anything and everything your husband wants." *Blah, blah, blah. I'm not doing that anymore.*

◆

The next morning, Julie dropped her daughters off at Miriam's and drove to the hospital thinking about the heap of manure her life had become. The stench was getting to her and she wished someone would come along and shovel out the mess. *I seem to have misplaced my glass slipper, and I'm at the wrong end of the horse.*

At morning break time, June Harrison walked up to Julie wearing an amusing smile and carrying a mug of coffee and a Hershey's bar. She held both hands out to Julie. "You look rattled. Want to pick your poison?"

June had this flair for showing up when Julie needed her. *How come I never realized how much she reminds me of Glo?*

"I'll take both."

June sat down across from Julie at a small, white, metal table.

"Julie, would you like to come to a prayer group that some of us are thinking about starting? No pressure. If you'd like us to pray for you, we would do that." June fumbled through her purse for a notebook and pen.

"No. I mean yeah, I don't want you to just pray for me. I actually think I want to go with you. When and where is it?"

June set her purse aside and looked intently at Julie. "The first one will be tomorrow at six-thirty in the break room, and then probably every Friday morning from now on."

"I'll be there." Julie crumpled up her candy wrapper, tossed it into the garbage can, put her coffee mug into the sink, and headed back to work.

"Thank you Lord," whispered June.

♦

At six-twenty the next morning there were already a dozen people gathered in the break room when Julie walked in.

"Hey, Julie, glad you could make it."

"Actually, June, I'm not really sure why I'm here. I've never prayed out loud before—"

"And you don't need to start now if you don't want to. We're here to help each other along, to grow together. We all struggle with jealousy, and resentment, and anger, and gossip. We pray so that we can ask God to take those things from us and make us look more like the people He wants us to be. Some of us will pray out loud and others will follow those prayers silently."

"That's a relief. I'll be one of the silent ones."

"Cool."

Julie got a cup of coffee and sat down next to June. "Can I ask you something?"

"Shoot."

"How did you get here?"

"You mean—"

"To wherever you are in your life."

"Well, I'll give you the two-cent version now, and someday when we've got more time I'll give you the expensive one."

Julie laughed.

"My dad was an alcoholic."

"*Was?*"

"He died about ten years ago from cirrhosis of the liver."

"Sorry."

"Don't be. By the end of his life he had made himself right with God and it was a blessing that he didn't keep living any more in constant pain."

"Oh."

"When I was about twenty-five years old, I realized that I spent my childhood feeling out of control, so when I became an adult I tried to make up for it by being obsessed with perfectionism. I drove everyone crazy, I was extremely unhappy, and I didn't feel like I could trust any man, including the one I was married to."

Maybe there are more people rowing in my boat with me after all. "So what changed?"

"A caring and honest friend told me that I wasn't a little girl anymore. No matter what had happened in my childhood, I had a will that needed to be bent toward God, just like everyone else in the world. I had hidden behind perfectionism and resentment and 'righteous' anger—but God saw me as someone who needed the same kind of forgiveness as everyone else."

One of the older men in the group broke into everyone's conversations and asked them "to come together now so that we don't fall apart later." A short time of sharing illnesses and financial needs, emotional struggles and 'praises' was followed by about twenty minutes of the most honest and vulnerable praying Julie had ever heard. When a younger gal prayed for the strength to love a father who didn't deserve her love, Julie's mind drifted back to Bret's talk. *Didn't he say God was a perfect father? I've tried this long enough on my own, God ... 'Abba' ... it's time for me to find my way to You. I'm sure You can do a better job with my life than what I've done.*

When the prayer time was over and everyone headed out to the time clock and the start of their shifts, Julie felt wrapped in a kind of peacefulness that had been mostly unknown to her in her life, especially as an adult. She'd for sure be at the prayer meeting again next Friday.

That Sunday Julie began listening to her pastor's sermon with a different attitude; and the next time he challenged the women of the congregation to honor their husbands as though they were honoring Christ, Julie decided that she had nothing to lose by trying it God's way. She knew that her stony heart needed some softening, and if she focused on that, then it was God's business to work on Tom's words and attitude.

◆

Maybe Tom would settle down if he had a son. Julie knew Tom's number one dream was to pass down their farm that had been owned by the only person who had ever created good memories for him. *I can do this for Tom. It's totally in Your hands, God. This is all new to me ... but I believe ... I* want *to believe that You know what's best for me—for us.*

By the time Julie, Christina and Emma made another trip to Dr. Johnson's office the following month, Julie knew it was a formality: she had all the signs of being pregnant and she absolutely knew she was carrying a boy.

◆

Unaware of the lengthening days and more robust smells of spring, Julie shifted to autopilot and opened the door of the hospital's employee entrance one May morning. *I need to rest my feet. Did I really want to be pregnant again? How long until lunch? I'm already starving.* At eleven-thirty, she navigated through the accumulation of male patients—many of whom were social misfits from the fourth floor Chemical Dependency Unit—forming a broken line in the second floor cafeteria. All patients were expected to step aside and make room for hospital employees on their half-hour lunch breaks. Julie had finally gotten used to the catcalls, gestures, and recent additions of poking and rubbing her growing belly. *The presumed mating activities of the species.*

Julie was at the head of the line, reaching for a plastic tray when she received a sharp crack on her backside. Reeling around, she faced a man slightly taller than she was, with greasy looking, graying hair, and an unkempt beard.

"Hey Sandy, who's the hot chick?" The man smirked as the guys standing around him whistled and yelled.

"That's no chick!" The whistles grew louder. "That's my *kid!*"

Julie stood in paralyzing horror. *That son-of-a … why is he here?* She evaded Danny's outstretched arm and ran out of the cafeteria, eyes burning in tears of anger and shame, and collided with her supervisor. Grabbing her arm and dragging her into a nearby conference room, Julie slammed the door behind them.

"Jennifer, do *not* give out any information about me to Danny Sandford—not where I live, anything about my girls, my life, or my home…not even about my car…nothing." She left Jennifer with the responsibility of picking up her jaw while Julie found an office to file some reports. Her hunger would have to wait.

◆

Although the cruder male patients moved on to a different object of ridicule, Julie couldn't avoid Danny as she performed her daily duties. He often looked at her with an unreadable expression on his face, but didn't attempt any conversation. Even though patients' records were confidential, their bragging usually allowed the staff to know more than they really wanted to about any given patient. News traveled quickly about Danny—mainly that he had three DUIs and faced either jail time or ninety-days detox in the hospital.

Julie saw Danny sitting alone at a table farthest from the vending machines. Julie approached him, dropped her tray on the table and glared at the broken-looking man sitting hunched over his lunch. *God, I do not want to feel sorry for him.*

"So what was up with Grandma Hagstrom?"

Danny looked up at Julie; no surprise showed in his face at the out-of-the-blue question. "*Leona* was no mom. My family told me all about her." He stabbed a glob of congealed macaroni and cheese with his fork.

Julie sat down across from him and opened her carton of milk.

"She slept around, married some guy, shacked up, had me, kept sleeping around, and her old man died when I was six months old." Danny set his fork down and pushed his tray aside.

"Where did you and your mom go after that?"

"Who knows where *she* went? All I know is I was juggled between an aunt, an uncle, a grandma, and friends. They all told me I had cute hair and I was a happy baby—but they were all a bunch of drunks."

Have you looked in the mirror lately? Julie sighed. "How come Grandma came to live with us?"

"Beats me. Your mom invited her—felt sorry for her or something. We didn't know she was going batty—"

"Which explains why I overheard Mom saying she had 'awful hard arteries,' and that she was 'looney.' She must have had hardening of the arteries, and could have used some real help."

"I wasn't going to do *anything* for her."

"But why did you let her baby-sit Dan and me? Most of the time she was passed out on the couch while we did guerilla warfare. You never knew that we drowned every turtle we had in the toilet."

Danny chuckled.

"It was like 'Cuckoo's Nest' around there." Julie shook her head, got up, and left her food untouched on her tray as she walked away.

♦

Danny left Fairview cleaned up and sober, and connected with an AA chapter. By the time he had earned his thirty-day sobriety pin he had also regained his license from the Steamfitters Union, reclaimed his old job and went looking for Arlene. Julie figured her mom must have been in serious financial or emotional trouble—or both—to open her door to him.

"So your dad—"

"*Danny*—" Julie crooked the phone under her chin as she washed dishes.

"Whatever. He says, 'C'mon, babe, let's put the past behind us. I'm different now, changed, and my life's good. I can give you the stuff you always wanted.'"

Isn't that what it was always about anyway—your *stuff?* Julie heard Arlene's end of the drama and got a mental picture of Danny sitting on the top seat of a teeter-totter with Arlene at the bottom dragging her feet in the dirt. *No good can come of this.*

233

Within one month, Danny had worn down all of Arlene's defenses and arguments. They rented an apartment together and re-married on a blustery day a week before Christmas.

CHAPTER TWENTY-TWO

ENCORE

J ulie's desire was for each of her children to have unique names, which would reflect unique identities. No Julies or Toms. Never an Arlene or Danny!

"Oh, baby," Tom pleaded. "If we have a son, please let me name him after me. That's all I've ever wanted." Julie finally caved, trying to weave any thread of peace into their marriage. Their son Tom Allen was born on a bright January morning shortly before Julie's twenty-fifth birthday. This time she took maternity leave and stayed home with her three kids. *Tom might not like it, but he's got his namesake, so we'll both be happy. And my baby boy will always be 'Tom-Tom' to me.*

♦

For three months after Tom-Tom's birth, the Dietrich home was blanketed by calm. Even the clouds cooperated by carefully releasing huge flakes of snow, which Julie loved to watch while she rocked her baby in the nursery. She looked at the bright yellow ducks on the wallpaper border against the pastel blue walls, and at the stuffed teddy bear sitting on the refinished, painted dresser. *I am really a mother,* Julie mused, with a contentment she had never felt after the birth of her girls. Endless days were spent in the house playing dolls with Christina and Emma as they watched their new little brother making faces and smiling at everyone. Sometimes Julie's daughters wrapped their arms around Tom-Tom and her heart was flooded with a new kind of love for all three of these blessings. *Maybe I can do this mothering thing in a family that's not like anything I had growing up. Words will be kind and love will fill the rooms.* Tom came home every night for dinner with a light in his eyes and a hug for all of them.

♦

A March thaw left muddy ruts behind slow-moving tires. The mounded snow melted into clumps of grass, sand, candy wrappers and fast-food containers while Julie's joy slowly disappeared under piles of diapers and unpaid bills—*both stinky.* A nagging feeling of uselessness gnawed around the edges of her contentment.

Tom's attentiveness also began fading as he was drawn back to the bar and his buddies. An April Fool's Day trip to town for a quick beer ended three hours later with Tom barreling into their backyard riding a John Deere tractor.

A John Deere cap ... undeserved respect? Forget it! Julie waited in ambush for Tom to enter the mudroom, bend over and untie his boots.

"Tom, I quit work to stay home and take care of our kids. How much did you pay for that tractor? How come there wasn't money for me to go to beauty school? How can we afford a tractor?" Julie shifted her baby in her arms and patted his back with the intensity of her rising anger.

Tom threw his boots into the corner, rose up and glared at Julie. "I make all the money; I can do anything I want with it! I'm not going to stand here and listen to any more

236

from you! I'm hitching a ride back to the bar where I left my truck. Don't wait up for me."

Julie turned in time to see her daughters peeking around the corner at her, their eyes filled with fear. She reined in her rage, wanting desperately to protect her children from the anger and abuse that had defined her childhood. Setting Tom-Tom in an infant seat, Julie told her girls to go find their dolls. She ran into the kitchen and pulled the church directory out of a drawer. With trembling fingers she picked up the phone and dialed her pastor's home phone number.

"Pastor." Julie skipped introductions and social niceties. "Tom bought a tractor and we have absolutely no money to pay for it. We're up to our eyeballs in debt." Julie wasn't sure what pastors were used to hearing, but she didn't figure this was a time for sanitizing the truth. The vultures were circling.

"Julie." Pastor Hines cleared his throat. "Tom was the one who bought that tractor. It's up to him to figure out how to pay for it. It's his responsibility. God will make a way through this for you; you can trust Him on behalf of your whole family."

I wish I could tell you my faith has replaced my worry. I'm afraid worry is winning this battle.

"Okay, well, thanks." Julie hung up as her girls came into the kitchen dragging plastic crates filled with their dolls and doll clothes. *After seven years of marriage our house is still cluttered with second-hand furniture, and the only reason our kids have decent clothes is because I sew everything. And yet we own a new tractor and chain saws. Something is messed up somewhere. God, are You still paying attention?*

◆

A fierce storm howling over Lake Michigan brought gale force wind and rain that pounded against trees, houses and cars. As the temperature dropped to thirty-two degrees, icicles transformed trees and power lines into chandeliers, and Mother Nature became a diamond-bedazzled, treacherous woman. People stood at their windows watching branches crack and topple—sometimes in slow motion—and it was another twenty-four hours before they ventured out to view the damage. When the temperature rose, falling ice chunks littered the ground like shattered glass.

Within a week, power had been restored to most homes and Julie's anger had melted along with the ice. When Tom suggested a five-mile drive to visit his Aunt Lucille and Uncle John, Julie jumped at a chance for a family outing, thinking maybe this was God's way of giving Tom that soft heart she so desperately wanted for herself.

Nothing as big as a tractor purchase stayed a secret in Kale. John and Lucille knew about the tractor without knowing how angry Julie had been because of it. When she showed up at their door with dark circles under her eyes, they assumed the cause was full-time mothering fatigue. John's foolproof cure for all ailments was a glass of his homemade plum wine. Julie hadn't had any alcohol during her last pregnancy and was ready for something sweet.

By the end of the small talk, Julie had consumed wine and a glass of homemade German beer. She was so starved for adult conversation and her husband's attention that she was oblivious to glass after glass set before her: piña coladas, Brandy Sevens, and wine. It had been a long time since she had felt this good, laughed this much, and had Tom's arm around her. While Julie stayed glued to the couch, Tom occasionally got up and checked on the girls, who eventually fell asleep on the rug in the den, and on baby Tom-Tom who slept in an old playpen, which had last been used by John and Lucille's children.

It was after midnight when Julie tried unsuccessfully to read the numbers on her watch. "Tom, I think it's time to go, don't you?" Julie laughed uproariously.

Tom seemed barely tipsy. "Yeah, it's almost one. You stay here and I'll get the kids settled in the car."

"Okay, José." Julie smiled and fell back on the couch while Tom's aunt and uncle tiptoed out of the room. Ten minutes later, Tom brought Julie's jacket to her, helped her put it on, picked her up, and got her into the car. A storm was dumping heavy, wet snow on fallen trees that hadn't yet been cleared away from the ice storm, which made the ten-minute drive take forty-five minutes. By the time they pulled into their driveway, Julie had passed out. Tom shut off the engine and left the keys in the ignition, got out and raced around to Julie's side, lifted her out and carried her into the house and upstairs where he plunked her down on the floor outside the bathroom. He quickly ran back down and out to the car, cradled a girl in each arm and fought the wind as he took them in the house and left them on the living room sofa. He then ran back out, unbuckled Tom from his infant seat and heard his daughters screaming even before he opened the front door. There, at the bottom of the stairs, Julie lay in a heap, hood pulled over her head, mumbling and groaning. Tom handed his son to Christina and knelt down beside his wife.

"Tried to crawl … bathroom … wrong way … dark … stairs …" Tom checked for signs of broken bones, sprains, or bruises. Julie tried to sit up, rubbed her elbow, hiccupped, belched, and went limp. "Listen Gumby, you're not going anywhere." Tom gently lifted Julie and carried her back upstairs.

"I'm nota rolla sod."

Tom laid Julie carefully on their bed, then went back downstairs, calmed his daughters and tucked all three children into bed. No sooner had he collapsed next to Julie than she got up and stumbled to the bathroom, which is where Tom found her when he awoke to the wailing of his son an hour later. Tom somehow coaxed Julie awake long enough to nurse their baby while he helped her sit up on the cold tile floor. The girls awoke when the sun was high in the sky; the baby slept twelve hours. When he needed to be nursed again, Tom brought him to Julie, who had somehow managed to crawl back to their bed. She was in a state of near panic at the thought that she may have killed their son with all of the alcohol he had absorbed through her milk.

For the next three days Julie lived in a stupor. She nursed her baby when Tom brought him into the bedroom; she was vaguely aware of being spoon-fed soup a couple of times; and she wondered, as consciousness gradually returned, how skin could hurt so much. When her mother showed up to help with the kids, Julie thought she might be hallucinating. *Apparently I'm looking in a side view mirror, since my mom is closer than she usually appears.*

CHAPTER TWENTY-THREE

STORM CLOUDS

⸎

The alcohol burned out of Julie's system and left a residue of loneliness. The women from church were kind and encouraging, but none had been let into the vault of Julie's soul—a place where not even Julie felt comfortable. And since Julie hadn't gone back to work yet, she deeply missed June and the others from the Friday morning prayer group. Tom's attentiveness had faded within a week of Julie's drinking episode; and as much as she loved her children, something was still missing.

Jamie Anders! I'd forgotten all about her! I would never have made it through my senior year without our conversations during homeroom every day. Marriage and jobs and babies had taken Julie and Jamie in different directions, but Julie thought they could easily reconnect. Julie certainly needed it, even if Jamie didn't.

After a quick call to Miriam Evans to arrange an afternoon of day care, and a hasty gathering of toys, extra clothes and a diaper bag, Julie settled her kids in the car, drove to Miriam's, left her kids and headed to Jamie's. She had nothing to lose!

Deep purple thunderclouds were heaped on the horizon. *I should buy one of those purse-size umbrellas next time I'm at K-Mart.* By the time Julie pulled into Jamie's driveway twenty minutes later, her car's windshield wipers were going at warp speed while lightning flashed around the darkening sky in spontaneous outbursts of power. Julie had always been mesmerized by thunderstorms ... there had been something strangely calming about them during her childhood, almost like they could overpower the chaos in her family.

Julie opened her car door against horizontal, driving sheets of rain. Since it was July, it was a hot rain; Julie expected to get instantly drenched anyway, so she tilted her head back and yelled, "Lay it on me!" into the rain. She walked to the front door, flung it open, slid inside and closed the door behind her, rain cascading off her clothes onto the tiled entryway.

"Yo! Jamie!" Julie shouted above the storm. "It's me, Julie Dietrich—Julie Sandford! Are you home?" Julie stood still and listened, feeling foolish for not having called ahead.

A television clicked off in another room, and a tall gal wearing cut-off denim shorts, a t-shirt that said, "If a Finn marries a Greek, you get a Freak," and entered the room. All of Jamie's friends knew they had an open invitation to come into her house anytime without knocking or ringing the doorbell. Jamie reached back to tighten the rubber band around her high ponytail, her face lighting in recognition.

"Julie! Julie Sandford! How have you been, friend?" She ran up to Julie and wrapped her in a hug. Both girls laughed as Julie's clammy, wet clothes stuck them together.

"Get down with your bad self, girl!" Julie rattled off the line that the two of them used to throw at each other. They had become really close for a short time, even discovering that Jamie's mom and Arlene had been childhood friends.

"Jewel, let me go find you some dry clothes. As soon as I get back, I'll make coffee, and we'll raid the pantry for

Mallow-cups, like old times!" Jamie ran out the kitchen, through the den, and up the stairs.

Julie watched the rain beating against the kitchen window and thought about the time she and Teddy had driven his Firebird through a car wash. *There must be a hole in the ozone—too many memories are getting through.*

Over the sound of the driving rain, Julie heard a knock at the back door at the same time it pushed open. A man burst into the house like she had done ten minutes earlier with water dripping off his raincoat and puddling around his feet. His umbrella had obviously lost a battle with the wind; the nylon drooped in defeat and the metal frame resembled the spokes of a broken wheel. The man dropped the hood of his jacket to reveal a full head of dark, wavy hair. His face was gentle, his complexion was ruddy, and his eyes were the deepest brown Julie had ever seen. He looked about six feet tall; with his broad shoulders and full chest, he reminded Julie of one of those handsome heroes in the old war movies she loved to watch.

The stranger made a valiant effort to wipe his face with a soaked sleeve. As though the weather was of no consequence, he casually said, "Excuse me, and is Jamie here?"

"Sure, hang on a minute and I'll go get her." Julie skipped out of the comfortable kitchen and stopped in the living room to dig her bare toes into the shag carpeting. In spite of the heat, she began to shiver from her wet clothes. She quickly ran up stairs, spotted a closed door and took a chance that this was Jamie's bedroom. Knocking on the door and shouting, "Girlfriend, some man is here to see you," Julie sailed back downstairs, plopped onto a kitchen chair and waited. The stranger stayed in the entryway; Julie ignored him and absentmindedly thumbed through a pile of magazines on the corner of the table.

Five minutes later, Jamie entered the kitchen armed with a folded pile of dry clothes. She stopped and stared, first at

Julie, then at the man. Her eyes grew huge, and her normally light complexion turned several shades of red.

Glancing up from her magazine, Julie grew alarmed. "Jamie, what's the matter?"

Unaware of any unfolding drama, the man looked at Jamie and said, "How's it going with you, Jamie? And what about this weather? Anyways, Barbie sent me over to ask if you'd like to go to dinner with us sometime this week."

"I'm not sure," stammered Jamie, as she collapsed into a kitchen chair and hugged the clothes. She looked again at Julie and then at the man. "Have you two met?"

"We were waiting for you to do the formal introductions," joked Julie.

Struggling to keep her voice calm, Jamie introduced the man to her girlfriend. "Julie, this is Elliott. Elliott, this is Julie." Elliott muttered a hello, ducked his head, threw aside his useless umbrella, pulled his wet collar up to his ears, shrugged his shoulders, and opened the door. "Barbie and I will call you later, Jamie," he said as he was swallowed up by the storm and closed the door behind him.

Putting her head down on the table, Jamie sobbed, "Oh, Julie, I'm so sorry. I didn't know what to think, or say, or do—"

"About what?" responded a befuddled Julie.

Jamie raised her head, looked at Julie through a blotchy, tear-streaked face, and almost screamed, "That was *Elliott!*"

"I know. You introduced us."

"No, you don't understand. Everyone calls him *Elliott*, because his last name is Ness. You know, like the guy who chased after Al Capone."

"That's funny! Why are you so upset?"

"Because his *real* name is Eugene—Eugene Ness, your biological father!"

Julie's pulse exploded in her ears.

Jamie plunged ahead. "Don't you remember when I used to tell you about Eugene and Barbie Ness ... how they would come over and take me out to dinner ... and how they would buy me presents for my birthday? They've been friends of my family for years. Eugene has always treated me like a daughter. I thought ... I thought ..."

Julie jumped out of her chair. "What? You thought I knew this guy was my father? How the heck would I have known that? No one ever told me his last name!"

"You remember when we were at that Youth For Christ meeting, and I said, 'I'm sorry he abandoned you?' I was talking about Elliott. Eugene. I'm so sorry."

Julie grabbed her purse, hung the strap over her shoulder, and headed for the door. "Look, James, I've got to go. Let's stay in touch, okay?"

"Please don't be mad at me."

"I feel a lot of things: disappointed ... bothered ... confused ... betrayed." She blew out a long breath. "But I'm not mad at you. It was never your responsibility to tell me about Eugene. I need some time to figure all this out. See you later." Julie opened the door and walked out into the storm, a perfect picture of her life. *How could that man stand in the kitchen and look at me and not tell me who he was or try to make any connection with me? And* why *has he treated Jamie like his daughter all these years?*

During the short drive to the daycare, Julie thought back to the first time she, her mom and her brother had made their midnight escape to Michigan. The day after they had arrived, Grandpa and Grandma Cerbé had taken them out to Burger King with two old people who had been introduced to Julie and Dan as 'Grandpa and Grandma Ness.' Every Christmas in Michigan, the Sandfords, Cerbés, and Nesses had been together. *How could my mom have done that to herself and to me? No wonder she always looked so uncomfortable. I figured she was comparing her clothes to the other ladies and didn't think she measured up. But this—I don't understand this at all. And where was Eugene all those times? Where were Eugene and Barbie? God, please help me.*

Later that night, after her kids were in bed and Tom had gone out looking for his drinking buddies, Julie grabbed a can of Sprite, plopped down on the couch, and listened to the rain tapping a steady rhythm on their roof. It was satisfying to have the weather outside reflect her inward emotions.

Julie's thoughts needed a diversion. She picked up the morning paper and flipped through the pages as she sipped her soda. At the back of the local news section were the obituaries—and Julie experienced the second shock of the day: Teddy Tannenbaum had fallen asleep at the wheel and been killed by a grain truck driver.

Oh, Lord, please let this day be over.

CHAPTER TWENTY-FOUR

"GO WEST, YOUNG MAN"

J ulie tried to push hard enough to squeeze all of the air out of her past. The approaching Christmas holiday needed to be different than anything she had ever known in her childhood—and as far as she knew, different than anything Tom had known, as well. A veil of sadness usually covered Julie from mid-November to mid-January; this year would be the pattern-breaker. If Danny could act like a reasonable father and grandfather, then Julie would do the 'normal' thing and invite her parents over for Christmas dinner. Since returning to work in September, she had had to work whatever shifts she was given, and she was scheduled to work graveyard on Christmas Eve. But she would be home Christmas morning to pop a turkey in the oven and make all the other fixings for a perfect holiday meal. There were wrapped presents for her kids under the tree, and no person or gift would be abused in her house.

It was three days before Christmas; Tom was sitting at the kitchen table watching Julie put a hot dish into the oven.

"Julie, that dad of yours—or I should say *Danny*—is a drunk."

You should both be comfortable around each other.

"I don't want him in my house. If you want him here, I'm gone."

Why am I pulling for the dark horse? Julie's wobbly voice reflected her confusion. "I'm not sure why I want to do this. I guess I feel like our kids deserve a grandpa like Grandpa Cerbé was to me. Or like Grandma Emma was to you." *But I won't let him out of my sight with our kids. One of these days I need to tell Tom what Danny did to me.* Julie sighed deeply.

Tom stared off towards the wall clock and breathed evenly. "Then I guess maybe I could stay. I've always gotten along okay with your mom. I sure can't figure out why she remarried that creepy guy, though."

Julie rolled up a dishtowel and threw it at Tom's head. "Heck if I know!"

"Hey!" Tom got up, went into the kitchen, grabbed Julie's shoulders and spun her around. Julie threw her arms around Tom, the man who had promised to spend the rest of his life taking care of her.

"Come here, you." Julie led Tom back to the table and motioned for him to sit down. "I want to tell you a story I heard from my cousin Vicki."

"I didn't even know you *had* a cousin Vicki."

"She's about twenty years older than we are, and I haven't seen her since the first time we moved to Michigan. I had actually forgotten all about her until she called me out of the blue last week."

"What did she want?"

"I don't know. It was still good to hear from her."

Tom got up, went to the fridge, popped open a can of beer and sat back down at the table.

God, I hope he stops drinking someday.

"So?"

"Well, my family usually lived in houses or trailers that should have been condemned. Except for the time we lived near the Andersons, I thought everyone lived like we did."

"This house must seem like a palace to you!"

"I really am grateful for it."

Tom drank the rest of his beer in one gulp. "I like it too."

"My mom always told me that we had to move because Danny was offered a better job somewhere, but Vicki knew that we moved because we had been evicted."

"*That* will never happen to us."

"But wait! It gets better. Apparently Danny has a half-sister, Pat, who married a guy named Mac when she was only fourteen, and he was only fifteen!"

"No way!"

"*And,* Pat and Mac divorced and remarried each other four times! Mac eventually made his fortune in construction, and then he and Pat bought a Caribbean island! And their financial help probably kept Danny out of jail a bunch of times!"

"That's freaky. You got any more strange relatives? How about rich ones?"

"I wish."

"Did Vicki say there would be any money coming our way?"

"Nada."

♦

Christmas dinner was the first of many shared between the Sandfords and the Dietrichs during the next few months. Christina, Emma and Tom-Tom loved their funny and charming 'Pop-pop.' Arlene usually distanced herself from Danny and the grandkids, apparently storing up her relentless criticisms of Julie's parenting and housework for the "day-after" phone call.

Julie wondered more than once if Danny would ever find an opportunity to apologize for his hurtful words and grotesque actions during her childhood. She knew there were times when something Tom said or did triggered horrific memories that would cause her to lash out at him, and they'd both end up confused and hurt. *And the real target is my children's grandfather.* Julie was still searching for a way to close the early chapters of her life.

♦

"Julie, Danny's gone!" Arlene was sobbing over the phone.

"What do you mean 'gone'? You were both here for dinner last night." Julie was rolling out dough for cinnamon rolls, helping Christina with math homework and half-listening to her mom over the sound of Pac-man coming from the living room.

"I mean 'finnito.' Vamoosed. When I got back from the mall, his clothes, his work boots—everything was gone."

I didn't even like *the man—yet he managed to abandon me anyway, just like Eugene.*

"I'm sorry, Mom, but I need to go. Talk to you later." Julie hung up before she was dragged into another conversation about what a wonderful husband Danny was.

♦

She had never thought of herself as superstitious—but to be safe, Julie considered climbing into bed and pulling the covers over her head on April Fool's Day. It had been a year and some change since Danny had disappeared, and her mom had seemed not only to accept it, but also to enjoy the freedom of supporting herself. When Julie had told her kids that their Pop-pop was out on a grand adventure, they, too, accepted it with a resilience that Julie had never felt as a child.

Julie promised her kids a fun, trick-free April Fool's Day at Nana's house and told herself that she would once-and-for-all let go of her ridiculous and irrational fears. As soon as the kids were settled with their toys and games, Julie joined her mom at the table for a cup of coffee and a slice of home-made banana-nut bread. When the doorbell rang, a state of comfortable lethargy kept everyone glued to their respective places until the persistent visitor rang three more times.

"I'm coming!" Arlene got up and stepped around several pairs of shoes on her way to the door.

"Open up, Arlene. It's your old friend Doug."

Arlene opened the door and smiled. "As I live and breathe, I never thought I'd see you again. Where's your partner, the Pillsbury Doughboy?"

Julie saw what looked like worry on Officer Seaver's face.

"I wish I didn't have to do this." Doug gingerly placed an envelope in Arlene's hand.

"You want some coffee?" Arlene's voice trembled slightly.

"No, I've got to run, thanks anyway." Doug turned and almost raced back down the sidewalk.

Arlene opened the envelope, unfolded a thick pile of papers, stared at the top sheet and dropped everything on the floor. "Doug, wait!" Officer Seaver turned around just as Arlene ran and vaulted herself into him, throwing her arms around his neck and hugging the living daylights out of him. "*Thank* you!"

Julie ran to the front door, bent down and picked up the papers her mom had dropped. The top page was a summons for divorce proceedings.

"Mrs. Sandford," Doug gushed, "I've been doing this kind of work for twenty-five years and no one has *ever* thanked me!"

"At least I know that that worthless man is in Wyoming. I hope he stays there until he falls into the Grand Canyon."

♦

So Danny's in Wyoming. Maybe it's time to find him. Julie was tired of shouldering a hundred-pound burden of anger, and the only way she could think of to get rid of it was to confront Danny. *When I finally face him I'm going to say 'Danny, do you* know *what you did to me all those years when you were drunk, or did you black out and forget everything? Because the truth is that I wish I could black out, but I've had to live with my memories for too many years. One of us has to lay them down, and I'm willing to. I know you're not my real dad, and I'm trying to forgive you for what you did.'* Julie was ready to throw off the victim identity and pick up a new one—if only someone would tell her what that was.

Every time Julie thought about trying to locate Danny, she got wrapped up in her job, children and husband; but when her frenetic level of activity slowed down, her anger came up for air, and then she would deal with migraines. The accompanying sleep that should have brought relief from the pain ended in nightmares in which she was trapped in a burning building, waiting to be rescued by Mr. O'Keefe or Mr. Thomas or Mr. Koski—or sometimes a dragon-like creature. This cycle of fighting and fleeing lasted a year and took the place of Julie actually pursuing Danny.

♦

It was a beautiful, clear morning at the beginning of May, and Julie willed herself to recuperate quickly from a pulled back muscle so that she could return to work. Lilac-scented air drifted through the open windows, and it was one of those days that made Julie glad to simply be alive.

Julie was startled out of her thoughts when a large man in a dark blue uniform suddenly filled the space in front of the screen door. She painfully rose to a sitting position and recognized a county sheriff.

"Oh, no," Julie muttered, "Did something happen to my husband?"

The sheriff spoke in an efficient and unemotional tone.

"I'm looking for a Julie Sandford."

Julie fought to keep her breakfast down. "That's me, but my name's not Sandford. It's *Dietrich.*"

"Is your father's name Danny?" the sheriff replied in the same monotone.

"Well, yes, he's my adoptive father."

"I'm sorry to have to be the one to tell you this, but your father died March twenty-second, and you're the only next-of-kin we've been able to track down."

"Did you try to contact my mother?" whispered Julie.

"Yeah, we tried, but we didn't have an address for her."

Julie sought refuge in trivia. "No, I guess you wouldn't have known that after her second divorce she changed her last name back to her maiden name of Cerbé."

"Can I come in?" Without waiting for a reply, the sheriff walked in, let the screen close behind him and walked over to Julie. He handed her an official-looking certificate and said, "I'm sorry to have to add to your grief, but your father is being cremated today."

♦

Julie counted on the gathering of information to absorb her shock; before the sheriff was out the door, she had picked up the receiver from the phone sitting on the end table and called information. The sheriff had said that she might be able to get some answers from the chief of police in Casper, Wyoming. *I wonder how much this call is going to cost me. Seems like I've spent my whole life paying a price for Danny's mistakes.*

Several different connections and ten minutes later, Julie was talking to a Sergeant John Mollen. "My name is Julie Dietrich. I live in Michigan. My ... *father* ... Danny Sandford ... died somewhere in Wyoming in March. Can you help me?"

"Hang on a minute. It's here somewhere." Julie heard the sound of rustling papers. "Here it is. Seems your dad was married to a Native American woman named Chondra."

"Does your report say when he was married?"

"Records show it was about a year and a half ago."

He wasn't legally divorced until a year ago. "Any idea where he worked?"

"Seems he was working construction jobs until he fell off a roof on a job site and broke his back. He got a two-hundred thousand dollar settlement for that."

My mom certainly never saw a dime of that money. Julie took a deep breath. "What happened to Danny?"

"He and Chondra were in some seedy motel—"

"Spending two-hundred thousand?"

"Who knows? You can blow through that kind of money pretty fast if you want to. Anyways, the manager was doing his rounds to collect the week's rent; when he couldn't get an answer from Danny and Chondra, he opened the door with his key and found Danny lying on the floor next to the bed. The ambulance responded within ten minutes to the manager's call to 911. According to the M.E., Danny died twelve hours later in a local hospital. The autopsy showed acute alcohol blood poisoning resulting in septicemia and pneumonia. The report also says he looked like a concentration camp victim."

"Has anyone found Chondra?"

"Not as far as I know, no. And I hope I don't see her name on another report from the M.E."

"Thank you."

"Do you want the ashes sent to you?"

"No." Julie expressed her thanks again and hung up. She lay back down on the couch and stared at the ceiling. *Having an alcoholic father was like being handcuffed to a rattlesnake. I spent my life trying to avoid its bite until one day it slithered out and attacked itself with its own venom.* Julie pumped her fist in the air. "Yes, yes, yes! That creepy, horrible, despicable, nasty, awful man is *never* going to hurt me again. Ever! It's done! It's over!" And then Julie began sobbing uncontrollably as the sky tore open, drowning her house, her yard, and her soul in a flood of sympathy.

CHAPTER TWENTY-FIVE

CLOSED DOORS AND
UNOPENED WINDOWS

Depression moved in and set up house in Julie's spirit. Since her friends assumed that Julie would feel vindicated by Danny's death—the ultimate 'what goes around comes around'—she assumed an attitude that wouldn't disappoint them. *But I feel out of control again ... his death was the ultimate one-upmanship. How am I ever going to win now?*

On Friday mornings, Julie tried to be at work by six-twenty so that she had a chance to talk with June before prayer time started. Every time June shared about how much her pastor had helped her deal with anger towards her father, Julie considered seeking the same kind of help. *Maybe this is the right time. Besides, I've been going to First EV Free a long time now. I should move out of the pew and formally meet Lance Johnson.*

♦

"Pastor Lance." Julie sat in an easy chair in the pastor's study early one Saturday morning and assessed her comfort level. One wall was made up of built-in shelves holding unadorned hardcover books, a scale model of a red, classic Corvette convertible, a framed picture of a petite, blonde woman with a small boy, an unopened box of animal crackers, a stack of cassette tapes, a carved, wooden cross on a stand, and a pair of headphones. The paneled walls displayed framed diplomas and certificates, and crayon drawings of praying hands, trees, and people. An older typewriter perched atop a metal desk defied modern technological advances. Julie relaxed and looked openly at her pastor. "I have a friend who's gotten help from her pastor, and I was hoping maybe you could do the same for me."

"I'm glad you came."

"You may not feel that way by the time I unload."

"My feelings won't matter at that point; the Bible says we're supposed to help carry each other's burdens."

"Mine have been weighing me down for too long." Julie rubbed the vinyl on the wide arm of her chair.

"Which load is the heaviest?"

She continued smoothing out invisible wrinkles.

"Probably the bucket of blame I've been lugging around since I was about eight years old."

Lance cupped his chin in his hand as his eyes opened wider in sympathy.

"And shame. Blame and shame."

"Go on."

"My father hurt me. For years."

"How so?" Lance spoke softly.

"He called me ... bad stuff." Julie stared past Lance out the window behind him. *What if Mom finds out I'm here and accuses me of betraying the family?* "I'm not sure I should say any more."

"Everything you say here is confidential."

Julie shifted her focus back to Lance, who dropped his hand and rested it on his desk.

"I haven't had many men in my life I could trust."

"I'm sorry."

"I am, too." Julie crossed her ankles and looked down. "My father abused me ... and then left me."

"Was that a relief?"

"Yes." She shifted in her chair. " No."

Pastor Lance folded his hands on his desk.

"I've felt like damaged goods for most of my life." Julie uncrossed her ankles and bent down to straighten her sandal.

"Take your time."

"If I smoked, this would be a good time for a cigarette." Julie and Lance chuckled together.

"How about a cup of coffee?"

"Great."

"Be right back." As Lance walked around his desk, past Julie and out the door, she fought the urge to flee. *What if I'm opening a box I'll never be able to close again? What if I don't like what comes crawling out?* She leaned her head back, closed her eyes and remembered the time she had sat in a chair like this in a waiting room, right before she got the news that she was pregnant again. That had been a frightening time for her, but having Emma had turned out to be a joy, and maybe something good could come of this time, too.

Lance came back in the room with two Styrofoam cups. "Is black okay?" He handed a cup to Julie.

"That's the only way to drink it. Thanks."

Lance sat back in his chair, took a sip of coffee and turned sideways to look out the window. "June's a great month. Do you have a busy summer planned?"

"Working, raising kids, gardening, farming ... 'Do it and get through it,' like my mom always said."

Lance swiveled his chair back around to face Julie. "Do you ever—"

"To be honest, I feel like I'm trapped in a room with no inside handle on the door, no windows, and it's getting hard to breathe." *Maybe I'm saying too much. He probably just wanted to know if I take vacations or something. Stick to the questions, Julie.*

"I'd like to talk more about your father."

"The ... abuse?" Julie felt her face turning red.

"But not if it's too hard for you."

Julie curled a section of her hair around her ear. "Actually, I found out when I was in high school that he wasn't even my real father. He adopted me when my mom married him.

"How old were you when that happened?"

"My biological father deserted my mom and me when I was three months old."

Lance wrinkled his eyebrows. "So you were abandoned by your real father ... and then abused and abandoned again by your step-dad?"

"Yeah, then my step-dad—or who I call my *adoptive dad*—divorced my mom, remarried her after I got married, and took off a year later without a forwarding address. Much later, I got the news he had died in Wyoming. I never got a chance to confront him about what he had done to me, so I guess maybe it was my *hope for closure* that was abandoned."

"This is a tangled story."

"Got that right."

"What did—what's your adoptive father's name?"

"Danny."

"What did Danny do to you?"

"What *didn't* he do?"

"Emotional abuse, verbal abuse, sexual abuse?"

"Yes, yes, and yes."

Lance released a loud sigh. "Was there anyone who tried to protect you?"

"My mom's parents helped me out of some trouble. If they knew what Danny was really like, they never talked about it."

"Anyone else?"

"Danny's mom lived with us for a while when I was a kid, but she had all these confusing behaviors, and I learned a few years ago that she was an alcoholic and was suffering from some kind of dementia."

Julie finished her coffee, tore off little pieces of Styrofoam and dropped them into her cup.

"Julie?" Lance finished his coffee and waited for Julie to look at him. "How does your mom fit into the puzzle?"

Julie erupted in a derisive laugh. "That's a joke!" She crushed the rest of her cup and pitched it in the wastebasket. "Oh, I don't think I should have said that."

"There aren't any 'shoulds' here. Please go on."

"Okay. Well ... my mom was—*is*—the most self-absorbed and co-dependent person I know."

"How so?"

Julie got up, walked to the door, grabbed the knob and stared at it, while her back was to Lance. "The first time Danny molested me in my bedroom," she whispered, "I told my mom about it, and she said, 'Oh, he was just in the wrong room.'" She turned around and yelled, "The *wrong room!*"

Lance shook his head. "I've been in this profession a long time and heard many stories of abuse, but none that involved an excuse like that."

Julie walked over to the bookcase and picked up the model car. "And there were so many things I never even told Mom about." She set the car down and walked back to her chair. " When I was a senior in high school, I drove down to Detroit with a couple of friends so that we could visit our boyfriends. I was a victim again ..."

"Of—"

"Rape. Date rape."

261

I should quit now, before I get accused of telling lies and kicked out of here.

"Oh, Julie."

She plunged ahead. "When I got back from Detroit a day earlier than I was supposed to, Mom never asked me why I was home early or if anything happened. I used to think that if the water wasn't rocking her boat, she could pretend she was the only one floating." Tears rolled down Julie's cheeks as Lance handed her a tissue.

"Julie, are there books you've read ... or friends ...or *anything* that's helped you work through some of this?"

"I had one really close friend in high school whose experience with her grandfather was similar to mine. We didn't know how to help each other except to create a world for ourselves that didn't include many males."

"Completely understandable."

"And then I had some misguided friends, like this girl who introduced me to bulimia. She assured me that it would give me the control I was looking for, but all I got from it was more migraines, so I stopped purging after about a month. A couple of different times as an adult I tried it again. Once, I had a blood vessel in my eye burst from repeated vomiting. That scared me ... and when I prayed about it, I knew God had taken away the urge, and I haven't done it since."

"That's amazing that you could quit without any help from anyone – it shows that you have a good deal of inner strength."

Julie looked at Lance with mascara-smudged eyes. "I've never thought of myself that way. All my life people have told me I was too stupid to do anything."

"What people?"

"My second grade teacher, who made me sit in a 'Stupid Chair' and write my name in a 'Stupid Student Answer Book.'"

"No!"

"Unfortunately, yes. And then there was my father—I mean *Danny*—who was never pleased with my grades or anything I did ... and my husband, who once told me I was too stupid to pass a test for a job."

"Those words can really tear holes in you."

"They *can*—and they have."

"So your husband—"

"Tom."

"Tom hasn't been in your corner?"

"No, he usually paints me into one."

"You're very articulate."

"I pretty much know how to hit the nail with my own head!"

"And funny!"

"Well, I moved around so much growing up that I never had a chance to make friends as a little girl, and I really wanted this one special doll for a friend. But when my Mom wouldn't buy her for me, I started having mental conversations with her ... and I'm still doing it today."

"What would it take to get those conversations out where real people could hear them?"

"I don't know."

"Do you trust people to handle your words with care?"

"Not sure of that, either."

"Do you think your husband would help?"

"Heck, no."

"Does he know all the things you've told me?"

"Only a few." Lance noticed Julie purse her lips tightly together.

He looked thoughtful as he said, "What kind of family did Tom have growing up?"

"Better than mine, because he wasn't sexually abused— at least as far as I know. He just wasn't any better in the emotional department. After his dad died his mom married a guy who hated him."

"Have you and Tom tried any marriage counseling?"

"I wish!"

"Would it be okay with you if I prayed for you?"

"Now?"

"I'd like to."

"Out loud?"

"Only if you're comfortable with that."

"Sure."

Pastor Lance folded his hands and bowed his head. "Dear God, I'm astonished at how honest Julie's been here today. We want her to get healthy in every way, and to be able to deal with some of these traumas of her past. We know that *You* are the best Father, the heavenly Father who has watched over her and protected her, even when it didn't seem like there was much protecting going on. Give us wisdom to know how to best help her now, and thank You for loving her with an unconditional love. Amen."

Julie and Lance lifted their heads. "Julie, I wish I were the one to help you. I believe in honesty as much as you do, and I know someone who's immensely more qualified to help you than I am. He's a colleague of mine, Lars Olson, who's a very gifted psychologist. He has an office in Grand Rapids, and I've known him for many years. I would be glad to give you his number so you can set up an appointment with him. Call me whenever you want to and let me know how things are going." Lance got up and walked around his desk.

It feels like I'm being dismissed again. But if there's a chance that Lars could really help me, then maybe I should try it.

"Thanks for listening to me."

"And thank you for trusting me. That's a big first step for you, isn't it?"

"I guess it is."

"You bet it is. You may not have arrived yet, but at least you've left the station."

"Really?"

"Absolutely."

Julie shook Lance's hand and left.

♦

Lars Olson's office seemed more functional and less homey than Lance's. Julie doubted she would have felt initially comfortable in a place where she suspected she would have to take care of some serious business. She had spent years on an arid road with few watering holes, and she felt like tumbleweed, bouncing through life without any control, direction or sense of value.

"Julie, before we get to the real reason for your visit, I need to do an intake."

"I spent several years working in a hospital, so I'm familiar with that."

"Great. I'll try not to take too long with it."

The intake flowed into a larger river of confession and catharsis as Lars began gathering information on Julie's health, medications, family of origin, marriage, and work history. While she gave detailed accounts of the different incidences of abuse, the boyfriend triangle that preceded her marriage, her desire to find Eugene, her endless stomachaches and migraines, the feelings of abandonment, and a deep need to be loved—specially by a father—Julie saw her life like it was playing on a big screen in front of her. It was no surprise to her when Lars used the DSM-IV, along with his obvious intuitive skills, to hang a label of Major Depressive Disorder on her. It was with a sense of relief that Julie realized she wasn't crazy, or stupid, or inept. Her past had continually battered against any attempt on her part to build a foundation of worthiness.

♦

During her weekly sessions over the next few months, Julie gradually replaced her need for comfort in Lars's office with the belief that, finally, here was a man who had proven himself dependable and honorable. She settled into the upholstered armchair and waited for Lars to start.

"Julie, I'm a strong believer in the power of Christ in my life."

"If you had said that to me from the get-go, I would have probably been out of here."

Lars chuckled. "Why is that?"

"I've been burned too many times by Christians who are convinced they're God's fingers pointing out my faults, His voice shouting out my sins, and His arms folded tightly against my desire to be loved no matter what."

"I'm sorry that happened to you. Sometimes we're the ones most likely to shoot the foot soldiers instead of standing together against the real enemy—the one who wants to rob your joy."

"That ship sailed a long time ago."

Lars sat back and looked kindly at Julie. "What's your main goal for therapy?"

"I guess it's to find a way to heal the wounds of my past so they stop ripping open and bleeding into my present."

"You've already done a lot of the work by figuring out what you want." Lars scribbled some notes on his pad while Julie unzipped her down jacket. "I've never suggested this to anyone before, but because you're so thoughtful and articulate, I think this may work well for you."

"I'm listening."

"Have you ever been a journal writer?"

"As a matter of fact, I started keeping diaries when I was a little girl pretending to write to a doll named 'Thistledew.' Then, when I got older, the diaries became journals – and sometimes I addressed those journals to God, or to my best friend Chris."

"Then I think this will be perfect for you. I'd like you to write a letter to Danny Sandford, and tell him how angry you are at being robbed of your innocence."

"My life has been damaged by a lot of emotional shrapnel from him."

"Don't hold anything back. No one—not even me—will read your letter. I should tell you that you're about to stir a pot that's had memories sticking to the bottom of it for a long time ... and when those hardened, blackened recollections float to the surface, your life might seem worse than if you'd left everything alone. But I can give you some tools to help skim the debris off of your past and dump it. I'll describe more of that to you after you get the letter written."

Julie heaved a big sigh. "I can try it."

♦

The following week, Julie cancelled her therapy appointment so that she could finish her letter. It had been initially slow going and awkward, and Julie found herself dealing with weird feelings of betrayal; but, the more she wrote, the more it felt like a dam had broken open, and the words gushed out of her hand as quickly as she could write. When she was finally finished, she was amazed to discover she'd written ten pages.

"Here, Lars." Julie pulled a neatly stapled group of papers out of her purse when she was back in his office again.

"I told you I wasn't going to read your letter. I've given some thought about what I think you should do with it."

"Send it into orbit?"

"Close."

♦

Maybe I should have waited for a warmer day! After Julie's husband and children left the house, she bundled up and went outside, ready to follow Lars's last instruction about her letter. She laid the stack on top of a snow bank, pulled a lighter out of her pocket, and watched the flame quickly turn the letter into black ash. *Lars said that God would add the ash to the compost already in my life to grow a bounty of forgiveness in my heart, and that forgiveness toward Danny, God, and even myself, would heal the wounds.*

Using the end of a stick to dig a small hole, Julie scooped the ashes into it and buried them.

CHAPTER TWENTY-SIX

HUMPTY DUMPTY

*L*ars has always been honest with me; he never prom-*ised that all of my memories would* stay *buried.* Julie soon discovered that her sense of smell resurrected some of them. Every time Tom made sexual advances while he was drunk, the sour smell of alcohol on his breath flooded her brain with images of Erik and her father, and she'd end up running to the bathroom and emptying her stomach. When Julie mentioned this to Lars, he suggested that it might be time for her to open up as much of her past to Tom as she felt able to do, a little at a time. He also said that bringing her story out in the light would take away the power it still held over her in the form of guilt. The thought of talking to Tom was far scarier than writing her letter had been—but she knew that Lars was right, and that she could no longer carry the weight of secrecy about the molestation and abuse she'd suffered from Mr. Thomas, Mr. Koski, Mr. Bittner, Erik Martin, and her father.

By the end of six months, Julie was ready to be done with therapy. If Tom had been willing to go with her … but that wasn't something she ever expected to see. As she said goodbye to Lars Olson, she remembered the verse Pastor Lance often quoted to her: "The loving kindness of the Lord is from everlasting to everlasting; his mercies are new every morning; great is Thy faithfulness."

◆

It was the eve of their ninth wedding anniversary. Julie had spent half a year thinking about Lars's last 'homework assignment,' and decided this was a good time to start unlocking some of her carefully guarded shame. Tom's sobriety—usually hidden as well as Julie's past—wore down the last of her excuses.

As she finished loading the dishwasher, Julie casually said, "Tom, let's go for a drive. It's such a beautiful night, and we could ask one of your cousins to come over and watch the kids for a while." *Maybe it'll be easier to spill my guts to Tom if I don't have to look at him.*

"Yeah, sure." Tom folded up the newspaper, dropped it on the floor and got up to find their kids.

With warm air blowing through their truck's windows, Tom seemed content to look out at the neat houses and farms and fields lining both sides of the highway. *Maybe I should create a tidy, sanitized version of my memories ...Tom wouldn't know the difference, but I'm pretty sure Lars would say that I'm not going to unlock the chains of my past until I use the key of complete honesty.*

"Tom, I need to tell you some things I should have told you a long time ago." Julie turned her head to look out her side window as Tom whistled softly. *He's not exactly encouraging me; at least he's not yelling at me, either.* "You know my dad was an alcoholic."

"Yep. No news there."

This is going to be messy. "There are some things you don't know."

"What—he was a thief? He did time for robbing a liquor store? That wouldn't surprise me, considering how much he drank."

Again, the pot calling the kettle ... Julie pushed down her anger towards Tom and concentrated on the confession-at-hand. "One time when Danny got drunk in my mom's café, he ... raped me."

The whistling stopped.

"Another time ... actually, lots of times for a couple of years ... he would get drunk, come into my bedroom, and ..." There was a knot in Julie's throat that momentarily choked her words.

She turned and noticed Tom gripping the steering wheel tighter.

"So when you've been drinking, your breath smells like Danny's did, and then you come into our bedroom, and you want to—"

"What do I look like to you?" Tom banged his fist on the dashboard, turned his head and glared at Julie. "If I'd have known ... I don't know *what* I would have done to him. But I'm *not* him." Tom turned back and squinted his eyes at the sun setting out the front window. "Don't you *dare* compare me to that horny—"

"Stop!" Julie swallowed the lump in her throat and leaned her head against the door, thinking that this would be a good time for someone to reach across her and shove it open.

By the time they got back home and walked into their house, Julie had dried her tears and decided to hide behind a wall of functionality. If Tom didn't want to deal with her past, she would continue living in the present like a well-oiled machine—rising at six, making breakfast for him and doing jobs around the farm until eight, returning home and getting the kids ready for school and daycare, and then back to farm work until she showered and left for her full-time job at one-thirty. After work, she would can vegetables, make freezer jam, clean house, wash clothes, and collapse into bed at three in the morning.

Meals would be cooked to perfection. Children would be raised with precision. Sex would be given on demand and her stomach routinely emptied after each encounter. Intimacy would be protected behind the wall.

♦

It soon became obvious that a flat line was far worse than an erratic one—and that something was needed to shock Julie's heart back to life.

Flowers and leaves had shed their dormant state overnight, and the world was full of color. Julie faced a rare Sunday afternoon with nothing to do and was anxious to put some distance between her life at home and whatever she felt drawn to by the vibrancy of spring. Car trips with old boyfriends and her husband had never turned out well—so this time she would do a solo flight and maybe keep driving until she ran out of gas.

Right outside the town limits of Kale was a mileage sign for Cross River. Forty miles sounded like a good trip, so Julie headed in that direction. *I wish I had some clear mile markers in my life. God, where am I going?*

The previous night's rain was still evident in the deep puddles on the highway, and the bright afternoon sun made the air smell clean and unsullied. Julie loved fresh beginnings, but felt like she was the second generation in a family of dream-recyclers. Nothing in her life held any promise of newness.

Driving into Cross River, Julie passed a farmhouse with a 'for rent' sign near the mailbox. *Maybe that's what I've been looking for. I'm quite acquainted with farmhouses ... and even though that one looks like it needs a facelift, I'll bet I could fix it up.* Tom had fulfilled his promise to take care of Julie, which she now realized was his only way of covering all the bases in their marriage. His newest job was in insurance sales, where he quickly rose to the position of top salesman while continuing to work the farm. Both he and Julie lived life at the speed of sound, while only one of them experienced a deep sense of failure to be heard. *I've got a voice. I'm going to use it.* Julie pulled her car over to the side of the road, fished a pencil and piece of scratch paper out of her purse, and wrote down the phone number listed on the sign.

♦

As soon as Julie got home she called the number on the sign and arranged to meet the owner and pay the first month's rent. *Tom will have to run the farm by himself for a while—I'm going to need time to get ready to move in.* Julie spent every spare minute at the house, cleaning mouse droppings out of kitchen cupboards, scraping old paint, scrubbing every wall and floor to a sturdy shine, and painting all three bedrooms, the living room, and the bathroom. As soon as the paint was dry, Julie borrowed Tom's cousin's truck, loaded some of their furniture, clothes, and the kids' toys, and she and her kids moved to their new house. After all of the moves she had made in her life—including the midnight flight from Danny—Julie never expected to be moving again this way. At least with the other moves, there was a good reason behind them—eviction, job change, and hope of more financial stability. This time wasn't quite like any of those, but Julie didn't think she could tell anyone why she was leaving. *My friends would be shocked over me ditching a handsome husband and beautiful home.* Julie had heard that some of those same neighbor women were in abusive marriages, but she had learned from her own childhood that people carefully guarded that kind of secret.

273

◆

Julie wondered what Grandma Emma would think about her leaving Tom. It almost felt like the days with Mama T all over again: she didn't seem to mind losing the guy half as much as losing the mom. It was definitely time to give Grandma a call; she had put it off for too long, and the truth was that she really missed the elderly saint far more than she had been willing to admit.

◆

"Grandma Emma? It's Julie." Julie pushed the words through the golf ball in her throat.

"Julie? My liebchen? Oh, how I haf missed you!"

Tears ran down Julie's face. "Really?"

"I haf wanted to call you, but I vas afraid you would think I vas interfering between you und Tom."

"This isn't the old days anymore, Emma. You can cook for me anytime!"

Emma's chuckle was raspier than Julie had remembered. *She's getting older, and I can't even think about losing her someday.* "I know you und Tom haf been getting along nicht so much."

"No, Emma, Tom and I have been separated for quite a while."

"My Tom vill always be my junge, but he is not vell in his head and heart. I haf prayed for him every day since he vas small, and I vill keep doing it. But you, Julie, I haf loved for all dese years, and you vill always in my heart be."

"Emma, you are my special grandmother. You were there for me when no one else was. Did I ever tell you how much I love you?"

"Ja, but I haf short-term memory loss sometimes!"

"Then I'll just have to remind you often!"

"Vat do you kids alvays say? 'It's a deal!'"

"Can I come see you sometime?"

"Anytime. My door is open for you alvays."

"Danke, Emma."

"Guten nacht, liebchen."

Julie hung up the phone and hugged herself the way she knew Grandma Emma would have done. She started in to the kitchen to get a cup of coffee when the phone rang. *Emma must have forgotten to tell me something.*

"Hello, Emma."

"No, it's Tom."

One of these days, I may yank the phone cord out of the wall.

"Tom, I'm headed for bed."

"What? It's only ten o'clock. You're never in bed before three."

"Things are different now." Julie slid the pot out of the Mr. Coffee maker.

"So I've heard."

Julie ignored the sarcasm, poured herself a cup of coffee, opened the microwave door, slid in the cup and carefully shut the door before answering Tom. "What's going on?"

"I want you to come home."

"I *am* home."

"Why should you live in an old farmhouse? I thought you had enough of that in your life."

"I thought so, too. But this is different. It's peaceful here."

"I could pay more attention to you, and it would be peaceful here, too."

"Goodnight, Tom."

The conversation was a verbatim of the previous night, and the night before that. *He's been calling every night for weeks. Why do I keep answering the phone?*

◆

One night, the conversation took a detour.

"Tom, I told you I go to bed by ten."

"Yeah, whatever."

Is this how he plans on convincing me he's going to be a better listener?

"Julie, my Uncle Jack has invited me to come out and visit him in Kansas City. I really want you to come with me. You didn't get a decent honeymoon, and we've never had a vacation. Please come and we'll talk. I know we can work things out."

Julie's heartbeat increased.

"If I agreed, who would take care of the kids?"

"I've already talked to Emma, and she is willing."

"For how long?"

"Probably four days."

"And the farm?"

"My cousins will feed the critters for us."

"I don't know, Tom—"

"Please, babe."

"I've never been on a plane before."

"Me neither! It's time for some adventure in our lives."

"You mean more than living with you?"

Tom chuckled. "I deserved that. But if you come home, I have a surprise for you."

Not another tractor.

"I'll think about it."

◆

When Julie walked into her bedroom in Kale the next day, she saw a white pants suit spread out on the bed, along with sandals, purse, and a gift certificate for a manicure. Even though she didn't see a new dress, she suddenly felt like a happy little girl and hoped there were two more wishes left in her bottle.

♦

Uncle Jack and Aunt Suzanne met Julie and Tom at the airport, and the four of them hit the pavement running for the next three days. Their itinerary included a Royals game, Boyd's Bar-B-Q, the City Market, and jazz clubs on 18th and Vine. Julie hadn't known that married people could have this much fun together—and she certainly never expected Tom to be this attentive to her. She was back as an eighteen-year-old newlywed who had been rescued, only this time she had been swept up by a romantic guy, and she found herself unable and unwilling to catch her breath. *I wish this would last forever.*

♦

During the return flight to Detroit, Julie sank back into her seat in a state of happy exhaustion. Looking out her window on a checkerboard of farms and wheat fields, Julie wished for a life as ordered as the landscape. She turned and looked at her husband, a man who had seemed transformed during the past few days. He casually reached his hand into his jacket pocket, pulled out a small velvet box and flipped open the cover.

"Julie, you threw this at me when you left. Please take it back and come home. I'll go to counseling. I'll do anything. You know we're meant to be together."

My friends warned me about this. Julie smiled at Tom, leaned over, kissed his cheek, and let him put her wedding ring back on her finger. Tom laced his fingers in Julie's, and the two of them leaned back and closed their eyes.

♦

First Evangelical Free had recently called a new pastor. Julie had liked and trusted Lance Johnson—both rare occurrences where the men in her life were concerned. But if Tom was serious about going with her to counseling, she was willing to check out the new guy.

Pastor Tim was a recovering alcoholic, which was the only credential he seemed to need to earn Tom's respect. By the end of their first counseling session, the men were talking and joking like old friends, even after Tim gave his 'homework' assignment to the couple—which was to go on a date once a week.

Julie and Tom laughed their way through corny movies, ate at nice restaurants, rode snowmobiles around their land, and spent a lot of time holding hands. When Julie told Tom that someday she'd like to go to school for her nursing degree, he squeezed her hand and told her that she was smart enough to do anything she wanted to do. *Maybe this is my second wish.*

Tom was home every night for dinner, playtime and story time with his kids. Julie would climb into bed and wait anxiously for him, rarely suffering headaches and feeling better in every way than she had in a lifetime.

♦

The first time Tom missed dinner and stumbled into the house at eleven, Julie was willing to give him a chance to be human. Things were going so well for them that Pastor Tim had ended their counseling sessions. When it happened again a week later, Julie flipped back through her journal and read the pages where she had pleaded with God to give Tom the desire to be with her and their kids. It was a good reminder to her that Tom had come such a long way, and that everyone deserved a second—or third—chance.

When the same thing occurred three more times the following week, Julie knew that Tom's drinking had put a chokehold on her pipe dream. *I'll stay until Tom-Tom graduates from high school, but then I'm leaving, even if I only own the clothes on my back.* The earth outside their door was ready for plowing and planting, but Julie's neglected heart was stony and overgrown with weeds.

◆

There had never been any Hallmark moments in Julie's marriage, and she didn't think that would change on her tenth anniversary. During their months of counseling, Tom could have figured out that she wanted diamonds, or clothes, or books; but where did he get the idea that she wanted a manure spreader with a red bow taped to the top? *If this wasn't so pathetic, and Tom and I had any hope of some kind of decent marriage, we could at least laugh about this. I might even think he meant this as a joke. But I know he can't connect the dots, so I'm not even going to say anything.* Julie's friends teased her mercilessly while they waited for the punch line to her story. As word traveled back to Tom, he reconsidered his gift and presented Julie with an actual anniversary card and a hundred dollar bill.

"It's too late, Tom," Julie sighed. "I already bought a sapphire ring and matching earrings, wrapped them in a box, bought a card to go with the gift, and signed it, 'Happy anniversary to Julie, from Julie, love Julie.'" She tossed Tom's card onto the kitchen table. "Besides, I feel a little bit like the stuff you spread with that contraption."

CHAPTER TWENTY-SEVEN

"ANGELS WATCHIN' OVER ME, MY LORD"

Julie hated dentists with braces, ophthalmologists with glasses, and male gynecologists. Here she was working at a state hospital for the mentally challenged while her own mental and emotional state made her an accessory to the crime of hypocrisy. *Maybe I'll climb into one of the empty beds and pull the covers over my head, or take off all my clothes and bark at the moon, or have a heated discussion with a shadow on the wall. No one here will treat me like there's anything wrong with me.* A new Certified Nursing Assistant job had put Julie in direct contact with people who struggled to stay afloat in constantly churning water—and the job was more satisfying than anything else Julie had done in her life.

Bill Bradford was everyone's favorite patient on the long-term wing. Julie had learned that someone who was profoundly mentally disabled could actually look anywhere from twenty-seven to seventy-seven years old. Bill's slight paunch, stooped shoulders, and graying hair suggested a forty- or fifty-year old man. He had been given free reign to roam the halls as his padded slippers made a flapping sound when he shuffled. Bill was normally a passive man who only experienced psychotic episodes when frightening voices echoed in his head, and that had only happened once in six months. Julie felt protective of him and had grown to love the caring man who seemed happily ignorant of socially acceptable behavior.

♦

Marissa was agitated. There was a full moon shining into her room, and Julie had learned not to overlook the effect of lunar phases on her patients. *I hope I get out of here in one piece tonight.*

"¿Qué pasa?" Julie made eye contact with Marissa as she approached her bed. Marissa had no verbal expression, but her eyes were sophisticated communication devices of love and appreciation. "La luna es bonita esta noche." Marissa nodded slightly, then turned her head to stare at the moon. All of the staff had recognized Julie's gift for calming the patients.

I wonder what's going to happen in my marriage. Julie grabbed a bottle of lotion from the bedside table, flipped open the top, poured a dab into her left hand, and set the bottle back down. *What if I end up like this, in a hospital, unable to tell anyone where I hurt?* Julie began carefully rubbing lotion into Marissa's arms and legs. *But am I really capable of telling anyone where I hurt? I still can't get Tom to hear me.*

♦

Bill came around the corner, peered into Marissa's room, tipped his head forward, yelled, "Leave me alone!" and ran full-tilt at Julie, whose back was to the door. Ramming the top of his head into the middle of Julie's back, she catapulted over Marissa's legs into the opposite wall and crashed to the floor.

Bill backpedaled, turned, and shuffled down the hall a little crookedly, having left one slipper in Marissa's room. Marissa stared at Julie, whimpered, and visibly shook while everything around her was quiet, since most of the staff was in a meeting on restraints. After a few minutes, Julie carefully stood up and waited for the pain to hit. *I need to fill out an accident report and get home!*

Julie hobbled down a flight of stairs to the nursing supervisor's office on the first floor. Inside the office were two desks, a metal file cabinet, an old mimeograph machine, a worn, upholstered armchair, a large fish tank on a cart, and a framed picture of a lighthouse hanging on the back wall. A small meeting room off to one side had the door flung open to reveal a round, brown table, dingy, yellow plastic chairs scattered in disarray, and a narrow counter with a microwave and Styrofoam cups perched on top of it.

Julie attempted to ease into the chair as she began to sweat and the room started to spin. The lighthouse left the frame and whirled around her blurred eyes. Right before she passed out, a nurse walked in, looked at her in alarm and reached for her arms.

When Julie awoke, she was lying on a table in a small, bright room surrounded by a cacophony of noise. Bells, beeps and alarms competed with voices shouting for tests and x-rays. *If I die from the pain, at least things will quiet down.* A prick in Julie's arm suddenly muffled the noise — like she was hearing it underwater — and then the room went black.

♦

Julie stirred, opened her eyes to bright sunlight pouring into her room and heard clear, quiet voices.

" … blood clot lodged between her spine and sciatic nerve … size of a baseball … right sacral iliac … poor kid … terrible pain … Valium will help … three months of complete bed rest … probably never walk again …"

Stop! I'm here! Please talk to me! Julie was glad to see Tom listening intently to the doctor, because she couldn't understand much of what she heard; the only thing she knew for sure was that she wouldn't be walking away from her marriage anytime soon. *How am I going to depend on Tom to do everything for us? He never did anything when I was able-bodied. I'm not sure he knows* how *to do anything.*

Although the injury wasn't her fault, Julie nevertheless felt guilty about it, particularly when Tom turned and looked at her like he was inconvenienced. *I need to assemble my dream team before I leave here. There's Grandma Emma, Sharon, Miriam Evans, and maybe even Mom.*

The anxiety over the possibility of a Valium addiction increased daily during the following weeks, especially after Julie left the hospital and the careful monitoring of the nursing staff. *I'm not doing drugs and I* will *walk again. If that doctor had known how my husband treats me, he would realize I love a challenge.*

The excruciating pain of physical therapy shot fire down Julie's back with each labored step she took. But her resolve gradually won the battle until Julie could walk the quarter-mile down to her mailbox—and that became known as her 'recovery road.'

♦

On a glorious summer morning, Julie awakened to the sound of arguing blackbirds. The large numbers on her alarm clock displayed four-twenty, which meant she had another half-hour of sleep before she needed to get up for her first day back at work. She had agreed to fill in temporarily for someone on maternity leave on the day shift. After twenty minutes of staring at the ceiling, she decided she was ready to get up with the birds. Looking out her bedroom window, Julie saw thin clouds streaking across the sky, piercing the rising sun into a spectrum of pink, orange and lavender. *This is the day the Lord has made.*

After a hot, soothing shower, Julie dressed in her white pants, blue uniform smock, and comfortable shoes. She unwrapped her hair from the towel, bent over and shook it out. The loosely permed auburn hair was in her favorite pick-and-go style. Low maintenance had worked well during her recuperation, and she had decided to keep it. After applying very light make-up—mostly eyeliner and mascara around her deep brown eyes—Julie did a quick mirror inspection, turned off the bathroom light, peeked in each of the rooms of her peacefully sleeping children, and walked to the kitchen. She had often heard her pastor quote the verse, "His mercies are new every morning." Today, she was grateful for the mercy of a completely healed back.

Julie punched the 'on' button on the coffee maker, stepped outside the back door and walked her recovery road down to the mailbox for the paper. She impulsively reached her arms towards the sky, whispered words of thanks, spun a circle, and laughed out loud. This was, indeed, an awesome day.

Back at the kitchen table, Julie enjoyed a leisurely cup of coffee and a banana nut muffin. The dream team had all returned home, leaving Tom to get their children up at seven, give them muffins and cereal, and make sure they were ready for daycare before he took off for work. He had learned how to help meet their basic needs, and had even curbed his drinking during Julie's recuperation time while she had learned to appreciate miracles in all their forms.

When Julie eased into her car at five forty-five, the dew-covered grass was glittering like diamonds. Pulling out onto the highway, she saw the temperature sign on the Farm and Fleet store: seventy-nine degrees, unusually warm for this time of the morning, even in July. By mid-day, the thermometer would probably read close to ninety-five again like it had all week. That—combined with ninety percent humidity—would turn the air into a sauna. She was glad she'd be in the air-conditioned hospital for the next several hours. When she returned home in mid-afternoon, she would change into shorts and a tank top and sit in front of an oscillating fan with an icy glass of tea.

Julie could walk and work again. She was empowered to feed her family and her self-esteem, both of which had become a bit thin lately.

♦

Bill was still a patient at the hospital. Julie started out somewhat cautiously around him, but found herself relaxing more and more after that first day. All of the patients seemed relatively calm and she rejoiced every day that she walked into work. *The jury is still out on my mental health, but one out of two ain't bad.*

As Christmas drew near, Julie was in the same frenzy of activity that had everyone else in its grip. Patients and staff alike seemed to get caught up in the excitement of decorating the various units of the hospital, listening to carolers, and watching their confined world transform into a kaleidoscope.

Julie was glad her shift was almost over; she had at least an hour's-worth of shopping and other errands to do, and she needed to get home and hide some of her purchases before the kids got off the bus. *I'll check on the few patients still in their rooms; there shouldn't be too many, since it looks*

*like almost everyone is out in the main hall listening to the
carolers. Then I'll grab my purse and coat, and I'm definitely out of here!*

Tommy Jones was a favorite of everyone's, but he usually
stayed in his room when there was a lot of excitement. He
was at least sixty years old, which made Julie think about
the wry sense of humor his parents must have had to name
their son 'Tom Jones.' The name must have fit his destiny,
because he was obviously soothed by listening to Tom Jones
music. The staff made sure Tommy's eight-tracks were in
good working order.

When Julie peeked in his room, Tommy was pulling the
tape through the slots of the eight-track and wrapping the tape
around his neck. The tape probably wasn't strong enough to
do any real harm, but all of the staff had been instructed to
use the four-point restraint whenever it seemed necessary.
Julie dumped her jacket and purse inside the door, ran over to
Tommy's bed, and lightly touched his arm. He was normally
placid and could refocus his attention with touch—until
today. Tommy let out a shriek, raised both arms, and pushed
against Julie's chest. She hurtled back against the wall, the
air gushed out of her lungs, and everything went black.

♦

Julie awoke in an all-too-familiar room of lights and
noise, and knew that she was in the Emergency Room at
St. Michael's. Again. *This time I'm* really *logging frequent
flier miles.* When the test results showed no breaks in her
back, she cried in relief, but also in disappointment that she
was back in the first place. And Julie knew she wouldn't be
dancing out of here; it looked like she had severely sprained
a muscle requiring complete bed rest for several days. *I was
going to make Christmas traditions for my family that went*

beyond the violent ones I learned so well growing up. How am I going to do that now?

♦

By late January, Julie had returned to work. She was a team player; workmen's comp had adequately covered her bills and she was determined to make this job work for her. Friends at church, as well as coworkers, began questioning why she didn't quit her job; none of them knew that the only way she could leave Tom was to gain financial stability, and this job was the vehicle for that. *And besides, I really do like my job. The patients are far less violent and abusive than what I lived with growing up. That was a family full of 'buggers,' as Grandma Emma would say.*

♦

Julie re-injured her back four more times in less than four years. *God, I don't believe that You want me to be hurt, or are somehow causing me to get hurt. But maybe You're trying to get my attention. Is it time for me to find a new job? Is there some reason for me to be somewhere else—a person to meet, or something that will somehow change my life? I don't understand it all. Trying to walk Your path for my life is still pretty new to me. But please, please help me find a new job!*

Years of molestations and difficult child bearing had exacted a silent toll on Julie's body: At thirty-two years old, she had a hysterectomy, followed by strep throat and a staph infection just six weeks later.

Someone had uncrossed her fingers.

CHAPTER TWENTY-EIGHT

'TIL DEATH DO US PART

Julie was ready to embrace a new job and discard her marriage. Both thoughts terrified her, but she knew it was time for major changes. She loved her job, and assumed she would have it for the rest of her working career. The reality, though, was that her body could no longer handle the rigorous physical demands of the job. She had also always assumed that she would be married for life, but faced the likelihood that either she or Tom were capable of seriously injuring each other even more deeply if they stayed together long enough for all three children to graduate from high school.

Where ... how ... am I going to find a different job? I'm trained to work with mentally challenged people ... and I know restraints ... but is there a market for that outside of the hospital?

Julie desperately wanted to unload her burden on her friends at church, and even ask them to pray for a new job for her during the 'prayer and praise' time of the Sunday morning service. But it was still a stretch for her to show that kind of trust—both in God, and especially in people who had the opportunity to use her vulnerability against her. *God, these people have been kind to me and my family for so many years. What am I afraid of?*

Julie brought her attention back to Pastor Tim.

"There is a prayer request here from a teacher who desperately needs an aide for a seventh grade boy with autism in her class."

I never thought about a classroom. Kids with Autism or Down's syndrome can sometimes cause harm to themselves or others. I bet I could be that aide! Julie knew that she would have to get through the rest of the service, and then Sunday school, before she would have a chance to seek out the teacher who was looking for a classroom aide.

♦

Having recently agreed to be a substitute Sunday school teacher for the younger kids, Julie now wondered if she had made the right decision. Between her small group at church, the sermons, the love of the people, and the Bible Study at work, she had steadily grown in faith and confidence. There was still that feeling of walking too close to the edge of the cliff, but Pastor Tim had said that God loves a dangling Christian.

As Julie entered the Sunday school classroom at eleven o'clock—a little nervous and slightly out of breath—she saw a tall man crouch down to kiss his little boy goodbye. Both father and son had flaming red hair—

"Erik! Erik Martin!" The man stood, turned, and with recognition lighting his face, wrapped his arms around Julie, lifting her off the ground.

"I heard you were subbing today. I wanted to come and see you, but I was afraid to." With the exception of more smile lines and less freckles, Erik looked the same as Julie remembered him. When she was no longer airborne, she looked at Erik and smiled.

"What—how—tell me how you got here."

Erik laughed the familiar laugh of the guy who had told the punch line of a lame joke. "Julie, it's only by the grace of God that I'm here and not living a druggie life somewhere. All the time I was trying to get 'off the hook,' God wanted me 'on the hook,' dangling and depending only on Him. I should have been dead about six lives ago." Erik grabbed Julie's elbow and gently pulled her towards the corner away from the door. "Julie." He spoke softly. "I honestly can't believe what I did to you ... how I treated you. I know it doesn't sound like enough to ask your forgiveness, but that's all I've got. I really hope you can do it."

Julie didn't hesitate. "Erik, that horse is dead, and we aren't going to beat it anymore. It is so *cool* to see you here. And your wife?"

"Sue is waiting for me in the adult class. And that little guy over there is Kenneth, my pride and joy. My family is everything to me." Erik smiled and waved at his son. "If God took me today, I'd thank Him for them and for all of the second chances He gave me to find Him." His eyes filled with tears.

Julie was in a state of joyful shock. "Erik, say hi to your wife for me. And maybe our families can get together sometime."

"Okay, see you." Erik walked out the door, turned, and said, "Read it if you got it! It's the only thing you need!"

Julie's heart filled with an almost foreign sense of elation as she remembered a verse from the book of Joel that Pastor Lance used to quote—a verse that hadn't made much sense to her until now: "Then I will make up to you for the years the swarming locust has eaten." Lance had explained that God was like a farmer tilling and reclaiming ground. It had taken fifteen years for God to redeem her time with Erik, after Julie thought she would never forgive him for what he had done. After facing the darkness in her own heart, she was overcome with gratitude for God's forgiveness in her life.

♦

Why did I tell Erik we would have him and his wife and son over sometime? I know I wear a good mask for the world, but even I couldn't pull that one off. My marriage is done, and Tom won't be here much longer. Besides, I'm not sure he would be as forgiving as Erik, although Tom ended up with the 'prize.' I wonder if he thinks of me that way? Julie was sorting through her thoughts several days after she had seen Erik at church while she was glancing through the obituaries in the paper. *God, no! There's a picture of Erik!* Erik Martin had been electrocuted while on the job as a lineman. *God, my heart goes out to his poor wife and son.*

♦

Julie sleepwalked her way through the next day, seeking refuge in daydreams with happy endings. A real dream began with a motorcycle ride to her wedding with Teddy-Boy, with Julie holding her veil down against the wind. When the wind became too strong for her to fight, she tumbled off the motor-cycle and lay on the ground, arms splayed out at crooked angles, as Teddy stood over her, laughing a hideous laugh. Suddenly Erik was standing behind him, pinning his arms behind his back and threatening to break both of them. As Teddy's face writhed in pain, Erik turned into Tom, who let go of Teddy's arms, pulled a gun out of his belt and held it to Teddy's head. Julie found a gun next to her, picked it up, and shot Tom, who shouted, 'No, mom!' and became Tom-Tom before he slumped to the ground. Julie had shot her son, and stood in the kitchen screaming his name. She ran to the front closet, threw on her winter jacket, slid into boots and left the laces dangling as she grabbed keys off the hook near the door. *I don't know where I'm going, but I need to get out of here.*

Right outside of Kale was terrain that held a terrifying beauty. Highway eight followed the top of a ridge that dropped off into a ravine of glacier-formed rocks. The drive was eerily quiet as snow-muffled tires carried Julie's car into some unknown rest for her soul. *Driving off the shoulder has to be easier than waiting for my car to stall on train tracks. I can slam my brakes; skid and drop into nothingness; and everyone would assume I'd hit a deer or a patch of ice.* A lone bald eagle soaring high in the gray sky kept an eye on Julie's death wish.

A ten-point buck froze in mid-leap directly in front of her car. Julie hit the brake pedal and fishtailed across snow-covered ice, screaming as her car careened toward the edge of the road and then stopped suddenly, as though held back by a giant hand. When Julie's heart settled down to a normal rhythm, she opened her door, climbed out of the car and plodded all over the road looking for deer tracks. *Where's the buck? Where are the tracks?*

Back in the car, Julie heard a voice through the sound of her chattering teeth: "You need to trust me. I love you." *The car is off. The radio is off. Is that God's voice? Does He actually care what happens to me?* Julie patted her frozen tears and drove slowly back home with an awakening of what it meant to be humbled before a powerful God.

♦

"Melissa? This is Julie Dietrich. We go to church together, and I heard that you were the one who put in the prayer request for a classroom aide for an autistic boy."

"I absolutely did."

"That was three or four weeks ago. Has your school filled the position yet?"

"No, they haven't. My before-school prayer group has been faithfully praying for that need every week."

"Well—"

"Are you interested?"

Julie took a deep breath. "I think I am."

"What is your experience?"

"I don't have a teaching degree, or really any experience with kids outside of raising my own. I've spent the past several years working at Fairview State Hospital, and I have a lot of experience working with people with mental and emotional issues. I know first aid, and restraints, and I'm compassionate with those kind of people."

"Julie, why don't you stop by the school and fill out an application?"

"I forgot to even ask where the school is!"

"It's in Allen Park."

Twenty-five miles from here? How would I ever afford to drive there every day? "Okay, I'll think about it."

"Please do. I need someone ASAP."

♦

Julie's low-heeled shoes clicked against the tile floor of Martin Luther King, Jr. Middle School in Allen Park. She had been hired as a teacher's aide within a week of applying for the job. Unsure of whether she was that good, they were that desperate, or some of both, she forgot both thoughts in the flood of memories brought on by the smells of the school hallway. Part wax, part magic markers, part stale milk and tater tots … it all reminded Julie of third grade and Miss Meyer. *How do stupid people end up as aides? Will I be sent to the office if I'm too rough on this boy, or not strict enough—*Julie's thoughts were interrupted by the smile on the face of a slender woman with stylish blonde hair walking towards her. There was something familiar—

"Glo! Gloria Gustafson! You're so—"

"Skinny! And I'm Gloria Peterson now!" The early-arrival students turned and stared at the women whose hugs almost knocked each other down in the middle of the hallway.

"What—"

"How—"

"You first!"

"Glo! I can't believe it's you! You look fantastic! And the last I heard, you were living somewhere out east with your husband."

"We were. After Jim and I graduated from Michigan State, we got married and found jobs in New Hampshire. I taught school, he worked as an engineer, and we loved being out there. But we really started to miss our families, especially after our daughter Stephanie was born. We moved back last year, and I was blessed to get this job. Let's go to the lounge." Gloria linked her arm in Julie's. "We can sit down with a cup of coffee. I didn't even ask what you're doing here?"

"I'm the new aide in Melissa Jenkins' room for a boy with autism."

"You'll love Melissa. She's a new teacher, energetic, creative, kind, organized, and a really cool Christian gal."

"I know. We go to church together."

Gloria opened the door to the lounge, directed Julie to a chair and headed for the coffee pot. "You go to church?"

Julie laughed. "Don't sound so surprised! You and Bret and some others had a bigger influence than you realize, and I'm trying to find God's way for my life."

Returning with steaming Styrofoam cups of coffee, Gloria set them on the table. "This is suddenly like a dejá vu—you and I drinking coffee in the lunchroom at Fairview, and me asking you about your weekend with Erik Martin."

"I was just thinking the same thing."

"Julie, I'm sorry. That sounded judgmental. I know I was really hard on you then. I had some maturing to do." Julie took a sip of coffee. "I was so afraid I had hurt you, but I didn't have enough courage to ask your forgiveness."

Julie touched Gloria's hand as tears spilled from her eyes. "Glo, you were the best friend I had, and probably the only one who shot straight with me. I had no business going down to Detroit to see Erik."

"So, you didn't keep dating him?"

"I actually did, for a long time."

"And?"

"And, he proposed to me, along with Teddy Tannenbaum and Tom Dietrich—all on the same night!"

"No way!"

"Way!"

"Which one did you marry?"

Julie stared in to her cup. "Before I answer that, you need to know that I never thought you owed me an apology. You did nothing that needed forgiveness. I wish I had gone back to the YFC meetings with you, and learned more about how to live the kind of life God had for me. I was angry and hurt."

"Julie, 'if wishes were horses' … you're here, we've found each other again, and I can't wait to introduce you to the other Christian teachers who meet once a week before school for prayer and support and encouragement."

"And I can't believe we're here together!" Both women got up, hugged again, and opened the door to what Julie hoped would be a fresh start, at least as far as her job was concerned.

♦

Her marriage situation didn't appear to be as easy to change as her job. Julie had agreed to let Tom live in the basement for three months until he could save up some money and find an apartment. It was approaching the end of the three months, and Tom wasn't making any progress towards moving out. He usually came home late and staggered downstairs to turn the TV volume up to full blast, which was Julie's signal that it was safe for her to fall asleep. Occasionally he returned earlier when Julie was still meticulously cleaning every inch of the kitchen, and then she knew some kind of confrontation was not only inevitable, but didn't depend on her input, since Tom seemed hard-wired for verbal abuse.

This can't go on any longer. Tom is supposed to be out of here by now. No matter how things are when he returns tonight, I need to be up waiting for him. And then, somehow, we need to work this out. Julie was completely unprepared for his arrival that balmy, late spring night, as he burst through the door. Blood covered his face and arms and was smeared across his white t-shirt.

"Tom! What happened to you?" The amount of blood on Tom's shirt mocked the lack of blood in Julie's face.

"Need my gun." Tom was panting. "Rocky. Gotta go."

"Rocky—that deranged cousin of yours? Why?"

"Gotta kill him." Tom grabbed a dishtowel hanging from the stove handle, wiped some of the blood off his face, and threw the towel in the sink.

♦

While Tom ran outside and jumped into his truck, Julie dialed 911. *This is one thing I've had a lot of experience with.*

In the meantime, other police officers had been called to the Kale Bar and Grill, where Tom was waving his gun around, spouting obscenities, the safety dangerously off. As soon as he saw the officers he ducked out the back door and arrived home ahead of a car with lights flashing and siren blaring. Tom fell getting out of his truck, got up and swore, stumbled to his house, unlocked the door, opened it, walked in, pointed the gun at his wife and children huddled together on the couch, and passed out on the floor still gripping the gun.

◆

What good is a Restraining Order in this county? It's too big of an area for the sheriff to reach my house in less than forty-five minutes. By then I would be dead. When have I ever seen a Restraining Order work in my life? Julie had never trusted any person or system to protect her; she banked on Tom's unwillingness to keep her in his sights if the possibility of jail hung over his head.

During the ten months it took for the divorce to become final, Tom defied the Restraining Order almost every day by showing up at the house to play 'use-the-kids-to-blackmail-the-wife.' *This will never be over until I take the kids and leave. How can I do that?*

◆

"I need to tell you something, Julie," whispered Mari Larsen one Sunday after church. "When I lost my husband Ebel almost a year ago, you wouldn't *believe* the friends I lost, as well."

"For crying out loud, you're the church organist!"

"Doesn't matter. They were convinced I would become a husband-stealer since I was single, and they shut me out of their lives. Don't be surprised if it happens to you."

"Did people think you wanted to get married again?"

"Heck no! Everyone knew I had been married for forty years to a mean, ornery alcoholic. Some even knew that I felt this huge weight lift off me when he died. Speaking of *weight,* I lost weight and started doing my hair the way I had always wanted to, and going places I had wanted to visit— and people thought whatever they wanted to think."

Suddenly the possibility of collateral damage was far greater than the disintegration of Julie's marriage. Tom's cousins—whom he jokingly called the 'full catastrophe'— were not only their neighbors, but also their closest friends. Julie thought of them as her brothers and sisters, especially when they celebrated birthdays and weddings and graduations together. The gathering place was usually at Tom and Julie's, with Julie cooking enough food for two battalions of cousins. Every event was an excuse for a party; even cutting wood to heat all their homes ended in a hot coffee-and-gooey-cinnamon-roll feast back at the house. Now Julie was in danger of losing not only her family, but also one of the primary supports of her self-esteem.

♦

By the time Julie paid the bills, there wasn't enough money for heating oil, but her salary was too high to qualify for fuel assistance. Since the divorce wasn't final yet, she couldn't expect any alimony or child support. *I will* not *go back to eating Spam!*

Right before Tom left he had cut a fallen oak tree into huge chunks that were still out in the woods. Julie knew that any of his cousins living on either side of them would be willing to come over and help her haul the wood back to the house, and she would have heat for another three or four weeks.

Late in the morning, while the girls played in the woods, Julie put on one of Tom's old Carhartt bibs and found a lightweight ax. She was angry with him, herself, the world, and God; every swing of the ax intensified her anger. *This is going to take me* hours *to do! Whatever happened to Tom's promise to take care of me? I don't want to do this.* When Julie's muscles screamed at her a few hours later, she dropped the ax and trudged into the house with tears frozen to her eyelashes.

Tom's cousin Gary lived a quarter-mile down the road. Within minutes of Julie's phone call, he and his three kids pulled into her driveway in an old Chevy pick-up hauling an open trailer. Julie's kids and their cousins played football and buried each other in the snow while she and Gary loaded the wood into the trailer.

An hour later, Julie resurrected the family tradition of post-work apple pie and coffee. In thirty minutes, hands and feet were completely thawed, the pie tin was devoid of crumbs, and the kids were all playing games in the family room.

"Gary, I can't thank you—"

The back door burst open and Gary's wife Jayne stomped into the kitchen.

"Hey, Jayne, join us for coffee. Sorry the pie is all gone."

Glaring at the offending plates and cups before directing her venom, Jayne ignored Julie and hissed, "Gary, where have you been?" At opposite ends of the table, Gary and Julie simply stared at her.

"We just finished stacking wood and had some dessert." Gary sounded confused, and Julie noticed a decrease in noise from the family room.

Jayne's body visibly shook with the effort to maintain control as she clenched her teeth. "I've been calling and calling here, and *no* one has answered."

Please God, no. Tell me Jayne doesn't suspect us of fooling around. As some of the kids wandered into the kitchen, Gary's oldest son Eric took one look at his mom's face and slowly backed out of the room.

Julie was negotiating a hairpin curve. "Jay, we've been sitting here. The phone hasn't rung." Gary eased out of his chair, walked to the phone, lifted the receiver, held it out so that everyone heard the dial tone, hung the receiver back up and walked over to his wife.

"Jaynie"—a ring shattered the tension while Jayne's eyes bore holes into Julie's stricken face. Turning sharply, she threw open the door and slammed it so hard that the only formal portrait of Julie's family fell off the wall and crashed onto the floor.

Gary is a sweet, lovable, gentle soul safely hidden behind a homely face. If we were trapped on a desert island, population growth would cease. Gary and Julie looked quietly at each other, ignoring the phone still ringing in shrill vindication.

"Is what happened now what I think really happened? Did Jaynie think something was going on here?" Gary spoke gently.

"Yeah, I think so."

"I'd better go then."

"I'm *so* sorry. If there's anything I can do, please call me. I'll come back and explain things to Jay if she's willing to listen."

Julie had never felt so completely alone. *I am dead to Tom's family.* She got up to answer the phone.

♦

The next morning Gary dropped his kids off at Julie's to play in a fresh snowfall. While Gary and Julie stood awkwardly staring at each other, Eric said, "Hey, Aunt Julie! Boy, was Mom mad at Dad when we got home! First she threw a carton of eggs at him, and then she baptized him with a gallon of milk. After that she screamed and ran upstairs. Dad had a *gross* mess to clean up!"

I should make my life simpler and tattoo a scarlet 'L' for 'Leper' on my forehead. The first Sunday at church after the incident with Jayne, Julie assumed she'd find two groups of people: those who were related to Tom and felt a sense of loyalty to him, even though he had stopped attending church at the end of their marriage counseling; and those who were threatened by Julie's divorcee label. In both cases she saw herself as untouchable by the same people who had spent several years embracing her with love and affirmation. She knew that if Grandma Emma could safely drive, there would be at least one person in her corner. No one else was going to offer to help drive her kids home from school after soccer practice or piano lessons. If her car broke, it would be hauled to a junkyard. There would be no handholding to lessen the throbbing ache of her divorce. On top of all of that, she still had her job and house repairs—and three angry kids. *Note to self: never divorce the hometown boy.*

◆

The loudest echoes in the empty house came from the newer bedrooms added on after Tom was born. *This was supposed to be my dream house. Now it's going to be someone* else's *dream. God, what went wrong? Tom and I were so young when we got married. Did either of us know what we were getting into? How many times did I tell Tom I loved him, while inside I was screaming, 'Please love me* more*'?* Julie walked through the living room, across the thick carpeted floor into the tiled kitchen, and ran her hand along the side of the sage green, dual oil and wood burning stove—one of her prize possessions, and one of the few things Tom had bought for her that she truly valued. *Tom and I were like broken-winged birds when we got married, each hoping the other would find a way to help us soar above every hurt and betrayal that had defined our childhoods. It sure would have made sense for at least one of us to figure that out and say it. We were clueless about how to talk to each other. We did a fair amount of cussing in stereo, but it didn't help us communicate love, or compassion, or trust. I still don't know the right way to cry for help.*

Julie made one more sweep of the house, turning off lights and checking for closed windows. *For five years, I inhaled and held my breath, waiting for this house to be built. After I exhaled, I still wasn't in the place I think I was seeking—a place where I could withdraw more love than I invested, and where there would still be a surplus in my home account.*

CHAPTER TWENTY-NINE

FLAT TIRES AND INFLATED DREAMS

Some people in Julie's congregation used the Apostle Paul's description of the Bible—the 'sword of the spirit'—as an opportunity to sharpen their weapons of judgment. By further interpreting verses in the book of Matthew as a condemnation of divorce, even one fueled by adultery, they fulfilled Mari's 'prophecy' by thrusting their pointed words into Julie's heart. She gradually learned to draw a wide circle around them and cling to the people who embraced her with gentle arms of love.

An attractive, thirty-something, single woman was a rare species at her church, and Julie soon found herself in demand for after-church lunch dates. Sean Mills was tall, lean and blonde, with a whimsical, soft-spoken nature that captured the image of being the polar opposite of Tom. Julie was instantly drawn to him; after a half dozen dates she was held by his interesting stories. She had never known anyone who had lived in Alaska and worked on the pipeline—and for a long time, she ignored almost everything else to spend time with Sean.

After a pleasant dinner date one evening, Julie awoke from a dream in which she had been running away from Sean, only to have him reappear at every corner trying to throw a big net over her that she was barely quick enough to escape. She got up and went to the kitchen to warm up a cup of coffee; and when her brain was firing on all cylinders she faced the reality that her relationship with Sean had reached critical mass. He had shown every sign of someone about to propose marriage, and Julie suddenly realized she was in a battle between the need for intimacy and an equally strong aversion to it.

The church congregation had followed the whirlwind romance between Julie and Sean, with the sword-sharpeners quoting verses against re-marriage, while many others let them know that they were praying for the obvious leading of a wise God. When battle fatigue became visible on Julie's face, a discerning, older woman suggested that she spend some time focusing only on God without making any decisions about Sean, who had made it clear to Julie that he had waited thirty-two years to marry the right woman—and she was it. Julie's response had been that she had spent fifteen years in a wrong relationship, and wasn't sure who or what was *it*. Without a goodbye to Julie or anyone at church, Sean disappeared. Word around town was that he had moved back to Alaska.

What's wrong with me? I broke this guy's heart, and mine isn't in such good shape, either. I can't play this game the way I did in high school; I'm older and have a lot more at stake now, especially my kids' emotional safety. I need to get some things figured out, or stop dating. In the meantime, I've got children to raise and a job that needs some clear-headedness.

♦

The fifty-mile roundtrip from Kale to Allen Park became easier and cheaper when Julie found out that Butch Lane and Jim Newman—both from right outside Kale—were looking for a third person to carpool with them. And, because she had had very little experience or success with guys who were 'just friends,' she was pleasantly surprised when Butch and Jim turned out to be exactly that. The teasing banter made the trips to work pass quickly. It reminded Julie of those first staff meetings at Lakehaven Nursing Home. She teased these guys every time it was her turn to drive and they had to fold their lanky frames into the back of her Toyota Celica. After six months of carpooling, she hoped she would never have to return to the days when she drove alone.

One day in early September, the teasing took on a different tone.

"Julie, you need to meet Danny Lewis," said Butch.

"You mean the history teacher?"

"And soccer coach," added Butch.

"He's a great guy," echoed Jim.

"Isn't Nancy your cousin? I heard she dated Danny after her husband died, and she says he's 'fantabulous!'" Butch snickered.

"Uncle!" Julie laughed.

"Hey, he's six-one, and has one of those wide-open, honest faces that I bet everyone loves." Julie saw Jim's puckered lips in her rearview mirror.

"Why don't *you* date him, then?" Julie raised her eyebrows and wore a serious expression.

"I'm already spoken for." Jim put his arm around Butch.

"Ain't we cute together?" Butch laid his head on Jim's shoulder.

"You guys are morons."

"At least we're more *on* than *off*."

"Uncle again!"

"Do we win?"

"Yeah! Leave me alone!"

"Then drive on, oh faithful chauffeur," laughed Jim.

♦

The chilly October evening was already in the grip of winter when Julie left school and headed for her car. Butch and Jim were standing next to the car, stomping their feet and swinging their arms to ward off the cold.

"You have a very flat, right-front tire," they spoke in unison.

"Who are you guys—Dean and Jerry? Cut the comedy." Julie wasn't ready for any good-natured bantering until she was in a warm car.

"We're not teasing," Butch said. "It's as flat as most of Jim's jokes."

Julie looked at the tire in the gathering darkness, and burst into tears. "What am I going to do? I don't have any money or credit cards."

"Danny Lewis could fix the tire for you," said Jim, making a poor attempt at keeping a straight face.

"I won't owe any man *anything!*" Julie's voice was as taut as piano wire. "Sue can give us all a ride home tonight, and I can figure something out tomorrow. I'm quite sure things will get worse before they get better," she added ruefully.

As Julie and Jim climbed into the back of Sue Kendall's vintage Dodge Dart, Butch said offhandedly, "I need to run back to my room. I left some papers I need at home tonight. Be right back!"

"Hurry up—it's freezing out here!" yelled Julie.

Once inside the building, Butch took a few deep breaths, slowed to a saunter towards Danny's room and wandered in casually.

"Hey, Dan."

"Hey, yourself." Danny flipped his pen in the air, caught it and stuck it behind his ear. "What's up?"

"Well, Butch and I have been carpooling with Julie Dietrich for several months now. She gave us both extra keys in case she ever locked herself out of her car. And lucky you: that very car has an acute case of flat tiredness. Wouldn't she appreciate it being fixed—" He tossed the keys to an unsuspecting Danny, who instinctively reached up and snatched them.

The next morning Sue and company pulled into the parking lot right next to Julie's car. Julie reluctantly got out of Sue's car, willing herself to walk over to her own car and inspect the damages in the light of a new, but rather unpromising, day. In utter shock, she discovered a new tire on a newly washed car.

What's going on here? By the time she looked up, her posse was already headed in to the building. *Oh, well. Maybe one of them called triple A and had it fixed without telling me. Those people are really amazing. I'm lucky to have friends like them.*

During their lunch hour, Danny spotted Julie and walked over to her.

"I hope you don't mind that I washed your car while I was at it." He winked and smiled at her. *He's got amazingly clear, hazel eyes.*

"You?"

"Sure. I'm a handy guy."

"What do I owe you?" *Listen, buddy, I got nothing to give.*

Danny took a big sip of his coffee. "Nothing. It's on the house."

"Oh."

"Bye." Danny set his mug on the counter and walked out of the room.

What an idiot. 'Oh?' That's the best I could come up with? Would it have been so hard to thank him?

On the way home from work that night, Julie tried the casual approach.

"Butchie, what could I give Danny to thank him for fixing my car?" Julie kept her eyes focused on the road.

"Buy him a bag of Oreos, and tell him that that's the way a modern woman bakes," said Butch, a smile dancing in his eyes.

The next day Julie arrived in the lounge armed with Double-Stuff Oreos, figuring that exaggerating the thanks would include her in everyone's joke. The room was filled with laughter, and the Oreos quickly disappeared. Julie noticed that after she thanked Danny, he had to work hard to keep his face a normal color.

After everything I've lived through with men, I don't think I can trust my instincts. I need to maintain caution here. Julie felt like a giddy teenager every time she ran into Danny. *But my teen years slipped by without me ever feeling that way. Maybe this is God reclaiming more ground for me.*

Valentine's Day had always been just another day for Julie, who had learned, during her marriage, to grit her teeth and bury her expectations on February fourteenth. Since it was already early February, it was time for her to start flexing her coping muscles as she arrived at work. She sat down at her little cubicle in the back of the classroom with a fresh cup of coffee, stashed her purse in the back of her file drawer, and turned on her computer. While she was waiting for it to warm up to the day, she attacked her ever-present pile of mail and divided it into three stacks: Urgent, Useless, and Unbelievable. After sorting twenty different sizes and shapes of envelopes, she looked at a large manila one that didn't seem a likely candidate for any of her efficient categories.

Julie unwound the string on the clasp, flipped up the top, reached inside and pulled out a large, red, construction paper heart with a white ruffle material glued around the border. In neon green marker were the words: "I've been watching you—and what I see is nice." Julie turned it over looking for a signature, and didn't find anything. Up on the third floor, Danny Lewis was organizing his desk for the day. He picked up the pile of yesterday's tests and discovered a similar homemade Valentine underneath.

As tempted as she was to skip lunch altogether, Julie's curiosity trumped caution as she walked into the lounge at twelve-fifteen.

"Sue, do you know anything about someone sending me a Valentine that looks like a grade school boy made it?"

Sue flashed Julie an innocent smile. "Uh-uh."

"You would be able to talk clearer if you hadn't swallowed so many canaries."

"Umm … Danny Lewis?"

"Negative. We're not anywhere like that in our … friendship."

"Well, then, I guess it will remain one of America's great unsolved mysteries."

"Very funny!" Julie picked up a stale donut hole and launched it at Sue's head. As it missed and hit the floor, both women linked arms and walked out the door.

◆

By the end of the day, Julie was swallowing a large serving of pride. As she walked the long hallway to Danny's office, the pounding pulse in her ears drowned out every other noise. A large group of students was hanging around his desk, along with Sue, Butch and Jim.

Waving the Valentine over her head, Julie announced, "Does anyone know who sent this?"

Everyone in the room erupted in laughter, as Danny's face turned red. Brandishing his Valentine over his head, he replied, "Maybe the same person who sent me this one!"

Julie pointed her Valentine, first at Sue, then at Butch and Jim. "Okay, you louses, 'fess up."

Sue reached in her purse and pulled out a folded newspaper. "Here." She opened the paper and pointed to a circled paragraph in the classifieds.

Dropping her Valentine on Danny's desk, Julie grabbed the paper and read it out loud: "Danny, thanks for all the work you've done for me. I really appreciate all your help. Love, Julie."

"Ooh-ooh." The middle schoolers were poking each other in the ribs and making no attempt at hiding their shock. Julie looked around at the sea of faces and knew she should feel mad and embarrassed—but to her surprise, she felt excited and flustered.

"All right, citizens, return to your lives." Butch patted Julie on the shoulder as he followed the others out the door.

◆

Over the next few weeks, Julie's skepticism and fear were replaced by a growing attraction to a man who was kind and solicitous. Danny volunteered to change the oil in her car, also explaining that there was an air filter that needed changing, but basically everything ran well. When Julie offered to pay him, he refused to accept it—and he acted like a great sport when a bag of Double-Stuff Oreos magically appeared almost daily in the lounge.

"But enough about cars," Danny said one day during lunch. "What do you like to do? Hunt? Fish? Bike? Garden?"

Julie knew she needed to proceed with caution, so that no one would be injured in the making of this friendship.

"I haven't been interested in hunting or fishing. I've mostly worked and taken care of my kids."

"Who are your kids?" Danny leaned forward and looked openly at Julie. *I'm pretty sure I can see through his eyes down into his heart.*

"Christina's fifteen, Emma's fourteen, and Tom-Tom's nine."

"Divorced?"

"Yeah, not long ago." *Am I giving too much information? What are the rules for divorced people?*

"I've been divorced for about ten years."

"Kids?"

"I have eighteen-year old twin boys, Sam and Yam."

"Yam?"

Danny's laugh was full of unselfconscious joy. "When the boys were about four, I started reading 'Green Eggs and Ham' to them. And there's the line that says, "I am Sam, Sam I am." Well, Sam picked out his namesake, but Jeff thought I was saying 'Sam Yam', so he started pointing to the page and saying 'Yam.' It stuck, and I've called them 'Sam' and 'Yam' ever since."

"They don't mind?"

"They have great senses of humor, plus they're both over six feet and big, tough football players. Who's going to mess with them?" Danny's eyes twinkled.

The conversation momentarily stalled, although Julie didn't sense any discomfort in the quiet.

"Look, Danny," Julie ventured. "Our friends went to a lot of trouble to get us together. Why don't we go out once, and then they'll leave us alone? Besides, I'm getting fat eating Oreos!"

"Me, too! Okay, it sounds like a plan. How about a movie?"

"When?" Julie's hands were shaking under the table.
"This Friday?"
"Great."
"Bye, then." Danny got up and walked out of the room.
Real great. I've got nothing to wear but fancy clothes—not good for sending a casual message on a casual date.

♦

On the chance that she could find a way out of this date, Julie called Danny at home that night.
"Hey, Danny, it's me—Julie."
"Hi."
Is it a mistake to call him at home? Is that a more-than-casual message?
"Umm ... about our date—"
"Yeah?"
"Well, I know this is going to sound silly, but I only have dressy clothes that wouldn't be right for a movie. So we probably shouldn't go out Friday." *That is* so *lame.*
"Would you go if you had the right clothes?"
"I'm not—"
"Hey, I don't mind going shopping. How about if we go this Friday, and then we can catch a movie next weekend?"
Julie giggled. "A man-sighting in the mall!"
"Boggles the mind, doesn't it?"
"Lewis, have you crossed over to the dark side?"
"Luke, I am your father." Danny's attempt to imitate Darth Vader made Julie laugh out loud.
"Oh, man—you've been hanging around Butch and Jim too long. They got to you!"
Danny laughed. "I'll see you at work tomorrow."
"Night." Julie hung up and stared at the phone. "You're too nice for my own good."

♦

As they walked into the darkened theater, Julie thought back to a week earlier when they had had their 'shopping' date. It had taken an hour for her to be convinced that Danny really liked being with her, and that he actually enjoyed watching her pick out a pair of boot-cut Levis, a pale green turtleneck, and a black fleece vest. Afterwards, they had driven to Big Boy's and ordered breakfast at eight o'clock at night. They reluctantly left the restaurant at eleven, and Julie knew she was hooked. *This guy is handsome, and a gentleman. Where has he been all my life?*

Danny steered Julie toward empty seats in the middle of a row at the back of the theater.

"Do we have to wait until after the previews to dig into the bucket?" Julie didn't want to look greedy, but she figured half the fun of any movie was the hot, buttered popcorn, a huge cup of Dr. Pepper, and a box of Junior Mints.

"No way! Put it right between us!"

Julie laughed as she and Danny took turns holding their snacks while they took off their jackets and threw them around the backs of their seats. By the time they were settled, the credits were rolling for "Look Who's Talking Too".

♦

"I don't get it, Julie," whispered Danny.

"What?"

"I'm confused."

"Seriously?"

"Yeah."

Julie decided to have some fun and be coy. "How many kids do you have?"

"Two—you know that."

"How did they get here?"

"What do you mean?"

I'm probably enjoying this more than I should. But it's too much fun! "You need the egg, the sperm ..."

Danny's eyes got big as he laughed. "I can't believe how stupid I am!"

Julie put her hand on his shoulder. "No, you're sweet." She had never known a man who was embarrassed by anything, and it was endearing.

"Don't tell anyone about this!"

"I'd never *conceive* of the idea."

Danny slumped down in his seat, tipped his head back and moaned. "I deserved that!"

"Sorry—I couldn't resist! Butch and Jim and I have *pun-offs* every day—makes the long ride to Allen Park go faster."

"I'll have to get some tips from them if I'm going to try to keep up with you."

"Don't try. You're fine the way you are. Besides, you don't want to mess with the master."

By the time Julie and Danny had finished their light-hearted conversation, Julie wasn't the least bit concerned that she had missed some of the movie.

♦

As soon as Julie walked in her door later that night, she called Sue.

"Hi, Sue. I hope I'm not calling too late."

"Not at all! I want a report."

"I'm free-falling, friend, and there's no safety net anywhere."

"So you had a good time?"

"I loved it!"

"Knew you would."

"But now I feel dizzy ... and nervous ... and excited ... and my heart's racing ... and I'm really, really scared."

A few moments of silence passed.

"Sue?"

"Yeah, I'm here. I'm deciding whether or not I should tell you something."

Uh-oh. "Like ..."

"Like—did you know I used to date Danny?"

"I heard that."

"It was a long time ago. He's been divorced for ten years, and it was probably after he'd been single for maybe a year."

"Okay."

"I think I know how you're feeling about him, because I felt the same way. I actually proposed to him, but he said he could never marry anyone—that he had been burned once, and he would never put himself through that again."

Julie let out a long sigh.

"Please don't be mad at me." Julie heard the tremor in her friend's voice.

"No way! Now I know we can go out and have fun."

"You're sure you're not mad at me?"

"Heck, no! You helped me get some balance back in my life."

"Yeah?"

"For sure. And our next date better be bowling. No more movies for a guy who doesn't understand conception."

"What?"

Julie laughed. "Never mind. It's a long story."

♦

"Danny, thanks for another great date. I know it's only midnight, but you've got a long drive back home. And I'll see you at school Monday." Julie was standing at her door, whispering so she wouldn't wake her kids, and blushing like a teenager over her infatuation with this wonderful guy. *When was the last time I felt awkward around anyone? I don't want to blow it with him. He's sweet, and kind, and everything about being with him feels right.*

"I'll be there. Catch you at lunch time?"

"Yeah." Julie didn't trust her voice to say more. As Danny turned around, walked out her door and closed it behind him, she wondered why she didn't at least kiss him on the cheek. *I like him!* Julie absentmindedly wandered over to her kitchen, where she saw Danny's hat sitting on the table. She grabbed it, ran to her door and raced outside to the driveway.

"Danny! You'll need this!"

"Thanks," he whispered.

Julie reached up with both hands, put the hat on his head and leaned in to kiss him. His warm lips made her forget how much the rest of her body was shivering. She pulled away and ran backwards, shouting, "Be careful!"

"It's too late for that!"

Julie started crying, and turned to run the rest of the way to her front door before Danny could see her. *I'm not sure I could explain the tears to him. To be honest, I haven't experienced too many happy tears in my life—just enough to know that that's what these are.* Once inside, she dried her eyes on her sleeve and picked up her cordless phone.

"Mom? … I'm sorry, I know it's late … yeah; I'm fine … I'm more than fine. I think I know the man I'm going to marry—"

"Lord, no!" Arlene shrieked.

Julie slammed the phone down. *Why did I think she'd be happy for me?*

CHAPTER THIRTY

FATHER KNOWS BEST

Some of the great ironies of life seemed to camp on Julie's doorstep. She was determined to find the father who had abandoned her as a child so that he could give her away again as a bride someday.

Trying to locate Eugene was like playing a game of Clue, in which *motive* was more important than location of the crime—so Julie thought of it as a 'whydunit.' *Why did Eugene leave Mom and me? Why didn't he ever try to find me? Why didn't he know me when he was standing right next to me that day at Jamie's house?*

The first move was the easiest. Julie knew that Grandpa Richard and Grandma Rose were still friends with Eugene's parents, and they seemed almost relieved to give her his Washington address. Julie didn't know how long he and Barbie had lived there, but she would find him first and ask questions later.

Julie drafted a simple, one-page letter, telling Eugene everything she knew about him, and making it clear that she wasn't interested in his material possessions, only his presence. She dropped the letter in the outgoing mail at work and spent the next week focusing on her job, her kids, and Danny. She desperately wanted Danny to know what she was doing—and maybe he would encourage her attempt to sever the chains of deceit that had imprisoned her for most of her life. *But, all he knows is that my dad did 'some bad things to me,' and that he died in Wyoming. Danny promised me that the second 'Danny' in my life would trump the first one … that he would love and be gentle … and that all random acts would be only ones of kindness. I'll get this all figured out, Eugene will come here, and then we can get to our marriage and a new life. Pastor Dan used to quote a verse from First John about the 'evil deeds of darkness exposed to the light.' There will be time for all of that once I find Eugene, and then we can put it all behind us.*

♦

There was always the possibility that the letter had been lost in the mail, or that the address was wrong. After double-checking it with her grandparents, Julie composed another letter. *Maybe this time I'll start with 'Dear Eugene' instead of 'Dear Dad.' And I'll leave out the paragraph about what my mom did after he left her.* Julie finished the letter, dropped it in the mail on the way home, and counted on the same diversions to keep her thoughts clear. And, if either letter were returned stamped with a 'no forwarding address,' at least there would be some kind of completion. As she looked out her window at the spring rain pummeling the timid flowers, she suddenly remembered when connect the dots had been her favorite pastime, and a poor substitute for girlfriends and dolls. *I wanted a family like the Cleavers. Maybe I'm hoping that finding Eugene will bring me that family.*

Neither letter Julie mailed had been returned unopened or marked 'undeliverable.'

Now Julie wished she had let Danny in on her scheme. Would there be anything to tell him?

Julie mailed six more letters to Eugene; the first had been typed on her computer, and the remaining ones were copies. Julie figured that since Eugene had abandoned her, she could send him typed letters. *'Don't take it personally.' Is that what he said when he left me?*

♦

"Grandma, it's me again."

"Hi, Julie. I'm always glad to hear from you."

"Thanks. Grandma—"

"By the way, did you ever hear from Eugene?"

"That's kind of why I'm calling. No, I haven't."

"Did you try talking to Chuck and Nancy?"

"Who?"

"Didn't your mom ever tell you about them?"

"No." Julie could feel her heart beating a little harder.

"I don't understand her."

"Me either. I don't expect to anymore."

Rose let out an exasperated sigh. "Chuck is Eugene's brother."

"You're kidding!"

"No, I'm not. And he and his wife Nancy live in Coldspring."

"This is too much. They've lived here—"

"All their married lives."

Julie shook her head. "It would be nice to get *all* the clues for a change."

"I'm sorry I didn't tell you sooner; I assumed you knew about them."

"Grandma, don't assume anything like that anymore."

"Guess not."

"Do you think I could call them?"

"I'm sure you could. They're very nice people."

"So are you, Grandma."

"Thanks right back."

"Later."

Julie pushed the 'off' button on her cordless phone and pitched it on the bed. *Do I chance a face-to-face, or should I call these people? What if they don't even know about me?* Anything's *possible with this family, especially where my mother is involved. Thing is, I can't even ask anyone except her or Jamie. What will happen if I open Pandora's box?*

♦

"Hi, Jamie? It's Julie. Is this a good time to talk? I'm calling from school." Julie's hands were sweating.

"Oh, Jewel, I was *really* hoping you would call. How long has it been since you were here? I've wanted to call you, but I was afraid it might hurt you worse to hear from me." Jamie's gentle voice brought tears to Julie.

"James, I have a lot to tell you. And I need to ask your forgiveness for running out the way I did. So much has happened in my life since then."

"Girl, you're kind. No forgiveness is necessary."

"Thank you. Thank you so, so much."

"Welcome."

"Listen, we definitely need to get together. I've missed your friendship. But for now, I have a quick question to ask you."

"Shoot."

"Do you know Chuck and Nancy Ness?"

"Yeah."

She's probably dreading the other shoe dropping, since I already kicked her with the first one.

"I've been sending letters to Eugene for the past couple of months, and I haven't heard back from him. I just found out about Chuck and Nancy, and I wanted to contact them to make sure I have the right address for Eugene. Do you think it would be all right for me to do that?"

Jamie sighed in relief. "Absolutely! I've actually been with them a few times; they're cool people and I'm sure they would shoot straight with you."

Now it was Julie's turn to sigh. "Thank you, friend. You've taken a huge burden from me. I need to call them today."

"Go for it! Call me soon, okay?"

"Roger that." Julie hung up, ready to jump back into the deep end.

♦

As soon as she verified Eugene's address with Chuck, Julie printed another letter and mailed it off. *I wonder if Barbie has been intercepting the letters, and Eugene doesn't know anything about them? After all, Eugene's past wasn't hers.* Julie didn't want to fret needlessly. She needed to wait a little longer.

No letter ever came from Washington.

♦

"Julie?" Nancy had a naturally soft voice, especially on the phone.

"Yes?"

"This is Nancy. Nancy Ness, your aunt."

"Hey there."

"Have you heard from Chuck's brother yet?"

"No, no I haven't. Maybe I've finally hit a brick wall."

"I hope you don't think I've been too forward, but I decided to call Barbie yesterday. You sounded so anxious, so I thought I'd call and do a little digging of my own. Turns out Eugene spent several months recuperating from hip surgery, then knee surgery. That last surgery brought on an infection that went through his whole body. Barbie said they thought they were going to lose him a few times."

Before I even had a chance to talk to him? "So what happened? How is he now?"

"He's much better, and Barbie said she's finally ready to give him your letters."

"Oh, Nancy, you're amazing. I can't thank you enough for doing this for me."

"Please do me a favor?"

"Anything."

"Let me know what happens."

"Done."

♦

Julie had folded and unfolded and refolded the letter from Eugene so many times the past three days, it was already starting to tear on the crease lines. It certainly didn't matter, because every word of the letter was permanently etched in Julie's mind and on her heart.

"My dear Julie," Eugene had begun his letter. That could have been the beginning and end there, and it would have been almost enough. Julie had never had a father call her 'dear.' The love packed in that one word had erased several years of heartache ... of abuse and violence from Danny, the only father she had known until now.

"You are a beautiful woman with a beautiful family. I would never, ever have willingly given you up for adoption. I think your biological father was a Navy man from Pennsylvania."

The first time Julie had read that sentence, everything in her froze. Eugene's matter-of-fact words indicated his belief that this was old news for Julie. *Someone dropped the ball somewhere, for sure.*

"When people assumed I was your father," the letter continued, "I never corrected their thinking, because I wanted to save your mother any further embarrassment. When we married and moved out to Washington, I had never told her about the mumps I had as a twelve-year old, and that they left me sterile. That was wrong of me."

The constant re-reading of the letter had lessened some of the shock by now.

"Barbie and I have never adopted any children; I guess that's why we treated Jamie like our daughter. As far as my parents, brother, and wife knew, you were my biological daughter. I don't know why none of them ever learned that most men who had mumps as boys end up sterile. I guess we're all guilty of creating our own reality. Anyways, I'm glad I got a chance to tell you the truth. Maybe you can put an end to the lies that have followed me around for so long."

♦

Okay, God, are any more bombs going to drop on me? This is like "The Price Is Right." Do I look through door number three for father number three? I probably shouldn't be bargaining with You—but if You help me find my father, I promise I'll spend the rest of my life learning to live for You.

♦

Julie walked to her closet, reached up to the top shelf and pulled down a box her mom had recently given her. Most of it was filled with report cards—including the one she had wanted to tear to shreds—some artwork, and various school papers. Julie tossed the report cards in the trash, pulled out everything else and plopped it on the floor, and then retrieved her birth certificate from the top of the pile. *Why didn't I understand this sooner? Dan and I are sixteen months apart; if Mom's initial explanation about Eugene had been true, she would have had to divorce him, meet Danny, and get pregnant—all within one month. I could have figured this out back in high school ... but what difference would it have made? Maybe it was God's grace that kept my understanding clouded until I was old enough to absorb the truth about Danny and Eugene. What will I do with the truth?*

CHAPTER THIRTY-ONE

A LITTLE GESTURE

Julie was ready to pay an unannounced visit to her mom. *I'm not giving her any time to work up another fairy tale.*

"Hey, Ma." Julie poured herself a cup of coffee, sat down at the kitchen table, stretched out her long legs and kicked off her flip-flops. "The lilacs are beautiful, aren't they?"

Arlene lifted her hair off her neck, undid the top button of her blue-striped blouse and glared at her. "You're the only person I know who would notice flowers in this heat! Maybe you should pay more attention to your kids. Why don't they come to see me? Is Tom in trouble again? You know if you stayed home a little more often—"

"Ma, I didn't come here to be lectured about my kids."

"I can see that."

A tense silence fell over the room while Arlene fanned herself with a folded newspaper. *Will she* ever *stop harassing me about my kids? Does she have any idea that the reason they don't visit her is because of how nasty she treats them? I'm not dealing with that right now.*

"So Mom." Julie put on an innocent face. "I wrote a letter to Eugene a few months back."

Arlene's face turned ashen. "What?"

"I needed some questions answered." Julie pulled Eugene's letter out of her purse. "Imagine my surprise when he told me that he wasn't my biological father."

With trembling hands, Arlene dropped the paper, picked up a package of cigarettes from the table, pulled one out and attempted to light it; when she couldn't get her hands to stop shaking, she threw the pack and disposable lighter across the room. "Why can't you ever leave stuff alone? Even when you were a child, you could never," she pounded on the table, "never, never leave anything alone! You always had to ask 'why, why, why!'"

Julie looked calmly at her mom with a mixture of anger, humor and pity. "Well, Eugene must have been telling the truth."

Arlene exhaled a plaintive sigh. "I guess there's no reason to keep anything secret anymore." Holding her head between her hands, she choked out her story in a muffled voice.

"When Eugene—'Elliott'—and I moved to Washington, there was no house, no job and no money. When I found out that he would never be able to give me children, it seemed like the last of a whole string of lies and deceptions. When he was offered a construction job in Hawaii, I knew that I absolutely did *not* want to go with him."

Arlene lifted her head, got up slowly, walked out of the kitchen, and was gone for such a long time that Julie thought she was being dismissed again—which was the expected outcome every time a subject got too close to the bone. As she grabbed her purse and got up to leave, Arlene came back into the room cradling an old Florsheim shoebox. The women both sat down as Arlene set the box on the table, lifted the lid, dropped it on the floor, and began sorting through the contents of the box. *I've seen that box for years and assumed it had one of her many pairs of shoes in it.*

"Here. If you're so hell-bent on discovering the truth, you might as well have these." Arlene pulled out a stack of black-and-white photos and pitched them at Julie, who began laying out the pictures in front of her.

Arlene spun the photos back around and pointed to one of them. "That's Elliott and his buddies from the Navy, during the Korean War." She tapped the other picture with a sharply manicured, red nail. "This is Elliott and his mom, taken the morning he shipped out."

Julie couldn't believe what she was seeing. "Why didn't you ever—?"

"He was a handsome guy, wasn't he? Everyone said we were the perfect couple. We were elected homecoming king and queen our senior year."

"You told me about being homecoming queen when I was a little girl."

Arlene got up, walked to the refrigerator, pulled out a can of Diet Coke, flipped the top, took a long drink and returned to the table.

"Like I said, after Elliott left, I got a job at a restaurant-bar called 'Coasters.' Mostly servicemen came in there." Arlene ran her finger around the rim of the can.

Does she realize she's picking up a conversation she started twenty years ago?

"I was really lonely, and I wasn't about to sit home twiddling my thumbs while Elliott was swimming in the ocean in Hawaii. I was already twenty-seven, and I was ready for some of the fun he promised when we first moved out there."

Julie stared at the pictures.

"After I started working the night shift, this guy Andrew came in to Coasters. He spotted me, walked up to me, and said, 'Has anyone ever told you that there is a mysterious beauty about you?' Well, who could resist a line like that? He came back every night after that, and pretty soon we were dating. By the time I found out he was only nineteen, I was already carrying you."

Julie thought back to when she was eight, and her mom had tried to explain how Grandma Philips had been married twice, so that her last name was no longer Sandford. It was way too much information for Julie then—and she felt the same way now.

Arlene seemed to be on a roll. "Andrew was at Puget Sound for another nine months after you were born; when he was discharged, he assumed I'd marry him, and the three of us would go back to his home—I think it was Charlottesville, Virginia."

Julie felt like a lonely, abandoned girl. "Mom, why didn't you and I go with Andrew?" she whispered.

"Because," Arlene suddenly wailed, "I *hated* coloreds; I *hated* the South; I *hated* the heat!"

"And you were still legally married to Elliott?"

"That too."

"What did Elliott do when he got back and found out you were pregnant?" *I can't* believe *I'm asking her these questions.*

"He was mad, but he had always been even-tempered—not like Danny. He definitely wasn't like any of the other men I've ever known, either before or since that time. He seemed resigned to whatever I wanted. He didn't even fight for me. He never asked who the father was. When I demanded a divorce—well, that was fine by him. The only thing he asked was that I'd agree to give you his last name—Ness."

Oh God—I wish she had stayed single! "And then you married Danny?"

"I met him after Elliott was discharged and moved back to Michigan, and Andrew moved back to Virginia. By the time Danny asked me to marry him, I was carrying your brother. Danny legally adopted you, and I didn't care about keeping my promise to Elliott. I didn't think he deserved it."

The web of deceit that trapped her for so many years had also trapped me, and I never knew it until now. "Did Andrew expect you to tell me about him someday?"

"Oh, I figured since he was in the Navy, I could tell you he'd been killed in some kind of accident at sea."

Julie was sure her heart was beating louder than the ticking wall clock. "So ... all you know ... is that Andrew is from Charlottesville, Virginia? You don't know anything else about him?"

"Remember—it was the fifties, I was embarrassed, I was *never* going back to Michigan, and no one would ever find out about Andrew. I don't know why I ever moved back here ... it was a big mistake."

Seems your secret stopped several years short of your grave.

Julie thought this would be her last time to press any advantage. "Mom, can you *please* tell me everything you remember about Andrew? Like, what's his last name?"

"Little." Arlene finished drinking her soda.

"Don't make me play twenty questions." Julie focused all of her emotions into what she hoped was a direct hit on her mom's guilt.

"And he had brown hair and brown eyes. I think he was about five-ten." Arlene tossed her can into the garbage. "He was stationed at Puget Sound Naval Shipyard for three years, from '54 to '56. My friend Charlene from Bremerton is the only person who knew about him. Could be she remembers more than I do." Arlene got up, picked up her shoebox, and stepped on the top as she left the room.

I'm amazed it took her this long to leave.

CHAPTER THIRTY-TWO

CLOSE ENCOUNTERS AND
TANGLED BLISS

I should have left the box closed. Julie sought refuge from her churning thoughts in the security of familiar people — her co-workers, her children, and Danny. Throughout that summer, she and Danny began taking all five of their children on outings to the zoo, restaurants, and drives to the Upper Peninsula. Butchie had a large boat, and invited Julie and her 'full catastrophe' — his favorite phrase — to join him and his wife on their boat to watch the Fourth of July fireworks on Lake Michigan. The beautiful night, with the moon rising up over the water as the fireworks began, redeemed some of Julie's early years of unpredictability and deprivation. *I'm sure I could get used to this. Christina and Emma and Tom-Tom definitely like Danny and his boys, and Sam and Yam seem to like us. This is my second chance at a family.*

The following day, Danny invited Julie and her kids to his parents' house for a picnic. Julie knew that she should be past the point of nervousness — but the last time she had really cared about impressing anyone was when she had met Chris' parents in high school. *God, what if they're like my parents? Or worse yet: what if they're really nice, but they don't like me? I wonder how much Danny has told them.*

The playful respect between Georgia and Daniel Lewis was so sweet—and so encompassing of everyone around them—that Julie quickly forgot about herself and entered into the dynamics with happy abandon. By the end of the picnic, Julie realized that her love for Danny was the wrapping on a delightful family package.

♦

Danny and his boys had been making the drive in from Allen Park every Sunday morning to go to church with her, and usually spent the afternoon with her and her kids until it was time for everyone to go back at night for supper, Kids' Adventure Club, youth group and small-group Bible studies for the adults. Danny seemed comfortable and was definitely well liked at First Evangelical, and Julie no longer thought of him as a 'visitor' in 'her' church.

The church thirty-something age group had decided to get together for a cross-country ski outing on a Saturday in early December, ending with hot chocolate and a warm fire at the Kale Chalet.

As Julie glided across the new-fallen snow, she thought about how many things in her life—how many *bad* things—had occurred during the winter and especially around Christmas time. She had expected to experience her usual pre-Christmas to mid-January depression, and didn't think this year would be any different, although she sincerely hoped something would eventually break this cycle of defeat.

"A dime for your thoughts." Danny skied behind Julie, talking freely to her as they had dropped back behind the crowd.

"I thought it was supposed to be a penny."

"Your thoughts are worth more than that."

Julie silently watched the sun already dipping lower on the horizon, although it was barely past mid-afternoon. A sliver of moon was making its appearance in the opposite sky. She was extremely grateful for the guy behind her who was comfortable with silences, and who genuinely seemed to care about her.

"I was thinking about something Pastor Tim often says— that God chooses not to reverse consequences in our lives, but He does choose to redeem them." The trail led Julie out of the woods and into a clearing, and she waited for Danny to pull up beside her.

"I've thought a lot about that, too."

"Some of the things that happened to me were just that – they *happened* without my control or consent." Julie stopped, laid her poles on the ground and zipped up her vest. "That fire in the chalet is going to feel good!"

"You bet!"

Julie picked up her poles and started her easy glide again. "But some of the things were *my* doing, and they became my undoing. Do I have the right to ask God to somehow 'work those things for good' in my life?"

Danny slowed his pace to stay even with Julie. "When I thought my first wife was serious about kicking her alcoholism, I went to AA meetings with her. At first, I was so wounded, I couldn't think about anything else except being an expert victim. Then, when I thought about the wrong choices I had made in my life, I didn't figure God wanted anything more to do with me. If He didn't have a magic wand, I was doomed to spend the rest of my life continually suffering the consequences, like a real-life Scrooge."

"I love that movie! I cry every time I watch it!"

"Me too. But if you tell anyone, you'll regret it!" Danny grabbed a clump of snow from the high bank bordering the path and hit the center of Julie's retreating back.

"Danny, we need to catch up to the gang! Pretty soon it'll be too dark to see out here."

Danny and Julie were surrounded by puffs of exhaled air as they skied at a fast clip over the carefully groomed trail. When they were within shouting distance of the chalet, the skiers slowed down and Danny picked up the thread of their earlier conversation. "What really turned things around for me was finding a verse from the Psalms that says, "God redeems your life from the pit." I figured whether I was thrown into the pit, fell in accidentally or jumped in on purpose, He could still bring me out of it. It took me a long time to realize that He doesn't grudgingly pull me up and then dangle me over the pit, threatening to drop me if I step out of line."

Julie was overcome by love for the man who had pulled up and was now skiing next to her—a man who might be willing to spend the rest of his life always at her side. "Danny, have I told you that you're the one for me?"

Danny made a noise that sounded like a half-laugh, half-cry. Julie stopped skiing, suddenly alarmed. "Danny, what's wrong?" *Did I say too much again?*

Tossing his poles into the air, Danny threw his arms around Julie and enveloped her in a massive bear hug. "Last week, I asked my dad how I would know if you were the right woman for me, and he said, 'She'll tell you!' And he was right! And you're right!" Danny pulled off his gloves and took Julie's hands. "Julie Marie Dietrich, will you marry me?"

Julie looked at Danny's brown eyes, remembering the first time she had met him and thought his eyes were attached to his heart. "On one condition."

Danny lowered his head.

"That it happens before the end of this year."

Danny lifted his head, let out a war whoop, raised his fist and yelled, "Hey, guys, we're getting married!" The group gathered in front of the chalet broke out into wild cheering.

♦

First Evangelical Free Church was filled with garlands, pine wreaths, candelabras, red satin bows, and white, glittery lights. It was Christmas Eve, and Julie was standing outside the double doors at the back of the sanctuary. She had assumed that a Christmas Eve wedding would bring a small gathering while most of their church friends would be home celebrating with their families. As much as she had wanted to share her wedding with friends who had become her true family, she could never be angry with them for choosing their biological families over a Christmas Eve wedding. *If I had had a loving, together family during any Christmas growing up, I certainly would have wanted to be with them at any cost.*

After Julie had told Danny about all of the times her 'adopted' dad had destroyed their Christmas tree and presents in the middle of one of his drunken rages, Danny had convinced her that God could redeem those memories with a wedding on Christmas Eve. Julie was initially hesitant, knowing her mom would scoff at how unconventional it was, and 'just plain wrong.' *But, my mom will find something else to complain about, anyway—and Danny is the sweetest man I've ever met.* It turned out to be easy for Julie to agree to the wedding date.

And now, standing at the back of a sanctuary packed with people who had spent the previous three weeks sending Julie e-mails that said, "Who are you kidding? We would never miss your wedding!" Julie was once again overwhelmed at God's goodness to her. She knew that somewhere near the front of the church sat Grandma Emma, Georgia and Daniel Lewis,

Grandma Rose and Grandpa Richard, Danny's grandparents, and Arlene Sandford. Christina and Emma were standing at the front, Tom-Tom had ushered everyone in, and Sam and Yam were standing on either side of Julie. Sweet Stephanie Peterson was skipping down the aisle, spreading rose petals from her basket onto the floor, oblivious to Gloria's smile of encouragement. If there had ever been a more magical evening in her life, Julie didn't know what it was. *God is good—all the time.*

Julie struggled to lock her thoughts on the ceremony— not out of reluctance, but because she had had very little experience with the joy that filled the church. The hesitations in her first wedding ... the marriage to an alcoholic ... the mistakes she had made ... the empty places in her spirit which she had tried to fill by controlling all of the outcomes in her life ... none of those things mattered tonight. She was marrying a man who had promised to draw her closer to a 'second-chance' God—not a God of 'seconds' or 'left-overs,' but a God who would draw her to a continual feast at His table of redemption. Danny had said it was God's 'extravagant grace,' and Julie was more than ready to find out what that meant.

"Tonight's message to Julie and Danny is going to be 'The Back Side of Christmas and Marriage.'" Danny squeezed Julie's hand as they turned and faced Pastor Tim. "We are standing in a building filled with poinsettias, sparkling lights, lit candles, and the fragrance of pine. We also know that the tables in the fellowship hall are filled with every kind of cookie and baked good imaginable. And let's hope there are a few fruit cakes there!" The congregation laughed at their beloved pastor's quirky sense of humor.

"I suspect that our homes are decorated in similar ways. We want to show only the good sides this time of year. If a batch of cookies is burned, we might still save it, but we certainly wouldn't waste icing or cinnamon candies on it. If there is a crooked side of our Christmas tree, or a side with gaps in the branches like missing teeth, we turn that side towards the wall and don't waste any ornaments on it.

"At our family gatherings, there might be a drunk Uncle Joe who becomes the elephant in the living room. We try to ignore his behavior, and hope he'll quickly retreat to a place where he will pass out alone.

"There can be depression, discouragement, and a blind hurtling towards a new year filled with hopelessness. We ignore that side of our spirits for 'the sake of the season.'

"There is the precious, infant Jesus in a stable which has been sanitized and stilled, worshipped by tame animals which, if we believe the crèche scenes, know exactly where to stand around the manger.

"But what is the back side of Christmas? It is the *back* of the baby Jesus, which was ripped open by a leather whip. It is the symbol of our forgiveness. It is certainly the side the world needs to see.

"In the same way, there is a back side to marriage. Danny and Julie have each experienced some of that back side in their first marriages: alcoholic spouses, emotional and mental abuse, days and months and years of hopelessness. They are bringing God into their marriage as one strand of the 'three-fold cord not easily broken'—but we know that there will still be trials. There will be times when they see only the knotted back side of their marriage—like the back of a needlepoint design—and become overwhelmed with despair." Pastor Tim looked at the couple before him. "Don't ever forget that the back side of your marriage is the same as the back side of Christmas: It is the torn back of Jesus—the only One who is able to bring you forgiveness and strength. The book of Lamentations says 'His mercies are new every morning.' Hallelujah!" The congregation broke into spontaneous applause, and Julie was surprised that it had taken so long for her eyes to spill over with tears of joy.

Rings and vows were exchanged; Danny and Julie were announced as "Mr. and Mrs. Daniel Lewis; and Julie floated through the rest of the evening feeling like a life-size doll with the perfect dress.

CHAPTER THIRTY-THREE

THE CHARLESTON TWO-STEP

Buying a house in Allen Park had made sense to Julie and Danny, since their drive to school together would be less than five miles. Julie had been deeply grateful for Danny's understanding of her need to start fresh in a place without any memories for either of them. Their house was a simple, three-bedroom ranch, built in the 1970's and obviously maintained well over the years. Sam and Yam were at the University of Michigan in Ann Arbor, and Christina, Emma and Tom-Tom were busy with school and all of their extracurricular activities. Almost a year had passed since her wedding—and although Julie was content with her husband, job and family, she had never stopped thinking about her biological father. She had desperately wanted him to walk her down the aisle at her wedding, but hadn't found either the time or the courage to look for him before the big day.

Sitting in their cozy kitchen on a Saturday morning, looking over her Christmas shopping list and marveling over Danny's willingness to shop with her—even after they were married and he no longer had anything to 'prove' to her—Julie thought about what it would be like to have her *real* dad coming to spend Christmas with them. Unless records were tightly sealed, it should be easy to confirm that Andrew

Little had been stationed at Puget Sound sometime in the mid-'50's. Knowing how many times her mom had lied to her, Julie wasn't sure this bit of information was true, but it was at least a place to start. Monday morning, during her lunchtime at school, Julie would use her cell phone to make a long distance call to Washington.

◆

It was twelve-thirty Eastern Time, which made it nine-thirty Pacific Time. Julie hoped the base office opened before ten.

A very short phone call with a helpful clerk at Puget Sound showed no record of any Andrew Little ever having been there. *Have I hit a wall already? I've been waiting to find my real dad since high school, back when I thought I would someday meet Eugene Ness. It* can't *end this way.*

If Danny wondered why he never saw Julie in the lounge during lunchtime anymore, he never mentioned anything to her, other than an occasional comment that he thought she was losing weight. It was easy for Julie to answer with, "I'm just making sure I fit into a special dress," and Danny seemed okay with it. The truth was that Julie began using all of her free time to stay in her classroom and surf the Internet for addresses and phone numbers for The International Adoption Agency, The U.S. Adoption Agency, and various agencies in Virginia. Julie drafted a simple letter on her computer giving her name, date and place of birth, her desire to find her biological father who had been stationed at Puget Sound Naval Shipyard from '54 to '56, and her home phone number. After mailing five letters, she switched her focus to work and her family while often daydreaming about her *real* dad.

Julie received form letters expressing sympathy for her search, but telling her that her request had been denied.

Undeterred, she called the agencies, got different contact names, and mailed the letters again. *Maybe the left hand doesn't know what the right hand is doing.*

After each rejection letter, Julie broadened her search—to the vital statistics office in Bremerton, the base historian who looked through yearbooks of the USS Missouri, other base personnel—anyone and everyone who would listen to her story. When phone calls and letters began to have a common thread—that they couldn't do anything without either Julie's real birth certificate or Andrew's social security number—she decided to write to Eugene and ask him to mail her a letter granting her permission to obtain her birth certificate.

For the next few months, Julie continued to leave a paper trail, eventually buying a large plastic bin to store all of the weekly letters she received. On Good Friday, she walked in to her kitchen in time to catch the phone before the answering machine took over.

"Hello, is this Julie Lewis?" The voice sounded young and hesitant.

Julie dropped her keys on the counter and distractedly shuffled through a pile of leftover junk mail. I w*onder what she wants? A donation for St. Michael's? A promise to vote for her favorite democrat? Money for new vests for the local police force?* "This is she."

"My name's Sheila, and I work in Military Records for all of the naval bases in Bremerton."

Julie dropped the mail. "I didn't think you would return my call. I've gotten so used to riding the red tape express."

"I know how that goes."

"What can you tell me?" Julie closed her eyes and knew that everything she valued was tied up in the answer to that simple question.

"Probably not what you want to hear."

"Andrew Little is dead."

343

"No. I mean, I don't know." Sheila let out a big sigh. "This is hard."

"Whatever it is, I need to hear it."

"Seems like someone could have easily told you this months ago."

"Yeah?"

"Absolutely. You see, back in '73 there was a fire in our building, and all of the files with last names ending in K through Z were destroyed."

"Which includes the Ls for 'Little.'"

"Uh huh."

"Why *didn't* someone tell me this sooner?"

"I don't know ... national security, privacy, incompetence ... who knows?"

"Well, Sheila, thanks for telling me. I don't know what I'll do next, but at least I know what I *won't* be doing anymore."

"Good luck to you, Julie."

"Luck, prayers, I'll take them all."

♦

Julie crawled into bed that night with a heavy heart. *I should have told Danny before this, because now it looks like I was trying to keep something from him.*

"Hon?" Julie turned on the nightstand lamp, propped her pillow against the headboard and sank into it.

"What, babe?" Danny put one arm under his pillow and used his other hand to rub Julie's arm.

"There's something I need to tell you."

"Now?"

"I should have told you a long time ago."

"You're not sick, are you?"

Julie heard the loving concern in her husband's voice, which increased her levels of both comfort and guilt.

"No, not physically. My heart is sick."

"What do you mean?"

"Do you remember me telling you about my biological dad, Andrew Little?"

"Sure. You said you would like to try and find him someday."

"Well, actually, I've been trying to since Christmas time. I want my kids to have another grandfather, and I want something I've never had in my life—a father who loves me."

"What have you done so far?"

"I've written tons of letters, made phone calls, and surfed the net—and today I found out that Andrew's military file was burned in a fire at Puget Sound Naval Shipyard."

Danny started rubbing Julie's arm again. "Hey, maybe you could call your mom. She probably knows more than she's told you."

"Tomorrow." Julie reached over and turned out the light, knowing that she wasn't ready for another confrontation with her mom until she was intimate with this loving, tender husband who shared her heart.

◆

"Happy Easter, Mom."

"What's happy about it? You couldn't bother to bring your family over here."

Julie bit her lip. "I told you, we've been invited over to Danny's parents' house, and you are invited, too."

"And I told *you* that I don't enjoy myself over there. I always feel like a fifth wheel."

"But it's not just a couples thing. Your grandkids will be there."

"They don't have time for me."

What if you made time for them? That's the way it's supposed to be. It's what I wanted all my life … but I don't think you get it.

"Maybe you'll want to come some other time."

"Not likely." Julie could hear the door of her mom's heart slamming shut.

"Well, can I ask you something?"

"It seems to be what you're good at."

Julie ignored the sarcasm. "What was your friend Charlene's last name?"

"Hoffman."

"Where is she living now?"

"Brother, here we go again." Julie thought her mom sounded more tired than annoyed.

"I promise it's the last question."

"Charlene Hoffman lives in Corbett, Oregon. "

"Great. Goodbye."

"Why did you want to know?"

Julie took secret pleasure in the rare experience of being the one to withhold information. "Just curious."

"Figures." Arlene hung up before Julie could say anything else.

I'll give her that one.

◆

Julie knew that she and Danny had accumulated a fair amount of vacation time, and that they had never had time for a honeymoon. When she suggested to Danny's mom that the three of them take a trip out to Oregon to visit her sister Pearl, Georgia sounded thrilled at the opportunity, yet hesitant to be a burden. Julie reassured her that she and Danny would leave her at Pearl's, go off for a week of sightseeing and romance, and then return to get her. Georgia responded to Julie's offer by booking and paying for three roundtrip tickets to Portland.

◆

Julie figured she had enough adrenalin to fly to Portland without benefit of an airplane. As soon as they settled in their seats in Detroit, Georgia put her head back and fell asleep, and Danny concentrated on his Field and Stream magazine. This was Julie's first honeymoon, and first trip back to the Pacific Northwest since she left at eight years old. She wasn't going to sleep through any of the adventure.

Planning for the trip had been a whirlwind of excitement. Everyone at school had given Julie suggestions for what to see and do in Corbett, which was twenty miles east of Portland. She and Danny had reservations at the Brickhaven Bed and Breakfast overlooking the Columbia River Gorge. During their week in Corbett, they would see Multnomah Falls, the Washington Park Rose Gardens, Mt. Hood, the Bonneville Dam, and anything else that looked fun and interesting. And of course, they would pay a visit to Arlene's friend Charlene.

Maybe Andrew—my dad—*got tired of Virginia and moved back to Washington a long time ago. If Charlene has kept in touch with him, we could contact him and go see him! I know I shouldn't be getting my hopes up. I can't help it.*

As the flight attendants were collecting the lunch trays, Julie realized she hadn't paid attention to either the food or the scenery outside her window. Her mind had been too busy creating a scenario of a reunion with a loving father.

◆

Their first night at the Brickhaven B&B was even better than Julie's expectations. The inn had been built in the '50's using recycled bricks, and with a conscious effort to copy the design of Frank Lloyd Wright. Every room was decorated in an English country décor—and several rooms overlooked the Columbia River Gorge. Julie knew Michigan had the beauty of inland lakes, as well as miles of magnificent shoreline. She had simply never seen a view this wild and spectacular. *I could live here. I wonder if Danny would be willing to move.*

◆

The directions from the Triple A Auto Club were neatly folded in Julie's purse, although she had already memorized them during their flight. As Danny drove their rental car up into the Cascade Mountains, Julie put her head back and felt the cool, foggy May air hitting her face.

Danny's voice broke through Julie's reverie. "You got the directions?"

"We're looking for Summit Road. We should see a sign in about a mile."

There was a kind of haunted desolation that shrouded the car as Danny drove the last mile and pointed to a sign for Summit, nearly buried behind overgrown branches. As soon as they turned on to the gravel road, they saw a beat-up house trailer partially hidden behind a growth of bramble.

Charlene lives in a trailer? I'm not sure what I expected. At least I'll feel comfortable here.

Danny glanced at Julie. "Is this the right place?"

"It's what the directions say." Julie opened the door as a large, mangy dog limped up, staring at her with glassy eyes.

"Maybe we ought to go," whispered Danny, when a woman wearing jeans and a pink t-shirt appeared at the screen door. Her silvery hair fell in thick waves on her shoulders, pulled back from her face by a pair of glasses propped on her head.

"Julie, is that you? Darn if you don't look like Arlene did forty years ago!" Charlene pushed the door open and ran down the steps in a pair of blue flip-flops. She embraced Julie, then turned toward Danny and flashed a bright smile. "And who is this handsome guy?"

"Charlene, this is Danny, my husband."

"No one has called me 'Charlene' in years. My name is 'Charlie'. And since we don't stand on formalities, I need both of you sweeties to always call me Charlie." As Julie and Danny each hugged Charlene, she said, "I hope you can stay for lunch." She spun around and stepped carefully toward the trailer. Julie didn't know what was going on, but she made sure to step in Charlene's footprints.

♦

Not even a comprehensive thesaurus would have contained the words to accurately describe the assault on her senses when she walked into Charlene's kitchen. A large cage was home to two yellow-faced cockatiels with orange cheek patches, squawking as though their spiky hair had been styled against their wishes. The bottom of the cage was covered with pieces of carrot, broccoli, spinach, and congealed rice. Several dogs of different breeds wandered in—and as Julie and Danny were led into the living room, it was obvious that the dogs had staked territory away from a number of cats of various sizes and colors. The only other rooms in the trailer were a bedroom, bathroom, and small sitting room, each filled with a box, bowl or cage holding a ferret, tropical fish, guinea pig and turtle. Swarms of flies were everywhere.

"I know some people think I'm a fanatic, but these critters all needed a home, and they're like my family."

Julie wished she had worn enough perfume to mask the smell of Charlene's menagerie. "I'm not sure—"

"But enough of that. I hope you came with an appetite, because I got a real good lunch made."

Standing behind Charlene, Danny looked at Julie and shrugged his shoulders. Julie smiled back. *At least I won't embarrass myself by overeating.*

"Make yourselves comfy at the table, and I'll be right back." Charlene pushed aside a large dog and disappeared into her bedroom.

Julie trusted neither her thoughts nor her voice as she dug around in her purse for a tissue and wiped off the seat of a vinyl chair. An uncovered casserole sitting in the middle of the table looked like it had already been tested by one of the cats walking around it. *God, please tell me that this trip was worth it.*

Charlene came back to the table carrying a large shoebox. "Do you mind if we wait to eat until I show you something?"

"No!" Danny and Julie answered in unison.

Charlene laughed. "How long have you two been married?"

"Long enough to know that we can wait to eat until we've seen whatever it is you have in the box." *I hope it's not another animal.*

Setting the box down, Charlene took the casserole to the kitchen and came back a minute later with three cans of soda. "I don't think these have had a chance to get cold yet, but I thought you might be thirsty anyway."

"Thank you, Charlie. It really was nice of you to invite us here."

"I'm tickled that you found me." Charlene set the cans down and opened the shoebox. "I haven't looked at these pictures since I knew your mom in Washington, Julie." Charlene pulled out a black and white picture. "These young bucks are my husband and your daddy. They were on the

350

Missouri together. Unfortunately, your daddy is the one looking down."

Julie choked down her disappointment at not being able to see any facial features.

"I wrote to your mom every year since she left Bremerton, and I always asked her if she'd told you about Andrew, and if you'd ever met him."

A yellow lab walked up to Julie and nuzzled its nose into her elbow. Julie reached down to pet the dog and looked up at Charlene. "What do you mean, *every year?*"

Charlene suddenly wore a hurt expression. "I'm sorry I missed a few years; one time Arlene must've gotten mad at me for pushing her too hard about Andrew, because she didn't write back to me. Instead of writing to her again, I called her at your grandma's house, only Rose wouldn't let me talk to Arlene for a long time." Tears were forming in Charlene's eyes.

"Charlie, wait! Have you been feeling guilty about this?"

"Yeah, I have. I've been waiting for Arlene to bring it up so I could apologize, but she likes to bury her head in the sand whenever anyone gets too close."

Overcome with affection for this kind woman, and ashamed at her unwillingness to see past the chaos and filth of the trailer, Julie sprang out of her chair and hugged Charlene tightly. "You've got *nothing* to worry about with me. As for my mom, you certainly have her pegged. I've spent my life trying to find her good side and stay on it—and I'm no longer sure she has one." Julie turned her chair around to face Charlene, sat down and grabbed her hands.

"Julie, I still feel—"

"Listen to me. Mom lied to us. She told me she hadn't heard from you since she left Bremerton. And after her stroke a few years ago, she has a hard time remembering many details about those years, except your last name and where you lived.

"What did she tell you about Andrew?"

"Only that he was from Charlottesville, Virginia."

"Julie! He was from *West* Virginia."

"*West?*"

"Oh, dear, I should have told you the truth myself a long time ago."

"Do you keep in touch with Andrew? Did he move back here?"

"I don't know, Julie. I never heard from him or saw him again after your mom turned down his marriage proposal. He may have finished his time and headed back home. I couldn't figure out why Arlene married that no-good, drinking, street-fighting man. What was his name?"

"Danny."

Charlene looked at Danny. "Do you ever resent sharing his name?"

"Never thought about it."

"Good, because you don't look anything like him, and you sure don't act like him."

"At least he's out of my life," said Julie.

"Why?"

"Long story." As Julie began to spill the major parts of her life to Charlene, she realized that Danny probably hadn't yet heard everything she was sharing. By the time Julie was done talking, she noticed that the dogs and cats were all sleeping in different places around the room, and even the birds were quiet.

Shadows were falling across the walls when Julie and Danny hugged Charlene one more time and left for the long, winding drive back to their inn.

The rest of the sightseeing was done without the enthusiasm Julie had had on the plane trip to Oregon. All she wanted to do was go home and look for Andrew. Again.

♦

A high-ranking naval officer—Julie could never keep the levels of rank and authority straight in her mind—in Military Records in Georgia heard about Julie's search and told her that, after doing some of his own digging, he had reached a dead end without Andrew's social security number. When he suggested that Julie hire a private investigator, she politely thanked him for his help and hung up. *Money may be no object for him, but it's the object* and *subject for me—and I'm sure for Danny, too. It wouldn't be a problem for rich people or celebrities, like Oprah Winfrey.*

♦

Sam and Yam called the summer weather 'splendacious'. Julie set aside her father search and focused on the blessings which daily surrounded her. She and Danny had several free weeks without needing to spend time on seminars or teaching-related activities. Both of their jobs were secure for the fall, and Danny had promised Julie, before they were married, that if they could, they would spend their summers doing house projects, taking short day-trips with whichever of their kids was still at home, and being together. When the temperature climbed into the 90's, they headed for the town beach; during the cooler evenings, they had barbecues for their kids and a variety of their friends of all ages. On the fourth of July, Christina and her boyfriend Stuart, Emma and her boyfriend Dusty, Tom-Tom and his gang, Sam and his girlfriend Josie, and Yam and his girlfriend Janice all converged at the Lewis house for a picnic. It reminded Julie of times she had spent with Tom's cousins—except that there was no alcohol this time around. As Tom-Tom said, they were all 'high on life,' and it was a healing, refreshing season for Julie's spirit.

When school resumed in the fall, and everyone headed back to one school or another, Julie's thoughts turned toward her father—the one factor still missing in the equation of her life. The idea of contacting Oprah—an idea that had seemed so absurd in May—seemed more plausible. It would be easy to cut and paste parts of various letters she had already written and compose one to the producers of the "Oprah" show. Hers was a compelling story of three fathers, with the hope that the third one would be the charm. *While I'm waiting to get a response from the show, I can lose a few pounds and be prepared for a television appearance.*

Julie hadn't ever been told that it was against some kind of rule to receive personal mail at school; and, since she wasn't ready to spring her new plan on Danny, she decided to use the school address on all of the return labels. It made for nail-biting tension over the weekends before she could get to school Monday morning and open up any letters that would help her find her father.

Even though a month had passed since she had mailed a letter to Chicago, Julie refused to feel discouraged. She was becoming an expert in the long shot, and decided to send another copy of her letter to the producers of "Unsolved Mysteries." *I'd love to meet Robert Stack! In the meantime, maybe I'll still hear from Oprah. Then I'll need to decide which show will get my business!*

Just before the Thanksgiving break, Julie accepted the probability that her letter to the "Oprah" show was either sitting in a stack of junk mail on someone's desk, or had long ago become fodder for the circular file. She would check her mailbox one more time before leaving for the four-day weekend, and find time before returning to school Monday to let Danny in on what she had been up to these past months.

♦

"I'll catch up to you in the parking lot, Danny. I'm going to check my box before we leave."

"Are you expecting a dinner invitation from the president?"

"Maybe! Why not?"

"Why not, indeed? Thing is, you're too classy for the White House!"

"A girl could get used to you."

"That's the plan."

As Danny turned and jogged toward the front door of the school, Julie pushed open the door to the office, greeted the steady, cheery, overly capable secretary, and pulled out the papers from her mailbox. There was a monthly newsletter for people who worked with autistic kids, the December school lunch menu, a sheet of announcements for all of the holiday festivities, an Avon catalog, and a plain brown envelope with a return address from "Unsolved Mysteries." Julie's hands shook as she opened her large canvas bag, shoved everything inside and headed out to the car.

♦

Julie had spent all week looking forward to a quiet, romantic dinner with Danny on Wednesday night, before the cooking-and-eating Thanksgiving marathon began. She knew now, however, that she would not be able to focus on either Danny or the simple restaurant fare. She wanted to go home, eat a piece of leftover pizza from the previous night, get the ingredients for rolls into her bread machine—*I wish I knew what to do.* If the letter was one she had been hoping for, she could still shred it, or she could pursue Andrew after she had had a chance to talk it over with Danny. If, on the other hand, it was a rejection letter, it might not be significant if one of the other countless phone calls or letters yielded a new clue.

355

Julie had easily convinced Danny that she had too many preparations and house cleaning chores left to do to have time to go out for dinner. He graciously understood and offered to help Julie with whatever she needed. Together they spent the evening vacuuming, sorting through teenaged clutter, and washing all of the china and serving dishes that would be used the following day.

It was close to midnight when Julie was sitting on the edge of the bed, listening to Danny humming in the shower while she held a small envelope with the potential for a large impact on her future. She looked at Danny's side of the bed and thought she knew what he would say if she asked him about whether or not to open the letter— 'You do whatever you want'—the most loving, yet maddening, response she could imagine. *I was attracted to him because he had no desire to control me, but a little decisiveness would help right now.*

When the shower water stopped, Julie put the letter back in her purse and tossed it on the dresser. *Tomorrow.*

◆

Regardless of the outcome of the sealed letter, Julie decided that she needed a break. She had spent the past ten months actively searching for Andrew; during that time she had lost weight, lost sleep, and gained a bin of letters suitable for wallpapering her house. It was time to see whether or not this last letter would be added to the bin.

The producer of "Unsolved Mysteries" informed Julie that the show would soon be going off the air permanently, and that they couldn't take on any new cases.

Julie's train of thought was headed toward mental derailment.

◆

Julie had never been close to Jim, one of her ex-husband's distant cousins. When she heard his funeral would be the first Saturday in December, she saw it as an opportunity to cry out her anguish over her 'lost' father, while everyone assumed her grief was for a very different reason.

Settling in to a church pew near the back of the First Evangelical sanctuary, Julie was surprised and relieved to see Grandma Emma walk in. She walked over to Julie with the same look of stubborn love that had won over Julie's heart so many years before. The two women hugged and then sat back to listen to the contemporary piano music.

Pastor Tim must have had another commitment today. There's a new man walking to the pulpit. Where have I seen him before? Waiter? Salesman? Insurance agent? That's Darrel Larsen from Channel Ten! I had heard he was an ordained minister, but I didn't know he officiated at funerals.

◆

'The Lord is my shepherd; I shall not want.' As Julie recited the familiar words during the service, and listened to Grandma Emma's broken English, her mind was suddenly distracted by a new plan. *Darrel Larsen is on TV, and probably has a crew and money to work with. His station could do a search for Andrew as a human-interest story. It's worth a shot!* 'Yea, though He leads me through the valley of the shadow of death …' Julie was ready for a shepherd to lead and guide her to her father.

As the mourners quietly stood in line waiting to extend their sympathies to the family, Julie considered introducing herself to Mr.—*Reverend*—Larsen, but then decided that there would be no way for her to keep from asking him about her plan, and this wasn't the place to pursue it. Instead, she slipped out of the line, hopped in her car and raced home, firing up her computer before she had even taken off her coat. For once, she was glad Danny hadn't come with her, although he had been concerned that she would be ostracized at the funeral. After her reassurances that she could hold her own, he had followed through with his original plans to go bow hunting with Tom-Tom. The house was empty, which was a noticeable contrast to Julie's filled head.

With a little tweaking of one of her many form letters saved on the computer, Julie was able to compose what she hoped was an informative, clear and interesting letter to the news producer at Channel Ten. *Cross my heart, hope to die.* Julie printed the letter, put it in an envelope, found a stamp in the desk drawer, and decided that a brisk walk to the mailbox across town would be good for her racing heart. *Lord, I can't put off telling Danny any longer. Please give me the strength to approach him tonight. I don't want to do this alone anymore.*

One long week later, Julie received a letter with WNBI in the return address. This time, she had a clean conscience, having told Danny about the rejection letter from "Unsolved Mysteries", and about this latest scheme. She was no longer using the school's computer and return address, having decided that her home—a home she shared with a loving husband and family—was the best place to chase her dream.

'It is with great joy and anticipation' the letter began. Julie threw it in the air and danced around her living room. "Yes, yes, yes!" She shouted and sobbed in relief, as months of accumulated work and stress suddenly fell from her shoulders. "I finally have help!"

◆

"Gloria! Do you have time to stop by my room after school?" Julie was putting the plastic lid back on her container as Gloria walked into the lounge. "I have some great news to tell you, but I have to get back to give Repete a test while the other students are watching a video in history."

"He's a great kid."

"And I know it sounds crazy, but I love the fact that he has a nickname. When I met his father, I knew why they nicknamed him 'Repete.' Pete and Repete have the same hair color, same crooked grins, same funny personalities. I know I'm supposed to be the one watching out for Repete, but sometimes I think he's the one who blesses me more."

"Every time I see him, he asks me if he can come into my classroom and feed Rosie, our pet tarantula. Most of the kids—especially the girls—admire Repete for having the courage to hold Rosie. It seems like he and that hairy creature somehow understand each other."

"I'll let Repete share that experience without me, thank you very much!" Julie had an involuntary shiver, and Gloria laughed.

"So, what's the big news?"

"Can't tell you now—I really do need to get back to class. Catch me after school!"

"I'll be dying of curiosity the rest of the day!"

"You'll live!"

♦

"Bye, Miss P.!" Repete slapped Gloria's hand in a high-five as he ran to meet his dad. Glo walked into Julie's room and stood quietly as Melissa Jenkins gave Julie a new book to be used with Repete the following day. "Don't forget to lock the door when you leave."

"Thanks, Melissa."

"Thank *you*, Julie. You are amazing with Repete. His father is happier now that his son has someone to stay with him all day."

I wonder what that would feel like …

When Julie and Gloria had settled in to padded chairs, Julie exploded with her news. "Gloria, channel ten is going to help me find my real father!"

"What? How? Who? I don't know what you're talking about!"

"Right about the time I met you in high school, I found out that the man I assumed was my father—the man who had been abusing me and grinding my self-esteem under his heel—wasn't my biological father. It took me about twenty years to fill in all the pieces for me, and for a long time I thought *another* man was my real father, but it was actually a *third* man who fits the description."

"That's almost an unbelievable story."

"Sometimes I have a hard time believing it myself."

"What does your dad—your 'first' dad—think about your search for your biological dad?"

"He died many years ago."

"Did you ever forgive him for what he did to you?"

"Yes. Or no. I tried. I think I have. I'm somewhere in the process of forgiveness, which may not be complete for the rest of my life."

"Should I pray for this search?"

"Absolutely. I'm counting on it."

♦

The TV news producer's offer was even more generous than Julie had thought possible. Not only was he putting together a film crew to interview her at her house, but he was also prepared to hire a private investigator. Best of all, he promised to air 'before' and 'after' segments, regardless of the outcome of the search. *I'm going to need at least one new outfit for the 'reunion' show. And, since Andrew—my dad—is only five-ten, I'll make sure I wear flat shoes on the show and let him enjoy his height advantage.*

It had been difficult for Julie to wait for all of the details necessary to set up the interview. She had been ready for the news crew to show up at her house the day after she opened the letter—but there were legal matters and scheduling issues—and sometimes, just when everything was set, it would be pre-empted by a more important story. Finally, when the windows of her house were open to welcome the warm spring air, the station called and said they would be out the next morning. The secrets of the buds were ready to reveal themselves in daffodils, irises and tulips that would wrap the house in a profusion of color, while inside sat a lone figure, topped with auburn hair, and adorned in white pants and a peach shirt. Everything in Julie's world reflected the dazzling promise of new birth.

♦

The young man running the video camera didn't look much older than Julie's son, which put her immediately at ease. He introduced himself as 'Leo' and had a nervous habit of pushing a lock of wavy hair behind his pierced ear as he absorbed rapid-fire directions from the interviewer, an equally young-looking woman with hair color and a body build similar to Julie's.

As Julie unfolded her story to Susan, Leo looked like his mind was on the post-interview ham and rolls she had baked and left sitting on top of the stove. She was surprised when Leo initiated a conversation with her as soon he began packing away his equipment.

"Can I ask you something?"

"Sure."

"Why is it so important to find Andrew?"

"Well, because he's my *real* dad." *Weren't you paying attention?*

"I know—but I'm adopted, and I really love my parents. They're the only parents I've ever had."

"I'm happy for you." Julie sighed. "Maybe because you had such a good, adoptive family, there's no gaping hole in your heart, like there is in mine."

"What do your parents think about your search for your bio dad?"

"That would be another long story, and probably not one you would want to tape."

"Oh."

"If you're interested, come back someday and I'll tell it to you."

"Maybe I will." Leo looked thoughtful as he pushed his hair behind his ear.

"I really am happy for you, but you might need to think about how many reasons there are for adoptions—and sadly, not all of them are about love."

"Why else would someone spend all of the money and time it takes to adopt, if it wasn't something they really wanted to do?"

"In my case, I was adopted by the man my mom married—and I wish—"

"Is it okay if we eat?" Susan called from the kitchen. "This was so nice of you, but we have a schedule to keep."

Leo held out a tissue to Julie, who hadn't realized she was sweating. "Another time, Leo?"

"For sure."

◆

Julie hadn't given any thought to how her mom might react to the Sandford story broadcast around the area; and, although she knew this would likely break a forty-year cycle of deception, she also knew it wasn't her goal to unnecessarily hurt her mom. It occurred to Julie that she might find help from her mom's brother Johnny and his wife Caroline, who lived in Tennessee. Julie hadn't been with Johnny and Caroline more than a half dozen times in her life, but she knew that her cousin—*I wish I could remember his name*—had been adopted, and so they might be sympathetic to her search. Julie also remembered hearing that Uncle Johnny was a retired high-ranking Naval officer, and she wasn't about to turn down any offers of help.

E-mail seemed like a good way to communicate—somewhat personal, without being overly intrusive. Johnny and Caroline could collaborate on their advice, and then one of them could write back to Julie when they were ready. Julie sent an e-mail the day after the taping at her house.

♦

As soon as Julie turned on her computer and opened her e-mail account the next day, she noticed the fire extinguisher hanging on the wall next to her desk. Looking back at the screen, she prepared herself for the words to ignite the desk.

"How *dare* you do this to your mother, after all she's done for you! How could you embarrass her like that? Don't you even *think* of running that on TV! Your father was good to you, too." Since the e-mail was unsigned, Julie didn't know if the inflamed diatribe came from Johnny or Caroline.

Thank you, God, that I didn't get that kind of reaction from my family. I never tried to drive a wedge between my kids and their Pop-pop, even though they don't remember much about him. But, I also never sanitized the truth. I didn't think it was necessary to give them the sordid details, but they know he molested me. And Danny—bless him—knows that when I'm in a season of obsessive cleaning and organizing, I'm usually trying to make up for the lack of control I had as a child in Danny Sandford's house. He doesn't criticize me or dismiss me. He takes my hand, leads me to the couch, sits down next to me and asks how he can help. Maybe he can help me through this.

"Julie?" Danny shouted from the kitchen door.

"Hey, hon. Where were you?"

"I told you I was going out for a run." Julie sighed. "I guess I forgot."

Danny walked into the den. "Are you okay?"

"Not really." Julie began rubbing her forehead.

"Another migraine coming on?"

"No. That would almost be easier to deal with than this."

"What?" Danny stood behind Julie and massaged her shoulders.

"Look at the screen—but be prepared for spontaneous combustion."

Danny read the e-mail.

"Let me guess: Uncle Johnny and Aunt Caroline?"

"Yep."

"You're probably not going to be on their Christmas card list anymore."

"Nope."

Danny swiveled Julie's chair around. "I'm sorry. I can't imagine how much this must hurt."

Julie tipped her head back and closed her eyes. "I try not to live like a victim—"

"I know that."

"But this almost feels worse than the abuse."

Danny tipped Julie's head forward and kissed the top of it. "Maybe you could try calling them," he whispered. "People tend to be less rude in person than when they have the anonymous cover of the computer."

Julie opened her eyes. "You think so?"

"It's worth a try. And if you'd like, I'll sit next to you when you're on the phone."

Julie reached out and hugged Danny around the waist. "Thank you."

♦

"Aunt Caroline?"

"Is this Julie?" Julie thought Caroline's voice was impaled on barbed-wire fencing.

"Uh-huh. How's Uncle Johnny?"

"We're fine. But apparently you're not."

"I need to explain—"

"No, you don't. I'm so sick of hearing about abuse! Everybody I talk to has been abused. And I watch the same shows they watch. *You've* been abused. *I've* been abused. You're forty years old. Get over it already."

"But Aunt Caroline—"

"Don't you *dare* embarrass your mother like this."

"*Me* embarrass *her?*"

"Exactly. She gave up a lot for you."

Drawing her words like a loaded gun, Julie aimed and fired. "I really don't care what you think about me or my family—"

"Now just a—"

"You've never been there for us—"

"You can't—"

"You never helped us—"

"I expect you—"

"And you've never been anything to me." Julie was almost more frightened by her boldness than she expected her aunt to be.

"You're a little—"

"It won't be necessary for you to hear from me again." Torn between the desire to slam the phone down or throw it through the window, Julie compromised by hurling it across the room, where it smashed against the wall. *This must have* been how satisfied my dad felt every time he destroyed our phone. When Danny offered Julie the comfort of his arms, she pushed him away and wept.

♦

"Mom?" Julie wiped her nose again and willed herself to stop sniffling.

"Who is this?"

"Julie." *I keep forgetting that her stroke has done some weird things to her memory.*

"Is everything okay?"

"Yep."

"Kids fine?"

"Uh-huh."

"You haven't broken anything?"

"No, Mom." *No sense worrying her about my tendon.*

"Why'd you call?"

"I need to tell you something."

"I figured you didn't call to ask how *I'm* doing."

"How are you doing?"

"Not good, but no one really cares."

We could be on this ride all night.

"Listen, Mom, I did something last—"

"What? You're not pregnant again?"

Julie ignored the memory loss, or sarcasm, or whatever it was that made her mom ask the most over-the-top questions. "I'm going to be on TV."

"What did you do wrong?"

"Nothing."

"There's no *good* news on TV any—"

"Sometimes there is."

"Like what?"

"I was interviewed by—"

"What for?"

366

"Let me finish!"

"Have it your way. You always do."

Are you kidding? "Channel Ten is going to run a story about me trying to find Andrew."

"Andrew *who*?"

"Andrew Little—my dad."

Silence.

"Mom?"

"Do you wanna find me dog dead in the car tomorrow morning?"

"What?"

"I said, 'Do you—'"

"I heard you."

"Well?"

"Why are you doing this?"

"Why am *I* doing what? How could *you* do this to *me*?"

Did Aunt Caroline call her before I could? Julie knew that, although the threat wasn't empty, her heart suddenly was. "No, ma'am, I wouldn't do that to you."

"All right, then."

"Goodnight."

♦

The phone call to Darrel Larsen the next day was one of the hardest Julie had ever made. She briefly explained that there were 'personal reasons' that made it impossible for her to let the station run the story. Darrel sounded disappointed, but reassured Julie that they would still run the story in the future if things changed for her.

CHAPTER THIRTY-FOUR

"YOU'VE GOT A FRIEND"

May had always been one of Julie's favorite months: the air was fragrant with the smell of lilacs; the temperature was warm enough to take long walks at night without the annoyance of mosquitoes; and school was closing in on its summer vacation. But in her state of emotional rigor mortis, Julie was hard-pressed to awaken any of her senses. *Why did I care about not wanting to hurt my mother? If the shoe were on the other foot, she would have taken it off and beaten me with it. And now I've lost the only chance I had of finding Andrew Little.*

"Glo? It's Julie."

"Do you have good news for me again? When is the show going to air?"

"It's not." Julie felt her eyes filling with tears, which she thought might be a good sign that she was coming out of her emotional deadness.

"How come?"

"My mom."

"She put the kybosh on it?"

"Yep."

"Oh, Julie, I'm really sorry."

"Ditto."

"What are you going to do next?"

"Nothing. I don't know. I'm tired of fighting everyone. I didn't even tell you about a conversation with my aunt and uncle."

"What's that about?"

"They were defending my adopted father's right to be part of the human race."

"Ouch."

"It wasn't worth the effort trying to get them to understand what my childhood was like."

"They probably wouldn't have believed you, anyway."

"I'm *sure* of that."

"Julie, my practical, engineering husband is a problem-solver with the most upbeat attitude of anyone I've ever known. He would probably say that you should go back to the drafting table again."

"I still can't afford a private investigator."

"No, but you still have access to your computer."

"I've tried the Internet for adoption agencies—"

"Maybe it doesn't have to be that complicated. You could type a flyer with your name, birthplace and date, phone number, e-mail address, and any info you have about Andrew. You could use the Internet to find addresses of Littles in Virginia and West Virginia."

"If I did that, I wouldn't leave Danny out of the loop this time. Some private stuff would be out there, and it would affect both of us."

"That's a wise idea."

"Glo, what would I ever do without you?"

"Miss me!"

♦

Julie counted on Danny to bring up all the scary sides to her plan. She might anger her mother again; she could open a hornet's nest in innocent Little families; they could get some creepy person calling them, or showing up at their house, trying to somehow extort money or threaten them; or, worst of all, there might not be any response from any of the flyers.

"What about your brother?"

"I haven't seen him since the day of my first wedding. He didn't even graduate from high school. He just took off and joined the army, and then disappeared. He despised Danny Sandford's life as much as I did, but my mother says he's been drinking, been married twice—"

"And Andrew Little is only *your* father."

"That's right. I'd be willing to have my brother back in my life ... and maybe Andrew would be able to be some kind of father to him, too."

"But first things first: we pray."

They talked and prayed about Julie's idea, and enlisted the thoughts, prayers and advice of Pastor Tim, as well as trusted church friends. Julie had learned to value a simple Proverb that said, "There is wisdom in many counselors." Her children—and Sam and Yam—were also informed of her idea. Christina and Emma voiced approval at their mom doing whatever it took to find her father. Tom-Tom didn't seem to have an opinion, although Julie suspected that he didn't want to see her experience any more pain or rejection. Sam and Yam said there was always plenty of food to feed one more relative—and Julie chuckled over how everything for them came down to how much food was served at picnics and holidays.

◆

With a green light from her family, and the support of her friends, Julie searched the Internet white pages for all of the Littles in the United States. *Four hundred forty? Wow!*

When she narrowed her search to Littles in Virginia and West Virginia, there were seventy. *Still too many!* A further search of 'Andrew Little,' 'Andy Little' or 'Drew Little' yielded forty names. Julie printed forty copies of her flyer and mailed them out.

Having played this waiting game before, Julie was impatient for some kind of response to the flyers. Every night after school, and several times on the weekends, she checked the mailbox, her e-mail account, and the telephone answering machine as soon as she walked in the door. After a week had passed, she decided it was time to turn up the heat under the pot. She got back on the Internet and printed out phone numbers for all of the Littles who had received flyers. *I'm glad I have a cell phone with unlimited long distance.*

As soon as Julie introduced herself and explained who she was and what she was doing, mostly angry responses were accompanied by definitive phone slamming. Julie hated to think that her simple phone calls might be the cause of blistering marital arguments for some of the Littles. *Deeds done in darkness are exposed in the light. Maybe some good will come from whatever doors were opened through my calls.*

♦

It was early September, and Julie's usual excitement over the beginning of another school year was dampened by an apparent dead end as far as the flyers were concerned. She had only had four responses from Andrew Littles, none of whom were *the* Andrew Little.

"Hi, Miss Julie!"

"Repete! How was your summer?"

"Fine. I got to go swimming, find crickets, and play with Jimbo."

"Who is 'Jimbo'?"

"My new friend who lives next door."

"That's great."

"Are you still my teacher?"

"I am. The school said I could stay with you this year."

"Good."

"I think so, too." *It's very good for me. I can start focusing on someone besides me again.*

♦

Mrs. Hammond, Repete's new classroom teacher, walked in and introduced herself to Julie. "I'm glad you're here. I want to tell you about something before all of the students get here."

Julie threw her purse in her bottom desk drawer and straightened her hair. "Shoot."

"I just heard about a statewide convention for parents, teachers and aides of autistic children. It will be held in Grand Rapids at the end of September, and I'd love to see you attend."

"I'd be happy to do it, but our finances are a little tight right now. My two stepsons are in college, my youngest daughter has a high-maintenance lifestyle of cheerleading uniforms, homecoming dresses—"

"Actually, the grant we received last year would cover your expenses for registration, hotels and food. I can't get away, but I'd really like for you to bring back information and tools that would help us both work with Repete this year."

"I'll talk it over with Danny and let you know next week."

♦

Although most of her time would be spent attending seminars, Julie was still excited about the upcoming convention. She needed something to steer her attention away from Andrew Little, and she knew she had been starting to take out her frustrations on her family. Tom-Tom would come home from school and ask her how her 'Little' problem was, and everyone else tried to get to the mail before she did. *If I drive away my family trying to find a father who may not want anything to do with me, I haven't really gained anything, and I have a lot to lose.*

As she was packing her garment bag and overnight case, Danny wandered into the bedroom. "If you get a letter from an Andrew Little, or Andy Little, or Drew Little, please call me on my cell."

"Julie—"

"Last week Emma gave me an unopened 'return to sender' letter from an Andrew Little in Virginia." Julie pulled up the zipper on the bag.

The ringing phone interrupted their conversation. As Julie pulled the receiver out of the holder, she noticed a long-distance area code on the caller ID.

"Hello?"

"Yeah, hello. This is Andrew Little."

Julie heard a voice that sounded like Danny's ... too young to be her father.

"I understand what you're trying to do; but there's no way my father could be *your* father. He was married during that time period listed on the flyer."

"Well," Julie replied, not unkindly, "I don't want to make you feel bad, but my mother was also married during that time."

The silence was potent.

"Well, I'm in my forties," replied Andrew.

"So am I," countered Julie. "Was your father in the Navy during that time?"

"Yeah." Andrew hesitated.

"Was he stationed anywhere near Puget Sound?"

Another silence.

"Well, I don't know about that for sure, but it's quite possible."

"Does your father have blondish-brown hair?"

"Yes." Julie heard the air escaping from Andrew's lungs in a slow leak.

"Does your father have brown eyes?"

The remaining air was forced out of Andrew in one relieved "NO! Thank God! They're blue!"

"Are you absolutely sure?" asked Julie.

"Yes, yes, they're blue, blue, blue!" answered Andrew triumphantly.

Julie sighed. "Well, thank you for being willing to talk to me. I hope I haven't caused any hard feelings between your parents!" Andrew good-naturedly wished Julie luck in her search.

♦

The four days spent at the conference were a wonderful reprieve for Julie. In meeting many parents of autistic children, Julie realized—for the first time in her life—that she had never had to deal with serious special needs in her own children. The chaos and anguish of her first marriage would never have stood the added stress of raising a child with cerebral palsy, or epilepsy, or Down's syndrome, or autism. The parents she met were gracious, kind, and obviously in love with their children—but they all wore the look of parents who were hanging on to slim threads of hope.

During the forty-five minute drive to Christina's house after the convention, Julie pondered that last phone call she had had with Andrew Little. *God, if I get home and there aren't any letters or phone messages, that's it—I'm done searching. This door will never be opened again.* Julie was tired of invading Little families like pepper spray, and knew that she needed to refocus her life on her own husband and children. She was looking forward to this weekend with Christina and Stuart.

◆

Tom-Tom absentmindedly answered the phone while watching TV.

"Yo."

"Hello?" A southern drawl stretched out the word to a length unfamiliar to him.

"Yeah?" Tom-Tom reached for his sandwich.

"Is Julie there?"

"Nope."

"Okay, I'll call back later."

"Wait—" Tom-Tom heard the dial tone, shrugged, hit the 'off' button on the cordless phone, and pitched it on the couch.

Danny walked in to the room. "Who was that, T?"

"Heck if I know. Sounded like some country hick."

"Who did they ask for?"

"Mom."

◆

When the phone rang again the next night, Emma grabbed it in the kitchen.

"Hello?"

"Is Julie there?"

"No, but—"

"I'll call back."

"But—"

Emma heard a click and stared at the phone.

"Was that some dude who talked like Gomer Pyle?" Tom-Tom was sitting at the table eating popcorn and watching a "Starsky and Hutch" rerun on a small TV in the corner.

"Yeah, it was."

"He called last night, asked for Mom and didn't say who he was."

"Weird."

♦

"Andrew," said Eunice with a steely glint in her eye, "why don't you tell these people who you are when you call?"

"Because," Andrew patiently explained, "suppose her mama and daddy, aunts and uncles, brothers and sisters, husband and children—suppose her family doesn't know she's looking for me? It could cause problems for her."

♦

When the phone rang the following evening, Danny made sure he answered it this time.

"Hello?"

"Hi. Who is this?"

"I'm Danny."

"Are you Julie's—"?

"Husband. Who are you?"

"My name is Andrew. Andrew Little. I was born in Charleston, West Virginia, and I've lived here all my life, except for a short time when I was stationed in Bremerton, Washington. I have several reasons to believe I'm your wife's father—and I'm really anxious to talk to her. But I'd like to be the one to tell her who I am."

Danny sucked in his breath. "Andrew, she's staying in Grand Rapids until Sunday night. I'll try to get her to come home Saturday instead. It won't be easy, especially since I can't tell her why. I'll do my best."

Danny's sweaty palm almost dropped the phone before he could push the 'off' button and toss it distractedly on the bed.

◆

With the windows up and the radio blaring, Julie alternately pounded the steering wheel and shook her fists in the air. "God, you allowed me to suffer through abuse for so long; I lived through a hell I can't even explain to anyone; why won't you let me find my real father? It's the only thing I've ever wanted."

Julie dragged a defiant mood into her house late Saturday afternoon. She didn't know why Danny had been so insistent that she come home a day early; he always had a long list of 'honeydew' projects—and other than going to church without her on Sunday, he was perfectly capable of feeding the kids, washing a couple of loads of clothes and making sure his soccer schedule was set for the fall. *It's not like him to be so strong with me. I hope he's not starting to show colors I didn't see before we got married.* Julie was so seldom angry with Danny for longer than a few hours, that it made her world feel off-center.

Walking in the door, Julie tossed her keys onto the couch, kicked her shoes off at the door and then walked over to the counter to glance through a high, uninviting stack of mostly junk mail. Suddenly, her eyes lit on a return address from an Andrew Little in West Virginia.

"Danny," Julie yelled through the house, "why didn't you tell me about this letter from Andrew Little?"

"I'm sorry, honey, it must have been caught in the rest of the mail. I didn't see it."

Her usually meticulous personality traits set aside, Julie didn't bother hunting for her sharp letter opener; instead, she tore open the envelope, almost ripping the letter in half in the process.

"Dear Julie,
My name is Drew Little. My father is Andy Little. He organizes Little family reunions in West Virginia every year. After receiving your flyer in the mail, he asked me to write to you and explain that he is not the man you are looking for.
Good luck in your search.

Sincerely,
Drew"

God, I promised that this would be my swan song—and I meant it. Julie considered climbing into bed and pulling the covers over her head. *The world wouldn't stop spinning if I checked out for a while.* Going back out to the car to get her luggage, she was met by Tom-Tom, who casually reminded her that his car was still in the shop, and he needed a ride to work in ten minutes. Julie decided it wasn't worth making an extra trip into the house; she would leave right then to take Tom to work and deal with everything else when she got back. As mother and son were backing out of their long driveway onto the main highway, the cordless phone chirped in the bedroom.
"Hello, is this Danny?"
"Yep."
"This is Andrew again. Is Julie home now?"
"No, Andrew, but you could try calling back later tonight."
When Julie returned thirty minutes later, Danny said, "Some guy's been calling for you, and he said he'll call back later." Julie missed the shakiness in Danny's voice.

It's probably Drew Little, calling to find out whether or not I got his letter. I can certainly ignore him until tomorrow.

Tom-Tom was scheduled to work until ten o'clock, but finished his shift an hour early. Julie was too restless to come in for a landing and do anything productive, so when he called home looking for a ride, she decided to pick him up from work. As soon as she backed her van out of the driveway, the phone rang in the bedroom again. Danny ran into the bedroom, kicking himself for not volunteering to get Tom-Tom himself. "One of these days I'm going to hurt myself from serious brain activity."

"Hi, Danny?"

"Yes?"

"It's Andrew again. I'm sorry if I'm bothering you."

"No, you aren't at all. Julie had to leave again. I *promise* she'll be back soon!"

"Is it okay if I call back?"

"Absolutely."

When Julie returned home, Danny said, "That guy called back for you. He's still going to call you later tonight."

"Danny," Julie flatly responded, "I'm not talking to *anybody*. Whoever it is can call me back some other time. All I want to do is take a shower and go to bed."

As the steamy water coated the shower door, Julie was lost in a world impenetrable by the shrill noise of the phone. She heard the door open, and Danny shouting, "Yeah, she's here; I'll go get her." Extending his arm around the bathroom door, he said, "Julie, take this call."

"Get out!" screamed Julie. "I'm not talking to anybody!"

"Take this call!" insisted Danny.

"Get out of here! What part of 'no' don't you understand? Get out!"

"You *will* take this call," demanded Danny.

Julie stepped out of the shower, dripping wet and heaving with frustration. She was mad at Danny for seeming so insensitive, and mostly mad at herself for being impatient with her kind husband. She grabbed two towels, threw one around her body and the other around her head. Grabbing the phone out of Danny's hand, she yelled "Hello! Who is this?"

A small voice laced with a thick southern accent replied, "Hello, Julie, this is Andrew Little."

"I got the letter from your son."

"What son?"

"Drew."

"I don't have a—"

"Maybe you didn't know he wrote it."

"Wrote what?"

This guy tap dances like my mom.

"The letter telling me you're not my father."

"But that's why I'm calling. I believe I *am* your father."

Julie sat on the bed and started to feel her heart beating faster. "But I thought he said you *weren't* my father."

"Julie. Take a breath, and let's start this over again. My name's Andrew Little, and I got your flyer in the mail last Wednesday."

"That's what your son said in the letter."

"I don't *have* a son named 'Drew'! My sons are Owen Lee and Ira Van!"

Another phone clicked on, and a genteel southern voice said, "Well, hello, Julie, this is your Mama Eunice, and I'm so pleased and proud that we finally found you. Andrew and I have been looking for you for a very long time."

Julie was glad she was already sitting, because her legs suddenly felt like molten liquid. All intelligible speech left her.

"Julie, are you still there?" Andrew sounded alarmed.

"I am. And I hope this isn't some kind of a hoax."

"It's not," said Andrew. "When you were born, I told Arlene that I thought you were the most beautiful thing I'd ever seen."

There wasn't anything on the posters that told my mom's name.

"I've been trying to find you for a year. Actually, I think I've been looking for you all my life." Julie started to sob.

Eunice quietly asked, "Girl, how come you never came to West Virginia looking for your daddy?"

"How much ... time ... do you ... have?" Julie choked out the words.

"As much time as you need," answered Andrew.

Julie excused herself to get on her nightgown and unwrap the towel from her head, and then settled into bed and picked up the receiver. The time flew by as she shared the highlights of her life with Andrew and Eunice. Julie noticed that Andrew listened without responding while 'Mama Eunice' laughed, exclaimed, cried, yelled, and seemed to focus on every word. At the end of the conversation, Julie was convinced that the best parts of Mrs. Ryczek, Mrs. Anderson, Mama T and Grandma Emma had all been resurrected in Mama Eunice—and that 'finding' her was almost as wonderful as finding her biological father.

There was no sleep for Julie for the rest of the night; it was the most welcome insomnia she had ever experienced.

♦

Julie, Andrew and Mama Eunice exchanged letters and phone calls. Julie's every waking thought was an overwhelming desire to fly to West Virginia. Although she knew she couldn't afford it, she also knew something about scheming, and wishing, and a little more about trusting in a God who had brought a huge miracle in to her life.

♦

"Julie, we've missed you at our weekly prayer meetings."

"I know. It seems like every Monday morning I'm running late, or Danny's running late—and I hate for us to drive both cars when we only live a few miles from here."

"Understood. I'm just glad you could make it today."

"Me too."

"Do you think Danny will ever come?"

"I'd like for him to. He just ends up having multiple responsibilities before school. His soccer players look to him for so many things—things that maybe their parents could deal with."

"That's what makes Danny so great. He is much more than a soccer coach, or history teacher, and the kids all know it. You got yourself a good one there, friend."

"I know—he's a keeper because he's too big to throw back!" Butch did a rim shot on the table. Julie felt her face turn red and was relieved when Mr. Hedstrom, an English teacher, motioned for everyone to pull chairs up to the table and be ready for a time of prayer and encouragement before the first-period bell rang.

"I'd like to ask a favor of everyone."

"Julie, prayers aren't favors, they're privileges."

"Good enough. I'd like to give someone the *privilege* of praying that *I* have the privilege of making a trip to West Virginia, so that I can meet my father and his family." Everyone at school had rejoiced with Julie when she had finally found Andrew Little. As others were sharing prayer requests, Gloria whispered, "Call me tonight."

"Why?" Julie whispered back.

"Tell you later."

"I hate it when you do this to me!"

"You started it when you waited to tell me about the Channel Ten running your story, remember?"

"No fair!"

"Fair!"

♦

"Julie?"

"Gloria! I'm so sorry I forgot to call you! I went to Danny's soccer game after school, then dropped Tom-Tom off at work—"

"Time out! I didn't call to send you on a guilt trip. I just couldn't wait any longer to tell you my idea!"

"I need a cup of coffee."

"You're killing me here, girl!

"I can listen while I pour."

"Sure?"

"Absolutely."

"Okay. Here's my plan: My sister lives right outside Charleston, and she's been begging me for a year to come and visit—"

"How nice for you." *Does she remember that my dad and his family live in Charleston, and that I've been trying to get there? I wouldn't think Gloria would just be rubbing my face in something.*

"Let me finish! This morning, when you talked about praying that you could find a way to Charleston, I realized that you could come with me! I'm planning on flying to West Virginia during the Michigan Teachers' Convention at the end of October. It would be a wonderful four-day visit with Suzi."

"But Gloria—I still can't afford to fly down."

"Yes, you can, because I'm buying your ticket."

"You can't—"

"Can. My husband has a good engineering job, and we've been talking about doing this for you ever since Andrew contacted you.

"Gloria," Julie sobbed, "thank you, and I love you."

♦

How long ago was I flying out to Oregon, hoping I'd find my father out there? Here I am on another plane ... and this time it's really happening. I've been waiting for this moment for years ... and I think I'm going to be sick! Julie moved in slow motion, like so many of her dreams in which she was being chased and couldn't run fast enough ... only this time she was the chaser who couldn't catch a man walking slowly, but always ahead of her reach. And she was out of breath, gasping and holding her side.

"Sorry—I didn't mean to elbow you."

Not realizing she'd fallen asleep, Julie awoke with a start. "That's okay—these seats are small."

Gloria returned to her book, and Julie stared out the window, amazed again at God's provision. She had found her dad, and everything in her life had telescoped to this precise point in time. She tried to picture herself meeting Andrew in front of a TV camera that would capture every emotion showing through her eyes and smile. It was like every 'reunion' show she'd ever seen—yet not like any of them at all, because this was *real life*, and it was hers!

Reaching under her seat for her purse, Julie pulled out a small mirror and looked at her tanned face. She had never resembled Danny Sandford—a fact that had left her feeling like an orphan for years, until she experienced God's grace in being able to disassociate completely from a man who had treated her like flotsam and jetsam.

Andrew and Julie had the same facial features, cheek-bones, wavy, brown hair and brown eyes. For the hundredth time that day, Julie pulled out her wallet and carefully removed the picture of Andrew and Eunice Little. Andrew had on a white shirt, maroon tie with a gray paisley design, navy sport coat and slacks. Eunice wore a pastel blue dress with matching shoes and purse, and a pearl necklace and bracelet. Her brown hair was meticulously styled, and make-up carefully applied. Apparently Andrew was only five-feet six, which meant Eunice was probably five-feet four. *Mom had a baby with Andrew, and didn't even remember his height!* The day Julie had received the picture of her dad and Mama Eunice in the mail, she had yelled out loud, "That's it! *Now* I know who I look like! I finally have an identity!"

Willing herself back into Eastern Standard Time, Julie felt the landing gear open and the plane eventually touch down smoothly. She watched the filled-to-capacity cabin empty of passengers, knowing that she was also ready to enter the covered walkway, yet wishing she could stay seated a while longer. *I'm headed for the terminal … feels more like a gangplank. There's no going back now.* Julie stepped into a time warp, slogging through quicksand as people rushed around both sides of her, clipping her feet as they pulled their wheeled luggage. *I'm not sure I can go any further.*

As Julie and Gloria made their way into the terminal, Gloria spotted her sister. "Bye, Julie! See you back here in four days! Call me at my sister's if you need anything!" Julie hugged Gloria tightly, crying for what she knew wouldn't be the last time that day. As Gloria turned and ran to her sister, Julie spotted a couple standing quietly behind the ropes. Gasping for air, she heard, "Oh, my goodness, Drew, she looks like you!" As Eunice was yelling excitedly, Julie and Andrew found themselves standing face to face.

Julie had spent countless hours rehearsing profound words—and all she could say now was, "Boy, you're short!"

"Boy, you're tall!" Andrew happily responded. And then they hugged, while Eunice fussed with an uncooperative camera. Julie didn't need a camera to capture a scene she would never forget. She wanted to touch Andrew's face like a blind person, memorizing every feature—yet something compelled her to act with restraint, knowing that the last thing she wanted to do was embarrass her new family.

The half-hour drive from the airport to the Little house was the first of many surreal experiences for Julie. Since her mind was already saturated with the newness of this life, she tipped her head back, leaned it against the cool leather upholstery of her *father's* car, and closed her eyes.

When the car turned into a driveway, Julie lifted her head and saw a brick bungalow nestled among magnolias and dogwoods, rock gardens, flowerbeds, and carefully manicured grass. The inside of the house displayed a gentle perfectionism of Mediterranean décor—and Julie wondered if it was a reflection of Andrew's personality, Eunice's, or both. *If it's from Andrew, at least I know where mine came from.*

An unbidden and overwhelming sense of loss threatened Julie's happiness. *Look at this house. Why didn't I grow up here?*

CHAPTER THIRTY-FIVE

PIVOTAL PEOPLE —
PIVOTAL TIMES

"Make yourself at home, dear. I'll get us some iced tea. Are you hungry? Supper won't be for a while yet."

"No, Mama Eunice. I ate a bag of peanuts on the plane."

"Goodness! Couldn't they give you real food?"

"I wouldn't have been able to eat, anyway."

"Well you let me know if you're hungry."

"I will."

Eunice disappeared through one door as another one burst open, and a dark-haired, muscular, broad-chested guy bounded into the room wearing a black t-shirt and khaki shorts. *He's over six feet tall! How can he be so much taller than his father? I wonder if he's Owen or Ira.* Julie was mesmerized by his dazzling white teeth and huge smile, and was getting ready for a formal greeting when he walked over, said "Hey, I'm Owen Lee, but everyone calls me 'Tiny'!" and lifted her off the floor in a massive bear hug. Julie laughed as she looked over his shoulder at another guy with the same build entering the room. His hair was more reddish-brown, his jaw was a bit squarer, and Julie assumed this was her half-brother Ira Van, who apparently went by 'Pokey'. As Tiny set Julie down, she was expecting the same greeting from Pokey—but he simply said, "Hello," and sat down on the soft leather sofa across the room. *Okay, so maybe he wasn't looking for another sister.*

A younger gal walked through the front door swinging long, blonde hair across deeply tanned shoulders. Julie saw her own face and body shape about fifteen years earlier. "Julie, this is your little sister Cissy," said Andrew, as Francis Jane walked slowly to Julie, gave her a perfunctory hug, and sat down next to Ira Van.

"No one but *Daddy* calls me 'Cissy.' I'm 'Francis Jane' to everyone else."

Or maybe the 'Ice Queen.' Julie felt as though she were standing naked in this room full of people who were alternately accepting and skeptical of her sudden presence in their lives. *I'm sure they aren't all happy about having an extra place at the table tonight.*

Owen—*Tiny*—grabbed Julie's hand and sat her on his knee in a large, easy chair. "C'mon, ya'll, let's catch Julie up on our family."

"If we tell her about the whoopin's, we'll be here all night!" Ira—*Pokey*—chuckled softly.

"Daddy was a believer in the rod of correction!" Everyone laughed as Eunice came back into the room and sat down next to her husband.

"Especially for you, Tiny," teased Pokey.

"The biggest rod was for you, Pokey," Tiny shot back.

"Time out!" said Julie, as she held up her hands in a t-shape. "Why 'Tiny' and 'Pokey'?"

"I was only four pounds when I was born, so I was called 'Tiny' by the end of the first day."

"You definitely aren't tiny now!" said Francis Jane.

"Except for maybe that thing between his ears," said Pokey.

"And you," Julie pointed to Ira. "Why 'Pokey'?"

"When Mama and Daddy brought me home from the hospital, Tiny looked at me and said, 'Pokey.' For some reason, the name stuck."

"You guys don't mind those nicknames?"

"Look at us: We're big enough to take on anyone we want!"

"You remind me of my stepsons, who go by 'Sam' and 'Yam.' They are also big bruisers, so no one messes with them, either!"

"The four of us will be a great team!"

Julie glanced at Francis Jane, noticing the almost imperceptible scowl on her face. *I'm guessing she's not going to be a part of that team anytime soon.*

"My brothers are both full of it," muttered their sister.

"Cissified girl, watch it!" Pokey threw a pillow at Cissy, who ducked just in time.

"*This* is why we needed the rod," yelled Tiny and Pokey in unison.

I wouldn't have minded the 'rod' from a loving father. Looks like you guys turned out okay. A mother, dad, and three siblings surround me. What else could I want?

♦

Late every afternoon, Julie was whisked off to another relative's house for supper and introduced like a debutante into Little society. Back at home with Daddy and Mama Eunice, Julie felt like she was living on Walton's Mountain, a peaceful place that was the fulfillment of her every dream. She slept in Francis Jane's bedroom—a room beautifully decorated in French provincial furniture. Cissy had her own apartment on the other side of the city, and Julie hoped she didn't mind having an interloper sleeping in her bed. *A Goldilocks from Michigan.* Her first evening in the house, Mama Eunice had been helping Julie settle in, when she turned and saw tears in Julie's eyes.

"Julie, what's the matter?"

"Oh, Mama Eunice, that Victorian dollhouse—"

"Should I get it out of your way?"

"No! I always wanted a doll growing up. I was going to name her 'Thistledew,' and her dress ..." Julie began to sob as Jean wrapped her arms around her.

"Darlin', this is your home whenever you need it. I can't undo years of wrong, but I hope we can make some good memories for you here."

"You ... already ... have..."

In bed that night, Julie was bombarded with thoughts and emotions. *Why did you let so many things happen to me, God? How come I didn't find this family sooner? I had a father who was horrible, another one who was non-existent, and one who gave up looking for me. I have a lot of 'whys', and no answers. The only thing I know for sure is that I'm a very stubborn person—so maybe it has taken You a long time to work in my heart and make it ready for the Father I've been learning about. And I guess ... as bad as things were, I still knew You were watching over me. So many things should have destroyed my life, my children, and me. But You spared all of us. I'm thankful for that. And now I'm here! It's amazing grace that brought me here!*

Julie fell into the sweet sleep that accompanies profound gratitude.

♦

Julie and Andrew were sitting on the back veranda during a pleasant fall morning, drinking coffee and watching hummingbirds sipping from the red feeder hanging above the geraniums.

"Daddy, this has been a wonderful vacation for me."

"Glad you liked it."

"At home, it wouldn't be unusual for it to be snowing by now. And here I am, sitting in shorts!" *God, give me strength.*

"I've always liked living here."

"I don't know when we'll have a chance to be together again."

"Hope it's soon."

"Me too."

Julie looked at Andrew. "Pop?"

Andrew set his cup down on the glass table and looked at Julie. "Yes?"

"Can I ask you something?"

"Yep."

"Actually, it's more than something. It's a big thing."

"Okay."

Julie took a sip of coffee. "Can you tell me about your life after you left Washington?"

Andrew stared off for such a long time, that Julie was sure she had offended him. *God, I asked for strength. Maybe I should have been content that the family has begun to accept me.*

"Well." Andrew's clear eyes reconnected with Julie's. "I was discharged from the Navy at twenty years old. I really wanted to marry Arlene, but she didn't seem to want to have anything to do with me, my family, or West Virginia."

"She told me something about that."

"When I came back home, I was confused and depressed over leaving my infant daughter behind."

Julie's eyes filled with tears, but she remained silent.

"I went to college for a business degree, and got my life back on track—but I never stopped thinking about you. I tried to find you through a friend in Bremerton, but it seemed like you had disappeared."

Julie sniffed. "I was already adopted by a man named Danny Sandford by then, and he had my name legally changed."

"Well, that clears up a mystery."

I don't know if he knows anything about Eugene, but I'm leaving that one alone.

"So ... when did you meet Mama Eunice?"

"It was around my junior year in college, and we met at a church social. While we were engaged, I told her about you, and that I hoped we could find you someday. She loved me, and reassured me that she would love you, too."

"She's a wonderful woman."

"Amen to that. We were married right around your third birthday—and I kept wishing you could have been there to be our flower girl."

"Oh, Daddy, me too!"

"But I began to have the feeling that you would never know anything about me, and I didn't see any way of finding you. Maybe I should have told my parents about you, and they could have helped me ... but I didn't. I thought maybe someday I could hire a private investigator to try and find you, but the finances never worked out for us. After I graduated from college, I got a job with an insurance company, and I worked for them for several years."

Andrew stopped talking, got up and invited Julie to join him as they walked around the house admiring the exquisitely crafted and painted birdhouses, particularly the martin houses. *If he takes this much care with the birds, imagine how much care he would have taken with me!*

When they had settled back into their patio chairs, Andrew picked up the story. "When I was forty, my company was down-sized, and I was out of work for ... a very long time. We had no money, and I figured the chance to find you was long gone. Eunice and I often talked about whether or not *you'd* try to find *me*."

"Believe me—if I had known about you, I would have looked for you!"

"And I still would have looked for you, but when I got into a new business ... well, let's say everything went south." Andrew reached out his hand and gently touched Julie's. "I can't forgive—"

"Daddy, this is a 'guilt-free' zone. There's nothing we can do to change the past, but hopefully we'll have lots of time to reclaim what we lost. Deal?"

Andrew squeezed Julie's hand. "Deal."

♦

By the time Julie left Charlotte, she knew she had made some headway into the family's inner circle. Relatives and friends alike had all expressed what seemed like a genuine desire to have her visit again. There were quiet evenings, after returning from the round-robin suppers, when the family— including Tiny's wife Lily and Pokey's girlfriend Cheryl—sat around the Little living room and shared stories, accompanied by photo albums carefully organized and labeled. When they spent an entire night looking through Tiny's and Lily's wedding album, Julie wondered why Pokey wasn't in any of the pictures, either as best man, or even as an usher. *Maybe he was away at college, or in the service ... but I don't feel comfortable asking about it right now.*

The return flight to Detroit was even more difficult than the flight to Charlotte had been—because this time Julie had begun to know and love the family she was leaving behind, and she didn't know when she would see them again, or how Danny would feel about embracing the Littles. Tiny had been like a big, lovable teddy bear; Pokey was beginning to soften, although he had initially told Julie that he

"… ain't lookin' for no new sisters or friends;" and Francis Jane was still keeping an emotional distance from Julie, who recognized signs of hurt and insecurity. *God, let me see them again soon!*

Sometimes I think I would change places with Repete. He lives in a world he creates and controls. If things get out of balance, he escapes until everything makes sense again. I would like to do that with the Little family, except that I'm not sure how I would tell when the scales were tipping in my favor.

"Miss Julie?"

Julie shook herself out of her reverie. "Yes, Repete?"

"Can I go feed Rosie after school?"

"Absolutely."

As Julie and Danny walked to their car after school the last day before the break, they were greeted with kids yelling at them to have a Merry Christmas. They were heading into the holidays full throttle, preparing for a houseful of people, and hoping to find time to celebrate their second anniversary within the whirlwind of excitement. Julie was reaching the place where her horrendous memories of childhood Christmases were being replaced with loving, joy-filled times. *Thank you, God.*

During the ten-minute ride home, Julie's mind was racing with all of the things she needed to do—cooking, cleaning, and shopping. She was wondering if the Littles would like the gifts she had mailed when she and Danny walked into their kitchen through the garage door.

"Mom! Phone for you!" yelled Tom-Tom from the living room.

"I thought you wouldn't be home until late?"

"I'm here for a forty-five minute break, and then back until ten." Tom-Tom strolled into the room balancing a peanut butter sandwich, glass of milk, banana and cookie.

"Where's the phone?"

"I couldn't carry it! It's on the couch." Julie could never stay mad at her son, especially when he wore a silly, crooked grin, which seemed permanently etched on his face. He had all of the charm of his father, but without the need to fuel that charm with alcohol. Julie had never been able to tell him that without sounding like she was putting Tom down. She was grateful beyond words that none of her children had followed in their father's staggering footsteps.

Julie took off her jacket and scarf, hung them on a hook by the back door, and squeezed her son's shoulder as she passed him on her way to the phone. "Hello?" Julie cradled the phone to her ear as she picked up a paper and pencil from the coffee table, prepared to jot down a "to-do" list as she answered this call.

"Is this Julie?"

"Yes. Who is this?"

"It's Francis Jane."

Julie dropped the pencil and paper, grabbed the phone and stood up. "I'm sorry I didn't recognize your voice!"

"That's okay. I haven't exactly made a habit of calling you."

"Is anyone sick?"

Francis Jane laughed. "No! This isn't an emergency call."

"That's good." Julie wanted to say more, but wasn't sure of what was happening.

"Listen, Julie. I think it's time for us to get together. I know I haven't been fair to you—"

"Oh, Francis Jane—"

"I want to start over. I'm flying in to Detroit on a business trip on January third. How far would it be for you to drive down and meet me?"

"It takes less than four hours, depending on the weather."

"I'll be staying at the Holiday Inn at the airport. My meetings will be through by supper time Friday night."

"I teach Friday. If I leave right after school, I could be there by seven."

"What would you say to a late supper?"

"I'd *love* it!"

"Thank you for being so gracious to me."

"Water under the bridge."

"Daddy told me he's amazed you're not bitter, after everything you've been through in your life."

"We'll talk when we're together."

"I'm looking forward to it."

"Me too!"

"I'll see you in a couple of weeks."

"Absolutely."

Julie punched the 'off' button on the phone, placed it back in its holder, and yelled for her husband through a haze of happy tears.

♦

Charlie's Chop House in the Holiday Inn was not more than half-full when Julie walked in at six forty-five. When the hostess led her to Francis Jane's table, Julie was equal parts raw nerves and barely-contained excitement. She wanted this time with her half-sister to go well … to be a start of a friendship. Julie hoped to finally be accepted by this family member without having to compromise the growing, healthy self-esteem, which her husband affirmed in her every day.

As Francis Jane stood, Julie slipped out of her coat, and both women burst out laughing.

"We obviously shop in the same stores!" said Julie, as she saw her mirror image in the woman standing before her. Julie and Francis Jane graced their five-foot-ten frames with a beige pantsuit and light pink blouse. Julie's short, auburn hair and Francis Jane's long, slightly wavy blonde hair comprised the only difference in the reunion picture.

As the two hugged, Julie felt herself immediately relax.

"Julie, I know this is stupid to admit—even though I was twenty-five when you came into our lives, I didn't want to be dethroned!"

"And I was already forty—the queen of everything!"

The women sat down, lifted their water glasses and clinked them together.

"You're a *hoot!*" Cissy cackled. " Why was I afraid of you?"

"Lots of reasons: You thought I was a gold digger, or I wanted to claim some secret place in your dad's heart, or I wanted to break up your parents—"

"Oh, Julie, let's be friends."

"We already are."

"And please stop calling me 'Francis Jane.' I can't stand that hoity-toity, stuffy name. It sounds like something out of a Bronte novel. I'm just plain 'Cissy.'"

"Cissy it is."

♦

The women focused on their conversation far more than their food, although Julie noticed that Cissy ate slowly and then pushed half of it aside 'for later.'

"Cissy, do you mind if I ask you something?"

"Ask away. We've got all night. I don't need to check out until eleven tomorrow. You *are* staying with me tonight, right?"

"I am."

"So, what's the question?"

Julie took a sip of her Coke, put down the glass and played with the ice cubes, before looking up at Cissy.

"When I was in high school, I had some horrible experiences with my father ... at least, with the man I *thought* was my father."

Cissy pushed aside a crouton with her fork and stared at Julie. "You mean—"

"Yes. And I also had painful experiences with guys, particularly with my first husband for many years. I *know* our father was good to you, but did we wear ruts in the same road when it came to guys?"

"What ... what do you mean?"

"When I needed to get control of my life, I experimented with anorexia and bulimia for a time. I was past that long ago ... but I think I might be seeing signs of it in you."

Cissy's eyes brimmed with tears.

"Ciss, I didn't mean to offend you! If I'm wrong, please forgive me!"

"You're not wrong. I went through counseling and conquered it, but I find it really easy to slip back into it if I'm not careful."

"Can I help?"

"You already have, just by being so honest with me about your past."

"We would have to stay up all night for me to tell you the whole story."

"I am so sorry for you."

"Sometimes I still am, too ... but I'm not going to wear those memories like a pity sack. I'm learning about forgiveness and healing and unconditional love through my husband, my pastor, my church friends, and the middle-school boy I work with. I'm not going to let my past have power over my present."

Cissy grabbed Julie's hand and squeezed it. "Thanks for coming into my life."

"*I'm* the one who's thankful for finding my sister."

◆

Julie drove home the next morning on three-hours sleep, a quart of coffee, and with her intake valve open and overflowing with gratitude for her time with Cissy. *The scale is tipping in my favor.*

CHAPTER THIRTY-SIX

"IF WISHES WERE HORSES ..."

"**D**anny, I'd love for all of our family and the Littles to meet in Myrtle Beach for a reunion over spring break.

"When did you get that idea?" Danny was working on his snowmobile in the garage.

"I've been thinking about it ever since Cissy and I were together in January. Christina and Stuart can afford to buy plane tickets, and so can Sam and Yam. That would leave Emma and Dusty, Tom-Tom, you and me."

"That's still almost two thousand dollars."

"I know."

"I've been thinking and praying about something, and I think I just got the answer."

"What's that?"

"We don't do much snowmobiling anymore, and Tom-Tom is into his own stuff. One of the teachers at school is interested in buying all three of ours. If he wanted to buy them right away, we might have almost enough money for those tickets."

"Danny!" Julie threw her arms around him. "A girl could get used to you!"

♦

"Hey ya'll! You must be from somewhere like Minnesota or Alaska! We'd never swim in water that cold!"

As beachcombers taunted Danny, Julie, and their pasty-looking kids, Julie began to wonder if she had been crazy to plan this vacation. Not only had the Littles conveniently forgotten their promise to pay for everyone's food and lodging, but the chilly ocean water—although warmer than Lake Michigan—mirrored their attitude as well. Wrapping a towel around her and walking alone along the beach, Julie figured herself for a slow learner. *One of these days I'll stop trying to create the family I want. Why do I keep setting myself up for failure? My half-brothers make lots of comments about poor people and trailer trash folk. Have they forgotten where I came from? They have so much money, yet seem so unwilling to use any of it to make this vacation easier on me. What good is their money? God, why did you let me find these people? They don't share any of my values. They don't seem to even care about me.*

In spite of the fact that the Michigan and West Virginia blended family shared good food and hearty laughs for four days, Julie was unsure of their future together. *There are such interesting family dynamics going on here. I thought I fit in when I was in West Virginia, except with Cissy ... now she's the only one who seems to be reaching out to us.*

♦

"Those people—"
"My *family*—"

"Your *family* better act nicer than they did in Myrtle Beach, or I may not want to be with them again."

It was uncharacteristic of Danny to be unkind or ungracious to anyone; and, although Julie knew he was trying to protect her emotions, it dug a deeper trench between her loyalty to her second husband-children-step-children and her biological family. *When did things get so complicated? I bet my life would have been far different if I had found the Littles when I was a teenager.*

"Hon, everyone deserves a second chance." Julie and Danny were driving to the airport in Grand Rapids to pick up Daddy, Mama Eunice, Tiny and Lily. It was the last weekend of August, and her parents, half-brother and sister-in-law had decided it was time for them to visit Julie and her family in Michigan. Julie wasn't sure what Arlene was thinking ... or whether she and Daddy would cross paths ... or what Mama Eunice would think about that ... or if this visit would really be different than Myrtle Beach.

Danny let out a sigh and turned up the air conditioning.

"I just don't want you to be hurt again."

"I love you, Danny."

"Love you back."

♦

The sultry air that blanketed Michigan held its breath under a blazing sun. Most of the countryside was brown and parched; Julie was certain that her southern family would not be expecting to pull into her driveway and see lush, green grass sloping gently down to a flowing stream behind her home. She had designed and planted and maintained gardens that were an array of varieties and colors: pink and blue delphinium, red roses, creeping geraniums, daisies, orange day lilies, veronica, purple petunias, majestic lupines, magenta and yellow pansies, and white bellflower.

As they all stepped out of the cool minivan into the oppressive heat, Tiny shouted, "Ya'll MOW all this stuff?" Danny and Julie stared at each other. This was something they had never heard when people got a first glimpse of their house and panoramic view.

"Of course." Danny's tone of voice was the only chilly part of the day.

"Man, all ya'll are nuts! There must be an acre of grass here! Why do ya'll waste your time mowing?"

"Tiny," explained Julie patiently, "in the Midwest, people value their land more than the size of their homes. We like it that way. We love our grass and gardens, and especially our pole barns."

"Pole *what*?"

"Never mind! Come on, everybody. Dad, you're going to sweat to death in your suit coat. Let's get in where it's cool!"

♦

"I know it's hot," Julie began as she washed the pancake griddle the next morning, "but I'd love for us to go to the Kale Tulip Festival."

"Sounds good to me," said Dad.

"We'll do whatever you want, dear," Mama Eunice chimed in.

"Great! Where did Tiny escape to?"

"He's up on your deck. Said we could call him down whenever."

"Okay. I need to finish cleaning up the kitchen, hang out a load of clothes, and then we'll be ready to go."

As Julie lugged a heavy basket of wet sheets and towels out to the clothesline, she heard Tiny yelling down from the deck. "Ya'll have a clothes dryer?"

"Yeah, we have a dryer." *Where is this going?*

"Is it broke?"

"No. It's fine."

"Then for Pete's sake, why are ya'll hanging clothes out?"

"I like the smell of fresh sheets and towels. There's no better drug than climbing into bed and burying your head in sheets that have been hung out on a line, or getting out of the shower and wrapping an air-dried towel around you."

"Oh, yeah, when I took a shower this morning, the towel smelled really good when I was drying off," Tiny conceded.

Andrew came out the back door, made his way over to the clothesline and helped Julie finish hanging up the clothes.

"You know, Julie," continued Tiny, "in Charlotte you wouldn't be hanging clothes outside."

"Why not?"

"Because in Charlotte it would look like—"

"Trailer trash?" finished Julie.

"Well, yeah," replied Tiny sheepishly.

"You know, Tiny, I *was* trailer trash growing up. Even in Midwestern winters, we hung clothes outside on sunny days because we didn't own a dryer. During bitterly cold days, we slung all of the wet clothes over chairs and dressers and tables in the house, and then it was my job to iron things after they dried."

"Uh, yeah," broke in Andrew, "there're certain places in Charlotte where you wouldn't be allowed to have a clothesline. As a matter of fact, you couldn't even paint your house any color you chose. You'd have to go before the city council, and only a few colors would be approved. And, you could only have your yard a certain way—"

With a piercing look, Julie replied, "Well, Pop, I'm here to tell you that I would never live *anywhere* where I was told I couldn't hang a clothesline ... or I had to paint my house a certain color ... or I could only plant certain kinds of trees or plants, and certainly no vegetables. As far as I'm concerned, that's not living."

Andrew and Tiny were both silent.

"Mom, are we ready to go?" Emma was home for another week before classes started at Central Michigan University. "Dusty wondered if we could swing by and get him."

"Let's saddle up!"

CHAPTER THIRTY-SEVEN

THE PRESENT IS NOT A GIFT

Julie held a picture in her mind of going under a limbo stick to reach her family, only they were backing away from her even while they were cheering her on, while Danny was lowering his side of the stick faster than she could pass through. Would Danny's ambivalence towards her family propel her towards people who didn't seem sure of what to do with her? This was all supposed to be happy and uncomplicated, but somehow the uncertainties of life got in the way of her plans.

Tiny had generously mailed a plane ticket for Julie to be able to participate in Cissy's November wedding as a reader. *Did she know how desperate I was to be a bridesmaid?* At least Julie was being included. Danny had been excluded from the plans, which increased the tension in her home. *Maybe when I return from the wedding, I should pack my clothes and confusion and move to Charlotte permanently. But I would* never *leave Danny!*

♦

Cissy's wedding was simple and beautiful, and Julie had been so proud of being included in the rehearsal dinner, wedding, and the day-after gift opening and family celebration. She had spent that weekend feeling like the wheel had stopped spinning and the arrow was pointing to a Caribbean cruise—a valuable prize she had won just for being in the right place at the right time. Tiny, Pokey, Cissy and their spouses had shared many inside jokes; Julie had submerged any sense of being left out for the goal of being welcomed unconditionally into the Little clan.

Until she returned home to Michigan.

It was close to her third anniversary, and Julie wasn't sure how or *if* she and Danny would be celebrating this year. Their house was no longer filled with wall-to-wall kids, kids' friends and a frenzy of activity. She and Danny were bona fide empty nesters, and doing a good imitation of a married couple occupying the same space without sharing the same heart. They hadn't had a conversation about anything more important than car repairs and replacing their washing machine since Julie had returned from West Virginia almost a month earlier.

And now, sitting at her desk preparing for the last shortened week of school before Christmas vacation, Julie tried to sort through her jumbled mess of thoughts in the hopes that the ache in her head would lessen. *God, I'm tired of being pulled between my father's family and my husband, not that either one is fighting for me. They are both assuming that I'm fine with the status quo, but actually I'm feeling more miserable than I have in a long time.* Julie glanced outside at the overcast sky, thinking back on Decembers from her childhood filled with sadness. *I should have called in sick this morning ... my head is throbbing and my heart hurts.* She turned on her computer, waiting for it to boot up and wishing the school could afford high-speed Internet. Pulling open her desk drawer and reaching for a bottle of ibuprofen, Julie felt a sudden, stabbing pain in her head. *What is that? Did something fall on me?* She grabbed her head with both hands and swiveled her chair as another sharp pain shot her out of her chair and on to the floor. "Oh, my God!" screamed Julie, as she writhed in a fetal position.

"Julie, what's wrong? Did you fall? Are you hurt?"

Julie stared at a pair of shoes, turned her head slightly, looked up at a halo of light, and thought it might be Barb, the teacher from the room across the hall. "My head ... feels ... like ... it's gonna ... blow ... off. Need ... bathroom ... help me up?"

"Are you sure?" Barb eased Julie up off the floor.

"If I'm not back ... in ten minutes ... come and check on me." Julie held on to the wall as she stumbled out of her room and down the hall to the bathroom. Once inside, the bright lights almost knocked her to the floor again. She leaned over the sink and supported herself as she tried to turn on the faucet. *I'll be okay if I can splash cold water on my face.* When Julie realized she couldn't feel anything in her right hand or arm, she began to panic. *This must be a stroke. Barb, come back now!*

Julie heard the door open and a voice saying, "I don't know what to do. Let's get you back to your desk, and I'll get help."

"I can't see anything!"

Barb guided Julie back to her chair. "I'll be back ASAP!"

I'll call Danny on the room phone. He'll know what to do. It would be helpful if I could actually see the numbers.

A shadow crossed Julie's peripheral vision. "I decided to come back and call Danny for you. Maybe we should drive you to the ER."

"Barb, I'm either having a heckuva migraine, or else it's a stroke."

Within five minutes, Danny was standing in Julie's room talking to Barb about whose car they should drive to the hospital.

"No," slurred Julie. "I want to go home. Bed."

"Really?"

"Yeah. No. I don't know. Call Dr. Beth."

♦

"Is Dr. Beth Steingard there? Tell her it's Danny Lewis, and it's an emergency." As Danny, Julie and Barb were pulling up to the Emergency Room door at St. Michael's, Dr. Beth was emphatic that that's where they needed to be. A half-hour had passed since the initial explosion in Julie's head, and her vision was beginning to return—but she was still numb and frightened.

The hour wait in the cubicle suddenly ended when Julie's face began to droop, and the numbness in her arm turned into paralysis. After a CT scan and the administration of something that made her feel loopy, Julie spent the night in the hospital wondering how she had ever thought any of her previous migraines had been the worst pain imaginable. This level of pain was horrific and relentless.

♦

"What we are dealing with is not good," began Dr. Meyer the next morning, as he stood quietly next to Julie's bed. "You have a blood clot. I don't know why you should, since you're young and otherwise healthy."

Go on.

Danny stood near Julie's head, rubbing her shoulder and smoothing her hair. *He asked me to forgive him for being distant, and for trying to force me to choose between him and my father. All I could do was blink my eyes. I can't tell him that I absolutely forgive him! And I can't ask him to forgive me for doubting his love. God, please let me talk again!*

"We'll have to run further tests over the next few days, but I suspect you have what's called 'Protein C Deficiency.' It predisposes people to blood clots. If that's the case, we can put you on Cumidin."

Three MRIs confirmed Dr. Meyer's diagnosis of a blood clot on the left venous cavus, the artery that drains blood from the brain. During the nine days over Christmas break that Julie spent in the hospital, she learned that the blood clot was affecting her speech center—so at least she knew she wasn't simply going crazy from the pain. At least there was an explanation for her total loss of speech.

♦

The doctors and nurses said I probably had a slight stroke. It's a good thing I've learned to have conversations in my head. It may be the only place I'll ever be able to have them again.

Julie was home, flat on her back, unable to handle any light or noise, unable to talk, and unable to process any thoughts except angry ones. *I've had thirteen medication changes, including anti-depressants and blood thinners, and nothing has changed. How many times, God, did I suffer pain with my back? Didn't you have enough of my attention? Okay, I'm here again. I can't walk, and I certainly can't run away from you any more. I can't even turn on the CD player to drown out Your Voice. I am totally helpless.*

Danny's mom, Georgia, walked into Julie's bedroom.

"Here, dear, I thought you might like some iced tea. I even found one of those bendable straws in a kitchen drawer."

Julie hoped her eyes showed her gratitude.

"Let me help you sit up, and then you can try and take a few sips." Georgia set the glass on the nightstand, pulled Julie to a sitting position and propped pillows behind her back. She brought the glass up to Julie, who took one sip from the straw and motioned her desire to lie down again. Georgia brushed a tear from her eye, set the glass down, made Julie comfortable, kissed her forehead, and forgot the glass as she walked quickly out of the room.

God, I am so thankful for Georgia—but I don't think I can be with anyone but You right now. I have so many things to figure out. I know that I can no longer lay blame for the rotten things in my life at the feet of my adoptive father, my first husband, my mother, other relatives, or the other men in my life. I have not only feasted at the table of bitterness—I also had a hand in cooking the meal.

Julie saw herself wasting away. She could barely walk from her bedroom to the bathroom; she couldn't lift a fork; her limited speech was mostly unintelligible; and her thoughts swirled around in her brain like a sandstorm. Her neurologist and the rest of the hospital staff voiced their dismay over trying to treat a blood clot that seemed resistant to medications that should have dissolved it by now. Every other week, Julie had a dejá vu in Dr. Meyer's office.

"Julie, I don't know why you're not getting better."

"Bad."

Danny reached for Julie's hand.

"You're frustrated?" continued Dr. Meyer.

Julie nodded.

"Let's increase the dosage on one of the medications, and see if anything has changed by your next appointment."

"Okay."

♦

God, I'm not living in the Dark Ages! They've tried everything but leeches with me!

414

Dr. Meyer walked into the exam room.

"Julie, your husband told me that you said the word 'Mayo' last night."

Julie made a partial fist and stuck up her thumb.

"I don't have a problem with you wanting a second opinion, but it's probably going to take you two to three months to get into Mayo."

Julie moaned and put both palms on her forehead.

Dr. Meyer looked at Julie with kind eyes. "Mayo takes patients based on identifiable symptoms, diseases, or illnesses, and you have nothing we can put a name to. Protein C Deficiency isn't enough."

◆

Dr. Bob Carlton, head of the University of Michigan School of Family Practice, was Christina's new father-in-law. *He must know a doctor at the Mayo Clinic in Rochester, Minnesota. I'm desperate. I'll do whatever it takes to get help. Christina could talk to Stu, who could talk to his father, who could plead my case with a neurologist at Mayo. I may only be three degrees of separation from someone who could tell me what's wrong with me. I just need to figure out how to communicate this idea!*

Julie had the shoulder and arm strength to write out her idea while Christina was spending the day with her. While both women were reluctant to take advantage of Dr. Carlton, they also knew that this might be the best and last hope Julie had of ever returning to a normal life.

Although she was accustomed to receiving phone calls from kind friends who regularly checked up on her, Julie was startled when Georgia brought the phone into her room the day after Christina's visit and announced, "It's Dr. Carlton!"

"Julie, Danny called and told me some of what you've been going through. Why don't you describe your symptoms to me?"

"Dr. Carlton, this is Georgia, Julie's mother-in-law. She still can't talk, so she'll write down the answers to your questions, and I'll be her interpreter."

"That sounds good."

The three-way conversation lasted forty-five minutes; by the time it was over, Julie felt confident that she had been understood, but no promises had been made about any future trips to Mayo.

♦

"Julie?" Danny walked into Julie's room carrying a cordless phone.

Julie grabbed her note pad, wrote 'Dr. Carlton?' on it, and held it up.

"No. It's a Dr. Binru. He says he's a neurologist at Mayo."

Julie drew a huge exclamation point on her pad.

"Should I find out what he wants?"

Julie nodded vigorously, and listened closely to Danny's end of the conversation.

"You want us down there *tomorrow*? But that's a whole day's drive!"

I don't know if my insurance will cover a visit to Mayo. I haven't had time to check on that yet.

"Julie needs to get copies of her x-rays, CT scans, MRIs …"

And that red tape could bog us down for weeks.

"No, she doesn't want to waste any more time, either."

Please, God, let this all be worked out.

"He will?"

Who will do what?

"Just a minute." Danny turned to Julie. "Dr. Binru said that Dr. Meyer promised to write whatever letters are needed to persuade the insurance company to cover his referral to Mayo."

Julie wrote '$30,000' on her notepad.

"I don't care. We'll mortgage the house if we have to. We're going tomorrow."

Danny held the receiver to his ear. "Dr. Binru, we'll be at Mayo tomorrow. Thanks for your call."

♦

It was a delightful May morning, almost five months after Julie's initial episode at school. *I'm glad I can walk steadily, feed myself and communicate through writing and some speech.* After being admitted to an exam room at the Mayo Clinic in Rochester, Minnesota, Julie and Danny were instructed to wait for a Dr. Johnson.

"We're finally here, Julie."

I can't believe it!

"Before Dr. Johnson comes, let's pray together."

Julie nodded her head. "Yeah."

Danny reached for her hand and bowed his head. "God, we've spent the last five months looking at the back side of our marriage. Show us Yourself in all of this. Please find a way to take away Julie's pain, and give her back her speech. Show me how to be the husband she needs ..."

"Amen." Julie carefully lifted her arm and tried to brush the tears from Danny's eyes. She kept missing and poking the bridge of his nose. Danny laughed and wrapped his arms around Julie.

"Have I told you I love you today?"

"Memory loss ..."

"Then I'll just have to keep reminding you!"

There was a quiet knock at the door. "Come in," said Danny as he released Julie and wrapped a stray lock of hair behind her ear.

A short, gray-haired man wearing a white coat with an identification badge pinned to the lapel walked into the exam room, shook Danny's hand and said, "I'm Dr. Johnson."

"Nice to meet you."

He continued looking at Danny and gestured towards Julie. "I heard she walked in on her own. What's she doing here?"

"Dr. Binru told us to come," responded Danny.

Dr. Johnson visibly stiffened. "How do *you* know Dr. Binru?"

"My wife's daughter's father-in-law is a good friend and colleague of his."

Dr. Johnson grabbed both ends of his stethoscope hanging around his neck

I wonder how he would talk about me without hiding behind his obvious authority.

"We don't function like that," he replied tersely.

Julie reached inside her purse, pulled out her notepad and pen, and wrote, "We're doing what we were told." She tore off the sheet and handed it to Dr. Johnson.

"Well, we'll see about this," Dr. Johnson muttered as he left the room.

Julie stared at Danny as tears sprang to her eyes. She shoved her pad and pen back into her purse, took out a tissue, and cried softly. *I guess it's good that my tear ducts still work. But this crying is going to make my head hurt worse.*

Ten minutes later there was another knock at the door. Julie looked at Danny and shook her head. "Yes?" A tall woman who looked to be in her fifties opened the door, entered the room and headed for Julie. "Julie," she smiled and touched Julie's shoulder. "I'm Cheryl, the nurse manager. We'll have a room ready for you shortly."

"What about Dr. Johnson?" said Danny.

"Don't worry about him," Cheryl replied cryptically.

♦

None of the tests performed on Julie revealed a blood clot. During her four days at Mayo she learned that she had probably suffered a basal artery migraine—a serious condition, which can mimic a stroke and cause facial drooping, paralysis, and loss of vision and speech. What immediately followed the new diagnosis was the administration of Depacote. Within twenty-four hours, Julie's pain had decreased from a ten to a five on the pain scale. Forty-eight hours later, she awoke without a headache for the first time since December.

Danny and Julie were almost home. The open windows of the minivan let in the sounds of birds singing, the distant whistle of a train, lawnmowers grooming humble yards, chainsaws cutting wood for the stacking of winter fuel—all a sweet paradise for Julie.

"Julie? Are you awake?"

Julie turned and looked at Danny. "I am."

"I was just thinking ..."

"Thanks ... for the ... warning!"

"Hey! That's my line!"

"Talk ... too fast ... for you?"

Danny laughed. "I could keep up with you when I had the advantage. You're going to get better quick, and then I'll be left behind again!"

Julie smiled a crooked smile.

"But seriously: When you had the MRIs at St. Michaels, was your head turned in the wrong position, so that it looked like you had a blood clot?"

"Don't know."

"Or, did you really have a blood clot that God miraculously healed?"

"Maybe so."

I wish I could tell him that I think God somehow allowed this long illness, or misdiagnosis, or whatever it was, to draw me closer to Him and to Danny. As far as the Littles go, I don't know what to do about them. I understand them not being able to talk to me on the phone these past several months ... but they never even called to talk to Danny. Cissy e-mailed once, and Tiny and Pokey e-mailed a few times ...Daddy wrote once ... but how could they have thought that that was enough? Anyways, whether my head was in the right or wrong position during the MRIs, it's in the right position now: turned toward God and wanting to go in His direction for my life.

♦

"Julie, you're not going to believe this!" Danny opened the garage door into the kitchen, and found Julie sitting at the table practicing her writing.

"What?" Julie looked at Danny in alarm.

"This!" Danny dropped an official-looking letter on the table. "It's a letter from our insurance company."

"How much ... did they pay?"

"Forty-five thousand dollars!"

"What?"

"They explained in their letter that there was such a discrepancy between the original diagnosis at St. Michael's and the accurate diagnosis at Mayo that they would cover the cost, even without the pre-authorization requirement."

"Praise ... God!"

CHAPTER THIRTY-EIGHT

'HONOR THY FATHER AND MOTHER'

The Rose Garden was a perfect name for the long-term care facility five miles east of Allen Park. It was obvious that someone with a knowledge and love of roses had designed the various gardens around the building for optimum appreciation, even including signs throughout the gardens describing the varieties of roses, and the year they were discovered. The calligraphic lettering on each sign boasted names like Lavender Princess, Forever Amber, Miami Moon, Chinatown, Matador, and Shocking Blue, all planted carefully in front of roses blooming in spectacular mauves, deep reds and oranges, delicate pinks, rich purples, bright yellows, unusual peaches, and innumerable variegated shades.

On this warm afternoon in early June, the lavish colors and luxuriant scent drew Julie to one of the wooden benches placed at the end of a winding concrete sidewalk. She had finally conceded defeat to her mom's determination to remain inside—even in the summertime—and remain gloomy. As Julie tilted her head back to revel in the bright sunlight, she drained the rest of the water from her Nalgene bottle and thought how much she would appreciate even a glass-half-empty attitude from her mom. Arlene Sandford seemed to be living under the conviction that her glass had *never* had anything but bitter water in it—and that it had long ago been emptied and discarded.

Walking through the front door of the nursing home, Julie thought again of the irony that she and her mom had both lost speech and movement within the same month – Julie's through her basal artery migraine, and Arlene's through a second stroke, this one far more serious than the first one several years earlier. Julie had been highly motivated to do whatever therapy it took to regain the ability to reconnect with her family and friends. Arlene had resisted all pleas from her doctors and nurses to do any therapy—except the exercises that helped her regain her speech. Julie had to admit that she wasn't always thrilled about that one remnant of Arlene's former self—particularly when Arlene's words were pricklier than ever.

Julie knocked on Arlene's partially opened door and walked in.

"Hi, Mom. What are you watching?"

"Oprah Winfrey. She has some good shows for a colored lady."

Ignoring the comment, Julie walked over to the window and raised the mini blind.

"Don't do that! It puts too much glare on the idiot box!"

"It's a beautiful day!"

"The sun is too bright."

"But in the winter, you complain that it's too dark."

Arlene pressed a button on the remote until the volume was quite high. "Okay, enough about the outside," said Julie. "I'm sorry."

Arlene hit the 'off' button and put the remote on her lap.

"Would you like something to drink?"

"No. Besides, the coffee is too hot and the iced tea is too cold."

Is the bed just right? "Do you have everything you need?"

"I guess. I'm used to doing without. It came from years of giving all my money to you for clothes and swim suits and record albums ..." *Her memory must have been affected by the stroke.* "And besides, I hated sending you to pay our rent. You probably never knew that."

"No, I didn't." Julie's head began to hurt under the pressure of fighting for control of her thoughts and emotions.

"When that vulgar Cliff Koski kept complaining about missing you ... and then he told me he was getting the checks in the mail ... I had to go down there myself with the money. He pawed me and practically molested me ... and I had to put up with it to keep our rent down. You have *no* idea what I went through."

"Are you kidding me?" Julie tried to relax her facial muscles. "I told you what he did to me, and you accused me of lying!"

"Well, you always thought everything was about you, so I never knew what to believe. Besides, he didn't get you pregnant, and I'm the one who would have looked bad if he had kicked us out of our house."

"Was that more important than protecting me?" Julie whispered.

"Maybe I made some mistakes, but I did the best I could."

Julie looked at her mom's cloudy eyes. "You made one *big* mistake in your life, and the mistake has a name. Her name is 'Julie Marie Ness Sandford Dietrich Lewis Little!' She was born April 1, 1956 in the navy hospital in Bremerton, Washington."

"Don't get sassy with me."

"I'm being honest. I think you've always seen me as a mistake."

Bret ... undeserved respect ... I always thought that only had to do with Danny Sandford. But it's about my mother, too. God, You've brought me so far. Please don't let Your love in my heart be choked by bitterness.

"The only *mistake* I ever made was thinking you cared about what happened to me." Arlene picked at a thread from the sleeve of her green robe.

God, I could rehearse my resentments. I have the right to do that. No one would blame me. "I care."

"You have a funny way of showing it."

"I suppose." *God, I will release my right to rehearse my resentments. I have never forgotten that challenge from one of Pastor Tim's sermons, and I need it now more than ever. You have brought me so far. I haven't arrived yet—but at least I've left the station! This train is barreling down the tracks!*

"Did you want something?" Arlene looked past Julie to the grainy picture of her and Danny hanging on the wall above the bed.

"No, Mom. I have everything I need." Julie smiled through salty tears of both sadness and joy. "I'll come back later." She got up and squeezed her mom's shoulder.

"If you can spare the time."

Julie walked out and closed the door behind her, resisting the urge to skip as she headed out to her car. The chains that had bound her to her mom's approval were beginning to loosen.

CHAPTER THIRTY-NINE

POKEY'S STORY

"**D**anny, I'm not sure I want Andrew in my life." Julie tied a bow around Danny's finger as he held the ribbon down on the wrapped Christmas present.

"Julie?" Danny slipped his finger out and touched her cheek. "What's going on?"

"Ever since you proposed to me, I've had Decembers without depression ... until now." Julie picked up the present and put it on top of the growing stack of wrapped boxes on the kitchen table. "Can you help me carry these to the tree?" After scattering the gifts under the tree, Julie and Danny backed up and sat on the couch.

"Did I do something wrong?"

"No, but you can't make everything right, either."

"With Andrew?"

"Him, the rest of the family—they still don't seem entirely sure of what to do with me. When they call, everything's pleasant, like talking to a cashier at Wal-Mart. I've spent so much time telling them about my life, and I just get these uncomfortable silences when I ask any of them about their past—especially when I'm curious about Tiny's and Pokey's teen years. And why won't anyone tell me why Pokey wasn't in Tiny's wedding pictures? If he was gone on

425

a trip or something, what's the big deal about that? Why all the secrets?" Julie got up and straightened one of the ornaments on the tree.

Danny stood behind Julie and wrapped his arms around her shoulders. "What do you think you'll do?" he whispered.

Leaning into his chest, Julie fought back tears. "I don't know. Maybe I should call Pokey before I decide whether or not to keep him on my dance card."

Turning Julie around, Danny kissed her. "You know what I love about you?"

"I feel the short-term memory loss coming back." Julie smiled.

"Just about everything."

♦

"Pokey? It's Julie." Julie turned her body sideways on the couch and tucked her feet under Danny's legs.

"Merry Christmas, Julie!"

"Thanks." Julie took a deep breath. "How are Dad and Mama Eunice?"

"Great. Everyone's getting ready for Christmas Eve. We always call it the big Little party."

"Sounds fun." Julie's voice lacked conviction, while her emotions were still parked in neutral.

"I wish ya'll could be here."

"Me too."

"Julie—"

"Pokey—"

"You first!" Julie chuckled.

"Naw! Daddy always taught me to let a lady go first."

"Okay then." *God, be in my words.* "I know something you could give me for Christmas."

"I already mailed—"

"What I really want are some answers."

"Like?"

"Like why aren't you in any of your brother's – *our* brother's – wedding pictures? Why does everyone get so quiet when I ask about your past?" Julie didn't hear anything, and thought maybe the connection had been lost. "Pokey? Are you there?"

"Yep."

"I'm sorry, I shouldn't have asked."

"I'm the one who's sorry. We should have told you before now. Daddy's been after me to talk to you, but I guess I was waiting for the right time."

"If it's too painful—"

"It was, but not any more. God has brought huge changes in my life."

"I've never heard you talk like this."

"That's because I'm afraid of what people might think of me if they knew the truth."

"After everything I've told you about my past? Do you think I'd judge you?"

"No, but you've said many times that you wish you had found us when you were in high school, and that cousin told you about your real dad. You probably thought our family was perfect, and if you found out otherwise, you'd be really disappointed."

"I'm not sure what I'll feel. I'd still like to hear the truth."

"When I was fifteen, I started dealing cocaine."

Julie felt a lump in her throat. "Oh?"

"I never did any, just dealt it. By the time I was twenty-two, I was living in a mansion with four Dobermans for security. I always carried a gun, wore a Rolex, and had all the girls and clothes and parties I wanted. Are you sure you want to hear the rest?"

"Uh-huh."

"I was called a lieutenant, the number three man in the drug ring. It was one of the biggest rings on the east coast, and I was in charge of two hundred eighty million bucks. I often flew to Bogotá and stayed in one of my houses, and when I was back here I recruited doctors, lawyers, and policemen for the drug ring."

"Were you ever afraid?"

"Only all the time. I got so paranoid that I slept maybe three hours a night. After years of living like that, the house of cards began to fall when I met with the number one and two men in the organization, out on abandoned farmland about fifty miles from here. They were as scared as I was, and number two shot number one. I got out of there before I was next."

"This sounds unbelievable."

"It felt that way, too. I was way past the point of no return, and stayed on the run for the next eight months, until I ended up in a cheap motel in Phoenix. I knew the FBI was following me, so I contacted Tiny under the radar."

"What did he do?"

"There wasn't anything for him to do. He said he hoped he'd see me alive again someday, and he broke down on the phone. I knew I had to quit running, but I was too afraid, and I didn't think I could trust anyone."

"So, what happened?"

"I was so desperate that I called my friend James—a guy I had known since first grade. I couldn't get at any of my money without being found by the FBI, so I asked James to mail money to me at the motel. By the time I had hung up the phone, I looked out the window and saw black cars with smoked mirrors pulling up in front of my room. Guys in black suits carrying Uzis spilled out of the doors. I loaded my 9-millimeter, opened the window and aimed. 'I can take three guys out from here!' I yelled. Julie, I figured I could kill myself after them. I was only thirty-seven years old, and I wasn't going to spend the rest of my life in prison.

"One of the guys started yelling, 'Mr. Little! We have a search warrant! Put your weapon down!' I didn't know what made me listen to them. I know now that God had big plans for my life, and that my folks had spent years praying that I would be protected from harm, but that God would allow whatever it took for me to become a broken man. I laid down my gun, and the agents came in, knocked me to the floor and handcuffed me. Long, long story short, Julie, was that I expected to stay broken. As soon as the other guys found out that I was *the* Pokey, I became the only cool white guy they knew. They elevated me to the status I had had as a lieutenant in the drug ring, and I went right back to the same pride that had gotten me in trouble as a fourteen-year-old kid."

"Did you ever feel bad for what you had done?"

"Not until I was transferred to Florida, and then Tennessee, and people stopped caring about who I was. There was a new kid on the block, and I was just another messed up inmate. I had resisted calling Daddy for all those years; suddenly I couldn't stand who I was anymore. I remembered reading the story of the prodigal son in Sunday school when I was a little boy, and I thought maybe my parents would forgive me for making such a mess of my life, and for bringing such shame on them."

"Did they?"

"Amazingly, they did. They both cried, and said they would be waiting for me however long it took me to get out of prison. Through a series of miracles, I was out after only three more years, and that was just a few years before you came into our lives."

Julie was crying freely by now. "Pokey, I used to wonder how I could fully believe in a God who didn't seem willing or able to protect me from the things my father and other men did to me. And, after I was told that I had a different biological dad, I never stopped wondering how different my life would have been if I had found him."

"Julie, I am really sorry for what your life was like."

"But see, Pokey! Do you have any idea how much God lead both of our lives? If I had found all of you when I was a teenager, I would have fled from one bad situation right into another. God's timing was perfect, and things are so different now for both of us. I can appreciate the Littles in a way I never would have before. There was stubbornness in my heart that needed to be dealt with. And look where both of us are today!"

"I know we haven't been very open with you, which was mostly my fault. I still battle crushing guilt over what I did to my family, and it's hard to talk to anyone about it."

"I understand that now. There is *no* way you're getting rid of me!"

"When I got out of prison, Tiny said that I should get baptized and show everyone that I was a clean, forgiven man. When that day arrived, my pastor baptized me in a lake during a pouring rain. He figured God was doing His job thoroughly!"

"Awesome."

"What about you, Julie?"

"What *about* me?"

"Have you ever been baptized?"

"No." Julie felt the depression gradually lift from her spirit. "But I think I want to be."

"We have some things to make up to you. You pick a date, and we'll be there, all the Littles, big and little!"

EPILOGUE

A hand reached down to guide Julie back up out of the water. The baptismal ceremony had lasted thirty seconds, but her mind had rewound the tape back to her childhood—through years of alcoholism, abuse, financial poverty, and emotional deprivation. New words of victory were now being recorded.

"We're praising God today for a different kind of birth on Julie's forty-fourth birthday," began Pastor Tim. "We've prayed her through these past months, and she has regained most of her speech and movement. She stands before us today as proof that God cares about her physical healing. The greater miracle—if there are such things as *greater* and *lesser* miracles—is that Julie found her father and his family, who are all here with us today." *My mother could have been here, too. God, please work a miracle of healing in her heart.*

"The greatest miracle is what God did in Julie's heart … what He does in all of our hearts when we trust in Him. The Book of Isaiah tells us that death is swallowed up by victory. Julie's victory is that she has been cleansed by water in the Word.

"Many of us may wonder—as Julie probably has over the years—why God chooses not to reverse consequences, some of which are very damaging and can last a lifetime.

431

We may never know the answer to that this side of heaven, but we can be assured that God *redeems* all of those consequences in such a way that our character is strengthened and our faith is deepened.

Pastor Tim put his arm around Julie's towel-wrapped shoulder. "Julie's desire is to be a 'wounded healer.' She believes God has sent people across her path who need to hear her story, and to know that He is Abba, protector, the perfect Father and the preserver of life.

"I now want to introduce you to Julie Lewis, a new creation!"